The Awakening Fire

The Awakening Fire

Kelley Pounds

Five Star • Waterville, Maine

This novel is a work of fiction. Names, characters, places and
incidents are either the product of the author's imagination,
or, if real, used fictitiously.

First Edition
First Printing: May 2004

Set in 11 pt. Plantin by Carleen Stearns.

Printed in the United States on permanent paper.

Library of Congress Cataloging-in-Publication Data

Pounds, Kelley.
    The awakening fire / Kelley Pounds.—1st ed.
        p. cm.
    ISBN 1-59414-203-3 (hc : alk. paper)
    1. Apache women—Crimes against—Fiction. 2. Murder
victims' families—Fiction. 3. Ex-convicts—Fiction.
4. Kidnapping—Fiction. 5. Nurses—Fiction. I. Title.
PS3616.O86A94 2004
    813'.6—dc22   2004040465

For Mom, who never let me get away with saying "I can't."

And for Carol Quinto and Rebecca Gault. I'm still listening to your voices of support and confidence.

I'd like to acknowledge Laura Baker, Janine Donoho, Melinda Rucker Haynes, Melissa Kerby, Julie Laub, Priscilla Maine, Debbie McSweeney, Robin Perini and Charisse Sprague for their friendship and support. Each of them, in one way or another, helped me see this project to fruition.

Special thanks to Carol Lee Smith, granddaughter of Geronimo, for sharing her insight and information on the Apache people.

Apache Wedding Blessing

Now you will feel no rain
for each of you will be shelter for the other.
Now you will feel no cold
for each of you will be warmth for the other.
Now there is no loneliness for you.
Now you are two persons
but there is one life before you.
Go now to your dwelling place
to enter the days of your togetherness,
and may your days be good and long together.

—Author unknown

Chapter One

New Mexico Territory, 1882

Buzzards circled. Soaring, spiraling pinpoints of death against the midday sky. Ladino watched them through slitted lids as he clawed his way to consciousness. No breeze blew, and not a cloud marred the perfection above him or shielded him from the harsh rays of the sun. He rolled his head across the rocky ground to avoid the glare. Pain slammed against his skull like blows from an Apache war club.

Damn! Why does my head hurt?

Where the hell am I?

Sucking a breath through clenched teeth, he forced his eyes farther open. His vision blurred as he scoured the landscape beyond his right shoulder. The bare, wagon-rutted earth of the road where he lay gave way to grassland surrounded by small mountains dotted with trees. He swiveled his head to the left. Rock-strewn hills enveloped the wagon path behind him. About fifteen feet off the road, nestled within a couple of large boulders and clumps of rabbitbrush, stood a single, dwarf-sized cedar.

One tree. One tree when he'd grown up hunting, hiding, and playing survival games in a forest. If he could recall visions of childhood, why couldn't he remember why he lay here about to die?

A breeze stirred, fanning the odor of death across his face. Ladino lifted his head and peered down the length of

9

his trousers and over the toe of his moccasin. A corpse lay sprawled across the deep ruts of the road. In this heat, the stench would soon grow unbearable.

Squinting to clear his vision, he scanned the body. When he discovered the wound sliced between the ribs, he recognized the work of his own blade. Efficient. Deadly. Yet as he encountered sightless eyes, infested with flies, staring back at him from the face of a boy barely sixteen, his jaw fell slack with shock.

Ladino lowered his head. He tried to swallow, but his mouth felt as if it were full of powdered gypsum. He fumbled at the waistband of his trousers, searching for his knife in its sheath on his gun belt. Missing. His gun belt was missing! Stolen? But wouldn't that mean the boy hadn't been alone?

He groped in the dirt, relieved when he touched something hard—the staghorn handle of his bowie. Grasping the knife, he brought it before his gaze. Dried blood, mixed with dirt, smeared the length of the blade.

Surely the youth had attacked first. Even among the White Eyes sixteen was considered manhood. Only a dead man refused to defend himself against a youth determined to fight with a knife.

Had the boy ambushed him? Ladino hated to admit it, but seven years in that damp cell on Alcatraz Island had dimmed his father's time-honored teachings. He had failed to sense the changes in his horse and the wildlife around him.

And where was his horse?

Nothing made sense. His memories were scattered, vague, like rippled reflections on water, the images skewed and trembling.

Focusing on his clearest memory, he dove after it,

seizing pieces before they could escape. An enormous rock surrounded by ocean, smothered with fog. A red-bearded guard unlocking the door to his cage. The surge of satisfaction. The blood lust and war cry of a wild animal freed. He had wanted to slake that lust on Red Beard himself, but that wouldn't have gotten him any closer to Smeet.

Smeet.

Yes! The name conjured images of brutality as clearly as if he saw them through a medicine man's crystal. Nigel Smeet, not the guard, deserved to die. And die he would.

Fed by his obsession to find Smeet, to make the man plead for mercy, Ladino summoned the return of damaged instincts. Lifting his head, he studied his surroundings with an intensity that matched the heat waves shimmering from the earth.

The midday sun seared his eyes, offering him no directional clue. But as he peered far beyond the dead man and the vast expanse of grassland, he recognized the jagged western face of the Sangre de Cristos. In the valley below those peaks lay Santa Fe.

Ladino didn't remember believing he'd find Smeet in Santa Fe, but at this point he wasn't sure what his reasoning had been. He imagined Smeet's pale eyes, his face wreathed in a mocking sneer as he watched Ladino die while vultures mutilated his body.

"Not yet, you filthy, murdering bastard," Ladino whispered, his voice harsh with promise. "Not yet."

One buzzard plunged from the circle. More followed. Ladino watched their wings spread to full six-foot spans as they flapped and hissed and grunted, scratching out territories atop the corpse.

He shuddered, chilled by sweat creeping over his skin, unable to bear the thought of being eaten alive, of entering the Land of Ever Summer with his skeleton picked clean. He had to get away. Had to hide himself.

The tree. With such meager branches it only pretended to be the hiding place he craved, yet desperation demanded he reach it.

When he lifted his shoulders and tried to turn over, the agony piercing his head shot its arrow into his stomach. He collapsed, forcing short puffs of air through his teeth.

He *had* to show the vultures he lived. Since he couldn't turn over and crawl, he'd pull himself back. He pushed up on his elbows. His arms shook. Pain ripped through muscle and sinew. He squeezed his eyes shut, gritted his teeth, and dragged himself backward a few inches. And a few more. Across the rut. Halfway there. Beside one of the boulders now, just a yard from his goal.

Ladino gripped the hilt of his knife, dug in his heels, and lifted his body for one final stretch. As he gained the tree's shade, a growl shredded his throat. He clutched his stomach, certain he'd torn himself apart. Between his fingers flowed a warm, sticky wetness. He jerked his hand away and stared at his palm. *Blood. His* blood.

Frowning, he glanced down at himself and saw the blood-soaked gash in his dark brown *serape*. He fingered apart the rip and noticed the still soggier slice in his dirty gray shirt. Beneath that, a bright red bolt of lightning slashed across his belly. A deep muscle wound, slow to heal. And what skin he could see through the slick smear appeared red and swollen.

"Stupid . . . stupid," he murmured, his voice slurred. "You should have stayed put."

Forcing himself into a better sitting position, he clutched the woolen cape and slit the neckline completely open with his knife. Something hit the dirt with a soft thwack. *Damn.*

He'd cut the thong of his medicine bag.

Later, he told himself. *Deal with it later.*

He pulled the *serape* from around his shoulders, cut the woolen fabric into strips, then opened the pouch of healing herbs he carried tied to a suspender button of his trousers. He sprinkled powdered acacia leaves into the gash. Rolling a *serape* strip into a pad, he pressed it to the wound, then wrapped another strip around his midriff to hold the pad in place. Clenching his jaw, he yanked the makeshift bandage tight and tied it off.

He fell back, still clutching his knife so tightly his fingers ached. In the sky, a few buzzards continued their circular dance, absorbing him in their pattern of flight. The earth spun, and his vision blurred. He was too tired to fight the blanket of unconsciousness. His eyelids drifted shut . . . until he heard the eerie rasp of feathers scraping against rock.

Startled, he turned his head. One of the scavengers perched atop the largest boulder and stared down at him, its wings outstretched. Black eyes glittered like Apache tears in a background of wrinkled red skin. Ladino saw no intelligence, no cunning. Just patience.

Patience . . . and hunger.

Chills prickled his skin as the buzzard hopped down from the rock. With a weak gesture he tried to scare the bird. But the vulture, which loomed just out of his reach, only spread its wings higher, wider, until a black, jagged shadow of death feathered Ladino's legs where the tree's cloak of safety could not reach. The bird hissed, then opened its mouth as if to laugh at the pitiful sight he presented.

"Touch me . . . and *bánaagúúya*—I'll fix you." He knifed a clumsy arc in the air. "Go away, *tseeshuuye!*"

Fighting light-headedness and the inevitable fall of his

eyelids, he cut another arc, weaker this time. The bird did not move. With a courage that drove slivers of ice into Ladino's veins, the vulture bided its time.

Can one serve God and resent Him at the same time?

Adela believed it could be true. Especially now, as she contemplated her first solicitation trip as a novice Sister of Charity. She and her companions, Sisters Blandina and Mary Antonia, had been traveling from mining camp to mining camp collecting donations for St. Vincent's Hospital in Santa Fe. After weeks of riding sore-footed mules, walking hundreds of miles over terrain meant only for mountain goats, and being driven in borrowed ore wagons —as they were now—Adela had reached the end of her physical, emotional, and spiritual strength.

Instead of drawing her closer to God, closer to being ready for full vows and the black habit, exhaustion hounded her with visions of hiding behind her homeless mother's skirts as she begged for work . . . or a warm place to sleep . . . or a scrap of bread. Though the anxiety Adela felt now only echoed the terror and helplessness she'd felt as a six-year-old child, she still couldn't forget the cold November day her mother had abandoned her at the convent.

"Look!" exclaimed Sister Blandina, interrupting Adela's thoughts. She pointed at the sky. "Vultures. Just over the rise. I wonder what they've found?"

O'Gilvie, their driver, stared up at the circling creatures. The jaunty Irish airs he'd been whistling died on the breeze. "With 'em hangin' right over the road like that, I'd be thinkin' it's a mule, or maybe a horse."

"The animal will be dead?" asked Mary Antonia, her voice a squeak as she tucked her chin into the white collar of her habit.

Adela smiled wistfully, feeling old and too wise, envious of Mary Antonia's sheltered life. She tried to be thankful her companion was a teacher at the orphan asylum and not a nurse—a nurse who tried to exorcise her demons by fighting for control over mortality.

"If not dead, then dreadful close," said O'Gilvie. "We'll be findin' out soon enough." He slapped the reins and urged his mules to climb the hill. "If ye've got handkerchiefs, ye'd best get 'em out in case the smell . . ." His words trailed into silence as the Santa Fe Valley spread before them.

"Holy Mary, Mother of God!" cried Sister Mary Antonia. She closed her eyes, crossed herself, and swayed in her seat.

"Whoa!" O'Gilvie pulled back on the reins, stopping his mules. "Bless me soul," he whispered.

"It's a man!" exclaimed Sister Blandina.

A man! Adela shot to her feet. Only a pair of boot soles peeked through the tangled legs of the carrion animals. Despite the heat, gooseflesh shuddered down her arms as she watched the mass of black wings and red, welted necks teem over what had to be a body. Only once before had she experienced a sight to match this barbaric scavenging of human life.

O'Gilvie gripped her arm. "Sit down, Sister Adela! We don't know how long ago this happened, and ye make a grand target for any brigand still hidin'."

Adela obeyed. Yet as she crouched in her seat, waiting to hear a stray bullet or see some sign of danger, the compulsion to battle death overwhelmed her.

"We can't just sit here." She touched O'Gilvie's shoulder. "What if he's alive? We have to save him!"

"Save him?" O'Gilvie gave a snort of laughter and shook

15

his head. "It's lucky we'll be to find all o' the man's bones."

Adela flinched. The ache of resignation settled in her stomach, and she turned back to face the Irishman. "If that's the case, surely enough time has passed for any danger to be gone. We can still keep the vultures from destroying what's left of the body."

O'Gilvie quirked his lips and nodded. "Aye, that we can."

He whistled at his mules and slapped the reins, but the animals refused to budge. Instead, they brayed and side-stepped in their harnesses, spooked by the miasma of death.

Adela tossed the corners of her habit cape over her shoulders and scrambled out of the wagon. As she ran down the hill, the ties of her outdoor bonnet came loose, and the oversized cap of brown serge flew off her head, leaving a tightly fitted bonnet of the same color to cover her cropped hair.

"Shoo!" Waving her arms, Adela rushed at the vultures. "Shoo! Go away! Shoo, I said!"

The creatures hissed, flapped their wings, scattered, moved afield, but refused to go farther than a few feet from the corpse.

When Adela saw the extent of the damage, she let out a cry. Enough of the face was still intact that she could tell he'd been only an adolescent.

As she smelled the first stirrings of decay, a convulsion tightened in her stomach. Adela gave way to instinct and averted her face, covering her watering mouth with her hand. Flies continued to swarm. The birds crowded back. Adela swallowed her revulsion and grabbed fistfuls of her brown habit. She flipped her skirt hem in the air, not caring who saw her petticoats and black stockings.

"Mr. O'Gilvie, hurry! I need help!"

Still unable to budge his mules, O'Gilvie tied off the reins and vaulted from the seat. He grabbed his rifle from the wagon bed and shot into the air. The mules jumped at each sharp report, braying even louder as they jerked in their harnesses. The vultures lifted to the sky, drifting on the final thundering echoes.

Adela turned and saw O'Gilvie help Sister Blandina down from the end of the wagon. Sister Mary Antonia grasped the boxboard and crept toward the tailgate, clutching her handkerchief to her face with her free hand.

"Leave Mary Antonia there," Adela called up the hill. "She shouldn't see this."

The frail sister sat back down, and even from this distance Adela could see her shoulders sag with relief. O'Gilvie trotted down the hill carrying a shovel. Sister Blandina followed, her petite form two heads shorter than that of the burly Irishman.

When O'Gilvie reached Adela's side, he shook his head and issued a low whistle.

"A boy, Mr. O'Gilvie," Adela whispered. "Just a boy."

"Aye, but old enough to fight with a knife," he said, pointing to the bloodstained blade just beyond the youth's stiff fingers. "It's still a shame the lad came to such a bad end."

Sister Blandina scooted to a halt behind O'Gilvie, breathing heavily and waving flies away from her face as she peered around his arm. Shock and horror flew into her wide hazel eyes. She spun on her heel, clutching her stomach. For long moments she remained motionless. When she turned at last, Adela recognized the stiffness in her shoulders, saw the effort it took her to school her features into a mask of acceptance.

O'Gilvie dropped the shovel aside. "We'd better get the

17

poor lad off the road." He sighed, lifting the stiffening body at the armpits. "You sisters take his feet."

Blandina knelt and grabbed one of the youth's ankles with both hands. Adela grasped the other, and together they helped O'Gilvie drag the body away from the road.

"I'll take a closer look at the area and see if I can figure out what happened after I dig the grave."

His words sent a visceral shiver through Adela. She glanced down at the mutilated body and began to pluck absently at one white point of her turned-down collar. Feeling a light touch on her arm, she lifted her head.

"Are you all right, Adela?"

She stared at Blandina. Seeing her companion's expression of shared understanding, Adela felt the familiar bloom of gratitude and admiration. However frightened Sister Blandina Segale might be, nothing daunted her when duty demanded. She always met her own fears with faith and courage, her actions challenging others to do the same. Never wanting to disappoint her mentor, to lose her respect, Adela tried. But death was so final. How could one have faith and courage, or feel anything but guilt and loss of control in its irrevocable presence?

She managed a nod. "I'm fine."

Blandina offered a gentle smile. "Then perhaps you can check on Mary Antonia."

Adela nodded again and hurried away, hating the relief that coiled in her conscience like a snake. As she gained the road and skirted the blood-spattered dirt, movement caught her eye.

A dusty, broad-brimmed black hat was caught in the limber branches of some rabbitbrush. The breeze was slapping the hat against one of two large boulders, and beside them, Adela recognized bloody scraps of material.

Clothing? And under the tree . . . another body?

She braced herself as she veered off the road toward the cedar, expecting to find only flies, picked bones, and gore.

What she did see defied imagination. This man had suffered no disfigurement whatsoever, though his savage looks made it even harder for her to keep from shivering despite the heat. Instinct told her this man had murdered the boy. But why? What had happened?

As if it were possible to find answers merely by looking, she searched his face and found his eyes closed. Yet his expression was feral, defiant of death and danger like a sleeping wildcat. A red band covered the expanse of his brow, while along his smooth jaw, dirt caked in dried rivulets of perspiration. A leather thong bound his hair at his nape, leaving a long tail of thick mahogany waves to trail over the ground. Blood smeared his shirt above a makeshift bandage, but there was no sense of death, no odor of its finality. Only the hint of sweat and leather and wounded flesh.

What if he was still alive?

That thought was all she needed to shove down her dread. She hurried to his side. In the loose curl of his bloodstained fingers rested a knife. Crusted at its hilt were traces of more blood, but the blade itself shone, no doubt cleaned of the boy's life fluid when this wild man had cut up his *serape* to form the bandage around his midsection.

She dropped to her knees. Avoiding his knife hand, she grasped his other wrist and gasped.

He had a pulse!

19

Chapter Two

Adela pulled his collar away from his neck to see if the pulse in his carotid artery was any stronger. Her action exposed a small silver crucifix on a fragile chain. She jerked back her hand, startled by the incongruity between the religious article and the man's barbaric appearance.

She glanced again at the crucifix. Perhaps God tested her. He jested with life and flaunted this vicious man's near-dead body for all her memories to see. She wouldn't put it past Him, not when He knew the depth of her fear.

Reaching out once more, she touched her fingers to the firm muscles in his neck just above the delicate chain. Here his pulse felt rapid and weak, but more viable.

Adela glanced back over her shoulder and saw Blandina rise from prayer over the boy's corpse. "Sister Blandina!" The nun turned at her voice. "Get the satchel. And the blankets. Hurry! This one's still alive."

Blandina threw a glance at O'Gilvie, who stopped digging and returned her gaze. They moved at once, Blandina clutching fistfuls of her black habit as she ran up the hill toward the wagon, O'Gilvie dropping the shovel and racing toward Adela.

Adela scanned the ground nearby, seeing nothing but the boulders and some insignificant rubble. "Mr. O'Gilvie, would you find some kind of flat rock on which to prop his feet?"

O'Gilvie hurried to do her bidding. She turned her attention back to her patient. Each breath barely lifted his chest. She lifted his earlobe and saw telltale bruising behind it. Looking more closely at his ears and nose, however, she saw no sign of the clear leakage often associated with skull fractures. She opened his eyelids. Unresponsive to light, his pupils were dilated, obscuring his irises.

"Can you hear me?" For a moment she waited for some kind of response—a flicker of his eyelids, a frown, a twitch. None came. "Wake up. Please, won't you wake up?" She patted his cheek. "Listen, I don't care who you are, or what you've done. You will not die on me!"

Adela tensed against the chills that flooded her body. She pinched his shins and thighs, feeling little skin or fat, only muscle. His face twitched with a frown. Relief washed over her. She pinched his abdomen, his chest, and finally his face. Each time he grimaced, encouraging her belief that his spine was intact. Still, she would take no chances.

Sister Blandina returned with three blankets and their satchel of medical supplies, which she opened at Adela's side.

"Steady his head while I roll him toward me," Adela said.

"Just tell me when you're ready."

Adela pulled a handkerchief from a pocket amidst the heavy folds of her habit skirt. Resisting a shudder, she plucked the man's knife from his bloody palm, wrapped it hastily in her kerchief, and shoved both back in her pocket. Looking up, she met her mentor's encouraging smile.

She nodded. "I'm ready."

Blandina held the man's head, moving with his body as Adela rolled him over and brought his chest to rest against her thighs. While Blandina supported his head, Adela pressed her fingers to the base of his spine just above his buttocks and palpated her way up the muscular cleft in his back. As suspected, she found no deformities. Bringing her attention to his head, she worked her fingers into the hair between his scalp and the ponytail tied by the leather thong. She felt a large knot on his skull, but couldn't inspect the injury thoroughly for the thickness of his hair.

She grabbed the largest pair of scissors out of the satchel and slid a blade into his tresses above the binding. She was about to cut when a ray of sunlight filtered through the cedar branches and fell on his head. The ray teased a vivid russet highlight. Disarmed by this glimpse of beauty, she realized the value he must place on his long hair. It was soft and clean. There were no fleas or lice as she'd seen on many a man's head in her days of nursing. He had hair that any woman would envy. Hair that many a man would ridicule. In that moment she realized she couldn't cut his hair. Not when she remembered what her own had meant to her once upon a time.

Instead, she wedged the point of one blade beneath a strand of the leather thong. She levered the instrument back and forth, cutting several loops until finally his hair spilled free. She parted his thick locks. No broken skin. Even so, she gently probed the area, feeling for loose bone. All felt stable, but swelling hindered a complete diagnosis.

Hearing heavy footfalls, Adela turned to see O'Gilvie approach, burdened by the weight of a rock.

"Jesus, Mary and Joseph!" he burst out. "That's why we found the lad gutted in the road. This man's a damned half-breed Apache!"

Adela stared at her patient's face, fully absorbing his features this time. High, wide cheekbones and a strong, straight nose reflected his Indian birthright, but hidden beneath the layer of dust on his skin she detected a golden bronze hue instead of the coppery brown associated with the usual Mexican-Indian blend. She guessed Caucasian blood shared this man's Apache heritage.

Half-breed Apache. No wonder he looked so fierce despite his unconscious state. Still, she cradled him gently against her thighs, disconcerted when his body heat began to ease her nervous chill.

"I'll just fracture his skull permanently." O'Gilvie hefted the rock. "None would blame me."

"No!" The cry ripped from Adela's throat as she thrust up one hand and leaned over to cover her patient's body with her own. "Put down that rock, Thomas O'Gilvie. He's a man first, and we're sworn to help him."

"I've nivver seen an Apache good for more than murderin' and butcherin' innocent people."

"In God's eyes you'd be no better for murdering him," Blandina said, her tone soft but uncompromising. "We don't know but what he suffered his wounds in self-defense."

Adela hardly dared to breathe as O'Gilvie held the rock. Silence stretched to the breaking point. At last he clenched his jaw and lowered his weapon, dropping it aside.

She lowered her hand and straightened by slow degrees, studying the miner for warning signs of another outburst. She knew firsthand how quickly an act of violence could occur—how quickly even one so kind as Thomas O'Gilvie could kill.

"I've yet to do in a defenseless man," he said, his voice as ashen as his hair. "Even an Apache. An' I'll not be startin' now." He took off his hat and clutched it to his stomach. "I'll do me best to help however I can."

Blandina nodded her acceptance. "Thank you, Mr. O'Gilvie."

Shaken, still wary, Adela nevertheless set her emotions

aside and took her cue from Blandina. "Mr. O'Gilvie," she began, "we'll have to use a blanket for a stretcher. Would you unfold one?" She swallowed past the wedge in her throat as she indicated the pile with a lift of her chin. "If you'll lay it lengthwise beside him, with the folds up against his back, we can roll him over on it, straighten it out, and lift him that way."

O'Gilvie stepped closer. "I've been carried out o' the mines that way meself a time or two."

At this, Adela found his expression contrite. His shoulders slumped with a shame she found unbearable to witness. He offered her a shimmer of a smile as he grabbed a blanket.

"He's much larger than the boy," Blandina put in. "We'll need Mary Antonia to help us carry him."

Grateful for the excuse to look away from O'Gilvie, Adela turned her attention to the elder nun still sitting in the wagon. "Four would be nice—we can keep him steadier that way. Do you think she can handle it?"

"If she knows she has no choice but to help, she'll be fine."

Adela nodded and turned again to O'Gilvie, forcing a steady gaze. "Can you bring the wagon closer?"

"Aye. The mules are probably calm enough to lead now."

"Good. We need to get him to Santa Fe as quickly as possible."

The Irishman nodded and seemed to take special care as he positioned the blanket behind the Apache. After they rolled him onto the gray wool and smoothed the folds beneath his body, O'Gilvie scurried to fetch the wagon.

Adela watched him, feeling her shame grow as she considered her own opinion of the half-breed. Savage. Vicious.

Adela admonished herself. In God's eyes she was wrong to judge. She hadn't witnessed the fight and didn't know who had instigated the attack. After all, O'Gilvie said the boy had been old enough to fight with a knife. Even so, she couldn't escape the belief that her patient's appearance hinted at superior experience in such fights. Nor could she discount the reports she'd heard of Apache brutality. Survival often depended on snap judgments based on first impressions.

Was that really so wrong?

Evading memories conjured by the question, Adela turned to something that offered comfort, complete absorption, and a way to make amends. Medicine. Duty demanded she do her best to save him, and what she could diagnose, she could control. Simple. If only religious faith were so easy to understand.

When she inspected his bandage, she discovered a long, angry gash across taut abdominal muscles. Though the wound had bled profusely, he'd suffered no injury to vital organs, and she saw no evidence of fresh seepage on the heavy wool. A good sign. Even so, with over an hour's rough ride to Santa Fe still ahead of them, she didn't want to risk rebandaging the wound. She opted to wait until their arrival at St. Vincent's.

O'Gilvie returned with the wagon, and as he helped Sister Mary Antonia alight, Blandina rose and went to meet them. She took Mary Antonia aside, and Adela could hear the meek nun's moans of anguish punctuated by Blandina's cajoling whispers.

The Irishman came to her side. "I'm sorry if I scared ye, Sister Adela." He removed his hat and crouched beside her.

She couldn't meet his gaze or acknowledge his apology. Both smacked of her own hypocrisy. Instead, she spread a blanket over her patient's body.

From the midst of *serape* scraps, she picked up a leather pouch. "Should we take this with us?"

He nodded. "That's a medicine pouch. Full of religious things and the like. Probably made by some family member."

Adela fingered the pouch, admiring the intricacy of the beadwork. Who had crafted so much love into such a tiny ornament? Mother? Father? Brother? Sister? Or perhaps a grandparent.

Family . . .

Mixed with her innate fear and distrust, a softness began to swell inside her—a softness she was stunned to recognize as a lonely kind of empathy.

"Do you know Apaches well, Mr. O'Gilvie?"

He hesitated and shifted his weight. "Ye mean personally?"

"No. Just anything about them. Surely they aren't all murderers . . ." She continued to study the pouch, turning it in her hand. At last she met his gaze. "Are they?"

Again O'Gilvie shifted his weight. Adela wanted to assure him she had no ulterior motive. Her questions weren't a test of his repentance; she only wanted to understand her own confusion.

"I suppose not, Sister," he said. "But I've watched 'em murder too many o' me friends to change me opinion now."

His words seeped into her consciousness, adding weight to her uncertainty. She dropped the bag into her pocket with the bloody knife as Blandina and the elder sister approached.

Mary Antonia wore a mock-brave face. "I'd like to help." She swallowed visibly, her effort not to look at the body all too obvious.

Adela let out a long breath and forced her anxiety aside. "All right." She pushed up from the ground. "Mr. O'Gilvie, you and I are tallest, so we'll take the corners at his head. Sister Blandina, you and Mary Antonia take the corners at his feet."

When they all moved to their positions and bent down, Mary Antonia gasped and scrambled away, stumbling over a mound of snakeweed. "Ohhh, I can't do this," she wailed, clasping her hand to her thin chest. "He looks like an outlaw."

"All men look like outlaws to you," Blandina retorted.

Adela flushed as if Blandina's admonition had been meant for her, an accusation comparing her to fearful Mary Antonia—or worse, to O'Gilvie and his brief descent into barbarity.

With a pout on her thin lips, Mary Antonia returned to her corner and grabbed the blanket with both hands.

"Ready?" Adela looked at each one, then ordered, "Lift."

Adela struggled to synchronize their lurching movements as they carried him to the wagon. She and O'Gilvie hefted the man into the bed, then climbed in, pulling the blanket, while Blandina and Mary Antonia pushed from the ground. At last they had him settled. Adela knelt at his side and wiped her forehead, trying to ignore the perspiration that tickled her scalp beneath her bonnet and soaked the linen bindings wrapped around her chest.

O'Gilvie jumped to the ground and propped his forearms on the boxboard. "Ye know, findin' this one's changed things. I'm thinkin' there was another besides these two."

"What makes you say that?" asked Blandina.

"The head wound . . . ?" Adela offered.

O'Gilvie nodded. "A lick like that was likely the last thing ta happen. Someone must've bashed him with a rock, and our dead lad's injury wouldn't've allowed him the strength to do such a thing." He rapped a knuckle against the rail. "I'd best have meself a look around." With that, he strode to the front of the wagon and crouched in the road. He touched the ground, straightened, then shaded his eyes as he scoured the expanse of grassland to the southwest.

When he moved away, his head down in search of tracks, Adela returned her attention to her patient. As she searched his face for some hint of the truth, the reluctant sympathy for him returned. Sighing, she denied further thought by gently turning his head to one side on the folded blanket until he no longer faced her.

She scanned the wagon bed. Amidst mining tools and sacks of ore samples to be assayed were the bags of beans, flour, and cornmeal they'd been given in lieu of money at one of the mines.

"Can you climb up and hand me a couple of those?" she asked Blandina, pointing to the sacks. "I'll prop them around his body to keep him from being tossed about."

After she and Blandina had arranged the bags, Adela perched on a sack of flour at the wounded man's side.

"What about the other one?" Mary Antonia tilted her head in the direction of the body. "Are we taking him back with us?"

"No," said Adela. "Mr. O'Gilvie will bury him."

"I'm thinkin' that will have to wait," O'Gilvie said as he returned to the wagon and dropped his shovel in the bed.

"Why?"

"I found footprints of a third man and three sets o' hoofprints headed south, toward Albuquerque. Maybe the boy's friend. Maybe a horse thief. But whatever happened here a few hours ago, the sheriff should know about it. Maybe he knows who the lad is." He shrugged. "Or maybe the half-breed'll know somethin' when he wakes. If he's willin' to talk."

"Well, he isn't going to be able to say anything if we don't get him to the hospital."

"Aye. We'd best be goin'."

Blandina climbed over the backrest and sat down on the bench seat while O'Gilvie helped Mary Antonia into the wagon bed. Once she'd huddled in the only empty corner available, O'Gilvie vaulted into the driver's seat. He slapped the mules on the rump with the reins and the buckboard jerked into motion.

"Who do you suppose he is?" Adela asked.

"Judgin' by his red headband, he might be a scout for the military," O'Gilvie said.

"Maybe one of the soldiers at the hospital will know him," offered Blandina. "Or perhaps he has something on his person that will help identify him. Why don't you check his pockets?"

Dismayed by her superior's suggestion, Adela reached into one trouser pocket and then the other. Though she was careful not to prolong contact with the muscles of his upper thighs through the thin material, a strange sensation shivered through her stomach. Relieved to find nothing, she yanked her hand away.

Swallowing the breath she held, she turned her attention to the leather pouch on his belt. It contained only herbs. She fished the other pouch she'd found beside his body out of her habit pocket. Inside she found plant pollen, two white arrowheads, four long, vicious-looking curved teeth— mountain lion?—and a small black rock with a hole drilled through its top. The rock looked like obsidian, but was smooth, less shiny, and shaped almost like a teardrop.

What mystery did these fetishes hold?

At the bottom of the pouch she found a tightly wadded paper. Unfolding it, she discovered a poster issued by a Colorado bank. The handbill offered a hundred-dollar reward for N. S. Randolph. The man accused of forgery looked to be about fifty, with light-colored hair, possibly gray or silver. He bore no resemblance to the injured stranger, and certainly none to the dead youth. What would something so concrete as a wanted poster be doing in a bag of religious items?

"Do you think he's a bounty hunter?" she asked Blandina, handing her the bill.

When Blandina took the wrinkled paper, the wagon jolted into a hole. The unconscious man groaned and began to move his head.

"He's coming to," Mary Antonia whispered from her corner.

Adela palmed his cheek and turned his head so he would see her if he awakened. "Sir, can you hear me?"

He issued a moaning sigh and slowly opened his eyes. His irises, a rich amber-gold like she'd never seen before, caught the sunlight, and he blinked repeatedly before frowning up at her.

"Do you know your name?"

For a moment he looked blank, confused. Then he grimaced as he reached to touch his head.

"You've suffered a head injury."

Her explanation seemed to satisfy him, and his arm plopped back to his side, atop a sack of flour. His eyes drifted shut again.

Adela spoke to keep him conscious. "Can you tell me your name?"

He struggled to lift his eyelids. "What?"

"Your name. Can you tell me your name?"

"Which one"—he swallowed—"would you like?" His groggy voice sounded as dry as the summer landscape.

Realizing he probably hadn't had a drink of water for hours, Adela grabbed the canteen, uncorked it, and with unsteady hands lifted his head. After she'd trickled a few sips into his mouth, she helped him relax back against the blanket. When his head touched the makeshift pillow, pain jolted into his eyes.

Adela smiled her sympathy, but as he stared up at her, his expression of agony shifting to one of intense searching, she felt her lips tremble and straighten. She was overcome by the impression that he thought he should know her, but couldn't find the place in his foggy thoughts where she belonged.

"You have more than one name?" she asked, disconcerted by his avid attention. A blush burned her skin.

Mesmerized by his golden stare, Adela was reminded of a mountain lion. A predator. He had the same watchfulness, the same instinctual readiness for danger. She felt her blush deepen, followed by yet another inexplicable flutter in her stomach.

"You have more than one name?" she prodded again.

"I call myself Ladino, but my first name is . . ." He frowned, and for a moment his attention relented its intensity. "Christian."

Christian Ladino. Christian Half-breed. Adela couldn't help but stare at him as the paradox pierced her. A literal translation full of contradictions. The name lent even more ambiguity to his possession of the crucifix.

Perhaps it was his name alone, or the odd way he continued to study her as if he knew her—as if he could fathom things about her she didn't dare admit to herself—but Adela's animosity returned. She tore her attention from his face and wished he would do the same, but he did not. To distract herself, she contemplated the bandage over his knife wound, curious about the motive behind his injury.

Aware she fell into false judgment again, a challenge jumped to her lips nonetheless. "Well, Mr. Ladino, 'All they that shall take the sword shall perish by the sword.'"

As soon as she spoke, she recognized her condescending tone as a means of defense disguised as piety. Defense against what? In his condition, he couldn't hurt her physically.

She dared to meet his gaze. His expression darkened. Gesturing at his bandage, she hoped to draw his attention away from her. It didn't work, and more ill-chosen words rushed out of her mouth before she could snatch them back.

"Have you ever heard that, Mr. Ladino? It's from the Bible. The book of—"

"Save the evangelism for someone who gives a damn. I *know* what book it's in." His weak voice barely contained his sarcasm. "I've read it."

Adela flinched, stunned by his vehemence, surprised by his knowledge when before he could barely tell her his name. "I-I didn't mean . . ."

His study of her face intensified again, obliterating her train of thought.

"You're a nun," he said. "A Sister of Charity."

"Y-yes," she stammered, unable to keep the surprise out of her voice. Because their habits had been fashioned after Italian widow's weeds and sported a bonnet instead of the customary *serre-tête* and veil, many people didn't recognize her order. His knowledge astounded her even more when she remembered that her habit was brown, denoting her status as a brown novice. "How did you know?"

Concentration etched a deep frown between his thick straight brows. She could almost feel him knitting the threads of his thoughts back together, even as he fought the droop of his eyelids and inevitable unconsciousness. "I was on my way to Santa Fe to look for a nun. A Sister of Charity. Like you."

Adela's attention shot to Blandina, whose eyebrows hiked. She offered a shrug. Adela turned back to the injured man, but his eyes had closed.

"Mr. Ladino, wake up." She patted his cheek. No response, physical or otherwise. "Mr. Ladino." Frustration mingled with anxiety as she looked up again at Blandina. "What could he possibly want with one of us?"

Chapter Three

"An eye for an eye" didn't begin to describe the wrath of an Apache when he set out to avenge the murder of a family member. And since learning of the half-breed's release, Nigel Smeet hadn't been able to shake the dread that ate at his soul like a disease.

The blackmail attempt would have gone according to plan if he hadn't allowed this panic-stricken limbo to cloud his judgment. Even now, as he sat waiting for Randall Wiggins, a man who would prove instrumental in pulling off his newest, most elaborate scheme yet, he could think of little else but his hope that the men he'd hired to kill Ladino had accomplished their task.

The door to the Devil's Dew opened, threading afternoon sunlight to the most dismal corners of the adobe barroom. Unaware he held his breath, Smeet looked up from his seat at a table in one of those dark corners, unsure whom he expected to see. Would it be Ladino himself, not dead after all?

When he recognized the silhouette of Wiggins—the plump upper body and protruding paunch emphasized by the tight frock coat—his breath escaped on a sigh of relief.

Nigel sneered at himself and muttered, "Grab 'old of yerself." In the privacy of the moment, he relaxed his affected British accent, betraying the tattered Cockney he usually tried so hard to hide. "It certainly ain't the 'alf-breed, unless prison's taken to servin' seven-course meals."

Wiggins closed the door behind him and searched the

barroom. Turning in the direction of the barkeep, Nigel raised a hand and gestured for the man to bring another shot glass. Wiggins saw the exchange, tipped his hat in acknowledgment, and squeezed through spaces between chairs as he made his way to Nigel's table. Once at his destination, he murmured his thanks to the bartender, who nodded and left.

"Mr. Wiggins," Nigel said, nodding a further greeting.

"Captain Smeet," Wiggins returned, smiling as he pulled out a chair and sat down. Nigel frowned at the man's use of his old cavalry rank, but Wiggins either didn't see, or ignored his disapproval as he swept off his derby, pulled out another chair, and placed the hat in the seat. "I've talked to my supplier. I can have the guns to El Paso a week from Saturday, Captain—"

"*Mr.* Smeet," Nigel corrected, his voice tight. None of the Cockney slipped now.

"Of course. How remiss of me. When you're accustomed to addressing a man by his rank, you tend to forget when it no longer applies." Wiggins twittered a nervous laugh, but when Nigel refused to smile, the man cleared his throat. "Well," he said, lifting his horn-shaped brows, the expression akin to a shrug. He glanced at the shot glass in front of him and then at the bottle of whiskey. "May I?" At Nigel's curt nod, he poured himself two fingers. "As I said, my men can have the guns for you Saturday, north of El Paso, just as you requested." Wiggins threw back the shot. With a flourish, he set the glass back on the table next to the half-empty bottle of whiskey. "And you have the money?"

"The first half. Five hundred dollars." Nigel pulled a black velvet bag full of gold twenty-dollar double eagles out of his coat pocket and pushed it across the table toward Wiggins.

"Well," Wiggins repeated, again with the shrug of his heavy gray brows. He smiled. "You've just bought yourself fifty .45-caliber Sharps single-shot rifles. And what a bargain I've made you—each rifle a quarter of its true worth. I've even thrown in plenty of ammunition for good measure."

"Enough of the belated salesmanship, Wiggins." Nigel tried not to look at the bag of coins. It had taken him a month of playing poker and faro to earn that money. Some of it he'd even won honestly. But Wiggins would expect the rest upon delivery, and Nigel didn't yet have a dime of the remainder. "I'm doing you a favor by taking the things off your hands. None but the Indians want them anymore."

"It's a good thing for my business they do," Wiggins agreed. He hefted the bag, shook it, and smiled at the metallic clatter. "Is that what you want them for? To trade to the Indians?"

Nigel leaned forward. "Come now, Mr. Wiggins, why would you say a thing like that?" His voice held a condescending threat. "Trading or selling firearms to the Indians is illegal. Neither of us would be involved in that sort of business, now would we?"

Wiggins's smile faded and he lowered the bag. Clearing his throat, he fumbled with his lapel, dropping the bag in his pocket. Nigel dragged his attention away and took a sip of whiskey.

Once again the *cantina* door opened. Startled, Nigel pulled the glass away from his mouth. He cursed as liquor dribbled down his chin and shirtfront. Pulling out his handkerchief, he dabbed at the spill while keeping his eye on the figure in the doorway. Sunlight caught golden fuzz along the boy's jaw and Nigel recognized him at last. Benjamin Duffy. The younger of the two he'd hired to kill Ladino.

When Nigel saw the unfamiliar black leather gun belt slung low on the boy's slim hips, he felt a shiver of anticipation. If the rig had belonged to Ladino . . .

He watched Ben remove his limp woolsey hat and cast a nervous search throughout the room. At last Ben's gaze found his. The boy stepped forward, but was stopped by the bartender. After a few words, Ben unbuckled the gun belt and handed it over. The barkeep returned to his position and placed the rig on a shelf beneath the mirror that reflected every table in the barroom.

Nigel turned back to Wiggins and found the man's lips twisted in a shrewd smile. "Your new friend is younger than Perry, isn't he?" He tilted his head in feigned interest. "By the way, how is Perry? Still spending the allowance you give him on the fruit of the poppy?"

As Wiggins's suggestive smile broadened into a leer, Nigel was torn between the desire to laugh at the man's superior attitude and the urge to reach across the table and rip out the man's throat. He tamped down his fury, reminding himself that a fool's underestimation of another man's power was the key to the fool's destruction.

Comforted by that thought, Nigel felt brash enough to play up his part as he cast a hungry glance at Ben. "We've concluded our business for now, haven't we?"

"Certainly." Wiggins patted his coat pocket. "I look forward to completing our . . . mutually beneficial agreement."

"As do I, Randall," Nigel said, letting his wrist go limp as he emphasized his intimate use of the man's name with a sly smile . . . a smile of double entendre. "As do I."

Wiggins flushed and cleared his throat. "Yes. Well." This time the eyebrow shrug was followed by a true lift of his shoulders, as if he'd suddenly grown uncomfortable in his tight frock coat. "Until Saturday."

Standing, he retrieved his hat. He wheeled about, almost toppling his chair in his haste to get away. Passing Ben amidst the maze of chairs, he nodded once and fled. Silent laughter shook Nigel's chest. Teasing the bloody fool had been rather cruel, yet he'd relished every moment of his performance.

By now, Ben had reached his table and stood behind the chair Wiggins had vacated. "It's done, Mr. Smeet." He licked his lips and swallowed. "I did it."

"Do you have the proof?"

Ben hesitated and began to fold and unfold his hat brim.

Smeet kicked the chair farther out and grabbed Ben's arm, forcing him down. "The proof, boy. The bloody half-breed's scalp. Do you have it?"

"N-no, sir." Ben closed his eyes as if fighting back nausea. "But after I whacked him on the head with a rock, I—I saw the death throes. I ain't never seen those before. I stole his gun, but he thrashed around so much I was scared—"

Like a striking snake, Nigel clamped his fingers around Ben's chin. "Let me understand this," he hissed into the boy's face. "You don't have the proof?"

"No, sir," Ben whispered, his voice a meek slur, his Adam's apple bouncing as he swallowed.

Nigel released his grip, sat back, and forced his panic to yield control. "Your friend," he began, his voice moderate now. "Does he have it?"

Ben stared at Nigel, his expression startled.

"Well?"

Ben dropped his gaze to his lap, but not before Nigel saw the boy's lips pull down at the corners. For several moments Ben remained silent as he traced a shaking thumb along his hat brim.

"Jim's dead," he said. "Ladino killed him."

The boy looked ready to cry. Nigel knew then Ben Duffy wasn't lying. He pushed Wiggins's empty glass before the boy and uncorked the whiskey bottle. As he poured, the amber liquid gurgled for air. Nigel filled the glass. For a moment Ben looked uncertain, but he lifted the glass at last and jerked back the shot. Derision crept into Nigel's smile as the youngster shuddered and licked his moist lips. Such a timid little rabbit.

For the hundredth time Nigel wondered if he should have hired a professional shootist. And for the hundredth time, he reminded himself professionals demanded higher wages and weren't nearly so malleable. Besides, if Ben Duffy had killed the 'breed and lived to steal his gun, he might not be useless after all.

"When?"

"This morning. About ten miles out of Santa Fe."

Too close. Ladino had gotten much too close.

Nigel closed his eyes.

"We couldn't shoot him like we'd planned," the boy explained. "Soldiers from Fort Marcy were close by. They'd've heard. So we ambushed him . . ."

As the boy rattled on, Nigel decided he needed another drink as well.

Too close. Ladino had gotten much too close.

The words became a litany, a taunting chant in his brain.

". . . We thought we had him just out of Silver City," Ben continued, warming to his tale. "In the Black Range. But he disappeared. I don't know if he figured someone was trailin' him, or if he just likes to be on the careful side. But we lost him. So we went to Hawley's cabin, figurin' he might be there—"

"And he'd already been there."

Ben looked surprised. "Yeah. Hawley said the half-breed threatened to kill him if he didn't tell where you was. Poor Hawley, he didn' know you was here in Albuquerque."

"So how did you decide Ladino would go to Santa Fe?"

"The newspaper article."

Aside from the half-breed, the botched blackmail attempt continued to be the scourge of Nigel's life, splattered across the front page of every newspaper in the Territory as it had been.

"Hawley showed him the paper. Ladino ripped out the article and took it with him. I didn' know Injuns could read." Ben frowned, then shrugged. "Anyway, we figured he'd head back to Silver City lookin' for the Westbrooks, but since we knew they'd gone to White Oaks to check on their mines, we decided he'd head for Santa Fe to see if the nun could tell him anything . . ."

Ben recounted the remainder of his story, his agitation disappearing under the influence of liquor as he related how Ladino had stabbed Jim, killing him.

"What a pity," Nigel said, shaking his head in mock compassion. "So you had to finish Ladino alone, am I correct?"

"Yeah." Ben smiled. "Half-breed didn't know what hit him."

The boy's bravado was apparent now. Nigel smiled. If a man lived past the nausea the first time, murder—with practice—could become second nature. Though Nigel had to admit extermination was simpler when one didn't believe a man to be as human as oneself. And what was a half-breed, but something only half-human? Yes, bravado was a start. True pride would come later for Ben Duffy.

Lifting the whiskey bottle, Nigel raised his eyebrow in question. At the boy's nod, Nigel poured, his smile widening into a malevolent grin. The ease with which he corrupted this innocent amused him. A little money, some whiskey, a listening ear, and the boy was addicted to the taste of power over the life of another human being. Still, it was wise to keep him wanting more. Keep him hoping for more.

But the boy hadn't gotten proof. For that he would have to be punished. Nigel knew just how to do it—and how to test him at the same time.

"Well, Benjamin"—Nigel poured a drink for himself and corked the bottle—"with Jim no longer in on the deal, that's fifty dollars less I'll have to pay, wouldn't you say?"

Ben fidgeted with the crown of his hat as he stared at Nigel, his expression screaming his eagerness to speak.

"Drink up, dear boy," Nigel goaded, smiling in mock innocence as he set the bottle aside and waited for Ben to gather courage.

"I-I was hopin' you'd give me his share, Mr. Smeet," began Ben. "B-bein's you was gonna pay a hundred anyway."

Nigel snorted, though he laughed inwardly. "Not bloody likely. Without proof, I may not pay you one red cent."

Anger ignited in Ben's brown eyes. "I told you, Mr. Smeet. The 'breed's dead. Bashin' his skull oughta be worth a hundred."

Ahh, so Benjamin Duffy wasn't such a timid rabbit after all. Of course he'd never tell the boy he would have paid more than a mere hundred dollars for the scalp of El Ladino Greñudo—the Long-haired Half-breed. Not only would the trophy have symbolized the Apache's humiliation, it would have provided the talisman he needed to exorcise the demon of the 'breed's grisly promise.

"I think you need to understand who is boss, Mr.

Duffy," Nigel advised, his tone grave with a veiled threat. "Greed is not something I will tolerate in anyone but myself."

Ben's face went slack for a moment, but his shifting expressions revealed a desperation to save the moment. At last he contorted his anger into a mask of disappointment and apology. Amused by the boy's obvious play at shrewdness, Nigel allowed himself a twitch of one lip.

"Still, I'm proud of you, Benjamin." Nigel prepared to inflict the punishment that would destroy one more degree of the boy's spirit. "Already the death of your friend means less to you than an extra fifty dollars."

Shock and grief obliterated Ben's pretense. Nigel felt himself soften. Such harsh truths about oneself were always the most difficult to accept. What could it hurt to let the poor boy believe he'd won this round?

"Don't look so glum, Mr. Duffy," Nigel cajoled. "How does seventy-five sound?" He looked at the boy's cheap hat. "And a brand-new Stetson?"

The boy stared at him for several moments, calculation at odds with a final shred of remorse. At last a sly smile coated Ben's lips like oil, reminding Nigel of Perry before the opium had claimed him. "Sounds fine, Mr. Smeet."

Shoving aside disturbing thoughts of Perry, Nigel pulled a deck of marked cards from his vest pocket. "All right then, my dear boy," he said. "I'll pay you as soon as I drum up a card game and win a few hands. Then we'll find a haberdasher."

Ben's shoulders slumped, and he fingered a hole in his hat. "You wouldn't have any more work for me, would you, Mr. Smeet?"

Again Nigel offered Ben a rare, genuine smile. Oh, how he liked easily pleased, groveling young boys. What was more, with Ladino dead, he could afford to concentrate on his most recent scheme. If all went according to plan, he'd be wealthy, no longer forced to pay his debts from game to game.

Best of all, his old friend, Jonathan Westbrook, would be a begging, broken man.

Nigel cupped his palm on Ben's shoulder. The muscles felt surprisingly strong for a young man of such slight frame. "Do you know anything about babies, Mr. Duffy?"

Adela knelt at the prie-dieu during the Office of Compline, the last liturgical hour before bedtime. A cool breeze wafted across the altar candles, quivering shadows on the pages of the prayer book open before her. While the sisters around her recited psalms, Adela's thoughts centered on Christian Ladino.

Upon their arrival at St. Vincent's, his care had been taken over by Sister Mary de Sales, who had refused Adela's help and had ordered her to get some rest. But rest and peace were impossible when all she could think about was the Apache's possible reason for seeking out a Sister of Charity.

A touch on the shoulder startled her. "Mother Eulalia wishes to speak with you in her office."

Dread flooded Adela's body as she glanced up and found Karen, one of the oldest orphan girls, staring down at her.

"Did she say why?"

At a stern look from one of the sisters, Karen shook her head and gestured for Adela to get up. Adela rose, threading her rosary through the belt at her waist with trembling hands. She followed the young girl through the groaning side chapel door and across the *placita* toward the convent and orphan asylum. Piles of cut stone and fresh lumber littered their path, materials from the new shell taking shape around the adobe parish church. Entering the old convent, they wended their way by candlelight through the rabbit's warren of thick-walled corridors.

When Karen reached the room she shared with four other girls, she stopped and turned in the open doorway. "Good night, Sister Adela. I hope all goes well."

Adela nodded. "Thank you. Give little Mary a good-night kiss for me."

Karen offered a tremulous smile and ducked into her room, leaving Adela to continue alone.

As her heels echoed on polished wooden planks, she filled her lungs with air that smelled of ancient earth and the comforting essence of lemon oil. But when she reached Mother Eulalia's office door and found it closed, her stomach throbbed. Mother Eulalia never shut her door unless she planned to reprimand a wayward nun. Her policy was one of little privacy—privacy being a vain indulgence that encouraged questionable behavior.

Adela rapped lightly upon the wood.

"Come!"

Stepping inside, Adela made her bow of obeisance.

"Shut the door behind you and take a seat."

After closing the door, Adela moved across the room to sit on a rough-hewn bench by the room's single, unadorned window. She remained silent, watching as Mother Eulalia wrote in her daily record book, her head bent at such a severe angle that her bonnet strings cut into her bird-thin neck.

Taking another deep breath, she tried to distract herself by letting her attention wander about the room. Other than the desk and the bench, the chamber claimed only a couple of chairs and a small bookshelf graced with neat rows of centuries-old religious tomes. Among the titles were water-stained editions of the *Summa*, the *Theologia Moralis*, and the *Virgini Deiparae*.

Adela jumped when Mother Eulalia stabbed her pen in its stand. "I have matters of some urgency that I wish to discuss with you." She capped her ink bottle and removed her spectacles, setting them aside. "One of these concerns your mother. She is due to visit tomorrow from Silver City."

Adela's entire body tingled with a strange, prickly heat. "Silver City? My mother?"

"Isn't that what I just said?"

"But—" *Silver City*. She'd just been there, soliciting hospital funds from the surrounding mines. Her mother lived there? How could she have been so close without knowing? How could Mother Eulalia not have told her before now?

Adela laughed, the sound a bitter rasp in her throat.

"I fail to see what you find amusing."

"After fifteen years, after so much heartache, she wants to see me now? Why?"

"You may find this difficult to accept or understand, Adela, but your mother has been sending us funds for your upkeep. She has always asked to be kept informed of your progress."

"And no one told me?" She shot to her feet. "*Why* was I not told? Why didn't she tell me herself?"

"Enough! Sit down and allow me to finish."

Jaw clenched, body trembling, Adela obeyed, perching herself on the edge of the bench.

"I do not claim to know why your mother has requested that her whereabouts be kept secret until now, but she has decided she wants to introduce you to her new husband and infant son."

"New husband?" She clutched the bench seat until her fingers ached. "Son?" More laughter threatened, and only a splinter digging into her little finger kept her grounded in reality. "My mother has a son?"

"Yes."

Waves of hot envy sluiced over the ache of cold betrayal, bringing the fury she thought she had smothered years ago back to life. Now that her mother had married, the baby would have the kind of home Adela had always longed for, a home filled with faith in the safety and security of a mother's love.

"But as important as this news is, it is the least pressing of my reasons for summoning you."

While Adela reeled from her superior's revelations, she watched Eulalia thumb through a neat stack of papers. At last the nun came across a scrap of newspaper, and another paper which looked to be a rumpled advertisement bill. She held up both.

"Have you seen these, Adela?"

Adela frowned at the advertisement. She recognized it as the wanted poster she'd found in the half-breed's medicine bag. But she'd never seen the newspaper. Except for the *Revista Catolica*, newspapers seldom found their way into the convent.

Mother Eulalia scowled her impatience and fluttered both papers in the air. On shaky legs, Adela rose to retrieve them. Glancing over them, she returned to her seat.

"I believe you found the poster concerning Mr. Randolph. But Sister Mary de Sales found the newspaper article later, in one of the Indian's moccasins. Read it."

Wondering what lecture Mother Eulalia could be leading up to, and puzzled as to how this could possibly pertain to anything she had been told about her mother, Adela looked first at the wanted poster. She still saw nothing about the man's features or name that tugged at her memory, so she studied the piece of newspaper. It had been ripped from the *Silver City Enterprise* and reeked of sweat and leather. Her mind numb, she noticed the engraving of some unknown Sister of Charity below the headline. Adela looked up at Mother Eulalia.

"Read it aloud if you please."

" 'Millionaire Mining Magnate's Wife Has Illegitimate Daughter,' " she read, her throat tightening on the implication. " 'Blackmail Attempt Goes Awry.' "

Blackmail?

"The article is about you."

Adela swallowed as she stared at the paper. The words shivered on the page as she continued to read.

" 'For the past fifteen years, Mrs. Jonathan Westbrook has been hiding her illegitimate daughter in the Orphan Asylum run by the Sisters of Charity of Santa Fe, and it appears this daughter has become a sister herself. Nigel Smeet, Westbrook's ex-partner in the Silver Samson mine, learned of this information from hired investigators and attempted to blackmail Mrs. Westbrook with his knowledge. Confronted with past sins, Mrs. Westbrook wisely decided to tell her husband, thus bashing Mr. Smeet's hope of material gain. When asked further details about her daughter, Mrs. Westbrook declined to divulge details of her youthful impropriety. Mr. Smeet, upon learning of his failed blackmail attempt, has disappeared.

" 'If you recall, Westbrook shocked everyone by marrying this woman from the streets . . .' "

Adela continued to stare at the wrinkled newsprint while the remaining words faded into obscurity.

"It doesn't mention you by name, Sister Adela, at least

we can be thankful for that."

As Adela handed the papers back to Eulalia, her heart battered her rib cage. Could she be the sister he was seeking? Beyond the information printed in the newspaper, what did the half-breed know about her mother? Or about her? What did he want? Did he have something to do with the blackmail attempt?

Stop!

Adela closed her eyes and held the barrage of questions at bay. She forced herself to calm, to consider logic and common sense in her approach. She swallowed her panic, breathed to ease her racing heart, and focused on her superior.

"Mother Eulalia, I'd like to ask him about this article."

"That wouldn't be wise."

"Why not?"

"I want you to stay away from him. He could be working for this Nigel Smeet, planning to harm you or your mother."

"If so, I'd like to know instead of wondering and waiting in fear."

Mother Eulalia's lips tightened. "You've always been such an impulsive, intractable child." She took a deep breath and let out a long, controlled sigh. "You're an excellent nurse, second only to Sister Mary de Sales, and Sister Blandina seems to think you'll make a fine Sister of Charity. I have my doubts."

"Yes, Mother." Adela bowed her head to show her penitence. Her nursing ability and Blandina's confidence were the two things that brought her to heel, and Mother Eulalia knew it.

"Under normal circumstances," Eulalia continued, her tone long-suffering, "I might not offer an explanation, but in this case I believe it advisable."

Mother Eulalia folded her hands and rested them on her desk. Adela knew this meant the discussion would continue at the mercy of the senior nun's need for complete control.

"Sister Mary de Sales tells me this man has the letter H tattooed on his forehead. Is that correct, Sister Adela?"

Adela frowned, wondering where this could be leading. "Yes, it was covered by his headband, but—"

"Do you know what that means?"

"No," Adela murmured.

"I talked to the sheriff this afternoon. He says military convicts are often marked with a tattoo of some sort as a warning of their unsavory character. He plans to investigate further, but right now he believes this man murdered the boy you found."

Hearing her own suspicion expressed by the sheriff, an authority, made her shudder anew. But if the Apache had murdered the boy in cold blood, why had he suffered injuries of his own?

"And that's not all," continued Mother Eulalia. "He suspects this man might have escaped from prison at Fort Yuma, or possibly even Alcatraz, since it is to these prisons that the military often sends its Apache scouts when they've committed crimes."

Murderer. Convict. Escaped prisoner.

Each word reverberated in Adela's mind, vividly reconstructing her first impression of Christian Ladino. The more she learned about him, the more questions followed, and the more confused she became. And now his possession of the newspaper article gave her one more reason to fear him. Still, because of the deep respect she held for Sister Blandina, for her mentor's objectivity, she chose to play devil's advocate.

"But what if he was *released* from prison?" Adela shrugged. "Before we assume he intends the worst, Mother, I think it would be more sensible to see why he has the article, or if he even remembers anything about this. Head injuries—"

"I disagree. If he has no recollection, so much the better. I don't want to take the chance of reminding him." She stood. "We don't know the circumstances behind his injuries. He's probably a murderer, and at the very least, his possession of the wanted poster tells me he's of a mercenary bent."

The wanted poster. N. S. Randolph. Adela frowned. *Could the initials stand for Nigel Smeet?*

"Mother Eulalia, if the Apache truly is a bounty hunter, isn't it possible that Randolph and Smeet are one and the same? Perhaps he's only searching for this person and thinks my mother or I might know his whereabouts."

"Be that as it may, I'm going to order that he be moved to a private room in the morning. The other nurses will tend him until he is well enough to be discharged. If my prayers are answered, he will be none the wiser about your identity. You are not to set foot in his room. Is that clear?"

Adela shook with suppressed fury. "Perfectly."

"Good. I'm glad you understand. I have the safety of the other sisters as well as yours to consider here, and your situation has always been especially trying." Mother Eulalia opened the door. "Now, it is time you retired for the night. I'm sure you'll want to be rested for your mother's visit tomorrow."

As Adela strode from the room, she did not offer Mother Eulalia the slightest bow, much less a genuflection. If anything, Mother Eulalia's edict only made her more determined to discover Mr. Ladino's connection to her and to this Mr. Smeet who had tried to blackmail her mother.

He could be perfectly harmless.

Or infinitely dangerous.

Chapter Four

Adela's stride devoured the short distance between the rambling adobe convent and the new three-story hospital. St. Vincent's shone white in the moonlight below its black cap of mansard roof and dormer windows.

Time and again Mother Eulalia had told her that unquestioning faith in her superiors would lead to greater faith in God, her ultimate superior. But to Adela, that kind of blind obedience—to those as mortal as she—just didn't feel comfortable sometimes, or even smart. Adela resented being badgered into submission. She resented being expected to become a spectator to her own life, an insensitive machine with no right to personal emotions. Most of all she resented Mother Eulalia's refusal to give her credit for having a mind of her own or the common sense to use it.

But this time, at least where the Apache was concerned, Mother Eulalia could be right. Having to admit the possibility made Adela clench her jaw and lengthen her gait.

Once she'd reached her third-story dormer room, she lit her candle and went about her nightly ritual with more energy than usual. In fantasy, she envisioned stripping off her habit and recklessly throwing each piece to a different corner of her stark chamber. In reality, she fumed but followed custom as she slipped her white cotton nightdress over her head and chastely removed each piece of her habit beneath the gown's voluminous folds.

She unwound the binding from her breasts, stripped off hot cotton stockings, and stepped out of layers of petticoats. After slipping her arms into the sleeves of her nightrail, she folded the habit pieces that lay draped across her cot. To each article—her dress, her cape, her white cotton undersleeves—she gave a perfunctory kiss. Opening the trunk at the foot of her bed, she placed the garments inside where they would lie fallow, waiting for her next trip abroad.

Realizing she hadn't yet removed her bonnet, Adela allowed herself one small mutiny. She yanked the bow loose at her throat, jerked the bonnet off her head, and threw it atop the folded pieces in her trunk. Like one element of her personality purposely askew, the rumpled headwear shouted its individuality amidst fragments of her barren self. She slammed the lid shut and flipped the latches.

Heaving a sigh, she plopped down on her cot, reached into the cool space beneath her pillow, and pulled out Abbie, her childhood playmate and confidante. She stroked the armless, legless corncob doll, remembering how she'd cuddled Abbie like the daughters of her mother's employers had cuddled their own dolls of fine French porcelain. She also recalled slamming Abbie against the wall during fits of rage over her mother's desertion. Adela could still feel the crack where Hermana Dolores had glued the doll's "head" back on her body after just such a tantrum.

Fingering the circle of faded calico around the doll's body, Adela remembered the day her mother had made Abbie's skirt out of a scrap from the only new dress Adela had ever owned. She'd been wearing that dress, a size too small and bloodstained, the day Minna had left her on the doorstep of the orphan asylum.

For fifteen years Adela had lived with shame for the part she believed she had played in driving her mother away. Still, she could understand why Minna had wanted a fresh start. Marrying someone as wealthy and influential as Jonathan Westbrook certainly explained why her mother had never planned a visit until now, when she'd been forced to acknowledge the truth about her illegitimate daughter because of a blackmail attempt and a mean-spirited article in a newspaper.

Had her mother really been so ashamed of her? Or had she kept her existence secret in order to avoid revealing the darker one they shared?

Adela tried to convince herself she didn't care about the reason for her mother's visit. She tried to convince herself that the convent was her home now. Perhaps it was just Blandina who loved her, but when she took the next step in her novitiate training by becoming a black novice, she would be that much closer to vows that would proclaim her a permanent member of the only family she had ever known. In addition, nursing was a justifiable calling. It had become the most vital part of her, for though she couldn't yet obey God in her own life, she could save the lives of others for His use. Surely He would consider that when she displeased Him with the weakness of her faith.

Faith. Too much pain filled Adela's heart for there to be room left for such a mutable emotion. Yet she yearned for its conciliation of soul. She prayed long and hard for its conviction to wash over her and cleanse her heart. She craved the assurance that she would never be abandoned again.

Standing abruptly, she combed her fingers through her hair, willing the confusion and anguish to leave her body. Her scalp tingled as short chestnut curls fell light and full and, best of all, *free* around her face.

Conscience told her she flirted with vanity. Mother Eulalia would not approve. But how could she be vain when her quarters boasted no mirror? Unless she counted the times she'd happened upon her murky reflection in her darkened window at night, Adela hadn't seen her face or body for years.

She moved into the dormer alcove and studied her image in the window glass. She touched the curling wisps of her hair. She smoothed a hand down her cheek. It was as if her features belonged to a stranger. And they did, for they belonged, at least in part, to her mother.

Mama, what will you look like now?

What will I say to you?

Do you think we can—?

No. She refused to waste any more spirit on childhood dreams . . . or nightmares. This new baby—this new *life*— was her mother's priority now, as becoming a Sister of Charity was her own. She would not allow herself to hope for more than the small corner she'd once occupied in her mother's heart.

As she continued to stand before the window, raking her fingers through her short tresses, her reasons for studying her reflection changed. She turned her head, glancing sidelong into the windowpane. Why should it be such a sin to enjoy the feel of her own hair? Or her own body beneath her gown?

Little hypocrite, a voice whispered.

Adela stopped. She lowered her hands. Unbidden, a vision of the Apache's amber eyes taunted her, shimmering with the knowing light of mischief. She balled her night-dress in her hands as heat radiated up her arms. For the first time she recognized the name of her newest fear. Attraction. She had reacted to him not as a nun, but as a woman.

Stunned by this revelation, she flung up the window

sash, destroying her image. Hoping to destroy his. Yet despite the cool breeze that burst through the opening, billowing muslin curtains into her eyes, she still saw his face, smiling at her.

So be it. She'd grown accustomed to God's antagonism in other struggles; she'd accustom herself to His antagonism in this one. Perhaps Christian Ladino would be the instrument through which she could prove to God the intensity of her will to become a Sister of Charity. No one had forced her to take the habit. Not Mother Eulalia. Not her mother. She had made the choice on her own.

Wheeling away from the window, she rushed back across the room and pulled the rubber mat and lye soap out of her nightstand. After slapping the mat on the floor beside her bed, she poured cold water from the chipped ewer into the basin, ignoring the water that sloshed over the lip. She yanked her arms out of her sleeves and bathed beneath her gown. The cloth chafed her skin until it stung, allowing no room for any sensation except discomfort. No room for any emotion except repentance.

Her rebellion tamped down, Adela covered her hair with her night bonnet and tied the white strings beneath her chin. From the center of her pillow she lifted her crucifix, gave it a reverent kiss, then set it on her nightstand. As she slid into her narrow cot and blew out the candle, she couldn't believe how comfortable her lumpy mattress felt after two months of sleeping on the ground. But her room had also hoarded the afternoon heat, and despite bone-deep exhaustion, Adela couldn't sleep.

Her thoughts circled back to Christian Ladino. Even if it wasn't wise, she felt a desperate need to know what he wanted. She feared him, yes, but she feared the unknown more. In this instance, even though she risked Mother

Eulalia's wrath, and possibly her chance of becoming a black novice, Adela preferred knowing what to expect, what to prepare for.

A scream rent the darkness. A slam and a crash followed. Adela knifed upright, instantly alert. She heard another scream from the hospital wards, recognized it as feminine, and hurtled out of bed. They had no female patients!

Grabbing the door frame, she swung herself into the hallway, her momentum propelling her toward the stairwell. Nightdress clutched to her knees, she flew down two flights of stairs. When she entered the main hospital ward, she drew up short.

Two rows of narrow cots marched down either side of the ward, pulling her complete attention past night-blackened windows to the far left corner of the room. The legs of a toppled table tilted at a crazy angle, and a puddle of water crept across the floorboards from an overturned blue and white enamelware basin.

Tangled in water-soaked sheets, the half-blood Apache had one muscular arm clutched about Sister Martina, who lay sprawled atop his semi-prone body. In his other hand he gripped a pair of scissors, points pressed against the nurse's throat.

Martina gasped as she groped at her captor's hands. Patients gawked from the safety of their beds, and the nurses stood stock-still, faces stricken with terror.

Adela scanned the room for Sister Barbara, the nurse in charge. Standing among the others, Barbara watched the scene as if nailed to the floor.

Finding no help there, Adela rushed forward. Her movement captured the Apache's attention. Lamplight glanced off the silver crucifix nestled in the V of his soaked nightshirt as he pressed the scissor blades closer to the erratic

57

pulse along Martina's throat. He peered through long strands of wet hair, insane terror and hatred shimmering in his predatory eyes.

"Don't come near me," he whispered, his voice weighted with deadly menace, "or I'll kill him!"

Cold. He was so cold. And hot at the same time. Ladino's body convulsed with the burning chill. He was in hell—the hell of a White Eye as fingers of fog rose off endless water, permeating his prison cell and creeping into his soul.

Forcing his eyes open, he saw light glint off metal. A knife! He grabbed the hand that held the blade above his head.

"Please let go," a voice said. "I need to cut your hair."

"No," Ladino said weakly, shaking his head. When he focused past the gleaming metal, a round, bodiless face, surrounded by white haze and lamplight, stared back at him. Where was Red Beard? Ladino's eyes hurt, and the face began to blur. He squeezed his lids shut, trying to clear his vision. Another spasm wracked his body, and his hold loosened. Again he shook his head. "No," he repeated, his voice a croak of distress.

He felt as if his mind were being pried apart from his body by cold, wet fingers. The hand he held tried to twist out of his grasp. A trick. He forced his eyes open yet again and clamped his hand around the escaping wrist. The face above him grimaced in pain. Additional hands, attached somehow to more disembodied faces, swarmed around him, grasping and clawing at his head, his arms, his legs, holding him down. Being too weak to fight increased his panic and fury.

"No!" he roared.

"*Please* let me go, Mr. Ladino. I need to cut your hair." He saw the knife move, separate, become two blades. *Beelédidili*—scissors. "It's for your own good—to bring down your fever."

Ladino felt his grip shaking, and his stomach muscles screamed in pain as he fought to keep his head raised against the pressure of hands forcing him down. Distant laughter from that place of fog and sleeping visions grew louder, clearer, until the sound coalesced with sea waves slapping against rock. The demonic mixture transported him once more to his colorless hell where yet another face, a different face—no, a handful of faces—stared at him.

Ladino sat in a chair, his neck bound to the ladder back by rope. He couldn't command so much as a hairsbreadth of movement. Shallow breaths were all he could afford. His chafed neck burned, and his wrists were bound so tightly they bled. He tried to move his feet, but strained at more rope binding him to the chair. A man in a dusty blue uniform sat on a stool between his legs, a bloody needle in his hand. Ladino felt another pinprick on his forehead, but refused to show pain or emotion.

"If it were my decision we'd be branding his arse instead of giving him that tattoo." The voice came from behind him, and Ladino realized the man held his head clamped between his hands, as if the rope around his neck weren't enough.

"Nobody could see it then," explained another.

"Oh, I don't know," came the lazy voice of the guard who stood next to the man wielding the tattoo needle. "His face, his rump, what's the difference? Injuns're all butt-ugly if ya ask me." He cackled in sly amusement.

Determined to force the cackler, his prey, into submission, Ladino focused energy from his entire being into the stare of his Mescalero namesake. 'Idui Bndaa'. Eyes of the Mountain Lion.

"You need a haircut, Injun," the cackler said, but his laughter had ceased, leaving an expression of apprehension in its place. The cowardly coyote backhanded the needle man's shoulder, almost knocking him off his stool. "Don't he need a haircut, Hugh?"

Frowning, Needle Man righted himself on his seat. "Just as soon as I give him this H for Half-breed." He pricked Ladino's forehead, and Ladino felt a trickle of blood between his brows before Needle Man wiped it away with a filthy, bloodstained cloth, damp from the pinkened water in the basin.

When the tattooist finished, one of the other guards, a man with a grizzled red beard, brought scissors. A chorus of laughter and whistles echoed in the small stone room.

"No!" Ladino yelled. He bucked in his chair and toppled over backward, almost strangling himself as he crashed to one side.

"Sittin' up, layin' down, I don't give a damn." Red Beard opened and closed the blades with malicious glee. "One way or another we're gonna cut off all that girly hair." He laughed, dribbling a stream of tobacco in Ladino's face.

"No!"

Ladino bucked again, scooting the chair several inches across the stone floor. The ropes tightened around his throat. Then, as if in a mystical dream, his bindings disappeared. He was free!

Ladino grabbed Red Beard's hand in both of his and wrenched the scissors from the guard's grasp. He clutched the man's shirt, and as they battled, Red Beard kicked over the table littered with needles and ink. Water from the basin splashed into Ladino's face. He yanked his tormentor close and held the scissors to the bearded man's throat.

Red Beard groped at his hands. Another guard came closer. Ladino trapped this new threat in his sight.

"Don't come near me," he warned, pressing the scissors into Red Beard's neck, "or I'll kill him."

The guard stopped, his face frozen in shock. But his inactivity lasted only an instant. He made a head signal to one of the others standing nearby. A white-clad figure sped away and Ladino grew suspicious. None of the guards had been dressed in white . . .

"What did you tell him to do? Where is he going?"

"Calm down, Mr. Ladino." The guard held his hands up in a gesture of surrender. "We mean you no harm." With each word, he eased closer. "Why don't you let Sister Martina go? She only meant to help."

Ladino frowned. Sister Martina? He clenched his jaw against the dizzy, floating sensation growing in his head. The faces staring at him grew fuzzy. Silence expanded. He strained to listen, but could no longer hear ocean waves slamming against rock outside. Instead, he heard crickets.

Squinting, he shook his head. "What are you trying to do, trick me?" Ladino's hand shook as he pressed the scissors ever farther into the guard's neck. Any farther and he'd draw blood.

"No! No tricks." The voice came quickly, an appeal to an angry god. "I promise."

Ladino's vision continued to blur, and the guard stepped closer. He, too, was clad all in white.

"None of this is real, is it?" he asked, his voice panic-stricken. "I'm dead," he offered as his own explanation.

"No, you're running a high fever, and you've been given morphine for pain. The combination is making you imagine things."

"But it really happened."

The guard began to shift shapes until he looked like a woman dressed in a voluminous white nightgown and white cap. The room swam and rippled like heat waves in dense fog. Impossible. Ladino blinked to clear his vision.

"What happened, Mr. Ladino?"

The voice was feminine, soft, low, full of concern, adding to his confusion. The woman garbed in white crept closer, inch by inch.

"They cut my hair and gave me this damned tattoo!" Ladino wanted to rub his eyes, but didn't dare lose his grip on the scissors, or his prisoner. "Who are you?"

"My name is Sister Adela."

As he considered this, the one claiming to be Sister Adela looked away. Ladino followed her attention across the room. The one she had sent on the errand stood framed in the doorway, lips clenched between teeth, leaving a white line where its mouth should have been. Ladino now realized this figure was that of a woman as well, not a prison guard as he had first believed. The timid woman held some kind of bottle and a white cloth curled into a cone.

So much white. White everywhere.

The timid one in the doorway edged closer. Ladino's pulse quickened, driven by his instinct for survival. He felt the powerful, animalistic urge to kill and bolt, but knew he'd never escape. His hostage remained his best defense.

"Now, Mr. Ladino, we just want to help you, so why don't you let Sister Martina go?"

Ladino brought his shattered attention back to the one who called herself Sister Adela. She didn't look like a nun. None of them looked like nuns.

"Where am I?"

"St. Vincent's Hospital in Santa Fe."

He peered around him. A long row of beds, most occupied by patients, lined either wall, and he realized she was telling the truth. He *was* in a hospital, not the infirmary on Alcatraz. The walls and ceiling looked too clean, too new. Painted plaster, not cold brick.

"Now, won't you please let Sister Martina go?"

He glanced at his prisoner and saw that she, too, had become a woman. She stared back at him like a frightened ground squirrel, cheeks full of seeds for the winter.

He focused on the negotiator. Maybe it was her voice, her gentle command, or maybe it was her large, brown doe's eyes that made her seem familiar and nonthreatening. Still, Ladino was not convinced these . . . dream ghosts . . . weren't trying to trick him somehow. He knew one way to find out.

"I'll let her go." He heard his prisoner's sigh of relief. "But you have to promise you won't cut my hair."

His negotiator said nothing. Instead, she sent a quick glance to the woman who had come from the doorway, giving her an almost imperceptible nod. Then, she locked her complete attention on his face. Could it be his imagination, or did she try too hard?

"All right, Mr. Ladino, but will you allow us to help you in other ways? Perhaps give you something to help you sleep?"

Ladino studied her, struggling with his faulty perception. He couldn't trust any of this. His head still swam in deep water. Could she be telling him the truth? He wanted to believe her. Something about her face drew him . . .

Her voice . . . so soft. So gentle.

So deadly.

Ladino tightened his grasp on his prisoner, the scissor handles burning his palm. Would he really do it if they

63

pushed him? The harsh reality of an Apache's life left no room for second thoughts. It was either kill or be killed. Yet what if this Adela told the truth? What if this wasn't a trick?

Testing his negotiator, testing himself, he said, "I once vowed to kill the man who cut my hair."

His prisoner gasped and began to mutter unintelligible words. If she truly were a nun, perhaps she prayed.

"We won't cut your hair."

She had reached his bedside and now stood right next to him. She did not blink. She did not look away. She did not shake or cower or stammer, but held her head firm and her chin high. An odd warmth spread throughout his chest. Admiration?

"You have my word," she said, her voice a solemn whisper.

Ladino released the nun, who scurried away. She tripped over her skirt, fell, and scrambled to her feet. From a safe distance she turned, clutching her hand to her throat.

The one who called herself Sister Adela held out her hand, palm up, the gesture an odd display of trust mixed with challenge. Ladino looked up into her deep brown eyes and saw the same emotions reflected there, though both a thin disguise for the glittering fury she'd hidden much better before. He thought he remembered a time they had challenged each other and he had incurred that same lethal glare.

Despite his training in emotional restraint, Ladino smiled. Then, returning her glare, he placed the scissors in her palm and said, "Remember my promise, Sister."

She curled her fingers around the blades. "And you remember mine."

As he continued to hold the scissors, playing out a small tug-of-war with her, testing her mettle, he was amazed to watch her regain control over the emotions in her facial expression. This Sister Adela suddenly looked just as hard, just as stoic, just as purposeful as the most seasoned Apache warrior. Admitting the feeling in his chest as admiration, Ladino released the scissors.

"One should always heed first impressions," he thought he heard her mutter.

Ladino had been so caught up in watching her, he wasn't aware the nun with the bottle and cloth had closed the distance and now stood over his bed. When the cone covered his nose, he jerked his head away and grabbed her wrist. But he was too weak, too drained. His hold slackened.

Replacing the cone over his nose, the nurse dribbled liquid over its point. Sweet fumes filled his nostrils, overwhelming his lungs and brain. Thought grew lethargic, and all movement proved impossible.

Barely able to keep his eyes open, he looked up at Sister Adela. "Thith izz how you . . . honor your vow . . . ? With . . . a trick?" He heard his own voice as if from a distance, the words distant and thick, oozing across his uncooperative tongue.

She was answering him, but he could not understand her. A descending buzz, like that of a hummingbird being pressed into silencing mud, swallowed her voice until he could no longer hear her. All he heard was echoing laughter as ocean waves pounded rock outside the walls of his cold white hell.

The scissors loomed closer. As Red Beard sheared him, Ladino fought his bonds, screaming his hatred and rage.

Chapter Five

Adela knew the danger of putting a head injury patient under anesthesia, but his violent episode had left her no choice. What if he'd tried to hurt someone else? Bending over his unconscious form, she checked his pulse. Finding his heartbeat strong and regular, she found some comfort in her decision.

She glanced up at Sister Lucia. The young nun clutched the open bottle of chloroform to her stomach as she stared at the half-breed. Barely eighteen and recently transplanted from the motherhouse in Cincinnati, Lucia didn't yet understand life in this violent land, yet she'd been a fully professed sister for a year—a position Adela had coveted for almost three.

"Cap the bottle, Sister Lucia, before we all pass out."

"What? Oh!" she said, jabbing the cork in the bottle.

Adela peeled back the wet sheet and lifted one edge of his bandage. She saw just what she had feared—suppurated flesh weeping with infection.

"Let's get him to a private room and tend this wound." She faced the sisters standing around the bed. Sister Barbara, who should have been in charge, stood at the forefront. For a moment, Adela waited for the tall, bespectacled nurse to take control. When Barbara didn't move forward, Adela decided to claim the initiative.

"Sister Barbara, get some towels to clean up this mess. When you're finished, you, Martina, and Sister Mary Leo will help me move him to the empty second-story corner room." She looked past these three to Lucia. "I have to re-open his wound, and I need you to get the catgut and soak a small pair of scissors in some Lister's carbolic . . ."

As Adela watched each of them in turn, she realized they all stared at her, brows arched in disbelief, as if she had asked them to throw themselves to the lions. *Just one lion,* Adela amended. *One ferocious, powerful lion.*

"He's out," she explained, focusing on Sister Barbara, who licked her lips. "He can't do a thing."

Lucia clutched the bottle of chloroform. She shot a help-less glance at Sister Barbara before addressing Adela. "But he'll be angry if he wakes before we've finished."

"The longer we gawk at him like a bunch of frightened rabbits, the sooner he'll regain consciousness and catch us unaware." Annoyed by Sister Barbara's continued reluc-tance to step in, she sighed. "Are none of you willing to help me?"

"I'll help."

Startled, Adela turned. The reply had come from Sister Martina, who still held a hand to her throat as she moved closer. Adela searched Martina's round, grandmotherly face. Tears brimmed in the nun's small cornflower eyes.

"But only if I don't have to care for him from this point on."

Sympathy swelled in Adela's heart. She pulled Martina's handkerchief from her habit pocket and handed it to her. The nun smiled as she took it and dabbed at her eyes.

"All right," said Sister Barbara, lifting her chin as she stepped forward. "If Martina can do this, I can too. But after we move him, I want nothing more to do with him. And I think we should restrain him. He's much too violent. I'm sure none of us want a second incident."

"No, I'm sure none of us do." Adela put her arm around

Martina and squeezed the nun's thin shoulder. "But we've all had recalcitrant patients—"

"Recalcitrant!" cried Barbara. "I wouldn't call holding a pair of scissors to Martina's throat 'recalcitrant.' Savage would be a better word. And I, for one, wish he were not here at all."

"You're a nurse, sworn to save lives. Have you forgotten? Or maybe you'd like to throw him out in the street."

"We all know he's a murderer, and that he came looking for you. How can you defend him when everyone knows why he's here?"

Sister Barbara's words caused a sickening quiver to course through her veins. For a moment Adela couldn't respond. When she did, she fought to keep her voice calm. "I defend him because right now he is helpless—"

Sister Barbara snorted in disgust.

"—and we hold his life in our hands. I couldn't live with myself if I let him die just because he frightened me."

Barbara's lower jaw shifted to one side, making her bony cheekbones even more prominent. "If you're so determined he live, why don't *you* take care of him?"

Adela blanched. "I can't. Mother Eulalia forbade me to be in his presence."

"So you *could* let him die if Mother Eulalia frightened you?"

Sister Martina stepped forward. "You're not being fair, Sister Barbara."

"Perhaps not. But she forgets herself. She and de Sales may be in charge during the day shift, but I'm in charge now. I say we tie him to the bed to keep him from injuring the nurses . . . or himself."

"And then you'll care for him?" Adela challenged.

Again Barbara's jaw tightened. This time her brown eyes

narrowed with anger and resentment.

"You know, Barbara, you could take a lesson in courage from Sister Martina." Adela faced the others. "I'll speak to Sister Mary de Sales tomorrow. She and I will take over his care, but that will mean increased responsibility for everyone else if she and I are less able to help in the wards."

"But what will we say to Mother Eulalia?" asked Sister Lucia.

"She ordered that he be moved to a private room in the morning so I could go on with my duties," Adela replied. "She won't like it that none of you are willing to care for him. If Mother Eulalia finds out what happened, and how we handled it, all of us will be in trouble."

Sister Lucia gaped. "Lie to Mother Eulalia?"

"No. All I'm suggesting is that when Mother Eulalia checks to see if we've followed orders, he'll be in a private room, just as she wanted. If anyone sees her coming when I happen to be tending him, just let me know so I have time to get away."

"I don't know . . ." said Sister Lucia.

"Fine," Adela said. "Let him die. I'm going back to bed."

Sister Lucia stopped her with a hand on her arm. "What do you want us to do?"

Feeling a twinge of guilt for manipulating the issue and usurping Barbara's authority, Adela caught the woman's gaze.

Sister Barbara shrugged, her eyebrows arched in sarcastic challenge. "Yes, Sister Adela, what do you suggest we do?"

Martina, ever the peacemaker, stepped to Barbara's side and sent a supplicating glance to Adela. "I think Sister Barbara made a good suggestion." Martina touched

Barbara's arm, and Adela witnessed a softening in the set of the nurse's sharp-boned face. "We should keep the man tied up. That way, as Sister Barbara said, he can't injure anyone. Would you concede to that, Adela?"

Nothing Adela could say, no concession she could make, would keep the distance between herself and Sister Barbara from widening into a chasm. She had hoped to make friends with the woman one day, but after this, the proposition seemed hopeless. Only with Mother Eulalia did Adela feel the same desolation, the same dismemberment, as if some crucial part of her were missing. If she could just find that part, whatever it might be, would she then belong? Adela didn't know. Until then, she could only hope to keep the peace. And the request wasn't unreasonable.

"Get a stretcher," she said at last, her voice soft with defeat as she met Barbara's smug glare. "We'll move him to a private room and get him out of this wet nightshirt. Then we'll tie him to the bed."

Hours after midnight, Ladino continued to thrash with fever, yanking against the bandages that bound him by his wrists and ankles to the head and foot rails of his metal bed. He muttered a smattering of English, Spanish, and what Adela assumed was Apache. She understood nothing, but his sharp tone and the fury etched on his face told her he continued to flounder in violent delirium. Even if she wanted to break her promise to the other sisters, the danger of untying him still proved too great.

As for her vow to leave his hair intact, she'd made a ridiculous mistake by giving in to his demands. Yet here she sat on a chair beside his bed, doing the best she could to reduce his raging fever by bathing him with cold water and vinegar.

Succumbing to a moment of strange absorption, Adela folded the cold compress over the tattoo on his forehead and combed her fingers slowly up and over the pillow through the damp waves of his hair. When she reached the curling ends, she repeated the motion as if stroking a feral cat into some degree of trust. His thrashing lessened to fainthearted jumps and tugs, while his harsh words softened to indistinct murmurs.

What, besides his animalistic terror and inevitable wrath, kept her from fetching the scissors?

Adela stopped, once again remembering why. Her mother had called her "Little Rapunzel." But the morning had come when she'd been forced to sacrifice her past in order to satisfy her calling. She remembered the feeling of nakedness, the frightening sensation of some essence lost when she'd watched her yard-long chestnut curls drift to the floor atop the stripped identity of the blonde novice who'd gone to the chair before her.

Like Samson's locks, the Apache's long mahogany hair might be the envy or pride of any woman but a nun. Like Samson himself, this man seemed to manifest his masculine power—his identity as a warrior—through the wild beauty of his hair.

But his hair also revealed his vulnerability.

As much as Adela hated to admit it, she began to understand him. She recognized his fear of powerlessness, his resentment of those determined to rule his life.

Was he really so different from herself?

Uncomfortable with the tangent her thoughts had taken, she pulled her hand from his hair and touched the wet towel that covered the poultice on his knife wound. Finding it cold, she peeled it away and soaked it in near-scalding water from the basin on the floor beside her chair. After refolding the hot toweling, she placed it back on his stomach. Despite her gentleness, he jerked. Adela winced, realizing the morphine she'd given him hours earlier had begun to wear off.

Steam rose from the plaster on his wound, and with it the hot herbal aroma of hollyhock, coneflower and *hediondilla*. The scent blended with vinegar and permeated every corner of the room, clinging to her patient's rumpled sheets and her own nightdress.

"I can't . . . feel my arms . . ."

Startled by this clear whisper amidst his mumbled words, Adela glanced up and searched his face. His eyes were still closed as he tugged on his bonds.

"I can't feel my arms," he repeated, his voice rising to a croak of panic and frustration.

Even in the dim lamplight his wrists looked red, chafed almost raw. His fingers drifted in the air, for he no longer clenched his hands into angry fists. Adela bit her lip, scooting closer to the edge of her chair. Before she could change her mind, she worked the knot loose on his right wrist.

His arm dropped to the pillow. She picked up his hand and pushed both thumbs into his palm, kneading for several seconds. He grimaced, and Adela imagined the prickling sensation ripping through his deadened limb. She massaged his entire arm before retying this wrist and moving to the other side of the bed.

She massaged the feeling back into his left arm as well. Just as she began to retie this limb, he escaped her grasp and clutched several folds of her nightdress. Tightening the fabric across her chest, he hauled her close. She gasped as the heat of his knuckles radiated through her gown. Mere inches from his face, she met amber eyes glowing with fury.

"Smeet," he whispered, his voice harsh with the fanaticism of hallucination. "I have to find Smeet."

Adela's throat dropped to her feet. Visions of his violence toward Sister Martina drummed warning signals through her memory. At last, his intense expression melted once more into confusion, reminding her he drifted under the dark spell of opiates and fever.

A long moment passed before Adela's throat rose back into its proper place, allowing her to speak. "Release me, Mr. Ladino." Her voice held a command she did not feel.

As if he slid down a rope, his grip slipped down the front folds of her nightrail between her unbound breasts, pulling the neckline taut against her nape. At last he let go, and his hand fell to the mattress.

Without a moment's guilt this time, she wound the bandage around his wrist, yanked the knot tight, and scurried to the foot of his bed out of his reach.

Once she began to calm down, she heard again what he'd said, not just the name he'd mentioned. Smeet. He looked for Smeet. Perhaps she'd been correct in wondering if he searched for this man regarding the blackmail attempt. Even so, he might still have another motive.

"Thirsty . . . water." He lifted his head and scanned the room. Finding her, he lifted his head farther. "Please. Water."

She stared back at him, considering. At last she edged closer and picked up the cup of tea from the bedside table. While holding the cup in one hand, she helped him lift his head with the other. He strained to sit upright, cursing when he couldn't pull his hands down to his sides. Anger snapped into his eyes, and he yanked his bandage bindings so taut they shook. As he raised his head out of Adela's hand, the compress fell off his forehead, revealing his blue tattoo in bold relief.

Adela stepped away. The white wrought-iron headboard creaked as he bent it forward. The effort to escape only tightened his bonds. Exhausted, he collapsed back on the mattress and growled his frustration. Twisting his head on the pillow, he pierced her with the malevolent glare of a leashed wildcat.

"Easy, Mr. Ladino," Adela said in a low voice, hoping her quiet tone would hide the lump of apprehension in her throat. "Let's try this again, shall we?" She stepped closer and eased her hand forward. He continued to stare. Adela swallowed and lifted her eyebrows into an encouraging expression. "It's redroot and sage tea," she offered, forcing her tight voice into a comforting tone, "flavored with *cota* and honey." Still he watched her, searing her with his distrust. "It'll help bring down your fever and relieve some of the swelling in your head."

Suffering his stare, she touched the cup to his lips and he opened his mouth. Her hand shook as she tilted the cup. He swallowed, but the liquid tangled with the breath in his throat. A cough burst forth, and red tea dribbled down his chin. Adela pulled back the cup while he coughed and gasped for breath to clear his lungs. In a few moments she tried again, this time sitting gingerly on the edge of his bed for a better angle and more control of the liquid flow. Now when he drank, the easy sound of his breathing amplified into the tin cup.

"There, that's better." She eased his head back to the pillow and set the cup aside.

Finding the compress cloth among his bedclothes, she swished it in the basin. An idea began to form. She peeked at his face. He continued to watch her, his expression suspicious and curious by turns. If she could coax the truth from him in his fevered state, she wouldn't have to confront his complete coherence or any true danger.

Adela licked her lips, squeezed out the excess water, and wiped the spill off his neck and chest, noticing again how the dainty silver crucifix rested on an old scar that jagged like white lightning across the muscle. She also noticed the puckered circle of a healed bullet wound on his left shoulder. "Tell me about Smeet." She hoped her quiet voice projected only conversational interest. "Why is he so important to you?"

The subterfuge sent shivers down her arms. But as she continued to rub his chest and shoulders with the cool cloth, a strange heat replaced the chill, altering her steady breathing to a lurching rhythm. In that moment she realized her physical reaction had little to do with her earlier fear.

"Where am I?" he demanded.

Adela stopped rubbing his chest mid-stroke. For five quickening heartbeats, he imprisoned her in his gaze. Just as she feared, his strange eyes revealed his returning lucidity.

"St. Vincent's Hospital in Santa Fe," she answered at last, struggling to keep her voice from cracking.

"How long have I been here?"

"It's early Wednesday morning now, and we brought you in yesterday afternoon. Do you . . . remember?

In the space of a few seconds, a new confusion stole across his face. "I remember the buzzards," he replied, his expression becoming contemplative. "And I remember you."

She teased him with a tight laugh. "You remember me and the buzzards. I should be offended." She lifted the compress from his chest. "So you don't remember what happened before that? Anything about how you were injured?"

"Not sure," he said, frowning. "Ambushed, I think."

"Ambushed?" she repeated, feeling a relief she didn't fully understand, didn't want to probe. "Why? By whom?"

He shook his head, grimacing when his swollen wound came in contact with the pillow. "I . . . don't know."

"Do you remember your name?"

A weak grin fluttered over his strong features. "Which one?"

Despite herself, Adela smiled too. "I think you re-member more than you let on. Is that true?"

He didn't answer, but continued to study her, squinting now. "You haven't spent your whole life in a convent, have you."

It wasn't a question.

"What do you mean?" Her smile faltered as she imag-ined herself about to step into his carefully laid snare.

"Only a woman who's known a little more than life among a bunch of half-women would have shown the same spirit. Last night, when I was in a different room, a room with many beds, you . . ." Like glass shards in a kaleido-scope, his expression shifted. In awe, Adela watched as memory exploded on his features, replaced by betrayal, which just as suddenly changed to rage. He tugged at his bonds. "Untie me."

Disoriented by his sudden switch in moods, Adela opened her mouth to speak, but couldn't.

"Untie me, I said."

"I—I can't," she stammered, staring at him with wide eyes.

"Untie me, damn it. Now! I'm not some wild animal!"

Anger rushed to replace Adela's worry. "I'm sure Sister Martina would disagree." She flung the compress cloth back into the basin. Cold water splashed into his face. "You almost cut her throat with a pair of scissors!"

Beads of water danced on his sculpted cheeks and across his strong nose where his nostrils flared with fury. "She was going to cut my hair."

"*Well,* that explains everything! I'm surprised you admit to remembering the incident. I could have sworn you were out of your head and thought she was someone else," she goaded, her next words echoing her own fear. "Maybe it was an act, and you really are an animal who likes to terrorize women!"

He yanked on his bindings. The entire bed frame shook, threatening to collapse. She hopped off the mattress and retreated to a safe distance.

"I remember your promise. I want to see if you kept it." His voice turned low and deadly. "Untie me. Now. And give me a mirror."

"We don't have one." Her saucy reply belied the panic that rushed through her body.

He shook the bed frame again, using his legs now to pull against his bindings. Agony ripped across his face, and he fell back on the mattress, gasping. He closed his eyes and turned his head away from her, releasing one harsh breath on a moan. He breathed through clenched teeth as he clamped his body into a rigid column.

"Serves you right, you know."

He didn't answer, and Adela remained rooted where she stood. His breathing continued to slow, and by degrees his body relaxed. Still he did not look at her. Adela began to feel a twinge of pity for his suffering and masculine pride. Or perhaps it was Apache pride that wouldn't allow him to reveal his pain.

"Do you want more morphine?"

He still did not turn his head to look at her. "No." The

single word was a hoarse whisper.

"Are you sure?"

More silence. "Yes, damn it. I'm sure," he said at last. "Show me . . . you kept your promise."

All pity fled. An angry challenge rose to her lips. "Not until you tell me why I had to promise." She suspected the answer hid deep within his self-esteem and virility as an Apache man, yet because of his treatment of Martina, she couldn't keep from provoking him. She stepped closer. "You tell me why my promise not to cut your hair was so important you threatened to kill a woman who merely wanted to keep you alive."

He shifted his head on the pillow and glared at her. "I didn't threaten to kill—" He twisted his head away again. "You wouldn't understand," he said through clenched teeth. "What's more, I don't give a damn if you ever do."

Adela stormed back to the bed, lifted a lock of his damp hair from the pillow and shoved it before his eyes. "There. Are you satisfied? I did not cut your hair. If you weren't behaving like a two-year-old, you would have realized it for yourself."

She bent over and gave him her harshest Mother Eulalia stare. "And you know what? You may be Samson himself, but you are helpless to my whim while you're tied to that bed. I will not be bullied by the likes of you. Is that clear?" She straightened. "Now, you had better start being just a little bit nicer to me."

For several moments, while Adela stared at him, heaving deep breaths in her ire, he matched her fury with equal zeal. But by slow degrees his expression began to change to contemplation and wonder. He broke into a grin. It grew wider, and wider, and wider still until his broad chest shook with silent laughter.

Adela stepped away from his bed. She felt her scowl falter, and with it, all control of the situation. "What's so funny?"

"Is now a good time to start being nice?"

"What do you mean?"

"I . . ." He glanced away. "I need to . . . relieve myself." He swung his arms in the bindings. "And I'm at your whim."

At first Adela didn't know how to react. But then she lifted a brow and crossed her arms across her chest. "Mmm, so you are."

"So will you help me, or are you going to make me beg?"

"Begging would be a start."

He looked up at her white night bonnet, then ran a slow study down the length of her nightdress to her bare feet peeking out from under the hem. Adela curled her toes inward. He threaded his gaze to her face, and once there, his expression became hooded, lazy, but still almost predatory, evoking in her once again the frightened response of prey.

"Are you sure you're a nun?" He smiled. "Maybe you're Delilah, Samson's wicked temptress."

Adela's breath stuck in her throat as a hot flush raced through her stomach, her shoulders, her neck. Finally, it burst into her cheeks.

Having no response to his last comment, Adela rushed back to the nightstand, opened the door, and retrieved the urinal. "You should have just said something instead of teasing me. There's no reason to make such a fuss out of a natural function."

"Best way to make you feel as uncomfortable as I do."

"Well, you're only making this more uncomfortable than it needs to be for both of us."

"You should have untied me when I asked."

Adela refused to comment. Without looking either at his lower anatomy or at his face, she managed to pull back the sheet and position him into the receptacle.

"You're blushing, Sister Adela."

"And you're still delusional, Mr. Ladino. You've had too much morphine." Still she refused to look at him. "Are you finished?"

"Which is it—too much or not enough? Morphine, I mean," he clarified, tilting her a suggestive grin. "Minutes ago you offered more."

"Are you finished?" she repeated. Her ears felt so hot she feared they would ignite her bonnet.

"Finished," he said at last.

Adela removed the urinal, flipped the sheet back up into his face, and breezed to the door. "I'll be back in a few minutes," she mumbled over her shoulder.

When she had closed the door behind her, she leaned against the door frame. A pent breath escaped her as she stared up at the ceiling, battling to stabilize her racing heart.

"If I remember my lessons," he called through the closed door, "Samson's hair was cut and his eyes put out, but he still had the strength to push the temple pillars down."

For a moment he remained quiet. Adela didn't want to so much as blink an eyelash for fear he would hear her and know she still stood just outside his door.

"I know you're there, Sister Adela. I can feel you. I can smell the lye soap you washed with just hours ago."

More silence. Adela's breathing became too much for her chest to contain; she opened her mouth and let it out—slowly, so he wouldn't hear.

"Read 'Judges,'" he continued. "The sixteenth chapter."

Adela could no longer resist a retort. "Even the devil can quote scripture, Mr. Ladino. And the temple killed Samson when it fell. You might want to remember that."

Pushing away from the door frame, she strode away. Christian Ladino's demonic laughter nipped at her heels as she rushed down the hallway.

A repetitive dripping sound propelled Ladino back to the dungeon at Alcatraz. Fighting to escape, he awoke with a start to find shadows from the low flame of the kerosene lamp dancing on the closed door across the room.

When he turned his head, he found Sister Adela sprawled in the ladder-back chair, asleep. Light from the lamp's flame licked gold dust along the graceful curve of her smooth cheek and long neck, flickering bronze highlights in a tiny, springy tendril of brown hair that had escaped the nape of her white bonnet.

Though still clad in white, she no longer wore her nightshift, but a white habit like the rest of the nurses, the material crisp and clean under a bib apron made of gingham. His gaze traveled the length of her slim form and long legs. She also wore shoes—cumbersome shoes that hid her dainty toes.

When had she dressed? He must have been asleep when she had returned to his room. This time, along with visions of torture at the hands of his enemies, he'd been comforted by soothing words and cool cloths on his forehead, while the heat raging within him had come from a completely different source than the fever afflicting his body.

He laughed at himself. A nun. He was having carnal thoughts about a nun. Seven years without a woman was too long.

Still, he couldn't keep from looking at her, couldn't help

but watch her sleep, watch her breathe while he timed his own breaths to match each lift of her chest and stomach. In her lap, a basin rested precariously, the water level rising closer to the edge with each deep breath. Her arm hung at her side, and in long, tapered fingers she held a cloth, heavy with water that dripped on the floorboards.

So that was what woke him. His guardian angel had fallen asleep before wringing out his compress. Shivering now, he also became aware that the towel on his stomach felt cold, the clammy pressure another contribution to the atmosphere of his recent Alcatraz nightmare.

He was about to speak and wake her when he heard a creaking sound. The door opened, and a wedge of light cut into the room. Sister Adela slept on. Ladino feigned the same, and through his lashes watched another nurse, tall and thin, enter and tiptoe across the floor. She tapped Sister Adela on the shoulder.

Adela jumped, dropping the wet compress to the floor. The basin tipped, sloshing water into her lap. Ladino watched the water spot darken and spread, and he could imagine the cold moisture warmed by contact with her skin.

"Sister Mary de Sales," Adela said in startled recognition. "What is it?"

The woman put her finger to her lips, then pointed at him. Sister Adela followed her direction, and the dim light accentuated dark half-moons of lost sleep beneath her eyes.

Her drowsy gaze drifted back to Mary de Sales. "Has my mother arrived?" The tall one shook her head. Adela's shoulders slumped. "Of course not," she mumbled. "I'm being ridiculous. You'd think"—she yawned—"a fifteen-year wait would prepare me for one more day." Her eyelids began to drift closed.

Something niggled at the back of Ladino's mind. But

nothing that felt connected to the scene playing before him. Instead, he saw the cloudy vision of a face, a face different from that of the dead youth beyond his feet. Younger. Frightened. Desperate. But he sensed something else. Something to do with Smeet . . .

Damn! He couldn't remember, and it was right there! So close he could reach out and touch it if only he could gauge where and how far to reach into the dark caverns of his damaged memory.

"Sister Martina woke me." She took the basin from Adela's lap and set it on the nightstand. "I've come to relieve you."

Adela nodded, but remained sitting. With a sigh, Sister de Sales pulled her from the chair. While the taller nun retrieved the compress from the floor, Adela stretched, standing right next to his bed, so close he could reach out and touch the damp spot on her thigh if his hands weren't bound. She glanced at his stomach, blinked several times, and her eyes widened.

"Oh, no!" she cried, though her voice barely cracked a whisper. "I've let the plaster get cold. That's all we need to let him take a chill now."

"I'll tend to it, Sister." Mary de Sales tossed the cloth in the basin and herded Adela out of the room. "Now go. I daresay you haven't slept well in days."

As Ladino watched Adela's habit disappear around the door frame, the memory he'd been seeking burst back into his mind like an underwater swimmer coming up for life-giving air.

She had asked about Smeet!

But it was more than that. If he hadn't just recalled the newspaper article, and if he hadn't heard her ask about her mother, he might have pegged her question as another vague image from his earlier fevered nightmares. Added to that, he remembered the eagerness she had tried to hide when she'd mentioned Smeet, her intense curiosity mixed with fear of his response.

It all fit. She had to be the one.

Chapter Six

Carrying a ewer of hot water, Adela entered Ladino's room and found him asleep. She hesitated, glancing back at the open door. After one more peek at him, she retraced her steps and shut the door, deciding she'd rather risk being in a closed room alone with the trussed half-breed as have Mother Eulalia discover her presence in his room at all.

As she set her ewer next to the basin on the marble-topped nightstand, she studied him. His jaw had fallen slack, his long mahogany hair spread loosely over the white pillow, and both arms lay relaxed in their bindings. Exposed was the lighter brown, vulnerable-looking skin on the in-sides of his biceps—as vulnerable as that much latent power could look, even in repose.

Perching on the edge of his bed, Adela put the inside of her wrist to his forehead. Warm, but not unreasonably so. To make sure, she leaned over and touched her lips to the smooth skin of his forehead marred by the tattoo. Despite her care not to disturb him, her bound breast grazed his ex-posed chest. Tingling sensations suffused her skin, sub-siding into a pulsing heaviness deep within her body.

Mortified, she pulled back, letting her attention travel from his smooth, bare chest to his face, where she found his mountain lion's eyes staring into her own. Searching. Probing. Dangerous even in his injured state. Especially in his injured state.

And lucid like never before.

"You're awake." She rose quickly and poured hot water

from the ewer into the cool liquid already in the basin.

He said nothing, and she had the uncanny urge to cross herself as if she could somehow ward off complete absorption in his stare. And then his expression changed, calmed, flowed into something resembling compassion.

"Did you get some sleep this morning?" he asked.

Astonished by his concern, it took her a moment to answer. "Yes . . . I did. Thank you."

Eager to concentrate on anything but his concentration on her, she pulled back the sheet and lifted the edge of the clean bandage Sister Mary de Sales had put on that morning.

"Your knife wound looks good. The signs of suppuration are gone." She smoothed the bandage and replaced the sheet. "How does your head feel this afternoon?"

"Hurts like hell."

Adela lifted a single brow. "Did Sister Mary de Sales not give you more morphine?"

"I didn't want any."

"Why not?"

"Makes me feel groggy and confused. Out of control."

Adela met his gaze and found some understanding of herself mirrored there. She broke eye contact and turned his head to one side in order to inspect the fracture with her fingertips. The swelling hadn't diminished as much as she'd hoped. Now she looked at his eyes, noting that his pupils still appeared equal in size. A good sign.

"I have to ask a few questions I know you'll find repetitive, but they help me track your progress." She retrieved a bottle of vinegar from the bedside table and poured a small amount into the warm water in the basin. "Do you remember your name?"

He grinned, but said nothing.

Returning his smile, she put the vinegar away. "Perhaps one of these days you'll tell me what those other names are."

"Maybe I will." His grin widened into an open-lipped smile, and for the first time she noticed how straight and white his teeth looked against the warm glow of his skin.

Chastising herself for admiring such inconsequential details, she retrieved the oilcloth from the bottom shelf of the nightstand. After unfolding the cloth, she rolled his body away, careful to keep the sheet covering him even as she bunched one edge of the oilskin against his length. This done, she moved to the other side of the bed, rolled him away again, pulled the material under him, and straightened it over the mattress.

As he moved to help her as best he could, considering his bound arms and legs, the silver crucifix slid along its chain and fell into the hollow of his armpit. It amazed her how he could wear such a tiny thing when it seemed at such odds with his size and appearance of destruction under control.

"My mother's," he stated.

Her gaze drifted up to his face. "What?"

"The crucifix was my mother's. I've noticed how often you look at it."

"Your mother was Catholic?"

"That surprises you." He smiled. "She was also Irish."

"But you're—"

"A half-breed Apache. So I've been told in a number of imaginative ways." He issued a short, derisive laugh. "People usually assume a half-breed has an Indian mother."

"I didn't mean . . ." She shook her head. "But that would explain so much. Your knowledge of the Bible . . ."

When Adela saw his lips straighten and his skin tone

deepen, she decided she would be wiser to shut up and bathe him than to continue digging her own grave with thoughtless words.

She retrieved the basin of water and soaked the cloth. Squeezing warm water over the old bullet wound on his shoulder, then across the jagged scars on his chest, Adela marveled at the sight of clear droplets rolling to find every taut hollow in the muscle. She imagined her fingertips tracing those same paths.

Adela swallowed, dismayed anew by her fascination with him. She wanted to know more about Christian Ladino. Why he behaved as he did. Why he claimed more than one name. But most of all, why he had read the Bible, yet so forcefully rebuked its worth.

Despite Mother Eulalia's decree, she decided she would begin by working up enough courage to ask him why he kept the newspaper clipping about the blackmail attempt against her mother, and what he knew about Nigel Smeet. No more halfhearted attempts like this morning. No more allowing herself to be swayed by carnal fantasies about a man who could very well be the worst kind of savage, a murderer out to get her or her mother.

No. She wouldn't let herself entertain the possibility. Surely she wasn't so base, her mind so unbalanced, that she could feel stirrings for a man who wanted to harm her. Or worse, kill her. Could she? Dear God, let it not be so.

He was a test. Nothing more. She had to remember that.

Adela cleared her throat and forced herself to speak in a neutral tone. "Do you know what day this is, Mr. Ladino?"

"Wednesday."

"And the date?"

"All business now, aren't you, Sister Adela."

Again she noticed his habit of stating most questions as

matters of fact. "The date?" she repeated.

"June seventh. Why?"

She opened her mouth, but stopped, frowning. "Why the date?"

"No, why all business."

Nonplused, she shook her head, unable to answer.

"We both have more important questions we want answers to. You know it, I know it, so why don't you quit cat-backing and get to the point."

"I don't understand."

"All right, I'll ask the first question. Is Minna Westbrook your mother?"

Chills splashed Adela's body like sleet. "I—I don't underst—"

"Oh, yes. You understand. Untie me and we'll talk."

Ladino watched her, gauging her reaction as she pulled the cloth away from his chest and absently held it aloft. Water droplets made plunking noises on the oilcloth, and the moisture rolled beneath his ribs.

"I can't untie you," she murmured.

"You want to know what I'm after, don't you?"

"I can't untie you," she repeated, but this time she darted a furtive glance to his hands above his head. Then, with another surreptitious glance at the moisture on the oil-cloth, as if she just now heard the dripping sounds, she dropped the washcloth in the basin and peeked up at him through her dark brown lashes.

Ladino smiled inwardly but let nothing show on his face. He knew she wanted to untie him. He also knew that despite her bravado she feared him. Yet her fear was tempered with a bravery he'd never seen in another white woman. He decided to use this to his advantage. The way to do that best, he'd discovered, was to offer her a challenge and make her angry. Failing that, he'd use the next best thing—the fascination he suspected she felt for him. Or maybe a combination of the two would work even better.

"What happened to the spirit I thought you had?" he taunted. "Afraid of me?"

"Of course not." She glanced away for just a moment.

"Lying is a sin, Sister."

"And it makes you happy to think I can lie?"

At her left-handed admission, the beginnings of a blush crept across her high cheekbones. Ladino felt a tingle of satisfaction. Like picking a lock, he'd found just the right pressure, just the right position. Now to enter and steal what he'd come for.

"No. What makes me . . . happy . . . is seeing that even a woman like you is human, even if you won't admit it. Even if you feel it's somehow wrong to admit it."

Again her gaze skittered away. She dipped the cloth in the water, swished it around, wrung it out, and continued to bathe him without speaking. As she covered his chest with the sheet and moved to his right arm, Ladino thought he saw a slight lift at one corner of her mouth. The beginnings of a satisfied smirk? She slid the rag up to his wrist. Teasing . . . tormenting . . . so close to the knot in his binding, gliding over the top of it, and then . . . nothing. Slowly she moved back down to his shoulder.

"Who's cat-backing now, Mr. Ladino?"

Her voice startled him, low and provocative even if she didn't realize it. Or did she? Hadn't she already taught him in other ways not to underestimate her?

She stopped washing his shoulder and looked down at him. Wicked lights lurked in her eyes. Had she caught on to his game?

"All right, Mr. Ladino. Yes. Minna Westbrook is my mother. But you're crazy if you think I'm stupid enough to let you manipulate me with your odd attempts at flirtation, and even crazier if you believe I'm going to untie you before you tell me why my mother's name should matter to you."

"You will untie me if I tell you?"

Smiling, she shook her head. "You have to prove you can control yourself before I consider releasing you."

Humiliation and anger boiled just below the surface of his skin. "I already told you I'm not some animal, even if I acted like one last night. It won't happen again." He thought for a moment, hating to grovel. But he hated worse the degradation of being tied up like a dog vulnerable to anyone's whim. Her whim. Squelching his fury, he added, "You have my word."

"Tell me what I want to know, and then I'll decide."

Disgusted with himself for being caught at the bad end of a dirty bargain, he let out a long breath. "I'm looking for a man named Nigel Smeet. But you already know that."

Her eyes widened with unspoken questions, and Ladino welcomed the consolation of having taken her off guard again.

"Yes, I remembered what you asked me about Smeet," he answered. "But not until after you left the room. You must have seen the article," he added.

"But my name isn't mentioned. How did you know who I was?"

"You asked if your mother had arrived. You said something about not seeing her for fifteen years. It had to be you."

"What do I have to do with this?" She backed away, fear returning to her expression. "What do you want from me?"

"I thought Smeet might have come to see you—that he

might try to get back at the Westbrooks through you. Or that you might know where he is."

"Why are you looking for him?"

"That's my own business."

"But—"

"It has nothing to do with your mother—or with you."

"So . . . you're not involved somehow in the blackmail attempt? You don't work for Nigel Smeet?"

"Pretty high opinion you have of me." He released a short, bitter laugh laced with defeat. "Guess I deserve it."

"It's just that I assumed . . ." She shrugged. "You have to understand, Mr. Ladino. When we found you out there . . ." Her words faltered. "When Mother Eulalia showed me the article and the wanted poster, then told me the reason for your tattoo . . . she—I—*we* could only think the worst. And then the incident with Sister Martina, well, I thought you might be here to . . ."

As her convulsive attempt to explain trailed off, despondence tightened around Ladino's heart. It hurt to have anyone believe he could ever work for Smeet, but somehow, because it was her, it hurt even more. How could that be? He didn't even know her. Ladino turned away, no longer wanting to look at her, no longer willing to acknowledge his anger or his pain. He didn't care what kind of savage she thought him. She was merely a means to an end.

He heard her sigh as she moved back to his bedside. She lifted the sheet and folded it up to his knees. As she washed his feet, he hardened his resolve, determined not to give way to the tickling sensation or his own softening emotions.

"Damn it, stop that!" Ladino twisted his head across the pillow and opened his eyes, meeting her startled gaze. "Just tell me what I want to know. Has Smeet come up here looking for you?"

Anger sparked in her pupils. "No."

"What about your mother—has she seen him recently?"

"How would I know?" she snapped. Then she laughed, the sound harsh with pain and bitterness. "Don't you remember? I haven't seen or heard from my mother in fifteen years, so I couldn't possibly tell you whether she's seen him or not."

Adela yanked the sheet down over his feet, and as his damp body dried beneath the linen, he watched her snatch up the basin and stalk to the door.

Realizing how insensitive he'd sounded, how bluntly he'd demanded her response, Ladino felt a twinge of remorse. He closed his eyes, trying to shut out images of fiery Sister Adela as a little girl, pining away for her mother. He understood the kind of grief she must have suffered—the kind only destructive rage and tears in the dark seemed to appease.

A few moments later he heard her return. Sensing her warmth near his head, relief flooded him. "Adela," he began softly as he opened his eyes. "I . . ." His voice died when he saw the partially open pair of scissors in her hand. He jerked in his bindings, helpless to defend himself.

"I got a bit carried away when I retied one of these knots," she explained, and a wicked smile at his obvious discomfiture teased the soft curve of her lips.

As the memory evoked by her words disbursed his shock, Ladino stared at her. When her smile faltered, heat pulsed into his groin, and he wondered if she was remembering— like he was—how her warm, full breasts had felt against his knuckles when he had clutched the folds of her nightgown and pulled her close.

Her gaze fluttered away, and then he felt the sharp point of the scissor blade shake as she pressed it against his wrist.

She snipped, and the bond loosened, releasing his hand. Still avoiding his gaze, she moved to the other side and untied that knot. Ladino brought his unbound hands together. He rubbed one wrist and then the other, feeling his self-respect jump to the highest point in days.

Grimacing, he pushed himself upright on shaky arms, and the sheet fell to his lap. "Do you have something I can wear?"

Adela glanced first at his bare chest, then at his lower abdomen just below the bandage. Her throat spasmed as she swallowed and looked away. She dropped the scissors in her apron pocket and strode to the nightstand where she pulled a clean nightshirt from one of the drawers. "Do you need help?" she asked, handing him the garment.

"I'll manage."

Adela nodded, moving to the foot rail where she untied one of his ankles and gave it a quick massage. She had just moved to his other ankle when a shrill, feminine voice echoed in the hall.

"Why is that door closed, Sister Lucia? You know my rules."

The panel burst open, and two sisters—one old, the other young and timid—stepped into the room just as Ladino unfolded the nightshirt. A man followed, and the silver star on his vest caught the afternoon sunlight from the west windows. Adela straightened, her expression guilty and defiant at the same time.

"Sister Adela!" The elderly sister's small blue eyes widened. "What are you doing here?" She snapped her attention to Ladino. "And why is he undressed," she sputtered. "And untied!" Her surprise turned to an angry scowl. "Sister Lucia told me about the incident with Martina. She said Sister Mary de Sales had taken over his care!"

"Sister Mary de Sales must rest sometime, Mother Eulalia."

"But I expressly ordered you to stay away from this man."

Adela pierced tiny Sister Lucia with a withering glare.

"Sister Adela h-had no choice, Mother," admitted Sister Lucia, her head downcast. "W-we all refused his care."

Ladino peered at Adela. So, despite her fear, she had gone against orders to care for him? As he slipped the nightshirt over his head and settled the folds around his body, he couldn't keep the admiration for her courage from tilting into his private smile.

"We'll discuss this in my office, Adela. For now, I want you to retie those bonds. Deputy Latham wants to speak with him."

"Tying him down won't be necessary." Latham strolled farther into the room and assessed Ladino. A sneer twisted his blond mustache as he rested his hand on the gun strapped at his hip. "I can handle the 'breed if he gets out of line."

Mother Eulalia's attention dropped to the gun. "All right," she said, a hint of distress in her voice. "Come, Lucia—Adela." The elderly nun wheeled around, and Sister Lucia scuttled from the room in her wake, almost tripping on the woman's billowing skirts. When Adela did not follow, the elder sister turned, barely avoiding collision with Lucia. "Adela," she barked. "Come."

"Just a moment." Adela reached into her pocket for the scissors, brandishing them like a rebellious warning to the lawman before she snipped the last bandage that bound Ladino's ankle.

A cocky grin spread across Latham's face. "Run along

now, little sister. No need to worry. I'll take good care of him."

"See that you do."

He tipped his hat, but Adela's only acknowledgment of his gesture was an uptilt of her chin before she strode through the door and pulled it shut behind her.

Latham sauntered toward the bed and picked up the tail of a bandage still dangling from the foot rail. "Tied to the bed?" Toying with the cut bandage, he lifted his brows at Ladino. "I guess ya never know what kind of games a man can play in a place like this." A sly smile spread across his hungry features. "Damn, but that one with the scissors sure was a looker. And protective." He shook his head. "Mm-mm. I'd sure like to have all that protection wrapped around me."

"Shut your filthy mouth, White Eye."

The lawman lifted his brows even higher, his forehead wrinkling into his receding hairline.

"Just say what you came to say," Ladino urged. "It's about the dead boy. You think I murdered him."

Latham sucked his teeth, making a clicking noise. He turned around, ignoring Ladino while he pulled the ladderback chair close to the bed and sat down. "The Mother Superior tells me you were brought in yesterday afternoon. That right?"

Ladino cocked the lawman a sidelong glance. "That's right."

"Remember what happened to you?"

"It's coming back."

"What exactly does that mean?"

"It means things are still a bit hazy."

Latham sucked his teeth again as if he still cleaned them from his last meal. "You said I came here to talk to you about a dead boy. If you don't remember what happened, how do you know why I'm here?"

"My memory is unclear, not completely gone."

"All right. Tell me what you remember."

"I woke up to buzzards. My head hurt, and I saw the boy's dead body. He'd been stabbed, I found my bloody knife, so I figured I did it. I decided the location was ripe for an ambush and wondered if the boy had been alone."

"And was the boy alone?"

Latham's question prodded a disjointed image.

A couple of mourning doves burst into the sky, and as their wings beat the air, they called out frantic whuffling sounds of alarm. Two men leaped down on him from behind the rocks where the doves had been, knocking him from his horse. One pulled out a knife, slashing him across the belly before he'd been able to react. His first mistake. The second man hung back, waiting to see if his companion's attack would prove successful before he entered the fray. Ladino dismissed the boy as harmless. His second mistake.

Damn coward bashed me in the head with a rock! was the last thing Ladino remembered thinking before everything went black.

But he saw no point in enlightening Latham.

"You think I'd be here with my head bashed if the bastard was alone?"

Latham sighed. "So why are you so sure the boy, or they, or whoever, ambushed you?"

"Because I don't attack people without provocation."

"Hmm." The lawman rubbed his chin. "That's not what I heard. Maybe I should talk to that sister, what was her name—Martina?"

"I was hallucinating."

"I'll just bet."

Ladino clenched his jaw. He'd belt the man if he didn't believe it would land him tied to his bed again. Besides, he had only enough strength to make the deputy angry enough to kill him.

"I also hear you were carryin' a wanted poster on a man by the name of N. S. Randolph. You a bounty hunter?"

"Sometimes."

"I assume you know N. S. Randolph's real name is Nigel Smeet."

Ladino kept his expression stoic, allowing no emotion to slip past his rigid defenses. "Yeah, I knew that."

The deputy smiled, stretching back in his chair and resting his arms across his stomach. He peered at Ladino's forehead, squinting. "Nice tattoo. Where'd you get it— Yuma or Alcatraz?"

"Alcatraz."

"Released or escaped?"

"Released."

"I could have you checked out with the commander here at Fort Marcy. All it'd take is a wire to San Francisco to find out if you're tellin' me the truth."

"If you want to scare me, you'll have to come up with a better threat," said Ladino. "Don't you think I know you've already checked me out from here to Washington, just looking for an excuse to screw me over? I'll bet you even know why I went to Alcatraz."

Latham swung his lanky form off the chair and towered above Ladino's bed. "All right, you caught me. I don't cut much slack for murderers. The way I see it, any no-good Injun scout shoulda been shot dead or hanged on the spot for murderin' soldiers."

"Those bastards deserved what they got."

"And I cut even less slack for liars." The deputy began

to pace. "You ever work for Smeet?"

"No."

"That's not what the court-martial on you and Smeet said. In Smeet's records, he claimed he paid you a percentage for helping him sell guns and whiskey to the Mescaleros. He said he paid you to help him steal some horses and then kill those four soldiers when the two of you decided not to share the profit with 'em."

Ladino lunged from the bed. His legs shook and the room spun, yet he grabbed Latham by his vest lapels and shoved him back against the fireplace mantel just opposite the bed. "That's a damned lie!"

The lawman said nothing, but Ladino heard an ominous click and a cold, metallic pressure in his stomach.

"Back in bed, Injun, before I blow your patch job."

Ladino continued to hold the deputy's lapels, staring the man down. But he felt himself weakening, the edges of his vision turning black. Nausea roiled into his stomach. He released the deputy, intent on making his way back to the bed before he disgraced himself by vomiting all over the man's silver star.

Halfway to his goal, he collapsed to his knees. Using the foot rail, he pulled himself up on the bed, where he rested back against the pillow. Humiliated, he closed his eyes and breathed carefully, refusing to show further emotion as he willed his stomach to calm.

"Now why do you suppose Smeet would incriminate himself if what he said wasn't true?"

"Get out of my room." Ladino spoke low in his throat, his voice the warning growl of a wildcat. The room continued to spin, and he was terrified he would be sick despite his best efforts.

"Then there's that article about that blackmail attempt.

As I recall, Smeet was behind that. When did you get out of prison?

Ladino refused to answer.

"Two months ago? Three? Plenty of time to get back in with Smeet. 'Course, I can't figure out why you'd want to work for a man who'd say those things about you and have you sent to Alcatraz when all he got was a dishonorable discharge. Seems like an awful severe sentence for a soldier who sells whiskey to Indians—"

"Smeet was never court-martialed," Ladino said, trying to drown out Latham's words with his own voice. "Whatever you read is a lie, White Eye. He got no punishment for what he did."

"—But then there is that matter of him admitting to being your accomplice in the murders of those soldiers," Latham continued. Again he sucked his teeth, and Ladino wanted to rip them out of his mouth. "That makes me wonder why he didn't get sent to prison like you. Somethin's not quite right about all this. I still think you're lyin' about workin' for Smeet."

"Damn it! I don't work for Smeet!" Ladino's stomach cramped with suppressed rage. "I'll kill the bastard next time I see him, you can bet on that. And it sure as hell won't be for the measly hundred dollars on his head." Ladino threw his arm over his face. "Now quit spouting your filthy lies, White Eye, and get the hell out of my room."

"I'm not finished. Did you know the boy you killed was a horse thief with a two-hundred-dollar bounty on his head?"

"No."

"But I bet you'll admit to killin' the boy, now, won't you?"

"I guess I'll have to. He's dead. I'm alive. We were in the same place at the same time. That pretty much cinches it."

"If you're so dead set on not wantin' any reward money on Smeet, I sure hate to give you the two hundred on the boy."

"Then don't. Keep it. You earned it harassing me."

"Oh, I'd like to keep it all right, but the sheriff might frown on that." Ladino felt a thump on the mattress. Coins jingled. "Donate some of it to the hospital, gut-eater. It'll be the only decent thing you'll ever do. And maybe that pretty little sister'll be grateful if you could pay her for services rendered. That gold'll be all she'll want from you after she gets her ear full of information from the Mother Superior."

Ladino heard Latham click the hammer back down on his revolver, rendering it harmless. Seconds later he heard the deputy's boot heels across the wooden floor. The door opened, a slight breeze blew in, and then Latham closed it behind him.

With his bare, unbound foot, Ladino kicked the bag off the bed. Coins spilled loose, rolling and clattering across the floor until the sound sang through the room, an eerie counterpoint to Ladino's howl of fury.

Chapter Seven

Sisters quickly parted way as Mother Eulalia plowed through the convent corridors, Adela trailing in her wake. She knew by her superior's staccato steps that when they reached her office, even Archbishop Lamy's gardener would hear the reprimand.

At the last moment, Mother Eulalia ushered Adela in ahead of her. When Adela saw Sister Blandina seated in a chair before the desk, she stopped short. Mother Eulalia *couldn't* be so intent on humiliation as to reprimand her in front of Blandina!

"Take your seat, Sister Adela." Mother Eulalia indicated another chair which had been placed to the side of the desk like the witness chair in a courtroom.

Blandina offered a faint smile, and Adela returned the acknowledgment with a slight twist of her lips before she sat. Gripping the arms of the chair, she tried to prepare herself for what must surely come.

Mother Eulalia took her own seat behind the desk. "Before you left on your solicitation trip, Sister Blandina and I decided we would discuss your novitiate status upon your return."

Adela's attention darted to Sister Blandina, a silent question screaming to be voiced. Blandina bowed her head in assent.

Mother Eulalia unfolded her spectacles and perched them on her nose. "The date for this audience was set before I received word of your mother's visit, and before I learned of certain events of today." She stared at Adela, slamming open her record book as she spoke.

Dread flooded Adela's body. How easy it would be for her superior to strike her name from that book. How easy it would be to dismiss her from record and from memory, like an angry parent crossing through the name of a disowned child in the family Bible. Banishment. Its permanence was the most likely punishment for her blatant disobedience of orders.

"Sister Blandina and Sister Mary de Sales came to me three months ago with the request that you be allowed to become a black novice. Despite my misgivings, both feel you have reached a satisfactory level in your training for such a change. How do you feel about this, Sister Adela?"

Adela could only stare at Mother Eulalia in shock.

"Sister Adela?" prompted the superior. "If you aren't ready for this, perhaps I can talk to Archbishop Lamy."

"No!" The word burst from Adela's lips. "No," she repeated, her voice cloaked in a calm tone she was far from feeling. "It's just that—" *After your discovery of my disobedience I expected a dismissal,* she finished silently, sending a shaky smile to Blandina. "I'm honored that my sister finds me ready to accept the black habit. I've worked hard toward this goal, and I feel I'm . . . ready."

"This is not a decision to be made lightly," reminded Mother Eulalia. "Though we have no standard guidelines as to when a new black novice makes simple vows the first time, Sister Blandina has suggested that you might be prepared to take those vows by December eighth, during our celebration of the Feast of Immaculate Conception. Will you be fully ready by then, with only six months' preparation as a black novice?"

"I—I hope to be so, Mother Eulalia."

Blandina leaned forward, a gentle expression in her eyes. "Adela, faith and prayer will help you make a wiser decision than will mere hope."

"You're right, Sister Blandina." Adela bowed her head. "I have . . . faith—" She shook her head. "I mean . . . I will *pray* and ask God to prepare me by granting me the faith I need for such a momentous decision."

When she glanced up, she found Mother Eulalia assessing her over the wire rims of her spectacles. The elderly woman bent her head and wrote something in her book. "Then we'll have your ceremony on Friday—"

"Friday?" asked Adela, rubbing and pulling on her fingers in her lap. "This Friday?"

Mother Eulalia glanced up from her book. "Do you have a problem with the day, Sister Adela?"

"It's just that since my mother hasn't arrived, I've been worried she might be late." Adela realized she was just making an excuse. She had waited for this moment for years. So now that it had arrived, why did she feel rushed? Why did its impression of finality terrify her?

Like death.

Adela closed her eyes and shoved the thought from her mind.

"Though the Westbrooks did mention in their letter that they would be arriving this morning," Mother Eulalia was saying, "it is still quite possible they will arrive later today. I thought you might appreciate our effort to schedule the ceremony when your mother and her family could be here to witness the event."

"Of course. Thank you, Mother Eulalia."

"Sister Blandina has requested to be your sponsor. She will help you with whatever needs to be done. We're having a new black habit sewn for you, and it should be ready for pressing tomorrow."

Adela offered Sister Blandina another shaky smile to show her gratitude.

"Do we have everything settled?" After a quick glance at Blandina and then Adela, Mother Eulalia rose from her desk. "All right then, Sister Blandina, you may return to your students. I want a private word with Sister Adela."

Adela's stomach plummeted to her feet. She should have known she wouldn't escape this audience without some kind of punishment. She watched in trepidation as Mother Eulalia ushered Blandina out the door, closing it behind her.

At last the woman turned back to Adela, her expression pinched and harsh. "Do you enjoy making me feel and look the fool in front of the other sisters, Adela?"

"No, Mother Eulalia, of course not!"

"You deliberately deceived me and had the others participate in that deception. Only as I escorted the deputy to the Apache's room did Sister Lucia have the decency to explain what had happened with Sister Martina. Do you know how embarrassing that was, Sister Adela, in front of a complete stranger—what doubt it cast on my credibility?"

"With respect, Mother Eulalia, it was never my intention to cast you in a bad light. I only wanted to spare you—"

"No, Sister Adela, you only wanted to spare yourself this scolding. You knew how angry I would be that you went against my orders. Never mind that my orders are sensible, with the widest possible consideration for the welfare of all concerned."

"I understand that, Mother Eulalia, but I spoke to Mr. Ladino about the matter of him having the newspaper article—"

"You did what?"

"He said he had no intention of hurting me or my mother. He says he is only trying to find Nigel Smeet."

"Of course he would say that, Sister Adela, don't be ridiculous." She yanked off her spectacles and tossed them on her desk. "Do you think he would just come right out and say he intended you harm when you confronted him?"

"I didn't confront him, he confronted me. And I believe him."

"For your information, the deputy just told me that this Apache worked for Nigel Smeet. It seems your patient served as some kind of interpreter at Fort Stanton. He and this Nigel Smeet had numerous illegal business dealings with one another. In fact, his court-martial records say he murdered four soldiers on the orders of Captain Nigel Smeet. Mr. Smeet was dishonorably discharged following his testimony."

"Court-martial? You mean official records?"

Eulalia nodded, her expression smug.

"He was sent to prison for murdering soldiers while Mr. Smeet ordered the murders and suffered only a dishonorable discharge?"

"Whether you agree or not, Adela, the military in this lawless place administers its own justice any way it sees fit."

Stunned, Adela said nothing more. Something about the whole story was hidden out of reach, out of comprehension. She thought she had sensed the depth and truth of Christian Ladino's emotion, yet what did she really know of him? She realized he had only given her the assurances she had wanted to hear.

"I don't want you near the man, Adela."

"What choice do I have? The other sisters refuse to care for him, and we can't just put him out in the street. If he really wanted to, I'm sure he'd find a way to hurt me. But I don't think he has any such intentions."

"What makes you so sure?"

Adela had no response. She couldn't admit to Mother Eulalia how he had reached her . . . how he had touched her. She wished she didn't have to admit it to herself. For some reason she couldn't quite understand, she believed he had told her the truth. At least in the fact that he had no desire to hurt her.

"I just know," she whispered at last, dropping her gaze.

"You just know?" She barked a mirthless laugh. "You had better have a more convincing explanation than that, Sister Adela."

Sifting through the tumult of her emotions, Adela searched for some justification Mother Eulalia would accept. "All right," she said at last. "Common sense tells me that a man with Mr. Ladino's pride would not work for the man responsible for his court-martial and imprisonment. If anything, perhaps he searches for Smeet out of a desire for revenge."

Mother Eulalia pursed her lips. "And this is supposed to ease my concerns about having him in our hospital?"

"No, but perhaps he'll be intent on recovery and eager to be on his way now that he knows I've had no contact with Smeet."

Eulalia steepled her fingers against her nose and rubbed at the indentations left by her spectacles. "All right, Sister Adela." She sighed. "You win. You may resume his care. But I want him in restraints."

"No. I won't do that to him again."

"You will if I order it."

Nausea gripped Adela as she weighed the heavy price of disobedience. Nevertheless, she shook her head. "Even if you order it, Mother Eulalia, I'm afraid I won't do it. Not only does he find it degrading, but to attempt it I'd have to put him under total anesthesia again, which could worsen his condition."

"Sister Adela—"

"But I will keep his door open. I doubt he'll try anything. If he does, surely the other nurses will consent to help me if they hear me scream," she said, her tone laced with sarcasm.

Mother Eulalia's face darkened to the deep purple of apoplectic rage. Remorseful, Adela reached out, but Mother Eulalia shoved her hand away. Adela flinched. As Mother Eulalia retreated to her desk, Adela slowly lowered her hand, feeling the rejection like a well-deserved slap in the face.

"If I had not already discussed the matter of your black novitiate with Archbishop Lamy, and if I thought you were catering to the Apache for other than purely medical reasons, I would not hesitate to cancel your ceremony." She turned away. "Just remember, Sister Adela, I will be watching you."

Still struggling with his nausea a few moments later, Ladino heard the door open and someone step on one of the coins.

"What's this?" It was Sister Adela's voice.

"Reward," Ladino replied, lifting his arm from his eyes.

"For what?"

"The boy I killed was a horse thief." A sharp burst of disgust exploded in his throat. "Two hundred dollars. That's how much a horse thief barely out of baby-grass is worth. Twice as much as a lying, murdering son of a bitch who just happens to be wanted for forgery in Colorado."

He watched her bend over and pick up the canvas bag, putting coins inside. She didn't answer him. But then what could she say? What did he want her to say?

She held up the bag. "What would you like me to do with it?"

"Keep it. I don't want the bastard's dirty gold. And I don't want to owe you or this hospital a penny."

She made no comment as she walked across the room to his nightstand. Just as she reached out to open the drawer, he slapped his hand over hers and held it tightly against the wood.

"Mr. Ladino, I—"

"Keep it, I said! And close the damn door on your way out."

He felt her fingers curl under his own as if she abhorred his touch. When she looked down at him, he thought he saw distrust and betrayal in her eyes, heightened by the glaze of unshed tears. Had he made her cry? No. He didn't want the responsibility; it would only make him feel just as vulnerable. A trick of the light. That's all he saw shining in her eyes.

He released her, and she pocketed the drawstring bag. "I'll save it with the rest of your things," she said, her voice shaking. "You can decide what you want to pay when you leave. I just hope it will be soon!"

She turned and ran from the room, leaving the door open behind her—leaving his heart exposed to the drafts of disappointment, cold with remorse.

Adela reached into the pocket of her white nurse's habit for the hairbrush, touching her corncob doll instead. How cruel she'd been to herself for carrying Abbie with her. The doll only served as a constant reminder that her mother had not arrived yesterday as promised, and had yet to arrive today.

As she entered Christian Ladino's room, she found him sitting up in bed, gazing out the second-story window, where stonemasons atop the scaffolding beside the cathedral's new walls scurried about their work like ants building up their hill in preparation for a storm. Enormous clouds were building to the southwest, darkening the sky, charging the room with the smell of rain.

"What do you think?" he asked in an absent tone, turning his head to look at her. "Do they hurry for nothing?"

She smiled. "With the luck Archbishop Lamy's been having trying to rebuild the cathedral, I'd say we can expect Noah's flood."

Amusement flickered in his mountain-lion eyes. But as his study of her lengthened, his expression faded to passive stoicism, leaving Adela inexplicably bereft, as if the cathedral walls weren't the only barriers erected in sight of a storm.

Yesterday, everything had changed. He had changed. And today the puma had been too tame, his attempts at conversation too polite, his behavior toward her too courteous. So courteous he had been reduced to making trivial comments about the weather.

And she had been reduced to transparent excuses that brought her closer to him in the only way she knew how to be—as nurse to patient. She wanted more than this from him, but she didn't know what. Even worse, she didn't know why.

She fumbled for the hairbrush in her pocket and held it up for him to see. "I thought you might like me to brush your hair."

Like a mirage, the barest shimmer of a new smile rippled

across his features but disappeared so quickly she wondered if she'd seen it at all.

"Well, would you?" she prodded, feeling foolish for hoping that something so simple as brushing his hair would close the distance between them. Feeling even more foolish that the distance between them should even matter. In the rational, realistic realm of her thoughts, she knew it was better that they remain isolated from one another, but the knot in her stomach, the emotional ache for something she couldn't name, seemed to be telling her otherwise.

"Yes." He shot a glance over her shoulder before returning his attention to her. "But I want you to close the door first." The deep, soft timbre of his voice sent hot prickles down Adela's spine. "All day you've left it open. And you left it open yesterday when you left. Why?"

"Mother Eulalia's orders," she answered simply, though the answer didn't feel simple at all.

"She wants her nurses to gawk at the patients?" he exclaimed, the familiar antagonism sparking in his eyes. "Any other time I'd be glad for an open door, but I feel like I'm in a freak show. Hell, I *am* the damned freak show!"

His anger revived Adela's shame. She understood his anger. Ever since she'd untied him yesterday, several of the nurses—Lucia in particular—had overcome some of their fear and were making excuses to walk by and peer in at the "wild Apache." Their behavior embarrassed her because she understood it all too well. To them he was a beast to be watched from afar, dreaded, reluctantly admired for his ferocity, but otherwise avoided and kept in his cage.

With her understanding of her fellow sisters came a stunning self-revelation. She enjoyed sparring with the wildcat. She took pleasure in being the only one brave enough to venture so close. But she also found herself hoping she could tame him enough to look at the thorn in his paw, longing to coax forth the gentleness she sensed deep beneath his feral pride and violent past.

These aberrations, these paradoxes deep within her nature, seemed to be more tests designed by God to keep her restless and on edge.

"Be thankful it's only an open door," Adela said, her voice unsteady. "She wanted me to tie you down again."

"And you didn't agree?"

The soft, probing tone of his question added to her discomfiture. She couldn't meet his gaze. "I apologize for their behavior. I'll speak to them."

"But you won't close the door."

"I can't." She strode to his bed, struggling for a show of nonchalance. "Why don't you turn to your right and sit on the edge of the mattress? That way you can continue looking out the window if you like."

He pushed up into a sitting position and eased first one leg and then the other over the edge of the bed. His tense movements, with the greater part of his weight supported on clenched fists, made the firm ridges of his back muscles even more evident than usual beneath his nightshirt.

She eased one knee onto the mattress behind him so she could better reach his head. "You're moving a little better, I see." She recognized the affable tone of nurse to patient in her own voice and acknowledged her reaction for what it was—a desperate attempt to control the degree to which she allowed herself to become emotionally involved with someone whose physical presence unnerved her so completely.

"Well enough to try getting up and closing the door myself," he responded, his voice gruff. "But you ignored my question."

Adela's stomach fluttered. "What question?"

"You didn't agree to tie me down again. Why?"

Unable to think of a safe and quick response, she curled her fingers around his hair near his neck. "I told Mother Eulalia it would interfere with your treatment," she said at last.

She could offer more. She could explain how she had stood up to her superior on his behalf. She could tell him how she yearned to know the truth—*his* truth about Smeet and the murdered soldiers. But what if his explanation only made the barrier between them insurmountable?

Worse, what if his explanation drew them closer together?

Opting to say nothing for fear she would confess too much, she pulled the heavy waves over his shoulders and began the long brush strokes almost to his waist. She felt him shiver, and an answering quake trembled through her own body as the intimacy of the moment became almost unbearable.

She took several long slow strokes, careful to brush lightly over the swelling at the base of his skull. With each pass his shoulders dropped a fraction as he released his tension.

"Mmm." The sound was a low rumble in his chest, a purr that vibrated through his body and up her arm. "That feels good."

The fluttering heat in Adela's stomach grew. She had never felt anything like this with another patient. She had never been forced to question her motivation behind every action when caring for a man.

Ladino was perfectly capable of brushing his own hair. The suggestion that he do so flew to her lips, but she caught herself just in time. If she quit, would he wonder why?

Then again, would he wonder why she continued when he could handle the task himself?

Just as he might also wonder if she had been honest in giving her reason for leaving the door open. For her reason had little to do with the compromise she'd made with Mother Eulalia, and everything to do with her new fear to be alone with Christian Ladino now that he was free. Not because of anything he might force her to do, but because she might prove willing.

"Did you brush my hair the other night, when I ran the fever?"

Adela stopped for a moment and swallowed. The vivid memory of that first night assailed her, reminding her how his cool, silky wet hair had felt running through her fingers.

"No," she answered, ashamed of her half-lie. "I just found the brush today. Most of our patients prefer combs." She didn't tell him the brush she used was her own. "But at this point in your recovery, I thought a comb might be too rough."

Adela resumed brushing. Silence grew, broken only by the rumble of thunder and the crackle of static through his hair.

"The deputy talked to your superior," he stated. "She told you I worked for Smeet and that I murdered soldiers." His low voice tingled up her arm like the storm-charged atmosphere outside. "That's why the door's open, isn't it?"

He twisted around and gripped her wrist. Adela gasped, shock and fear slicing through her body. Once again he had stolen the advantage because she had been too afraid to take it for herself.

"Do you believe what she told you about me? Is that why you fled my room yesterday?"

Chapter Eight

Thunder continued to roll as Ladino watched her, waiting for her answer. He'd tried to be nicer to her. He'd tried to make her feel more at ease today, showing by his behavior alone that she had nothing to fear, no reason to cry. But he'd grown tired of skirting the issue. Experience had taught him that rough tactics would wrench the truth out of fear and surprise more quickly than gentleness ever could. It disgusted him to treat her this way, yet he couldn't seem to stop himself. He wanted answers. He *needed* answers. *Her* answers.

But why? He couldn't understand why it meant so much for her to accept him and his truth over the lies of anyone else.

"Don't be afraid of me!" he ordered, hearing the plea hidden deep within his anger and confusion.

"How can I be anything *but* afraid of you? You're behaving like a savage!"

Fury scoured through him. She had discovered the one word that always reminded him he would never belong to her world. "That's right," he said. "I am a savage. I'll always be a savage. Worse than that, I'm a half-breed, and I'm probably the furthest thing from civilized you'll ever meet." He shook her wrist. "I want the truth. Do you believe what she told you?"

"What does it matter to you what I believe?" she snapped, wriggling her arm as she tried to get off the bed. "Let me go. You're hurting me."

He shook his head. "Not until you tell me whether you believed what you heard."

"Should I have?"

Ladino felt as if she had kicked him in the gut and embraced him at the same time. Once again he wondered why it should matter. But it did.

"No," he answered quietly.

"Not even about the soldiers you murdered?"

Another kick. He released her, and she scrambled off the bed. She glared at him as she rubbed her wrist.

"I killed the soldiers. But I'll tell you what I told Latham. They deserved what they got."

"Oh? And h-how is that?"

He saw his grandmother's eyes, heard her screams. Terrified, desperate, she ran to him, emaciated arms outstretched as Smeet's bullet slammed into her back. And the others. Women. Children. All destroyed by the soldiers he had unwittingly led into camp. The blood from their bodies painted the field crimson and soaked Ladino in guilt.

"Mr. Ladino, are you all right?"

He felt a gentle pressure on his shoulder. Adela's hand. When her face came into focus, he realized she had sat down on the bed from her side. She peered into his face, her soft eyebrows arched in concern.

"Do you want to tell me what happened?"

He shook his head and pushed himself straight again. Her hand slid to his forearm and rested there. He stared at her long fingers, slim but capable, pale and soft against his deep brown skin.

"No," he said, his voice hoarse.

He wanted to forget. But he couldn't. Just as he had feared, the vulnerability he'd thought buried with so many long-ago deaths lived again. But he couldn't bring himself to kill it. Not yet. Not with her so close. So close that when he looked up at her face again he noticed for the first time the tiny chicken pox scar at the corner of her right eye.

Distraction was his only release, so he continued to study her, astounded by this unexpected glimpse of the soft heart she usually disguised so well behind her efficiency and authority. He couldn't understand it. She hid her femininity beneath the sexless garb of a nun, and the sharp lash of her tongue flayed open his pain, yet she cried out to his masculinity like no other woman he'd ever met.

"So if you didn't believe what you heard," he murmured, "why did you run out of this room so fast yesterday?"

She dropped her gaze, and he followed her attention to the hairbrush she clenched in her fist. "You hurt my feelings."

"I hurt your feelings?"

"Yes." She lifted her gaze to his, her expression defiant of his ridicule.

But he had no intention of poking fun, because her admission had opened something fragile in his heart. He reached up and touched the scar near her eye with his forefinger. If he had hurt her feelings, didn't that mean she cared—at least a little?

"You're beautiful," he said suddenly.

For a moment her face mirrored his own surprise. Then she frowned and pushed off the bed. "Flowers and trees are beautiful. I'm not. And belief in such vanity wouldn't be allowed even if I were." She propped her fists on her hips. "Now, if you want to keep that long hair you're so proud of, turn around so I can finish brushing it."

Ladino ached with the urge to grab her, to fling her on his bed and cover her with his body. He longed to convince her of her beauty—to convince her how wrong she was to deny the fact that the heat of one flame attracted the heat of another.

Nevertheless, he did as she asked, turning and presenting the back of his head as he crossed his arms in his lap, covering the evidence of his arousal.

What would she do? He conjured visions of her head resting on his pillow as she gazed up at him with those wide brown eyes, her full lips parted. And the lightning would flash outside, and thunder would roar, just as it did now.

And what would he do?

First, he would kiss her. Though Apaches found the act abhorrent, he had seen his mother kiss his father when they thought no one else watched. His father hadn't seemed to find the intimacy distasteful at all, at least in private.

But he'd never kissed a woman. He wasn't sure how to go about it. And she was a nun. Everything his mother had taught him about her religion screamed into his mind. Yet the longer he felt the bristles sliding over his scalp as she continued to brush his hair, the longer he listened to the rumble of faraway thunder, the more aroused he became, enough to take risks he knew he shouldn't take in his injured state. Enough to want to change images of fantasy to reality. Enough to formulate a plan.

"Would you help me walk?"

The brushing stopped. "I don't think you're ready. It's barely been two days."

He smiled to himself at the irony of her words. If she only knew. "Then just help me stand."

"No, I don't think so."

"I'll do it on my own when you leave."

She remained silent, and Ladino waited, willing her to relinquish her safe position so near the door and come around the bed, farther within his lair. She sighed, and he smiled at her obvious surrender.

"Oh, all right."

"Thank you," he said, angling his body for a better view of her as she stormed around the foot of the bed.

She stood before him at last, her lips set in an exasperated line as she set the brush on the bedside table. "I still think you're too weak, even with my help."

Privately, Ladino agreed, his strength still sapped after the episode yesterday with Latham. If the man hadn't made him so furious, Ladino doubted he'd have been able to get out of bed. But right now he was determined to show Adela he could walk a few paces. Just to the door.

"You can steady yourself with a hand on my shoulder."

He eased forward, to the very edge of the bed, and Adela grasped his large hands in her small ones, holding him steady while he pulled himself to a standing position.

His equilibrium dipped and his knees shook, threatening to dump him on the floor. He took a deep breath and placed his hand on Adela's shoulder. At his touch, she tensed in acceptance of his weight, her muscles jumping under his palm.

"How are you so far?" she asked.

"Fine," he offered, unwilling to tell her how dizzy he felt, or how much his legs trembled. She could probably feel the tremors as well as he could. He opened his eyes and the room spun. He jerked to catch his balance, feeling foolish for his belief that he could make it to the door.

"Are you ready to sit back down?"

He shook his head. "No. I think I can walk a few steps."

"I don't know . . ." She gazed up at him, her face close enough that he could kiss her now, if he thought she wouldn't back away and let him fall. "All right," she answered at last.

With slow, scraping steps, Ladino made it just past the foot of the bed before his knees buckled. He grabbed the foot rail. The flimsy iron shook under his weight. Adela clutched him about the waist and somehow managed to keep him on his feet.

"I think that's quite enough."

"No." He shook his head. "Not nearly enough."

"I disagree."

Before Ladino knew what happened, she deftly removed her arms and pivoted him on his left foot, plunking him down on the foot of the bed. Surprised, he wanted to startle her as well. He grabbed her wrist and hauled her between his legs.

She gasped. "Mr. Ladino!" She cast a frantic glance toward the open door behind him. "Th—the door!"

"That's where I was headed, to close the door." He laced his fingers behind her back and pinned her arms to her sides. "Would you kiss me if the door were closed?"

"Kiss you!" She wormed her arms free and pushed against his forearms. He could feel the panic in her shaking fingertips. "I-I'm a nun!"

"And I'm an Apache. That habit means nothing to me."

Mentally, he crossed his fingers behind his back, imagining his mother standing before him, scolding him for his blasphemy.

"Well, it does to me." Now she shoved at his shoulders, and the opposite force of her body pushing against his arms only sent the heat of her nearness straight to his need.

"You're not like the other sisters, Adela."

"I'm just like the other sisters." She flicked another horror-stricken glance to the door. "Let me go before I scream."

"You wouldn't do that."

"No?"

"No. I know a bluff when I see one." He gazed hard into her eyes. "I know more about you than you care to admit."

"Let me go, and I-I'll forget this ever happened." She darted another peek at the door. "If you don't, I *will* scream."

"If you really thought I wanted to hurt you, you wouldn't scream. You'd handle me on your own just as you always have."

Silent, she stared down into his face, her eyes wide and her lips parted. Her resistance weakened. He could feel it. Taking a risk, he loosened his hold on her waist and leaned forward, inhaling her body heat. Deep beneath the sterile scent of lye soap hid the sweet feminine excitement he had coaxed to life. This was madness. Intoxicating. The air quivered with her indecision, yet she made no effort to move away.

If she tried, he promised himself he would let her go.

As if he were taming a skittish doe, he eased his hands up on either side of her face and slid his fingers beneath the edge of her crisp white bonnet to caress the tops of her ears. She held her breath and closed her eyes. She grabbed his wrists, but didn't pull away. At each stroke of his fingers, more rigidity melted from her body.

"You are a beautiful woman, even if you refuse to admit it."

She opened her eyes. "Please . . . this isn't right."

"Then leave," he said. "I won't stop you."

He watched her throat tremble as she swallowed, and he wanted to press his lips to the gentle arch of her neck. Such beauty. Such fire. Such heat waiting to be unleashed between them.

"The Mescalero Life Giver, *Bik'éguindan-n,* meant for all his creatures to pay homage to the strength and beauty in others. Surely even your White Eye God didn't mean for you to become dead to yourself. You really are different from the others, Adela."

As if voicing agreement, Old Man Thunder boomed, closer now. The reverberation vibrated the windowpanes in their sashes.

Staring into her eyes, he pulled her face closer. For an instant her grip tightened on his wrists. "Mr. Ladino," she said, her voice barely above a whisper, "I don't . . ."

Their faces now even, her voice faded as she continued to stare into his eyes. He touched his lips to hers, carefully, softly, the brief caress like down from a cattail floating on a mountain lake. Despite the chaste contact, Ladino felt pure heat flash through his body. He drew away in awe, watching her as she searched his face, her expression full of unfamiliar wonder as if she sought answers to the same questions he could not voice.

This time, she initiated the kiss, her awkward hesitation just as untutored as his had been—just as virginal.

He deepened the kiss until her mouth shuddered open under his. Overwhelmed with the need to taste her, Ladino flicked the tip of his tongue across her upper lip, barely grazing her teeth. Adela moaned, and though she still held his wrists, she shifted, coming down on her knees before him, between his widespread legs. She dared now to touch his tongue with her own, even as she nestled her stomach against his groin.

Started by that bolt of lightning, desire raged through him like a crown fire through a forest, so hot it knew no bounds. He slid his hands closer to their coupled lips and touched the corners of her moist mouth with the pads of his thumbs. Her soft tongue brushed against the tip of one thumb. Just as he tasted the salt she had licked from him, she closed her eyes and grasped his wrists even tighter in her shaking hands.

The heat of her exhaled breath against his face as she pulled away startled him. She sat back on her heels and scrambled to her feet. Standing before him, she clutched one hand to her stomach. He knew she felt the same heavy, heated craving in her belly that he felt in his. Only he knew what they had awakened, and she was just discovering.

"I . . ."

She put her hand to her mouth, then jerked it away as if burned, rubbing the back of her neck instead. Incredulity and dismay chased across her features as she glanced behind him to the open door. She rushed from the room, and he twisted his body on the bed to watch her. Just as she wheeled around the door frame, he heard two bodies collide.

"Excuse me, Sister Adela," came a muttered apology.

But he heard no answer, and now one of the sisters paused in the doorway. Ladino watched as the nun straightened her gingham apron, her face in profile as she gazed down the hallway, frowning after Adela's retreat. When she turned her puzzled expression into the room at him, her face blanched. He recognized her as Sister Lucia, the nun who had held the cone over his nose that first night, the sister who had entered his room with Latham. He also recognized her as one of the nurses who had been making repeated trips past his open door.

"Is, um . . ." She pointed down the hallway, her gesture self-conscious. "Is Sister Adela all right?"

He shrugged, but felt none of the nonchalance he tried

to portray. "I don't know."

But he did know.

If Adela felt as shattered as he did by what had just happened between them, neither of them would ever be the same.

Friday afternoon arrived all too soon, yet not soon enough for Adela's years of preparation. One more stage, one more step toward her goal, yet she didn't feel worthy of taking it. Not after what had happened yesterday. Not after the kiss.

She stared at the black habit laid out neatly on her cot. The only piece missing was the bonnet—the symbol of consecrated virginity that Mother Eulalia would soon place on her head.

Adela fought an overwhelming urge to bolt from her room, away from this hypocrisy.

"Are you ready for me to help you dress?"

Startled, Adela whirled around and saw Sister Blandina in the doorway. Her mentor's smile exuded pride and happiness. She'd cleaned and pressed her black habit for the occasion, and the points of her white collar looked especially crisp.

Adela felt ashamed to speak—ashamed even to be in the same room with one whose faith never wavered. Yet because she idolized Blandina, Adela couldn't imagine letting her down. She'd be even more ashamed to admit yesterday's weakness and how it had swayed her vocation.

"Yes," she answered at last. She needed to know one more thing before she prepared to meet Mother Eulalia. "Has my mother arrived?"

Blandina crossed the small space between them and put a hand on Adela's shoulder. "No, Adela. I'm sorry."

Adela nodded. What else had she expected? "Perhaps

something came up at one of Mr. Westbrook's mines."

"I'm sure that's what happened."

Adela fought tears even as she forced a smile. "We'd best hurry. Mother Eulalia isn't too happy with me as it is." A nervous laugh accompanied her understatement. "She'll be even less so if I keep her waiting."

"Don't let her frighten you. I have faith in your ability to be a good Sister of Charity, to continue your growth on the path God has chosen for you. Taking this next step will help you see that. You have so much to offer, Adela."

She nodded again, unconvinced.

"*Believe* it." Blandina cupped Adela's cheek, and Adela was paralyzed by the intensity of the gentle contact. "Faith comes when you release control and allow yourself to believe that God wants to do good in your life, and that He wants to do good for others through your life. You may not see this yet, but God will help you understand."

She wanted to believe Blandina, but she still couldn't help but wonder if what God wanted for her wasn't what she wanted at all. What if it was His plan for her to leave the convent? What if He wanted her homeless and at the mercy of uncaring strangers? She wouldn't trust her life to such uncertain circumstances as He might force on her if she were to allow Him. She couldn't.

Yet Adela also knew she played a dangerous game. Judas had dedicated his life to Jesus, but that vow hadn't been enough to keep him from taking gold and betraying his Lord with a kiss.

Would her betrayal also be a kiss?

Chapter Nine

After the ceremony, Adela returned to her room and changed back into her nurse's uniform. As she folded the pieces of her new habit, the disappointment and disillusionment of the last few days enshrouded her. Sinking down on her cot, she lifted the black serge fabric to her face and closed her eyes as she inhaled. So crisp, so fresh, so full of promise, yet she still felt shabby and threadbare inside.

A light knock sounded at her open door. Startled, she dropped her vestments to her lap and looked up to see Sister Michaela's pale, thin face peeking around her door frame. She swallowed the sob that had been building in her.

"Sorry to bother you, Sister Adela, but Mother Eulalia sent me to tell you there is a man here wishing to speak to you."

"Is it Mr. Westbrook?"

"I don't know. Mother Eulalia didn't tell me his name."

"Is my mother with him?" In an effort to appear normal, she set the folded pieces atop the winter blankets in her trunk.

"Mother Eulalia didn't mention a woman."

"Tell her I'll be right there."

Sister Michaela nodded and disappeared.

It had to be her mother's husband. It had to be. Perhaps Minna rested at one of the hotels in town, while he came to give notice of their arrival. Or perhaps Minna waited as well, and Mother Eulalia had just purposefully not mentioned the fact.

Adela looked down at her nurse's uniform, then at the habit pieces folded neatly in the trunk. She thought about changing back into the black habit for benefit of Mother Eulalia, but decided against it. The new frock and cape still didn't seem as if they should belong to her. They would belong to her even less if she used them for the sole purpose of impressing her superior. Adela was out the door and down the first flight of stairs before she realized she'd forgotten her belt and rosary.

Only when she reached the long hallway before Mother Eulalia's office did she ease her pace, trying to catch her breath and slow her racing heart. It would never do to storm into her superior's office looking like a breathless fool.

This time Mother Eulalia's door was open, and she could see a man's black patent shoes and gray, pant-clad legs. No speech issued from the room, and Adela felt her wariness grow. Something wasn't right. Had Mother Eulalia left the man in her office alone? No, she heard the shuffling of papers from the part of the room occupied by her superior's desk.

Adela rapped on the door frame, not daring to peek inside to look at the man.

The ruffling of papers at the desk ceased. "Here she is," said Mother Eulalia, her voice filled with relief—an emotion that seemed strangely out of place.

When Adela entered, the man stood. She couldn't help but notice how he was dressed. His vest, coat, and trousers looked expensive, their fit meticulous, though wrinkled as if he'd spent long hours traveling. He was a tall man, and salt-and-pepper hair framed a strong-boned face, which seemed at odds with his kind blue eyes.

He bowed. "It's a pleasure to make your acquaintance,

Sister Adela," he said in clipped British tones.

Adela frowned. She'd learned that Jonathan Westbrook was originally from England, but she suspected this wasn't him. This man's air seemed somehow too formal to be addressing his wife's daughter. She cast a questioning glance at Mother Eulalia, but saw only an implacable grimness set in the straight lines of the woman's mouth.

"Might I speak to Sister Adela privately?"

"I'm afraid I can't allow that," said Mother Eulalia.

The man bowed his acknowledgment, then turned to Adela. "My dear Sister Adela, I wanted to see you in person. A telegram is so impersonal. My name is William Leeds, and I am—*was*—Mr. Jonathan Westbrook's attorney."

Adela pounced on the correction. "Was?"

He curled his fist over his mouth and cleared his throat. "Excuse me. Yes," he agreed, his voice a whisper.

Adela's throat and chest tightened. He seemed to notice her discomfiture and made an obvious effort to lower his hand and place it behind his back with the other, setting his shoulders as if preparing himself for the inevitable.

"Yes," he said again. "I'm afraid Mr. Westbrook has been killed—"

"And that's why my mother never arrived!" she blurted, unable to keep the grasping, panicked relief from her voice. "She sent you to tell me."

"Sister Adela!" Mother Eulalia scolded.

Horrified by her own insensitivity, Adela murmured an apology.

"It's quite all right. Your reaction is understandable considering you never knew Mr. Westbrook."

As sympathy melted into his forced smile, Adela fell back fifteen years, to her memory of the face of Hermana

Dolores, the sister who had comforted her and carried her
inside the orphanage, still wrapped in a bloody coat.

Even before Mr. Leeds resumed, Adela was shaking her
head in denial. It did no good. His face held the inevitable
sympathy, while his voice droned the unavoidable explanation.

"Unfortunately, that is not the only reason I've come."

Adela's body swayed. Mr. Leeds grasped her arm. She
looked down at his fingers curled about her forearm. She
felt as if he held someone else's arm, and she couldn't believe she still occupied her own body. Oh, Sweet Mary,
she'd never felt faint in her life. How could this be hap-
pening to her?

"I'll get a chair!" Mother Eulalia's voice held such sincere caring that Adela didn't recognize it, causing the whole
episode to seem even more nightmarish and out of kilter.

Something bumped against the backs of her knees and
she sat. She reached up and touched her cheek, surprised to
feel contact with her own skin as images, thoughts and
questions careened through her mind like thousands of
birds in a single cage.

Mama? Was. Killed? Unfortunately.

Abbie? Where was Abbie? She groped absently at her
pocket, but found nothing.

God. Resentment. Home?

A kiss, full of shame and wonder . . . and betrayal.

Punishment. She was being punished.

Mr. Leeds crouched at her feet and stared up into her
face, his thick black and gray brows meeting over the bridge
of his wide nose. He gave her arm a squeeze. "Are you all
right?"

As Adela began to resettle inside her own mind and
body, a tingling sensation pumped through her arms and

legs, while her heart slid into place last, beating furiously to make up for suspended time.

"I think so," she managed, her throat tight.

Preparing to stand, Mr. Leeds began to drag his hand from Adela's arm as he cast an earnest expression toward Mother Eulalia. "I can come back tomorrow."

"No!" Adela slapped her free hand over his. Was she ready to hear what he had to say? No. But she had no choice. "Please. I want to know why you've come."

He voiced a ragged sigh. "Your mother and Mr. Westbrook were on their way here when they were attacked by Apaches."

Adela closed her eyes, and a knot formed at the top of her stomach. "And my mother was killed."

"Sister Adela, please allow me to finish."

He hadn't agreed. Hope bloomed. Adela opened her eyes.

"Your mother and Jonathan Junior were taken captive."

"Taken captive! But—"

Mr. Leeds held up his hand. "Mrs. Westbrook is back at her home in Silver City . . . recovering." He cleared his throat and rubbed his upper lip. "But the Apaches still have Jonathan Junior."

The full weight of every layer of guilt Adela had experienced concerning the infant smothered her at once. She'd been envious of the baby. She had resented him being one of the reasons for her mother's visit.

"Oh, dear Lord," she said, covering her face with her hands.

"The attack occurred near Pinos Wells, about fifty miles north of Mr. Westbrook's mine at White Oaks," Mr. Leeds explained. "Attacks that far north are unusual, so Mr. Westbrook had only hired one escort. He and the escort were killed in the skirmish. Their remains were buried at the site."

Mr. Leeds stood. "Cavalry from Fort Bayard has been dispatched to search for the renegades. From your mother's description, Captain Grisham thinks the Mescalero Apache known by his Spanish name, Pajaro, is the leader of these 'dog Indians.' Several years ago Pajaro was accused of witchcraft, or some such."

"Witchcraft?" Adela knew belief in witches, the evil eye, and other superstitions were common among the Spanish families of the Territory, but she'd never imagined Apaches sharing similar beliefs. "Exactly what does that mean?"

"It seems the Apache believe that certain members of their tribe have what they call 'power,' which can be used for good or evil." Mr. Leeds rose and walked across the room to the window, then turned to face Adela. "After the mysterious death of a medicine man, Pajaro was banished from his tribe. I'm told banishment is a worse fate than death, and many accused of witchcraft avenge themselves on those responsible for having them sent away."

"Do the authorities know where these renegades are?"

"We aren't certain. Mrs. Westbrook was blindfolded when she was taken to their mountain camp, so she couldn't be specific about the location. But she claims it was early morning when she was left on the road near Lake Valley, and they had traveled at a steady pace all night." He strode to Mother Eulalia's desk and tapped his fingers on its surface. "From that information, Captain Grisham was able to deduct that the camp was somewhere within a twenty-five-mile radius, most probably in the Caballo Mountains. They searched for the renegades but found no sign. The Caballos are close to the border, so by the time Mrs. Westbrook was found and taken to Silver City, we believe they had already escaped into Mexico."

Adela closed her eyes, desperate to blot out the vision of her mother lying near death on the side of the road. "Why didn't he follow?"

"It's not that simple. The U.S. is not allowed to pursue criminals, or even Apaches, across the Mexican border. That's why they stay so close to our southern boundaries. If they raid one of our villages, they flee to Mexico, and if they raid a Mexican village, they slip back across the line to our side."

He threw up his hands. "Until policy changes are negotiated, the best Captain Grisham could do was notify the commander at Fort Stanton. He believes Pajaro might still have some connection with the Mescaleros."

Adela absorbed the lawyer's words for a few moments before speaking. "You say my mother is recovering. Did they hurt her?"

"She's suffering from broken ribs, a couple of knife wounds—"

"Knife wounds?"

"Yes, I'm afraid so. Your mother fought with the Apache woman who took her son." He sighed. "And, since your mother just recently delivered her baby, I'm afraid there have been some complications in that regard as well."

"What kind of complications?"

Mr. Leeds cleared his throat and darted a quick glance to Mother Eulalia. "The doctor who attended her lying-in claims she's not only depressed, but she is also suffering from—" He scratched his upper lip. "Well, it appears that before making this trip your mother was . . . not as fully recovered as she claimed to Dr. Clayburgh."

"Is this Dr. Clayburgh with her now?"

"Yes, but of course he has other patients he needs to attend, so he'll be unable to remain with her indefinitely."

Adela turned to Mother Eulalia. "Mother," she began, tipping her head in a respectful bow. "I would like to request a leave of absence so that I might care for her myself."

"I'm not certain that would be wise, Sister Adela. You've had no experience treating female patients. Surely the doctor who delivered the child is capable."

"Yes, but I want to help however I can."

"That is to be expected under the circumstances," Mr. Leeds reminded.

Mother Eulalia tightened her lips into a resentful line as she turned to Adela. "How long will you need?"

Adela considered for a moment. "Two weeks?"

"I suppose that will be fine. But keep in mind that Sister Blandina will be leaving for the retreat in Cincinnati at the end of the month." She tilted her head and lifted a brow above one wire rim of her spectacles. "I wouldn't want us to be left shorthanded. I'll send Sister Michaela as your traveling companion. Please tell her I wish to speak with her about it."

"Yes, Mother Eulalia."

"So it's settled?" Mr. Leeds asked Mother Eulalia.

"It appears so."

Mr. Leeds nodded, smiling as he turned to Adela. "I've taken the liberty of arranging for Mr. Westbrook's private car to depart with the three o'clock train. Can you and Sister Michaela be ready to leave by then?"

"Certainly." Adela gasped, just then remembering Mr. Ladino.

"What is it, Sister Adela?" Mr. Leeds rushed to her side and grasped her by the elbow.

Adela turned to Mother Eulalia. "Mr. Ladino. Who'll take over his care?"

"I'll see that he's taken care of."

Adela nodded, then thought of something else. A suggestion. She shouldn't push, but she couldn't help herself. "Perhaps Sister Lucia. She seems least frightened of him." Adela blushed, remembering the kiss. She didn't blame him, only herself. It wouldn't be fair to make him think she'd requested someone else to take over his care solely because she feared facing him. "And would you make sure he knows why I'll no longer be tending him?"

Fine vertical wrinkles tightened to deep slashes between Mother Eulalia's eyes. "I've already said I'd see to your patient, Sister Adela." She glanced quickly at the clock on her desk. "You have fifteen minutes to pack. I suggest you use the time wisely and not keep Mr. Leeds waiting."

"Yes, Mother." Adela genuflected and turned to leave.

"And Sister Adela," Mother Eulalia called.

Adela pivoted. "Yes?"

"Make sure you wear your black habit." She flicked a glance over Adela's attire. "And this time, don't forget your rosary."

Adela's blush intensified. She dropped one more genuflection and fled the office.

When Nigel Smeet reached the appointed place, he pulled out his kerchief and wiped the perspiration from his forehead. He saw no sign of Pajaro. No doubt the Apache was hiding, waiting for just the right moment to materialize. Nigel usually had the patience for the renegade's ghostly theatrics. Not today.

"Reveal yourself, savage!"

A raven soared in the sky, cawing in answer as Nigel scanned the surrounding hills. Whip-like branches of ocotillo swayed in the breeze above olive-drab greasewood bushes. The rocky terrain appeared undisturbed, but Nigel knew better. The raven cawed again, dove from the sky, and landed on a boulder near a clump of *sotol*. The bird tilted its head and opened its beak, assessing each member of Nigel's six-man party in turn. Then it dismissed them all and began to preen.

"Maybe he forgot this was the day—"

"Shut up, Benjamin!" Nigel snapped, yanking back on his mount's reins and wheeling the animal around. The horse tossed its head, whickering to protest the biting bit. Nigel pulled the rolled *El Paso Times* from inside his frock coat and backhanded Ben Duffy across the face with it. "If I want your opinion, you ignorant pup, I'll bloody well ask for it!"

The raven released a startled screech.

"*¡Dios mio!*" The wagon driver crossed himself and gaped, staring past Nigel and Ben.

Nigel turned in his saddle. An arm had emerged from the dirt and gravel beside the boulder, the hand clutching the raven by its feet. The startled bird flapped its wings and pecked at the fingers that held it captive. Dirt continued to shift and undulate like a living grave until the renegade's body emerged, the serrated blades of the *sotol* plant toppling to the ground from atop his head.

Nigel's heart pounded with fear, the sound echoing in his ears. No matter how many times he'd seen the tactic, it never failed to shatter his fortitude.

"Damned spooky savage," he muttered.

Still holding the raven by its feet in his bloodied hand, the Apache stroked the iridescent feathers with the other. He whispered and clicked his tongue, imitating the raven's own noises alongside its head. The bird calmed, but held its beak open and issued a sharp *tok, tok, tok* in warning.

135

Pajaro brushed away the dust that clung to his unbuttoned cavalry coat and calico breechcloth. He neared Nigel, and with a lift of his chin, gestured toward the wagon and the wooden boxes piled high in its bed.

"So, these are the guns you bring me?" he asked in Spanish.

Nigel shook with fury, yet knew he would have to regain control of his careening emotions if he was going to shift the balance of power to himself.

"Perhaps," he replied, forcing nonchalant contempt into his voice.

Though Nigel knew the savage couldn't read, for effect he tossed the newspaper at Pajaro's feet. It fell open to a recent picture of Jonathan Westbrook, the headline proclaiming his death during an Apache attack.

"I see all through the written messages of the White Eye," Nigel reminded, "just as your power enables you to see all through the eyes of birds. Killing Westbrook was not part of our plan."

"He would have killed one of my warriors. My band is small, I sacrifice no lives for your revenge." He strode to the wagon, still stroking the raven. "There are not enough boxes. Are you sure all are here?" Distrust radiated from his hellish black eyes as he turned back to Nigel. "Open them and show me."

Nigel shook his head. "No, One Who Speaks With Birds." Nigel knew he breached the Apache code of conduct with his deliberate use of the renegade's tribal name. "Not until we settle the matter of Westbrook's death and I see the baby."

For several moments the Indian remained silent, staring. Nigel had learned long ago how Apaches considered the act an invasion of privacy, just as disrespectful as speaking a warrior's name in his presence. Nervous under the renegade's scrutiny, Nigel shifted in his saddle.

Only one other man had ever mastered the same blood-chilling effect with his eyes. 'Idui Bndaa'. Eyes of the Mountain Lion. Ladino. He shuddered, but reminded himself that the 'breed was dead—no longer a threat.

Pajaro lifted his chin and whistled a quail call. The raven canted its head as if confused. In seconds, seven armed, mounted warriors and one woman appeared over the rise. Four of the warriors remained on the crest of the hill, rifles propped at the ready on their bare thighs. The other three escorted the woman down the rocky slopes and into the depression. A wide leather strap crossed the woman's chest. Behind her head and shoulders, Nigel saw the hooded top of a *ts'ál*.

At the renegade leader's command in Mescalero, the woman dismounted. The cone-shaped tin beads decorating her moccasins danced without making a sound as she walked toward Nigel and turned, presenting her back. Swaddled and bound to the cradleboard, the infant seemed content. His toes peeked out at the bottom. At the top, his right arm—his future bow arm—drifted freely. He gurgled in delight as he toyed with a beaded gourd rattle attached to the woven hood of the *ts'ál*. Nigel noted that the baby seemed large for his supposed age of less than three months, and the fair skin on his arm had pinkened from exposure to the sun.

Against his better judgment, Nigel gave in to the compulsion to touch the small fingers. The infant quit gurgling and dropped his hand from the rattle. He peeked out from under the hood, lifting his thin blond brows to stare at Nigel. Despite the baby's unformed features, his curious expression bore an uncanny resemblance to a youthful version of Jonathan Senior. It was almost as if Jonathan's spirit peered at Nigel through his infant son's blue eyes. Nigel stared at the child in wonder, his fury over the failed plan mixed with a sudden, unexpected burst of grief over Jonathan's death.

"There now, little Master Westbrook," Nigel said softly, fighting back the lump in his throat.

As if dismissing Nigel, the baby pulled his fingers back and made a fist. He dropped his brows into a frown and shoved his plump hand in his mouth. The image of the baby's father disappeared, and Nigel felt bereft, as if Jonathan had rejected him again. Cold anger settled in his chest as he realized this infant was now the only link he'd ever have to old memories.

He cleared his throat. "Is he sound?" he asked in Spanish. "I want to see his limbs."

The renegade perched the raven on his shoulder, and Nigel stared. Though he didn't believe Apache superstitions about power, he couldn't help but wonder in this one's case.

Pajaro lifted the *ts'ál* over the woman's head. He issued more orders in their native tongue and the woman took the cradleboard from him, setting it on the ground. She untied the crisscrossing leather thongs that held the baby in place. As she unwrapped the infant, shredded bark and grass fell to the ground. She held up the naked infant for Nigel's inspection. Nigel reached out to take the child.

The leader intercepted, grasping the boy himself. "Not yet, White Eye. Not until you show me what I have come for."

Nigel stepped back. "There's still the matter of Jonathan Westbrook's death. You knew I wanted him alive. You didn't keep our agreement to the letter, so I've reneged somewhat on mine."

"But I brought the child."

"Still only half of our agreement."

The renegade narrowed his eyes to angry slits. "To my people, a teachable child is worth more than the life of a grown enemy."

"Yes, but the Apache also value revenge. I once helped you get your revenge, and making Jonathan Westbrook suffer over the loss of his son was to be mine. A dead man no longer suffers. What use is his baby to me now?"

"Then you will not mind if I bash his skull."

Grasping the infant's ankles, the renegade dropped him upside-down, dangling him above a rock. Jonathan Junior burst out with a frightened squall, his face turning brick-red. Fear and fury bloomed in the woman's round face. She grabbed the renegade's arm, chattering to him in Mescalero, while the raven flapped its wings and let out a raucous screech. Barking a harsh command, the renegade pushed the woman away. She stumbled back, her jaw clenched as one hand hovered above the knife at her waist.

Pajaro's attention returned to Nigel. "What is it you White Eyes say about our babies? Nits make lice?" He lifted the infant higher.

"Do it, savage," Nigel challenged, though his heart plunged. "Just see where it will get you."

Ben Duffy dismounted and scurried to his boss's side. "But, sir, I thought you said—"

"Shut up, Benjamin." Nigel pulled his revolver and aimed at the boy's forehead beneath his new Stetson. "I've already told you once. I'll not tell you again."

"But he'll kill the baby, and—"

Nigel thumbed back the hammer. The chamber turned, clicking into place.

Ben fell silent, closing his eyes. Nigel shifted and pulled

the trigger. Ben jumped. The wagon driver clutched his chest and toppled from his seat. Ben's eyes fluttered open, his mouth widening in terror and amazement.

"That's right, Benjamin, you're still alive." Nigel smiled and lifted a single brow. "But just remember, my dear boy, when you cease being useful to me, you might meet the same fate."

Ben swallowed. "Yes, sir."

"Now step aside and let me handle this."

"Yes, sir," the boy mumbled, stepping several paces away.

Nigel spared a glance for the other riders surrounding the wagon. All returned his stare as if just realizing they were waking up to a rattler in their bedroll. Hoping his indiscriminate murder would tip elusive power back into his favor, Smeet dismissed them from sight and slid his attention to Pajaro. Clicking back the hammer, he trained his revolver on the Apache's chest between a silver *concha* necklace and a beaded rawhide war charm.

"You broke half of your agreement, so I broke half of mine. The remaining guns are in the wagon. They're yours. The baby is mine." He turned to the woman, skimming a disgusted gaze over her heavy breasts beneath the faded blue calico tunic. "And her. She comes with the boy."

Pajaro swung Jonathan Junior up by his heels, cradled his head, and placed him in the woman's arms. He muttered something to her and she glanced up at Smeet. She whispered something in return. Smeet strained to listen, but couldn't make out her words.

Cradling the naked infant in one arm, the woman used her free hand to pull new grass from the pouch she carried on the leather belt at her waist. She bent down and arranged the absorbent material in the swaddling blanket.

This done, she laced Jonathan onto the *ts'ál*. The leader helped her lift the cradleboard over her head and settle it on her back.

Turning to Smeet, Pajaro lifted the raven from his shoulder and resumed his absent stroking of the bird's black plumage. He appeared calm, even though Nigel's revolver targeted his heart.

"Show me the guns, White Eye. All of them. If half are there, as you say, I will honor this new agreement."

After today's near-fiasco, Nigel hated to turn his back on Pajaro's armed savages, but after ten years of successful dealing with the renegade leader, he felt he should continue to show a certain measure of confidence. He slowly re-holstered his pistol and turned to lead the way to the wagon.

Nigel ordered his men to unload all the boxes and pry off the lids. Pajaro's men inspected each weapon with extreme care, and Nigel's anger sizzled at the obvious affront to his honesty. After the dog Indians claimed all the rifles they could carry, Nigel ordered his men to re-nail the lids and reload the remaining boxes onto the wagon.

Pajaro spoke to one of his men, who nodded, then vaulted into the wagon seat and took up the reins.

"My warrior will take the wagon now, White Eye."

Nigel studied the leader for signs of trickery. "All right."

Pajaro nodded to his man, who lashed the reins along the backs of the mules. The wagon trundled up the rise, headed north toward the four who stood guard on the hill.

"I want your men to retreat." Pajaro lifted his chin at the woman. "She will go with you for as long as you keep the baby."

Nigel squinted, his suspicion growing. "You're being awfully careful, Pajaro—more so than in the past. Is it because you don't trust me, or because I shouldn't trust you?"

The renegade stroked the raven. "You try to hide it, but you feel a deep unhappiness in our agreement today. Like other White Eyes, you say one thing and mean another. Perhaps we have trusted each other too long."

Uneasiness coiled and rattled within Nigel's chest. He turned to his men. "Except for Benjamin, all of you leave. I'll follow in a few minutes."

His riders reined their horses around and headed back toward El Paso.

"Benjamin, fetch the woman's horse," Nigel ordered in Spanish for Pajaro's benefit. But he spoke his next words in English, knowing Pajaro couldn't understand well enough to decipher them. "And Benjamin," he added, "once you get back over the hill, take her knife away and tie her hands, otherwise she'll have you gutted and on a spit before you know what happened. Hold her at gunpoint if you have to, but don't let her escape." He allowed a sly, warning smile to rise to his lips. "I hold you responsible."

Benjamin swallowed, and his head twitched as if he started to dart a glance at the renegade leader. At the last moment he must have thought better of it, because he offered a quick nod instead. "Yes, sir," he said, rushing to do Nigel's bidding.

Once Benjamin and the Apache woman left, Pajaro turned to his men and issued orders in Mescalero. They wheeled around on their mounts and rode away, trotting up the steep incline. Pajaro waved at the group on the crest of the hill. They too disappeared.

"Are we finished here, Pajaro?"

"Almost, White Eye."

Pajaro released the raven. "White Eye!" the bird screeched, mimicking its owner. It flew straight at Nigel, beating its wings about his ears and slicing its talons across his face. The Englishman screamed. He twisted and turned, batting the attacking bird away from his head. At last the raven wheeled away, its beak open as it made the *tok, tok, tok* noise like laughter in its craw.

Wiping blood from his face, Smeet glanced to where Pajaro had stood just moments ago. He saw nothing.

The witch had vanished.

Chapter Ten

Adela alighted from the surrey with the help of Mr. Leeds and stared in awe at the enormous Westbrook home. Built in the Queen Anne style, with a mansard roof, gallery, and three-story tower, the house loomed above its neighbors, including St. Vincent de Paul's Catholic Church across the street. The tower's arched windows would afford a perfect view of the shade tree saplings and the fountain below, in which four winged cherubs held fish with waterspout mouths. Her mother finally had the castle she'd always talked about on their treks between towns and jobs.

"Are you ready to go inside, Sister Adela?"

Adela pulled her gaze to Mr. Leeds. "I suppose so."

He opened the picket-fence gate and ushered Adela and Sister Michaela up the sidewalk toward the front door. As they passed the fountain, Adela noticed the structure contained no water.

"Mr. Westbrook just had the fountain built," explained the lawyer. "It's not yet functional."

Her mother had always included just such a fountain when she'd described her dream castle. It was a shame, and sadly ironic, for the fountain to be empty. Adela fought tears as she held up her habit skirts to navigate the front steps.

She and Sister Michaela stepped aside for Mr. Leeds to use the brass knocker. In moments, the door swung open, framing a tall, thin woman in a gray dress and white apron.

"Good day, Judith," said Mr. Leeds.

"Good day, sir." The woman curtsied, then stepped aside to allow them entrance. Mr. Leeds ushered Adela and Michaela in before him, making introductions as they crossed the threshold. Adela absorbed the spacious foyer's atmosphere, noting the honeyed scent of beeswax, the tangy aroma of lemon oil, and the luster of sunlight reflecting on the curved mahogany staircase.

Mr. Leeds set the two black traveling baskets on the floor and hung his gray bowler on the mirrored hall tree. "How is Mrs. Westbrook today?"

Judith closed the door. "Dr. Clayburgh is with her now," she said, her voice bleak.

"Oh? I didn't see his buggy."

"It's in the carriage house." Her gaze shifted to Adela before it jumped back to Mr. Leeds. "Dr. Clayburgh stayed the night. After you left, he had to perform surgery."

"Surgery?" Adela cried. "What kind of surgery?"

Anguish creased the maid's brow. "I—I think you should talk to the doctor about that."

Mr. Leeds touched Adela's arm in a consoling gesture. "I'll take you right up to see your mother." He turned back to Judith. "Would you see that Adela and Sister Michaela have rooms?"

"Certainly." Adela thought she saw tears hovering at the brink of Judith's eyelids, but the maid bent so quickly to grasp their traveling baskets she couldn't be sure.

Michaela shot Adela a sympathetic smile before she hurried up the staircase after Judith.

Mr. Leeds turned to Adela, his expression grave. "Now I must warn you, she was not in the best condition before I left her yesterday morning."

"I'll be fine, Mr. Leeds. I'm a nurse."

"Yes, but this is your mother, and a reunion with her would have been emotional under the best of circumstances."

Eyes wide, Adela stared at him, determined not to allow any acknowledgment of her inner turmoil to cross her face for fear she would lose control. "Thank you for your concern, Mr. Leeds. I know better than to fall apart in front of a patient."

He patted her shoulder and offered a supportive smile. "Of course."

Before he turned away, Adela thought she saw a bit of moisture in his eyes. In a deep, selfish way she wished she didn't have to acknowledge, it hurt to know her mother's condition pained so many people—people who knew Minna so much better than she did.

Mr. Leeds gestured toward the stairs. "Shall we?"

Adela's stomach tightened another knot, but she nodded and led the way, fastening her attention on the dim light sifting through the stained-glass rose window at the top of the stairs. When they gained the landing, Mr. Leeds guided her across the carpet runner toward an angled set of double doors, both of which stood open to reveal the octagonal tower room.

A navy, garnet, and gold Turkish carpet covered much of the oak parquet floor, while a velvet-padded settee and a chess table with two wing chairs stood ready before the fireplace. Lace panels, flanked by heavy garnet brocade drapes, adorned the three tall windows, pulling Adela's attention to the canvas easel supporting a partially completed painting of the fountain. All evidence of oils and turpentine had been removed from the room, but a shade of their presence still clung to the air.

With a hand at her back, Mr. Leeds guided her across

the room to another set of double doors that stood next to the fireplace.

Mr. Leeds knocked lightly. One of the doors opened, and a flutter of nerves scattered to Adela's toes. The man's reddened eyelids hovered over piercing blue-gray eyes that glittered with annoyance. Thinning, iron-gray hair spiked in disarray upon his head, and harsh stubble sprouted from folds of weathered brown skin along his cheeks and throat.

Could such a disheveled ogre truly be her mother's doctor? After seeing how immaculate everything else in the house appeared, she found it difficult to believe. She reminded herself that she might be judging Dr. Clayburgh unduly. Perhaps caring for her mother left him little time to consider his appearance.

"Dr. Clayburgh," said Mr. Leeds, "this is Sister Adela Fremont."

The man raked his gaze over her. "I suppose you want to see your mother."

His breath reeked of cheap whiskey, causing anger to collide with the nausea already churning in Adela's stomach. Stepping back, he opened the door wider for them to enter.

Adela's pulse rushed to her throat as she stepped over the threshold. She could not distinguish color in the dim light, but the atmosphere of dark paneling, dark drapes, and dark carpet suffocated her. The enormous chamber boasted massive furniture, and an eight-foot headboard loomed above her mother's waxen face. The white gauze bandage on her left cheek provided the only bright spot in the entire tableau.

Though Minna slept, her teeth chattered despite the crazy quilt tucked up to her chin. She frowned and tossed her head, moaning as if her life ticked away in time to the mantel clock.

Adela turned to Doctor Clayburgh and whispered, "How is she?"

"Not good." He stalked back to the bedside. After wringing out a compress, he folded it and placed it on her forehead.

Adela stepped a few paces closer. "What is the diagnosis?" Her tone proclaimed self-assurance, but shame pierced her because she feared going near her mother's bedside.

"Broken ribs, high fever, nausea, acute mastitis, and excruciating pain in the lower back and hips. She screams unless I keep her dosed with laudanum. The vomiting has subsided, but only because she has nothing left to discharge."

Adela blinked at the assault of his words. She nodded, but more seconds ticked away on the clock before she could speak. "The maid, Judith, told us you performed surgery," Adela said. "Do you mind if I ask what you did?"

"I removed her uterus as a final effort to save her life."

"A final effort?" Adela exclaimed. "I don't understand. After all she's been through, was that kind of radical surgery necessary?"

Dr. Clayburgh jerked upright. As he strode toward her, the anger in his cold eyes made her shiver. Grasping her arm, he pulled her out into the tower room and closed the door behind them. "How many babies have you delivered at St. Vincent's?"

"None. Our patients are men. Miners, railroad workers, but—"

"Do you know anything at all about delivering babies?"

"I've studied anatomy. I've read—"

"You've read books. Does that make you an authority?"

"I didn't mean to imply—"

"Your mother is thirty-nine," he whispered harshly, standing so close she had to lean back to keep his liquored breath from turning her stomach. "Considering the difficulties she suffered during her first pregnancy, thirty-nine is not the optimal age for her to have borne another child."

Adela's cheeks stung as if he'd slapped her. She'd never known. But then birthing wasn't something a mother discussed with her small child—or even her grown daughter until she married and carried a child of her own. Instead of giving in to her overwhelming urge to cry, Adela swallowed her grief and anger until they hardened like rocks in her chest.

As if he felt chastened by his callous words, Dr. Clayburgh's manner softened somewhat. "Sister Adela, I realize that as a nun you may not be accustomed to such bluntness concerning matters of this nature, but as a nurse you should be prepared for what I have to say."

He gestured toward one of the wing chairs and waited until Adela had seated herself before he took the opposite chair.

"Jonathan Junior was a large baby. Ten pounds. After fifty-two hours of labor, Mrs. Westbrook suffered uterine tears and a prolapse upon giving birth. I prescribed a pessary and kept in contact with her for the first two months after her lying-in. I did not perform another internal exam, but she assured me the bleeding had stopped and that the pessary fit comfortably. I gave her permission to make the trip with Mr. Westbrook to check his mines, since she also wanted to visit you in Santa Fe."

Unable to meet his gaze any longer, Adela stared down at her hands clasped in her lap. She rubbed one thumb along the other until both grew red and sore.

"When she was found," he continued, "she had been bleeding. During an internal examination, I discovered her rough treatment had caused the pessary to injure her weakened organ. After trying unsuccessfully to stop the bleeding, I opted to perform the surgery."

For several moments all remained quiet—so quiet Adela heard the clock's half-hour chime beyond the closed doors of her mother's bedchamber.

Still staring at her hands in her lap, Adela spoke. "I apologize for questioning you, Dr. Clayburgh." At last she looked up. "I admit I have no practice in feminine matters, but I am a good nurse. I—I'll do my best to help."

"I'd appreciate that." He rose from the chair. "I need to tend an out-of-town patient—a boy with a bullet wound— but before I go, I'll show you what I've been doing to help her mastitis."

Where is she?

That had been Ladino's question for three days now, ever since Adela had rushed out of his room after their kiss.

Sister Lucia had taken her place. The first day he'd been too ashamed to ask about Adela, figuring she had just been upset after what had happened between them. By the second day, he'd decided she'd never be so spineless as to shun him, no matter how much he had upset her. By that night, he'd mustered the courage to ask Sister Mary de Sales, but she wouldn't tell him, and no amount of persuasion had enabled him to change her mind.

Now his only choice was to ask Lucia. If she wouldn't cooperate, he'd demand an answer—by force if he had to.

He didn't have to wait long. Sister Lucia sidled into his room moments later with his midday meal. Except for the dauntless Mary de Sales, Lucia did seem braver than the other sisters, yet he still despised the way she skulked around the corners, coming near his bed only when necessary.

Adela had courage. Adela had fire. This one had weak knees and a quivery voice. Despite his best efforts not to frighten her, he couldn't help but glare. If he were a more tolerant man, the sight of her discomfiture would be funny. With this one, he decided tact would get him nowhere. She'd never understand his efforts to be civilized.

She crept closer, gingerly placing the tray on his lap. Before she could flit away, he grabbed her wrist. Pulled up short, she gasped, struggling to wrest her arm free.

"Sister Adela has not come since Thursday," he stated without preamble. "Where is she?"

The nun ceased her fight, snapping her attention to his face.

"Well?" Ladino prompted. "I remember Sister Adela saying all the rest of you were too frightened to care for me, and now here you are, so something must have happened." He squinted, considering. Had someone learned of the kiss? Maybe Sister Lucia had seen it happen. "Was she dismissed?"

"No . . ." Sister Lucia shook her head. "Nothing like that."

"What then?"

"I-I can't say. M-Mother Eulalia's orders."

"Did Mother Eulalia tell you I wanted to harm Adela?"

The sparrow's eyes widened, giving him his answer.

"I have no intention of harming her. I just want to know where she is."

After one more glance at her arm, Sister Lucia met his gaze, and Ladino saw the little sparrow's allegiance to orders warring with fear. "Sh—she's in Silver City caring for her mother."

Surprised, Ladino let her go. She scuttled back, distancing herself several feet.

"Taking care of her mother? Why? What happened?"

"Apaches," Lucia stated, dropping her gaze. She peeked up at him again as if measuring him for possible violence. "They killed Mr. Westbrook and took the baby."

"When?"

"Last Monday."

Sinking back against his pillows, he tried to absorb the news while studying her face, searching for signs of dishonesty or deception. "Where did the raid take place?"

"North of White Oaks, near Pinos Wells."

Ladino nodded. He knew the land well; his father had been a warrior under the leadership of the Mescalero chief, Cadete. Their band had often camped atop the lone granite mountain before sweeping down into the valley and raiding horses from the village of Pinos Wells. Of course Cadete was dead now, murdered ten years ago. The Mescaleros had been confined to their reservation at Sierra Blanca, and the westernmost Apache bands lived at San Carlos. Even renegades rarely roamed that far north and east anymore, preferring easy escape into Mexico.

"Does anyone know which band was responsible?" He tensed, waiting for her answer, hoping his wounded mind hadn't led him down the wrong river of thought.

"I heard some sisters mention the name." She cocked her head. "Pajaro," she said at last.

Pajaro.

Ladino's nape tingled. Cadete's murderer. The witch would believe his evil power would make him invincible enough to attempt such an attack. Especially since Pajaro had once been a warrior in Cadete's band and knew the area around Pinos Wells.

And Cadete's murder would have also benefited Smeet . . .

"Are you certain of the name?"

She gulped. "I-I think so."

"I want my clothes and the rest of my things," he said. "Do you know where they are?"

"Y-yes, but—"

"Get them."

"B-but, Mr. Ladino, I don't think you're strong enough to—"

"Get them!"

"I-I'll have to talk to Mother Eulalia . . ."

Ladino set the tray of food on the bedside table and shoved aside the covers. Sister Lucia's eyes widened. She dashed toward the door. He lunged out of bed, then stumbled and staggered after her as a wave of nausea drove its fist into his stomach. Just as she gripped the door frame, he clutched her waist and dragged her back, whipping her body into his and kicking the door shut with his bare foot. Leaning against the door, he wedged it closed with his weight.

Lucia opened her mouth to scream, but he clamped his hand over her lips and pulled her head back until her ear rested close to his mouth.

"I don't have time for your hysterics. And I don't want to hurt you, but I want you to bring my things, quickly and quietly, or I'll make sure you regret it."

Her body shook in his grasp, and Ladino had no doubt she'd be more than willing to do his bidding if only to be rid of him.

As he continued to hold her, her face blurred and separated, becoming two faces. He blinked, shaking his head. When he opened his eyes, his vision had returned to normal.

"No more arguments, little sparrow. Just do what I say and you'll be fine. Understand?"

She nodded, squeezing her eyes shut. A tear streaked down her cheek.

He lowered his hand from her mouth and relaxed his hold by degrees. "Now, go get my things. All of them—even my bowie," he added, his voice still promising danger. "Can I trust you to come right back?"

"Y-yes," she choked out.

Ladino pushed away from the door and his knees collapsed. He tried to catch himself on the doorknob, but the room tilted up, then seesawed back and forth, dumping him on the floor. Ladino felt as if he were back on the deck of the packet that had taken him across the choppy bay to Alcatraz. He closed his eyes and reopened them slowly. Once again his surroundings appeared normal, no longer dipping and diving of their own accord.

Sister Lucia tiptoed forward. "Are you all right?"

"I'm fine," he gritted out, pulling himself up to his knees and finally to his feet. The aftereffects of his dizziness sent bile burning into his throat. "Just get my things." Tamping down his sickness, he forced himself to look at her, to study her. Concern and curiosity had replaced her fear. "I want to help Adela, but I can't do that here. I need to get to her."

"But why would you want to help Sister Adela?"

Ladino forced himself to stand a little bit straighter as the whirling sensation in his head filled his entire body. He tried closing his eyes and reopening them again, but this time the effort made no difference.

Because she needs me, whether she knows it yet or not.

154

"Because I think that Apache attack was planned by Nigel Smeet, the same man who tried to blackmail Adela's mother. And I plan to kill the bastard."

Chapter Eleven

The mantel clock chimed twice and resumed ticking as Adela stopped pacing and wilted at her mother's bedside. She soaked the compress in the basin of cool water, wrung it out, and placed it once again on Minna's forehead.

Dr. Clayburgh's sorrel poultices had proven worthless as a cure for her mother's mastitis, and when he hadn't returned from tending his bullet-wound patient, Adela had summoned the local midwife, a *curandera,* two days ago. She'd managed to coax a few sips of the woman's pipsissewa tea down Minna's throat and prepared numerous poultices using her herbs, but she'd seen little change in her mother's condition. Minna still hadn't awakened. Surely God wouldn't let her mother die, would he?

Not now.

Not after so many years.

Not while I'm caring for her.

"Mama, please don't die," Adela pleaded, sliding off the bed and slumping to her knees. "Please don't leave me again." She smoothed her mother's graying chestnut hair away from her face. "I'm sorry for all the things I thought about you. Most of all, I'm sorry for breaking Abbie," she said, her voice squeaking childishly as her throat squeezed shut. "I still have her." She pulled the corncob doll from her pocket and held it before her mother's face. "See?"

But her mother continued to toss and turn, oblivious.

Adela sighed, dropping Abbie back into her pocket as she rose from the floor. Ambling to the window, she studied her reflection in the night-blackened panes. For just a moment she was back in her dormer room at St. Vincent's, admonishing herself for her vanity even as Ladino's visage shimmered in her mind's eye.

"Jonathan?" came a croaking voice, and Adela whirled in time to see Minna swipe her hand along the opposite side of the bed. "The baby's crying. Would you bring him to me?"

Adela rushed to her mother's bedside. Minna's eyes opened, and she blinked several times, a frown creasing her pale face.

"Who are you?"

Adela's heart plummeted to her feet. As much as she fought it, she couldn't subdue her pain that her mother hadn't recognized her instantly, no matter how many years had passed. What had she expected? She should be elated her mother spoke at all. And she was. She just hadn't been prepared for the strange emptiness overwhelming that elation.

"Sister Adela Fremont," she said as if speaking to a stranger, not knowing whether her mother would even recognize the name in her current mental state.

"Adela?" Minna's eyes widened. "Is it really you?"

"Yes, Mama," she whispered to make sure her voice wouldn't break. "It's me."

"Not so tiny anymore, are you, my little Rapunzel?"

The nickname clenched Adela's chest and flooded her body with sorrow. She'd loved fairy tales as a child, and Rapunzel had been her mother's favorite to tell. Only in Minna's version, Rapunzel had never revealed the prince's secret visits. The witch had never cut Rapunzel's hair, nor forced her to wander alone in the wilderness. Instead, the prince had killed the witch so he and Rapunzel could live happily ever after in their tower, safe.

157

Minna pulled her hand from beneath the sheet and groped the air for Adela's. Time lapsed as Adela stared at her mother's hand, uncertain what to do. If she touched her mother now, she knew she would lose her tenuous control.

At last she reached out. Grasping her mother's hand in her own, she felt the blue veins so close to the surface, the dryness, the wrinkled texture from years of hard labor before this easier life had become hers. Of course her mother's hands had never been soft, even when she'd been a young woman brimming with dreams and fairy tales. Still, they were her mother's hands. Adela had memorized their feel. In the deepest recesses of her heart she'd never forgotten. Adela pulled her bottom lip between her teeth and tightened her hold, feeling as if the broken link of chain in her heart had been reforged.

"Oh, Mama," Adela spoke, the last syllable a croak in her throat. "I've missed you so much."

A wan smile drifted over Minna's features. "What a beauty you've become. I always knew you would. When did it happen? Where did the time go?" She tried to raise up in the bed, but couldn't. A distracted frown flitted across her features. "Have you seen your baby brother? Jonathan should be bringing him from the nursery any minute now."

Ice sliced through Adela's veins.

"He's a beautiful child," her mother continued, her voice losing strength. "Like you were. And big. Such a big boy."

Minna studied Adela's face, then shifted her gaze to the bonnet Adela wore. "Let me see your hair, my little Rapunzel. Your hair was always so beautiful. I loved to brush it because it curled all by itself, just like a French doll's."

Adela lifted her hand to the strings beneath her chin,

then stopped. No. She couldn't do it.

"Never cut your hair, my little Rapunzel," her mother had said, hugging her and kissing the top of her head. *"You may never have fancy clothes or fine things, but at least you'll have your beautiful hair. No one can ever take that."*

"It's still the same, Mama. Just a little darker is all."

Minna smiled. "Good." Her expression changed to another distracted frown. "I wonder what's keeping Jonathan? My breasts are so sore," she said, her frankness brought on by the high dosage of laudanum. "I need to feed the baby." Her eyes began to drift shut. "And I'm so sleepy. I wish he would quit crying. His father never can seem to . . . comfort him."

Minna's eyes closed and her grasp loosened. Adela's heart throbbed with panic until she shifted her hold to her mother's wrist and felt her pulse. Each steady heartbeat sent a degree of relief pouring back into Adela's chest. Another second passed. Another minute, until at last Adela could relax and replace her mother's hand beneath the covers.

Her mother was still alive . . . for now.

Adela felt a bout of frantic, gasping sobs coming on. Holding her breath, she rushed from her mother's chamber to the tower room, shutting the double doors behind her. She sank onto the settee and curled her feet up beneath her habit skirts, still holding the sobs inside her heart until her chest ached and her head felt as if it would burst.

Never cut your hair, my little Rapunzel . . .

The words spoken so long ago reverberated in her mind. Such a wonderful memory now turned so sour. She felt as if she had betrayed her mother. Not just because she had cut her hair, but because she'd shuffled so many other good memories aside, letting only the bad crowd into her mind and shape her life.

Adela gasped, releasing her first sob. Closing her eyes and lips, she swallowed the rest back until the pressure built in her chest and throat.

So much in her life felt like it was too little too late. For reasons she didn't understand, Ladino's face, in all its guises, teased her conscience.

Remembering him at his most violent, when he could have killed Sister Martina, Adela wondered how she could want him here with her now. How could she long for a man whose barbaric heart called to her deepest needs, even as her mother lay on the verge of death at the hands of an Apache witch?

Remembering him at his most gentle, when he had let her brush his hair, when he had kissed her, Adela sensed he would understand her confusion. But by the time she returned to the convent, he would be gone forever, their moments together forgotten—a thing of the past.

Another sob burst through her lips. She clutched her fist to her mouth, cramming back the rest until her body convulsed, determined to vent her emotions no matter how hard she fought to keep them inside. Her shoulders shook and her lungs heaved as she emptied fifteen years of misery from her soul.

Dr. Clayburgh pulled the covers back up to Minna's chest, straightened, and turned to face Adela. He shook his head. "I don't see much improvement."

"But just two nights ago she talked to me," Adela exclaimed. "She knew who I was." *She held my hand.*

"As a nurse you should know these things happen. A patient shows signs of improvement one day, and the next . . ." He shrugged, dropping his stethoscope into his black bag and snapping it shut. "You've done well under the cir-cumstances—just as I knew you would, or I wouldn't have stayed away quite so long."

Yes, and Judith tells me you spent your first day back in town in a saloon instead of making your rounds as you promised.

She wanted to say it. She ached to say it, but she held her voice. In her insecurity, she couldn't discount his abili-ties as a doctor solely because he chose to drown his sor-rows after the boy's death instead of caring for those still living.

"I don't hold much store in the witch-doctor medicine those *curanderas* swear by, but the mastitis does seem to be better, so maybe her advice wasn't a complete waste."

He tried to take Adela by the arm and lead her from the room, but she pulled her arm away, unable to abide his touch. He spared her a brief expression of annoyance, but other than that it was as if her action meant nothing. He kept walking, dismissing her.

Frustration and anger boiled in Adela's system as she followed him across the tower room and down the stairs. "But what do you think of what the *curandera* said about her kidneys?" she asked at last, disgusted because she still grasped for any help he could give her. "She hasn't pro-duced much urine over the last few days."

"Oh, that." He shook his head. "I'm sure you know it's not out of the ordinary for a bedfast patient to decrease uri-nation. And certainly your mother's earlier symptoms would indicate kidney problems, but knowing her case as I do, it's my opinion that her female problem is the sole cause." He shrugged. "You can continue to give her the tea, but I wouldn't put much hope in it as a cure-all."

Adela nodded, clenching her jaw. It was fruitless to argue.

When they reached the foyer, he turned to face her. "Adela, you can't fault yourself for your mother's lack of improvement."

"That doesn't make it any easier to accept."

"Just keep her comfortable," he said, patting her arm. "At this point, only time will tell." He plucked his bowler from the hall tree and slapped the hat on his head. "Fetch me if anything arises that you can't handle."

Adela fought a bitter laugh, nodding instead. "I will. Thank you for coming, Dr. Clayburgh."

Feeling cut adrift again, alone to struggle with untrustworthy emotions, she watched him stride down the walkway.

Just as he was climbing into his buggy, a horse appeared at the corner of the fence. Slumped over the animal's neck was its rider, his head wrapped in a red bandanna, while mahogany tresses trailed down the horse's shoulder.

Adela's breath caught in her throat. Ladino!

His head drooped lower, and lower still until he toppled from his mount. He landed with a whump, whipping up a cloud of dust from the hard-packed earth. The horse whinnied and blew in the dirt, nudging at Ladino until he rolled over on his back.

Adela ran down the sidewalk and hurled open the yard gate, almost colliding with Dr. Clayburgh, who had turned at the noise of Ladino's horse. She reached Ladino's side just before the doctor did.

"Mr. Ladino, are you all right?"

"You know this man, Sister Adela?" asked Dr. Clayburgh.

She nodded. "He was my patient at St. Vincent's." When she noticed how blood seepage had stained the shirt he must have been given at the hospital, she was consumed with anger at the nurses who had cared for him in her absence. "And he's not healed yet. I need to get him into the house."

"I don't think you want to do that. He looks like a rough character to me. Half-breed," he observed. "Apache," he observed further, his lip curled in contempt.

"Just shut up and help me!" she snapped. "Tell Judith to prepare my room, then ask her and Michaela to come down here."

When Adela turned and met the fury in the doctor's gaze, she knew she had overstepped her bounds, but she no longer cared. Where her tolerance with this man was concerned, Ladino's appearance had been the proverbial last straw. No matter how incompetent she might feel concerning her mother's illness, she understood Ladino's injuries too well to be intimidated.

"If he can't help, it'll take all of us to get him inside."

She continued to blast the doctor with her own stubborn determination until he clamped his lips into a thin line, rose, and hurried back to the house.

"I missed that."

Startled by the hoarse whisper, Adela looked back down at Ladino. He stared up at her as if he saw a miraculous apparition.

"Missed what?"

"How you boss people around."

"I don't—"

She ceased the argument as a gentle warmth engulfed her heart in the midst of emotional chaos. Until this moment she hadn't realized how much she'd missed him, or his antagonism. She hadn't realized how his blunt honesty and uncanny understanding made it impossible for her to hide her true self.

"All right, I do," she conceded, unsettled yet oddly comforted at the same time. "Nevertheless, you should still be in the hospital." She tried to frown even as a smile tugged at her mouth. "What are you doing here? Did they toss you out?"

"You might say I threatened my way out."

"But why?"

A faint smile teased his lips, but the expression dissolved into a grimace. "Help me up before the others come back."

"Really, Ladino, you've exerted yourself quite enough. Do you realize how far you've traveled? Over—"

"Two hundred miles," Ladino finished as he reached up and touched a finger to her lips, silencing her. "I know how far it is. Just shut up and help me."

Startled by his touch, Adela allowed her own gaze to be pulled into the depths of his. Though he had tried to tease, she could see an anxiety, almost a panic, glittering in his puma-like eyes.

"I can't stand the humiliation of being carried," he added in a softer tone. "Please, Adela. Help me up."

Moments crawled into eternity as he studied her, letting his finger glide slowly over her lips, tracing the curves. Though she wanted to force herself to keep looking at him, to show him how unaffected she could be by his touch—by memories of their kiss—her gaze sidled away, unable to uphold the lie.

"All right." She braved a quick peek as she grasped his hand and pulled it away from her mouth. He closed his long, strong brown fingers around her palm, and she pulled him up, maneuvering his arm around her shoulders. "Lean on me," she murmured, embracing his waist. "We'll make it together."

Ladino's chest filled with satisfaction to be walking up the sidewalk with Adela's help. Her lithe body fit so well within the circle of his heavy arm, as if only a feather helped him stand. But just like her spirit, her shoulders were strong. He knew he had missed her, but until this moment he hadn't realized how much.

Soon the others poured out of the house, the doctor leading the way. "I'll get my bag," he said, rushing to his buggy.

"Sister Michaela, tie Mr. Ladino's horse to the fence for now so it doesn't roam off." Adela turned to a pale blonde woman in a gray dress. "Did you ready my room, Judith?"

"Yes, Sister Adela." Judith hurried back to the door and held it open for them to pass.

"My bedroom is the easiest to get to. Just at the top of the stairs," said Adela, her breath coming in short gusts of exertion. "Can you make it?"

"Yes."

More dizziness careened through his head as she helped him drag his feet up the curved staircase. She gripped the railing, and he gripped her. At last they reached the landing, and she urged him to turn right. A doorway stood open at the end of a short, narrow hallway, but as they inched down the corridor, Ladino's knees buckled. He heard her soft grunt at the extra weight, yet she remained standing and helped him fight to regain his footing.

Once in the room, she guided him toward the bed. The counterpane and sheets had been turned back, and the pillows plumped against the brass headboard. After helping him sit on the edge of the bed, she crouched at his feet. With deft motions she pulled off his moccasins and lifted his legs up on the mattress. The nun and the maid stood in

165

the doorway, watching as she eased him back into the nest of pillows.

The physician entered, parting his way between the two women. He opened his black bag, plunked it on the nightstand and pulled out a stethoscope. Positioning the earpieces with one hand, Clayburgh pushed Adela aside with the other in order to unbutton the top two buttons of Ladino's shirt.

The man worked so quickly Ladino was too stunned to react. But when the cold metal disk touched his chest, he yanked the tubes out of the doctor's ears and flung the instrument back into the medical bag. "You'd be safer to leave me alone."

An angry flush stained the doctor's stubbled cheeks as he peered at Ladino. Contempt crackled in his cold eyes. Ladino stared back, determined to make this ill-mannered White Eye bow to the ferocity of his gaze.

The doctor shot his attention to Sister Adela. "You'll be sorry you let this man into the Westbrook home."

Adela lifted her chin. "I'll stand by my decision."

"Do as you wish." He snapped his bag shut and yanked it off the nightstand. "I'll be in to check on Mrs. Westbrook tomorrow."

Ladino saw anger and pain stiffen Adela's jaw and redden her cheeks. Sensing an undercurrent between her and the doctor that had nothing to do with his own presence, he glared at the man, issuing an unspoken warning. The physician met his threat for a moment before he turned and stalked from the room.

"Judith," began Adela, her tone grim with resignation, "why don't you tend to the horse, then see what you can find for Mr. Ladino to eat." When the one in gray disappeared around the door frame, Adela turned to the black-garbed nun. "And Sister Michaela, would you check on my mother? Call me if you think she needs me. Otherwise, bring my bag and come back as soon as you can."

"Yes, Sister," Michaela murmured, rushing from the room.

Alone again with Adela, Ladino noticed for the first time how weary she looked, how heartbroken. Even from her profile he could tell how hard she fought to repaint a mask of emotionless control.

He frowned, studying her more closely. Something about her had changed. At last he realized what. She wore black, like the one who had just stood in the doorway—not brown or white as he'd seen her wear before.

"Why are you wearing a black habit?"

Surprise flashed across her face. "I became a black novice just before I left Santa Fe."

"What does that mean?" he asked, fearing her answer.

For a moment she just looked at him, her brown eyes enormous. "I—I'm going to take vows as a fully professed Sister of Charity soon. This December."

Her bright, eager tone didn't quite ring true, and as he remembered the kiss he had initiated . . . the kiss she had returned, he questioned her sincerity. Too many times she had responded to him as a woman, making it easier for him to ignore her vows. But now, faced with the sight of her black habit, her words struck the dormant guilt and cold disappointment deep in his heart.

As much as he had always rebelled against his mother's religion, ridiculing it for its inconsistency, he realized he wasn't as immune to his mother's faith as he wanted to be. After all, he wore her crucifix not only as a respectful remembrance, but because he treasured the blessing she had given him when she had placed it about his neck. His unexpected reaction to Adela's admission only proved he couldn't escape the teachings his mother had instilled in him.

"May I take a look at your wound?"

Her question prompted him out of his thoughts and reminded him of the only acceptable bond between them. Closing his mouth in a grim line, he nodded.

She resumed the task of unbuttoning his shirt, and her fingers slid over his crucifix. A wistful smile touched her lips. Two buttons later, when her fingers grazed the mend in the leather thong of his medicine pouch, her movements halted. Hesitant but captivated, she stroked the beadwork with her forefinger.

Ladino frowned, bewildered by her behavior and the odd expression on her face. "My grandmother made it," he said, hoping the explanation would satisfy her curiosity. "Thank you for fixing it."

As if ashamed of being caught, she moved her fingers to the last button, slipping it from its hole. When she didn't respond, he wondered if something about his medicine pouch bothered her.

"You're the only sister who would have cared if I ever saw it again," he added, wishing she would look at him. Despite his newfound conscience, he couldn't deny his desire to renew the closeness they'd shared for that brief moment when he'd collapsed outside. He lifted her chin on the crook of his finger and baited her with a teasing smile, even though the words he was about to say already tasted bitter on his tongue. "The other good sisters would have done their duty to God and thrown it away, seeing it as a symbol of my heathen beliefs."

Instead of the dry retort he expected, she pulled her chin

away from his finger and averted her eyes. "Can you sit up?"

Confused by her behavior, overwhelmed by the sudden need to maintain contact with her somehow, Ladino grasped her hand. "This can wait, Adela. You need to quit worrying about me for a minute."

"No, what I need is to get your bandage changed."

"Tell me about your mother."

Her gaze jumped to meet his. Heartrending despair, so palpable he could feel it clutch his own heart, fluttered across her face. Yet like magic, she repaired her mask, hiding her injured soul behind it. She pulled her hand from his grip. "I can't. Not now."

"Adela—"

"Sit up so I can get your shirt off."

Giving in for the moment, he pushed himself up and swung his legs off the bed. She slipped first one arm out of a shirtsleeve and then the other, tossing the garment to the brass footboard.

"Let's unwrap the bandage. Hold your arms out of the way."

He did as she asked, and as she worked the knot at his side, the slender column of her neck came within inches of his mouth and nose, obliterating self-control and selfless concern. A fragile scent, suggestive of mountain lilacs, teased his senses. The fragrance suited her enduring strength as well as her delicate beauty so much better than the lye soap she had used before. Underlying that he still recognized an essence uniquely her own. He closed his eyes, trying to settle the elusive musk deep within him next to the memory of their kiss.

"Are you all right?" When he registered the concern in her voice, he opened his eyes. He could see his reflection in the mirror of compassion shining from her soft brown eyes. "I'm not hurting you with all this tugging and pulling, am I?"

"No," he croaked.

She met his gaze for an instant, then blushed and hid her embarrassment behind the curve of her eyelashes. He knew she must have undressed and tended hundreds of wounded men, yet as she embraced him to unwind the bandage around his midriff, passing the growing roll from hand to hand behind his back, she held her arms more gingerly than she ever had before. Her actions shouted her awareness of what a simple touch could ignite between them.

At last she set the bandage roll aside and removed the pad beneath. Ladino winced.

"I'm sorry," she murmured, her eyes full of regret as she peeked up at him. Then she straightened, her demeanor changing once again to the expert compassion of a nurse. "It looks like it's been healing well. Just a few of the scabs between the stitches have broken loose. Those are what bleed now."

With the poise and self-assurance that seemed to come more easily to her in this role, suspicion darkened her study of him. "Why have you come here?" she asked, her tone blunt and demanding.

Before he could answer, Sister Michaela returned, carrying Adela's satchel. "Your mother is sleeping," she reported. "She's still tossing a bit, but no more than she was earlier."

"Thank you, Michaela," Adela replied, her tone bleak, though she mustered a smile. "Set the bag on the bed beside Mr. Ladino. And would you hand me things when I ask for them?"

Sister Michaela nodded.

"I need a gauze pad and the carbolic solution."

Michaela uncorked the bottle and handed it to Adela along with the gauze.

"This might sting a bit," Adela warned.

He tensed his stomach muscles just before she pressed the wet gauze to his wound. *A bit?* A drop of the solution found a particularly tender spot and burst flames along his nerve endings. He sucked air through his gritted teeth.

"Damn!"

"I thought Apaches weren't supposed to feel pain," she retorted, her smile wicked.

"Must be the cowardly White Eye blood that burns," he croaked, closing his eyes.

A moment later he felt a hand on his thigh and a breezy sensation cooling the fire. He opened his eyes and looked down, seeing that Adela crouched between his legs to blow on his knife wound.

Pain caved in to the ache of desire. The cool breeze stopped. Adela blinked and stared at him as if awakening from a dream. Without saying a word she turned her attention over her shoulder. Sister Michaela looked from one to the other of them, her mouth forming an O of surprise. When she realized their attention had shifted to her, she feigned interest in the contents of the medical bag.

Adela cleared her throat. "I need the ointment in the white jar," she said, her voice revealing nothing of her discomfiture. But as her gaze met his, he recognized the deception.

Michaela rummaged until she found it. Opening the lid, she held out the jar. Adela took out a dollop and fingered it over the healing injury, her focus professional once again. A strange herbal aroma filled the air.

"Now I need another gauze pad and a clean bandage."

Michaela offered both, and Adela placed the gauze over the wound, rewrapping the bandage just as she'd unwrapped it before.

Though Michaela's presence heightened his sense of shame and exposure, nothing lessened the impact of Adela's touch. Her nearness sang desire along every nerve of his skin.

At last she finished and tied the knot. She rose, but remained standing before him. "How does your head feel?"

He waited until his breathing slowed to a normal pace before answering. "Still hurts, and I still have dizzy spells."

Adela frowned, reaching out to touch his head. She pulled back her hand, hesitating. Then, as if admonishing herself for her foolish behavior, she pulled her gaze from his and focused on some unknown point in the room as she ran her fingers through his hair.

Her black sleeve pulled back to reveal the white undersleeve, and when her blue-veined wrist touched his cheek at the same time she touched his scalp at the base of his skull, chills rippled down his arms. As hard as he fought against it, the impulse to press his lips to her pulse point overwhelmed him. Just before contact she pulled away, frustrating his yearning thoughts yet again.

Forcing himself to accept her effort at restraint, he held his gaze straight ahead. The only thing in his line of vision was her torso.

"The fracture still feels swollen. I had hoped it would be better by now. Of course it's only been a week since your injury," she added, her voice a rambling flutter of nerves. "Head injuries like yours can take months to heal completely. Do you still suffer nausea?" she added in a tone that indicated her struggle to regain detachment.

"Occasionally," he responded in kind, even as he struggled to ignore images of warm ivory curves hidden beneath heavy black serge.

"How is your memory?"

Right now he remembered how he had first opened his eyes to her face. Right now he remembered clutching the material of her nightgown between her soft, full breasts.

"Fine."

She stared at him for a brief moment. "Good," she said at last. "That's good." Turning to Sister Michaela, she smiled. "Thank you. Would you check on my mother? I'll be there in a minute."

Michaela nodded and left the room.

Adela turned back to him, her demeanor changed once again in her companion's absence. "This foolish trip of yours has done nothing to speed your progress," she admonished. "Why have you come?"

He hated to broach the subject with so little preparation, but her direct question made it impossible for him to be as gentle as he wished. "I'm here because Sister Lucia told me about the Apache attack."

She stared at him for a moment, then stepped over to the open medical bag where she began to organize bottles and instruments that likely didn't need such attention. "You had nothing to do with it, so if you've come just to apologize, there's no need."

"Apologize?" He grabbed her arm and pulled her back to face him, gratified to watch her eyes widen. Staring at her, he searched for the truth, finding it when her own search dropped to the medicine pouch hanging at the middle of his chest. So that was it. Like a traitor's blade, her unspoken condemnation sliced his heart in half. She had shown him so many times, but this time he had allowed his vulnerability to her blur that final line that still existed between them.

He released her arm. "I thought we had gotten past this."

Her gaze skittered from his medicine pouch to the window, evading his face. "There's nothing to get past, Mr. Ladino," she assured, lifting her shoulders in a small shrug. "Of course you needn't apologize. I'm sorry if you mistook my meaning."

"Oh, no. I didn't mistake a damn thing," he said. "You said it because you meant it. You may not hold me personally responsible, but you want to know why it happened. Why people whose blood I share could do what they did, don't you." He knew the answer; there was no need to state it as a question.

Her shoulders slumped in admission, and she crossed her arms across her chest, hugging herself. "Did Sister Lucia tell you it was a full-scale slaughter?" Fury lurked in her voice like an unseen enemy.

He remained quiet. The Apache half of him wanted to lash out, to destroy her naive little world by spilling tales of White Eye atrocities against his father's people. But he couldn't. Not when he saw a dimple form in her chin as she pressed her lips together to suppress their quivering. Ladino had to look away for a moment, too unsure of himself in his own pain to let her see it in his face.

"They murdered her husband before her eyes." She paused, and he glanced back up. "They stole her baby, and they cut up her arms and her face."

When she looked at him now, she held nothing back, her loathing of Apache brutality reflected on him. How many times had he and his people blamed all White Eyes for the crimes of one, just as she blamed him now. She did want him to apologize. She wanted someone—anyone—to pay for the torture her mother had been forced to endure.

"Then they dumped her on the side of the road." A tear finally escaped, streaming down her cheek. Adela swiped it away and shook her head. "Now she lies in that bed about to die, and when she wakes up she thinks her baby is still in the nursery, and that her husband has gone to get him to bring him back to her."

Adela clutched herself so tightly she shook. "They've taken her away from me," she whispered. "She might as well be dead, because those *savages* have taken her away from me."

Several minutes passed while he watched her rigid mask crumble bit by bit. Her body shook as if she'd taken a chill, and somehow, even though he knew she might push him away, Ladino wanted to offer her some kind of comfort, some brand of apology.

Biting back his pain and weakness, he pushed himself up from the bed and stood on his own. He crept closer, afraid she would run away, or fly into a million pieces before he could catch them all and help her pull herself back together. He touched her arm first, and she looked down at his hand, startled as her gaze then flew to his face. He pulled her closer, and he could feel her stuttering steps as she resisted, still clutching her own arms and hands around her waist. He embraced her, feeling shivers and starts throughout her body.

He stroked her back, but its unyielding column refused to allow her to lean into him. Lifting his hand to her head, he tested her reaction by stroking the snug-fitting black cap. And that was what did it. She broke, she released, she melted into his embrace, clasping her arms so tightly around him he could feel her fists pressing like rocks into his shoulder blades.

"My mother is going to die, and I can't do a thing to help her. *It's all their fault.*" She enunciated each word with an animosity so deep it touched the center of his own appetite for revenge. "And I wanted you here with me," she admitted, self-loathing and self-betrayal ravaging her voice.

It seared his heart to hear that she hated to need him, to think of him, but Ladino ignored his own pain and concentrated on hers, holding her as she sobbed.

Chapter Twelve

Ladino said nothing for a long time. Even when Judith appeared in the doorway with a tray of food and ducked back out, he ignored the intrusion, continuing to hold Adela as clouds shadowed the window and the sun brightened the room again. At last he pulled away, and Adela stared up at him as if coming out of a daze.

"I know who was behind this, Adela."

She frowned. "The Apaches—"

"No. Not completely. Nigel Smeet instigated the attack."

"Nigel Smeet?" Ladino watched Adela's eyes widen at the name, and then she frowned, shaking her head. "But . . . his blackmail attempt failed, and then he disappeared."

The clink of dishes and a timid knock sounded just outside the door. Adela stepped a respectable distance away from him and swiped tears from her eyes. "Is that you, Judith?" she called, her voice a thin thread unable to veil her embarrassment.

"Yes, Sister." Judith entered, her eyes downcast. The silver tray shook in her hands as she peeked up at Ladino. The glimpse became a startled study of his bare chest and the scars raking across its width. The woman forced her attention to Adela. "I brought Mr. Ladino tea and a roast beef sandwich."

"Thank you, Judith. Why don't you just set the tray on the bedside table while I help Mr. Ladino get settled."

The maid nodded and did as Adela asked, her gaze

averted as Adela helped him back to the bed, lifting his legs up on the mattress once again.

When Judith stepped back, Ladino glanced over at the table. On one corner of the tray, the staghorn handle of his bowie peeked from within the scalloped edges of a woman's white handkerchief. He couldn't explain how, but when Sister Lucia had brought him his things so he could leave Santa Fe, he had known the threadbare wisp wrapping his knife belonged to Adela . . . just as he knew she had mended his medicine pouch. The delicate white material had cloaked his guilt over killing the boy, softening it, just as the woman herself tempered his sharpest penchant for violence. Though her influence frightened him, made him worry about losing his edge, he hadn't been able to toss that handkerchief aside and shove the blade in his moccasin.

Adela turned and was about to lift the serving tray when her movements faltered, her fingers hovering above the handles. She tentatively touched her handkerchief, and any sentimental reason Ladino had entertained for keeping his knife wrapped in her kerchief withered when she met his gaze. *The bloody knife you used to kill that boy!* her wide brown eyes accused, as if their relationship had never progressed past her first instinctual fear. Too soon she slipped once again behind her disguise of detached competence.

"Would you like me to put your knife in the drawer?" she asked, her voice guarded as she lifted the tray and set it across his lap.

"Oh!" exclaimed Judith, stepping forward. "I—I hope you don't mind, Mr. Ladino, but I had my boy, Jaime, put up your horse. He found that knife in your saddlebags. The other things—food, water—are downstairs," she rushed to assure him. "And don't worry about your animal. Jaime's only nine, but Mr. Westbrook taught him the proper ways to groom and feed."

"Thank you." Ladino smiled, remembering how honored he had felt when his father had allowed him to help the other boys care for the horses when the warriors returned from a raid. He wished he could share with Adela the good memories of growing up Apache. "And thank your son."

Judith nodded, a speculative frown shadowing her face. She turned to Adela. "Is there anything else I can do before I go?"

"No, Judith. Thank you."

The maid tossed Ladino another considering glance as she turned. Adela had just slipped the knife in the drawer when Judith paused in the doorway.

"Yes, Judith?" said Adela. "Is something wrong?"

Judith pivoted on her heels. "Sister, I don't want you to think I make a habit of eavesdropping . . ." She blushed, lacing her fingers together at her waist. ". . . but I couldn't help overhearing Mr. Ladino mention Mr. Smeet."

Ladino glanced up at Adela and saw her face blanch with shock. *The embrace!* the alarm on her face screamed.

"Do you know him?" Ladino asked, hoping to distract the woman's attention from Adela.

Judith twisted her hands. "Not well, but . . ." She cocked her head to the side. "Are you looking for him concerning the blackmail attempt? Is that how you know Sister Adela so well?"

Ladino didn't answer. Adela's gaze jolted to his. Though she lowered her lashes as if to cover her abrupt behavior, a blush stained her cheeks.

"Yes," she answered for him, her eyes expressing the need to conspire. She turned to the maid. "At least partially. Mr. Ladino was my patient at St. Vincent's. He's also a bounty hunter."

The woman's pale face lit with inquisitive wonder.

Irritated by Adela's explanation as well as the woman's predictable response, Ladino frowned. "Do you know something about Smeet that might help me?" he asked, his tone gruff with the part Adela had forced him to play.

"I—I might."

"Well?" Ladino prodded.

"Well . . . before Mr. Westbrook . . . died, he entertained lavishly. Mr. Smeet was often a guest because of his mining partnership with Mr. Westbrook." She peeked at Adela. "They were also good friends."

"Friends?" asked Adela, her tone incredulous. "How so?"

"Both of them grew up in London before sailing to California and later coming here with the California Volunteers during the war. Mr. Westbrook was from the gentry, and I think Mr. Smeet's father worked in their household."

"But if they were such good friends, why would Mr. Smeet want to blackmail my mother?"

Judith wrung her hands. "I suppose it might have had something to do with the fact that Mr. Westbrook made a fortune from the silver mine he bought from Mr. Smeet."

Ladino squinted, trying to decide if the woman was lying or just evading the complete truth. "Why would Smeet sell his mine if it promised to make a fortune?"

"Mr. Smeet had gambling debts . . ." the maid answered vaguely, floundering under Ladino's stare.

"Didn't Westbrook pay Smeet well?"

"Yes, but it was more than that. Mr. Smeet was a jealous man. Jealous of—" The woman licked her lips, unable to hold her gaze steady upon his face. "Perhaps it isn't my place to say, but if Mr. Westbrook were alive, well . . . I—I'm sure he'd want me to tell what I know if he thought it would bring back his son."

Adela frowned and shook her head. "What do you mean, Judith? I don't understand."

Judith cleared her throat and glanced at the floor. "Seven years ago, Mr. Westbrook threw a party for several senators and other influential people hoping to sway their votes concerning the statehood issue. One of the guests wanted to leave early, so I came upstairs to fetch his coat. It didn't occur to me to knock." Blushing, she glanced at Adela. "I found Mr. Smeet upstairs. He was in a . . . a compromising position with a—with a . . ."

"With a man?" finished Ladino.

Adela snapped her attention to him, then back to Judith.

"Yes," Judith admitted. "I didn't know what to do. Mr. Smeet would have seen me if I'd gone in to get the coat. But I couldn't go back downstairs without it. So I stood out in the hallway, too shocked and afraid to do anything. Mr. Westbrook came upstairs with Senator Langdon and a Mr. Wiggins—"

"Randall Wiggins?" interrupted Adela. "Wasn't he a state legislator several years ago? I've heard he supplies guns for most of the mercantiles to sell."

Judith nodded. "That's him. He wanted his coat, and the senator was looking for his son. I tried to keep them from going inside, but—" She shook her head and closed her eyes.

Ladino didn't watch her as she continued the story, her voice a low murmur of embarrassment. "Senator Langdon beat his son and threatened to kill Mr. Smeet. Mr. Westbrook broke up the fight and asked the senator and his son to leave. Senator Langdon told Mr. Westbrook he could forget the statehood vote from him, and his last threat was to have Mr. Smeet court-martialed."

Revelation slid its icy blade down Ladino's spine. His thoughts spiraled back to the incident with the deputy at the hospital. Amid all the lies and cover-ups rested a glimpse of twisted truth. Smeet had been court-martialed all right, but only after Ladino had already gone to prison. But why had Smeet manipulated the facts by claiming Ladino worked for him, when Ladino knew full well Pajaro was the only Apache man who had ever been involved in business deals with the unscrupulous captain?

It almost seemed as if Smeet had been trying to protect Pajaro. But why? Other than being hunted as a renegade, Pajaro had no connection to the military, so it wouldn't have mattered what Smeet had said about the witch. Unless Smeet had known his punishment would be a mere dishonorable discharge. A minor inconvenience. Nothing to interfere with the contacts he shared with Pajaro, unless blaming Pajaro would have increased the need for the military to find and kill him.

And so, Ladino had become the scapegoat. Still, something didn't feel right about this. Some piece was missing . . .

"So what happened after that between Smeet and Mr. Westbrook?" he heard Adela say.

"Mr. Westbrook kicked Mr. Smeet out of the house and told him he'd buy Smeet's half in the Silver Samson mine. Mr. Westbrook said he'd pull what strings he could to cover up the true purpose for Mr. Smeet's court-martial, but only because he didn't want any scandal linked to him."

Ladino laughed, the sound deep and bitter. Adela stared at him, her face paralyzed in disbelief.

"I want to talk to Sister Adela alone," he said.

Judith looked at Adela.

"It's all right," Adela whispered, taking the woman's

182

arm and leading her to the door. "Thank you for all you've told us."

The maid cast an uncertain glance over her shoulder at Ladino, then left the room. Adela stood poised in the doorway, staring after the woman's departure.

"That son of a bitch lied at his own court-martial," said Ladino. "And Westbrook helped him."

"Mr. Westbrook was just trying to make the best of a bad situation," she murmured, glancing over her shoulder, but not fully meeting his eyes. "Just think of the scandal—"

"Scandal? Is that all anyone cares about? Is that all *you* care about?" Ladino shoved the serving tray to the other side of the bed and got up, ignoring his dizziness as he stalked an uncertain path across the room. "I don't give a damn about scandal," he said in her ear. "That bastard sent me to Alcatraz!"

"You murdered soldiers," she shot back, still refusing to look at him. "That's why you went to prison."

He laughed, the sound a bleak echo of his earlier bitterness. "It doesn't matter what race a woman is, she's still going to remember what she wants to, when she wants to, whenever it suits her purpose. You refuse to see what's right before your face. Instead, you're still angry and looking for a sacrificial lamb!"

Just as the words sprang from his mouth, full realization hit him. Her fear and anger delved deeper than her mother's torture at the hands of Pajaro . . . much deeper.

Ladino grasped her arm and whirled her around. Seeing the terror on her face only added pitch to his blazing emotions. Damn it! Was she so horrified by what she really felt for him that she found it easier to believe only an Apache capable of cruelty?

"You know what, Sister? You wouldn't have cared if I'd

been a scalping Comanche the day I kissed you. With my lips on yours, you thought nothing about my being a half-breed savage."

"You're disgusting," she said, her voice trembling as she yanked her arm out of his grip. "That is past. Done with."

"Is it?"

"Only a spiteful barbarian would bring that up right now!"

"You want civilized? Kiss a priest."

Her body went rigid. He expected a scream, a slap, a kick—anything. Instead, she clenched her teeth and stared at him with such destroyed trust he almost wished he could give her his knife and let her release her murderous intent.

"You don't know Smeet like I do," he whispered.

"And how would you know him so well unless you worked with him?" she asked, her tone treading the sharp blade of sarcasm. "Or was it for him?"

"Pajaro was the one who worked for Smeet. Not me. I was just convenient to blame because I was already on Alcatraz, unable to dispute his new testimony."

Exhausted, he returned to the bed and sat back down, staring at her. She met his gaze for several moments before she turned away, propping her elbow on a tightened fist at her waist and covering her mouth with her shaking hand.

Guilt ate at him. He wanted to tell her why he hungered for vengeance—why he longed to murder Smeet. It had little to do with court-martials, falsified records, or prison sentences. It had everything to do with the deaths of innocent people.

Some as young as her baby brother.

And then there was his grandmother . . .

He touched his medicine pouch, summoning strength from the prayers she had imbued into each and every item inside. His pain and guilt might not allow him to tell Adela why he wanted Smeet dead, but maybe he could make her understand why he thought Pajaro and Smeet could be working together now.

"Have you ever heard of Chief Cadete?" he asked.

Adela shook her head, her fingers still touching her lips.

"He was chief of the band of Mescaleros my father belonged to before he was killed. Pajaro was a warrior in Cadete's band, and he wanted to marry the daughter of our medicine man. The man refused, because his daughter and Pajaro were too closely related. I was not with the band at the time, but I learned later that the medicine man was found dead soon after."

Dropping her hand away from her face, Adela turned. "How?"

"The old one had caught an owl in a pine tree and was stealing feathers for a war bonnet. The owl escaped his grasp and flew in his face, attacking him until he fell to the ground. Someone accused Pajaro of witchcraft, and Cadete banished him."

Adela frowned. "But that's—"

"Ridiculous? Backward? Heathenish?" Ladino shrugged. "Maybe it is to you in your White Eye religion. Who's to say? It doesn't matter. The result was the same. Pajaro swore vengeance. A few months later, Cadete went to court to testify against some Mexicans involved in the sale of whiskey to the Mescaleros. In La Luz Canyon, on his way home afterwards, Cadete was murdered. Rumor said Nigel Smeet was involved with those Mexicans selling whiskey, but no one did anything about it. And Pajaro wanted Cadete dead. What does that tell you?"

She looked away, not answering.

"Believe me," said Ladino, "if Smeet thought nothing

about changing official records just to save his dirty white name, he would feel no remorse for having an old Indian man murdered. And if he thought it would get him what he wanted, he wouldn't think twice about killing your baby brother."

Adela flinched. "But if you really think Nigel Smeet is involved in this," she began, her voice ragged, "why hasn't he contacted us concerning ransom?"

"Maybe it's not ransom he's after. Maybe he wants revenge."

"But Jonathan Westbrook is dead, and my mother . . ." She swallowed. "I think we should notify Captain Grisham at Fort Bayard. He's already been working on this, but maybe he can do something more if he knows Nigel Smeet might be involved."

"What makes you think the military will do anything? There's no proof."

"But surely since this involves someone as prominent as Jonathan Westbrook they'll be willing to listen."

Ladino shook his head in disbelief and looked away.

"I—I don't know why you . . . murdered those soldiers," began Adela. "Maybe you had good reason." Her voice faltered, and a moment of silence passed. "I—I want to think you're a good man at heart. And I know our military isn't perfect, but just because things happened the way they did for you doesn't mean I should discount their help." She shrugged, the gesture hopeless and desperate. "I have no choice. What else can I do?"

Like Adela, he had once naively believed only his "better" side, his "civilized" side—his white side—would answer his hopes for peace. Even before his grandmother's murder, there had been his father's, and his grandfather's before that. Still he had chosen to trust the bluecoats. But seven years on Alcatraz had planted the deepest seed of hatred and vengeance in his heart. Death was his only answer.

"You could let me help you. I'd find Smeet and kill him with my bare hands before the cavalry would dirty their gloves."

He looked at her now and found her staring at him as she had that first day. Judging him. Accusing him of murder and worse.

"Whatever reason you might have for wanting to kill Mr. Smeet, it has no place in this," she said. "If you must have your revenge, get it some other way, but don't you dare use me or Jonathan Junior to do it." She averted her gaze, dismissing the subject. "I'm going to see how my mother is doing, and then I'll telegraph Captain Grisham." She stepped across the threshold, then stopped, turning. "Will you speak to him?"

"I have nothing to say to another bluecoat as long as I live."

"Then I guess I'll talk to him myself."

"That's up to you." Ladino shrugged, forcing a nonchalant attitude as he picked up the sandwich from the tray, smashing the bread in his grip. "But it's a waste of time. He won't believe you any more than you believed me."

"We'll see," she said, breezing out of the room.

Ladino cursed and took a huge bite of sandwich. As he chewed and swallowed, the roast knotted up in his throat just like the fury and frustration he'd forced himself to eat.

Nigel held his gun trained on the Apache woman as he watched her nurse Jonathan Junior. She reclined against the bed's white metal headboard, her feet bound by ropes to the footboard. Her behavior should have been meek, her gaze averted in modesty. Instead she stared back at him, delivering the most serious insult she could muster under the circumstances: invading his private thoughts with her unwavering glare.

"Quit staring at me, '*isdzáá*," he said in Spanish, using the Mescalero word for woman, "or I'll kill you."

Only when Nigel cocked his pistol, did she dismiss him, shifting her attention to the baby's head nestled at her full brown breast.

The longer he watched the dark Madonna suckle the pale, greedy child, the more he yearned to pull the trigger. No one would hear the shot, not from this abandoned two-room adobe, miles away from Albuquerque. He wouldn't tempt himself at all by holding the gun on her if she weren't always testing his authority, challenging his control. Once already she'd managed to slip away with the child as they'd waited to board the train departing El Paso. Luckily Ben had chased her down.

Shoving up from his chair, he strode toward her. "You've given him enough." He pounded his fist for emphasis against the chipping plaster on the adobe wall. "Give me the boy."

"No," she replied, her defiant expression a dare for him to take the child. "He has not finished." She pulled Jonathan away from one breast and shifted him to the other. Nigel shuddered, feeling bile rise in his throat. A knowing shimmer of a smile drifted across her face. Ever since that first day, she'd sought to break his control, tried to find a leverage all her own. Now she had. Her body sickened him.

That she could use it in such an intimate way to gain even the smallest amount of control infuriated Nigel—made him feel powerless, intrusive, and cut off all at the same time. Yet as much as he hated her, he needed her, and he knew she intended to play it to the last card.

"Cover yourself at least," he commanded. From the bed near her trussed ankles, he picked up the blue baby blanket he'd just bought and thrust it into her face. "And hurry up."

She yanked the blanket from his hand and draped it over herself and the infant. Keeping the gun aimed at her head, Nigel returned to his seat.

The woman smiled as if mocking Nigel's intimate secrets. She lifted the edge of the blanket and gazed at the baby beneath. Her casual air pretended contentment, but Nigel knew she'd never give up. She'd only find a new way to torment him.

Nigel also knew he was to blame—at least in part. After returning to Albuquerque, he'd bought diapers to replace the baby grass. Then the bassinet to replace the ts'ál. And just today he'd sent Ben after the blue blanket and a silver rattle to replace the old gourd the child was so fond of.

The woman might consider his purchasing of goods as a growing weakness for the child, but Nigel reasoned that a comfortable baby was a contented baby. And a contented baby would remain quiet, creating less strain on his nerves. He refused to acknowledge any other motives for his behavior.

He also refused to explore the recurring dreams he'd been having of Jonathan when they'd been boys together in London, and later young men in a new country. Still friends. Still inseparable. Before they'd formed separate lives and Nigel had been reduced to seeking comfort in second-rate proxies like Perry, whose damned politician father had destroyed his military career.

Disowned, Perry had turned to him for help. Perry had needed him once, where Jonathan never had. Now Perry needed only opium, and Nigel spent most nights dragging him out of Railroad Avenue's smoky dens. Disgusted with the trap he'd set for himself, Nigel wrestled his thoughts away from the young man who slept off his latest binge on a pallet in the kitchen.

Nigel closed his eyes. He'd thought himself past any feelings of softness where Jonathan was concerned. Yet he couldn't seem to contemplate, much less accept, the fact that Jonathan was dead. Gone forever. There would be no hope of reconciliation now. He shook his head in disbelief. He'd never wanted Jonathan dead. He'd only wanted to inflict pain—to humiliate, degrade, and force the man to beg. If he could never have earned Jonathan's love, then his hatred would have been a fitting substitute. Any emotion at all on Jonathan's part would have been better than the complete disavowal of their shared past and friendship.

Yet possessing the baby was revenge in itself, wasn't it? And he could still collect the ransom. He'd always envied Jonathan his money, his position, his luck. Well, that renowned luck had run out at last, and Nigel had only to wait just a little while longer. He'd let the Westbrook bitch worry and fret and cry about Jonathan's missing son and heir just a little while longer before he contacted her concerning the ransom.

At last the Apache finished and pulled down her calico tunic. Keeping his gun aimed at her, Nigel took the infant and carried him to the bassinet. He retied the woman's wrists to the headboard. Rendered helpless once more, she darted an anxious glance at Jonathan Junior, who now lay on his back, playing with his toes.

Intercepting her expression, Nigel had a flash of insight. He'd seen the same expression that first day, when Pajaro had threatened to kill the baby.

Feeling the subtle shift of power back in his favor, Nigel

smiled at the woman and spoke to her in Spanish. "You care for him, don't you, you heartless Apache bitch?"

She spat on the floor at Nigel's feet. "I care nothing for the White Eye child," she replied. "I feed him because you threaten to kill me. Watch me closely, White Eye, or I will bash his brains out on the floor."

Nigel lifted his eyebrows. "Maybe I'll do it first and save you the trouble, my savage Madonna."

Still smiling, Nigel strolled to the bassinet and lifted Jonathan Junior high above his head, gazing up into his chubby face. The infant studied the world from his new angle, unperturbed at being held so high in the air. Nigel smiled up at him, and when the boy smiled back through eyes so like Jonathan Senior's, Nigel shivered.

"Should I drop you, little Master Westbrook?" Nigel whispered in a singsong voice. "Should I let the bough break?" He frowned in mock seriousness, wiggling Jonathan from side to side. "Such a morbid lullaby, don't you think? Rather like that nursery rhyme about the egg." Nigel hummed the lullaby and Jonathan Junior cooed, still smiling as he drooled on Nigel's face.

Nigel accepted the mess in stride, surprising himself. He felt as if the infant, who looked so much like his dead father, had curled a tiny fist around his heart.

A sudden chill replaced the warmth he had been feeling. Nigel placed the baby back in the bassinet, tying him to the pillow as the woman had suggested in order to break him from his need of the cradleboard. Jonathan Junior began to squall, his face pinched and red with anger.

"Cry all you want to, Master Westbrook," Nigel said in English so the woman wouldn't understand. He retrieved his handkerchief from his pocket and wiped his face. "You won't make me feel a bloody thing I don't want you to."

The front door slammed and Nigel jumped, turning when Ben entered the woman's room.

Benjamin stopped beside the washstand, a newspaper rolled in one hand. "You ain't gonna like this, Mr. Smeet." The boy strode across the room and handed Nigel the *Albuquerque Daily Journal*.

When Nigel opened the newspaper and read the front-page headline, disbelief and fury scoured through his system. Jonathan Junior's cries screeched across his nerves.

"Damn it, Benjamin!" Nigel ripped the front page from the newspaper and flung the rest at the boy. "Pick up that child!"

Benjamin hurried to follow orders, slipping on discarded sheets of newsprint. When he swept the baby and his pillow up from the bassinet, Jonathan Junior only cried louder. "What do you want me to do with him, Mr. Smeet?"

"Walk with him," Nigel said absently. "Or give him to the woman. She knows what to do when he gets like this."

"But she's tied—"

"I don't care *what* you do, Benjamin," Nigel said through clenched teeth. "Just make the little bastard be quiet!"

Reading as he walked, Nigel found the chair and slumped down.

"Westbrook Widow on the Verge of Death."

Bloody hell! If the bitch died, he'd get no ransom money.

No. He would not allow that upstart maid Jonathan had married cheat him yet again out of his just due. By God he would think of something. He always had. This time would be no different.

Chapter Thirteen

By nine o'clock that night, Adela had given up on Captain Grisham's arrival. She sent Judith to bed and left Sister Michaela downstairs reading, while she trudged upstairs to sit at her mother's bedside. With her head on her mother's nightstand, she was just about to doze off when she heard the front door shut downstairs. Muffled voices followed— Sister Michaela's and a man's. She had told Captain Grisham to come at his convenience, but she had never dreamed it would be this late.

After a quick glance to see that her mother was as comfortable as possible, Adela kissed her forehead and left the room, shutting the double doors behind her.

As she crossed the tower room, she straightened her skirt and slapped at a wrinkle in her cape. Reaching the lamp table at the landing, she stopped and turned up the wick. Only then did she look up. Ladino leaned against one wall in the short hallway, his body bathed in the golden glow.

She gasped, stopping short as she lifted her hand to her throat. "You startled me," she muttered, her gaze wandering to his long, clean mahogany hair. The waves cascaded down his naked shoulders, hiding the ragged scars across his pectorals. Around his midriff, the bandage glared white in the semidarkness, and his trousers rode low on his hips. When Adela glanced back up, she felt fire radiate from his catlike stare.

"So Grisham has finally come," he stated.

"Yes," she said, recovering enough composure to lower

her hand from her throat. "Have you reconsidered? Will you talk to him with me?"

"Did you tell him anything about me in your message?" he responded instead, her own questions ignored.

Adela clutched her hands at her waist and rubbed one thumb with the other. "I said you knew both Pajaro and Smeet, and that you thought they might be working together on this."

"And are you going to believe what he tells you about me?"

"Are you going to give me a reason not to?"

"I can give you all the reasons in the world . . . if you really want to listen."

He crossed his arms across his chest. Adela had noticed the size of his forearms before, but right now, he seemed even more massive, more threatening . . . more virile.

"He's had plenty of time to check on me. Just like Latham," said Ladino. "So he's going to give you an earful. Parts of it will probably be true. But after he leaves, I want . . . I want you to come to me. I want you to hear the truth from me." As if realizing his voice had softened to a plea, he lowered his eyelids into an expression echoing his earlier anger. "That way you can't say I didn't try to tell you my side of the story."

Adela stepped forward. "Mr. Ladino, I—"

"Sister Adela?" came Michaela's voice. Adela turned and saw her companion at the curve of the staircase and climbing higher. "Sister Adela, Captain Grisham is here."

"I'll be right there."

Michaela nodded and turned back down the stairs. When Adela saw only the woman's shadow on the wall, she turned back to Ladino. He had vanished.

As she descended the stairs, pausing a bit at each step,

she tried to make sense of his behavior. After this afternoon, she had believed he would never want to speak to her again. She worried that she'd inflicted pain too deep to forgive, and in the process wounded herself.

Near the bottom of the stairs, Adela peeked into the parlor. Sister Michaela sat in a wing chair beside the fireplace, and the book she'd been reading lay open facedown on the doily covering the cherrywood table beside her.

Michaela noticed her presence and rose, so Adela swept down the final two steps and entered the parlor's double doors. Still wearing his gauntlets, the freckle-faced Grisham also pushed out of his chair on the opposite side of the fireplace. Fiery red wisps curled atop his head, and he held his scrunched-top forage cap beneath his arm, the black bill and crossed-sabre insignia facing her.

"Thank you for coming, Captain Grisham." Adela strode across the room and offered her hand. "I'm Sister Adela."

He clasped her fingers, but hesitated as if uncertain whether or not to raise her hand to his lips. Adela planted her hand farther into his large palm and shook his hand.

Captain Grisham released her, tipping his head in greeting. "Pleased to meet you, Sister."

She made a slight bow. "And I, you."

Now that she had him here, she had no idea where to begin. But because of the private nature of certain issues she might have to reveal, she decided it best to dismiss Sister Michaela.

She turned to her companion. "Would you see to my mother while I speak with Captain Grisham?"

"Certainly." Michaela nodded to the captain and drifted from the room.

Adela turned back to Grisham. "Thank you for coming,"

she repeated, gesturing toward his chair. "Won't you sit?"

Captain Grisham returned to his seat, and Adela took the chair Michaela had just vacated.

"I apologize for arriving so late," he said, propping his forage cap on a large knee encased in patched blue trousers. "I came as soon as I was able to do some checking on this Christian Ladino. Before we go any further, I think it only fair to tell you that you're harboring a convicted criminal—"

"I know about Mr. Ladino's imprisonment, Captain Grisham," answered Adela. "I also know he's been released, so there's no need to warn me; I've been warned quite enough already."

"As you say," he conceded.

"I've asked you to come because I believe I've discovered a development in the kidnapping of my mother's son."

"Hmm, yes." Grisham leaned forward. "You said Ladino told you a man named Nigel Smeet is behind it all?"

"That's correct."

He nodded as if he'd heard dozens of similar stories and found them all to be the ramblings of distraught women or lunatics.

"Sister Adela, there've been numerous Apache attacks where children and babies have been taken captive." A superior smile curved his lips. "The Apaches would never trust a white man enough, or vice versa, for them to be in league the way this Ladino claims. What would be the purpose?" He sighed. "Have you received a request for ransom?"

"No," she admitted.

"I still think it's the Apaches behind this. In fact, we recently received word from the Mexican authorities that Pajaro has been spotted near Casas Grandes. They're investigating now."

"Did he have Jonathan Junior with them?"

"No one saw a baby, or at least it wasn't reported to me."

"Then perhaps Mr. Ladino is right. He thinks the dealings between Pajaro and Smeet go back at least ten years to the murder of Chief Cadete. He claims Smeet used to sell whiskey to the Mescaleros, and that Pajaro wanted Cadete dead . . ." She paused, fury rising into her chest as she studied his bored expression. "How long have you been in the military?"

Grisham now leaned forward in his chair, and his sudden interest heightened Adela's ire. "Ten years. All of 'em in the Arizona or New Mexico Territories. That's long enough to've heard every lie an Apache ever thought of, and a few you wouldn't think they'd be smart enough to." He cocked his head, smiling with smug curiosity. "Why did you want to know?"

"I just wondered how long it would take a young man like yourself to develop such an insolent, overbearing attitude."

His smile straightened and he grabbed the bill of his cap, yanking the stiff blue material tighter over his knee. "I could ask you how long you've been a nun, but I imagine it hasn't been long enough to teach you a proper, quiet, pious attitude."

"No. You've picked the wrong novice to underestimate."
Mr. Ladino could have told you that.

Adela took a deep breath, pushing herself past the anger. "You're not even trying to have an open mind about this, are you?" She regarded him with incredulity bordering on contempt. "You've already formed your opinion, and you're not going to listen to a word I say."

"Not when it concerns the word of a savage in something

as far-fetched as this sounds." He smiled. If she had been a dog, she didn't doubt he would have patted her on the head. "Sister Adela, I know you mean well, but I wouldn't believe a damn word this Ladino says. Revenge is an Apache's greatest sport, and Smeet's testimony put Ladino in prison. By the way, has this Ladino told you why he went to prison?"

Adela began to rub one thumb with the other, conscious of her actions but unable to stop. Yes, she knew Ladino had killed soldiers, and his silence about the reason had done nothing to quiet her fears. Yet he had ridden all the way to Silver City, weak, wounded, and so exhausted he'd toppled from his horse, just to tell her of his belief that Nigel Smeet might be behind her baby brother's kidnapping. Why? Because he truly only wanted Smeet dead? No. She saw that now. He cared for her. And he also cared what happened to her mother. And she had shoved his help and his heritage back in his face. Why had it been so hard for her to listen to him? Because she had been terrified of caring too much—more than her vocation should allow?

Guilt scourged her, inflicting harsh penance. Yet she lifted her chin, determined to champion Ladino now, even if she hadn't earlier . . . when it had mattered to him most.

"I know what the court-martial records say, Captain Grisham, but they're wrong. Mr. Ladino did not work for Mr. Smeet."

"And I suppose he told you that?"

"Yes, he did," she said. "But let's put Mr. Ladino's word aside for a moment. Mr. Westbrook was a wealthy, influential man. Wouldn't it stand to reason that if Nigel Smeet's blackmail attempt failed, he'd try something else?"

"Maybe so, maybe not. But that puts us right back at the ransom that nobody's been asked to come up with. Besides, even if Smeet was involved, I couldn't do anything about it. That's a civilian matter, and Smeet's no longer in the military."

Adela's chest began to tighten and burn with fury. "Then what about Pajaro?" she demanded. "Let's say Pajaro does still have my baby brother. You do have jurisdiction where he and other Apaches are concerned, don't you?"

"We do when they stay on our side of the line, but I'll tell you just like I told Mr. Leeds—we can't touch them once they're in Mexico." He twisted his cap. "We'll have to wait for Mexican officials to handle it unless the dogs come back across the border. But that'll probably be a while; Pajaro will want to lie low. Most likely only a couple of scouts will return to assess the situation, maybe get supplies from their stronghold. Pajaro won't want to chance having his whole band wiped out. He hasn't remained free this long for lack of common sense."

"So you're not really doing anything about this at all."

"All I can tell you is that we'll keep ourselves posted. I've notified the commander at Fort Stanton, and I sent word to other areas where I think Pajaro might venture— even as far east as Fort Bliss. We've wanted to catch Pajaro for a long time, but he's not the only renegade we're dealing with. Nana and Geronimo also continue to elude us. I can't make any promises. And I certainly can't guarantee getting the baby back alive, Sister Adela."

"I can't believe a family like the Westbrooks can't get the military to work a little harder on their behalf. Surely you can convince the officials in Mexico to stretch the rules. I happen to know Mr. Westbrook had connections in our government. Why can't you use those?"

"We're doing what we can. I'm sorry I can't tell you more."

"Then why did you even bother coming?"

"I thought you might want to know what kind of man you've got under this roof."

"I may be a novice nun, but I'm not a lack-wit, sir. I know exactly what kind of man I have under this roof—a man who warned me what a narrow-minded tyrant you would be. You could learn a lot from Mr. Ladino about accepting the burden of responsibility."

Grisham lifted an eyebrow. "Is that so?"

Adela seethed. "You know, Captain, it's no wonder the Apaches continue to outsmart our government if you exemplify the intelligence of the entire military community."

His eyes glittered with bitter blue fire. "Since you seem to know so much more about what we should be doing than we do, Sister Adela, maybe we ought to let do-gooders like you lead the Indian campaigns. Do you really think that half-breed is telling you the truth?" He shook his head. "Gut-eaters are the worst. They'll tell you anything you want to hear until your back's turned"—he made a stabbing motion—"then in goes the knife."

Adela rose from her chair. "I'll take my chances."

Captain Grisham took her cue and stood. "And I suppose you're willing to take those same chances with your mother's life?"

Adela lifted her chin. "You have your hat; I suggest you see yourself out." Without another word she strode from the room.

Ladino heard her soft footfalls on the landing. An instant of indecisive silence followed, but then a board creaked in the short hallway. Moments later his door opened. Feigning sleep, he watched her through his lashes as she tiptoed inside, holding a kerosene lamp. She'd turned the wick down so low the golden glow touched only her fingertips and her face, leaving her black habit and bonnet a part of the surrounding darkness.

"Mr. Ladino, are you awake?" she whispered, creeping closer.

He felt a tentative touch on his shoulder and thought about letting her believe he still slept. What had possessed him to want to tell her? What difference could it possibly make? She was going to be a nun, and she would never understand why he had done the things he had done. If he just remained quiet, she'd go away, and he wouldn't have to reveal to her the guilt he'd lived with for the past seven years.

But she needed to know—to understand. He'd been just as unfair in his judgment of her as she had been of him, and he needed to give her the chance to accept him, even if he still found it too painful to accept himself.

"Mr. Ladino?"

"I'm awake." Opening his eyes, he rolled over on his back so he could look up at her. "So what did Captain Grisham say?"

Her shoulders slumped, and she set the lamp on his bedside table. "Nothing of any real use, I'm afraid. The Mexican officials claim to have seen Pajaro in Mexico. No one saw Jonathan Junior with them, but even that wouldn't convince him you might be right." From beside the nightstand she pulled a ladder-back chair close to his bed. Instead of sitting, she clutched the top rung with her hands. "He claimed they were doing their best, but that was it."

Pulling her skirts aside, she moved around the chair and sat down. "I'm so sorry for not being fair to you." The admission left her mouth as a miserable whisper. Keeping her chin tucked to her chest, she toyed with her thumbs in her lap. "And I'm not any more popular with him right now than I am with you." When she lifted her face, he saw a self-mocking smile curve her lips, as if she fought to hide overwhelming pain behind humor.

Catching her need, Ladino let out a chuckle. "What did he get his tongue-lashing about?"

At his playful return, her smile widened just enough to reveal a touch of relief. "His overbearing, patronizing attitude."

Ladino continued to study her, reveling in each line, each curve of her smiling face, just as relieved as she to be able to laugh at something—anything—again, if only for a moment.

Without warning, her seriousness returned, and she stared at the kerosene lamp. The golden glow highlighted her sculpted cheekbones, casting her long, graceful neck into shadow. And as she stared at the globe, a small flame danced its reflection so deeply in her brown irises Ladino thought he could see her soul, lost in misery and regrets.

"I'll get him back for you," he vowed, not thinking until after he'd spoken that she might refuse his help yet again.

Adela's attention shifted back to his face. A studied politeness touched the smile on her lips. "Thank you, Mr. Ladino, but you're in no condition to help me." Grimacing, she looked away. "Besides, what if he's already dead?"

"What if he's not, and Smeet has him?"

"Do you really think that's possible? I truly want to believe he's still alive." She shrugged, the motion anything but dismissive. "I—I need to believe you . . ."

"Then believe," he said. "Have faith—*ba'juudla*. And when I've recovered, at least think about what I've offered."

She nodded, but he could see she wasn't quite ready to put any real trust in what he said. And why should she? He had no proof, just a hunch and long knowledge of Smeet, which he hadn't yet fully revealed to her.

He rolled his head and stared up at the lamp globe's corona projected on the ceiling. "So did you ask Grisham about me?"

"No."

He turned his attention back to her. "No?"

"Oh, he wanted to tell me, but I'd rather hear it from you." She measured him with her gaze. "So I can understand you."

All traces of Ladino's resentment slid away. Not since they had been in St. Vincent's had he felt the same kinship with her, the same admiration . . . the same hope.

Ladino pushed back the covers and swung his legs over the edge of the mattress. He swayed, fighting a wave of dizziness. Adela rose to help, but he gestured her back with his hand. She resumed her seat, watching him.

"You already know I killed soldiers. Four of them." He let a moment of silence test her reaction and prepare her for more of his revelation. "I'm also responsible for the death of innocent women and children, and I might as well have killed my own grandmother."

A flurry of emotions raced across Adela's face. Shock burst forth first, followed by alarm. But when she looked at the medicine pouch gracing the middle of his chest, then lifted her lashes to meet his gaze again, he read her apology. He knew she was more sorry than ever for the hateful words and accusations that had passed between them earlier . . . just as he was.

"Mr. Ladino, being accidentally responsible for someone's death and committing murder are totally different things."

"Accident or not, death is death," he replied bitterly.

A strange expression crossed her face, as if what he had

said held a meaning for her that went beyond this conversation.

"And because I'm a half-breed, an abomination even among the Apache, I feel the dishonor of my betrayal all the more."

She said nothing, but continued to search his gaze as if desperate to understand him. "How?"

"How I killed so many of my own people—or how I came to the point of making such an unforgivable mistake?"

"I want to know as much as you want to tell me. I know I haven't listened in the past, but this time I'll try."

He laughed. "Is this like going to confession?"

"Hmm. I guess it is," she agreed, smiling as she settled her elbow on the nightstand and rested her head in her palm. Her teeth peeked through the crevice of her soft lips. "How did you know about confession?"

Instead of taking offense at her question, he saw it for what it was—her effort to know him better and dispel the heavy mood.

"Didn't I tell you my mother was Irish?" He returned her smile, grateful to her for giving him an easy way to begin his story. "As a child I lived with my father's people. But my mother secretly taught me her ways, too. She taught me about her religion, and she taught me how to read by drawing letters in the dirt."

"My mother taught me my alphabet the same way. When she was between jobs and we had no place to live." As she stared off at some point beyond his shoulder, her expression grew wistful, yet it was the hint of happiness remaining in her smile that made him want to touch her lips with his own. She shrugged and shook her head, looking back at him. "I'm sorry, go on."

"When I was nine," he continued, "the Mescaleros were

rounded up and taken to Bosque Redondo. Nine hundred Navajos, enemies of our people, were brought to live there as well.

"My father's people prefer death to captivity, and that's what Bosque Redondo meant to us. We were forced to live in filth because we could not move our camp, and we were given maggot-ridden beef to eat, and still we tried to cooperate and live by the rules of the White Eye. But when they began to throw dead bodies diseased with smallpox into the river—the water we drank—all the Mescaleros strong enough to leave ran away."

She leaned forward now, her brow creased with concern.

"My mother stayed," he said. "I was angry with her because my father had been killed by a bluecoat a short time before. I felt she had betrayed my father, and me as well. It wasn't until much later that I understood, because as much as I loved my father's people, I never felt like I truly belonged, either. So I went my own way for a while."

"What did you do then?"

"I became a bounty hunter, a man who doesn't truly fit on either side of the law. A necessary evil in a society that prefers to be ignorant of the true depth of violence. I adopted the name Christian Ladino. My mother called me Christian, and Ladino is short for my Mexican name, El Ladino Greñudo—the Long-haired Half-breed. It was a joke, a mockery I made of myself."

Adela frowned. "Why?"

Ladino shrugged. "I was angry. Bitter because I've never been the person I want to be—a whole person, not two halves of an incompatible mixture."

"You said you were considered an abomination among your father's people because you're a half-breed. Yet they kidnap Mexican and white children and raise them as their own. That doesn't make sense to me."

"For one, I'm the son of a slave—*naant'a-a*—one to be ordered about. So I'm illegitimate. A bastard. My father loved my mother, but the others never accepted her." He shrugged, displaying a nonchalance he did not feel. "It's true the Apache kidnap children and raise them, so why do my father's people consider me an abomination?" Again he shrugged. "For much the same reason White Eyes look down on those of mixed race. A child of mixed blood is seen as unreliable, never certain where his loyalties should lie. He is not one thing or another, but a confusion of both."

Adela studied him, and as Ladino absorbed her gaze, he wondered at her intensity. "So you went by the name Christian Ladino because you wanted to show people it didn't matter," she murmured, "even though it really did."

He nodded, unable to speak for several moments.

"I knew I could never be happy alone," he said at last, "but I thought I could at least be content. I felt like I had deserted my father's people. I thought perhaps I could help them in some way because I understood the white culture as well as that of the Apache. I went back to Fort Stanton and signed on as an interpreter. That's when I met Captain Nigel Smeet, although I was never assigned to work with him."

Ladino took a deep breath, then let it out, forcing fury and despair to yield to his command. No matter how many years had passed, he would never forget the incidents of the day that had cut apart his life and his heart forever.

"One day, seven years ago, the commander at Fort Stanton learned of a small band of Mescaleros who had left the reservation. He sent me to convince them to return peaceably. I made sure I wasn't followed; I'd heard stories about soldiers attacking helpless camps because they believed the Apaches had done some wrong, or because they thought force was the only way to bring them to heel."

His voice rose with his anger. "The people left because they were hungry and needed to hunt. The agency was supposed to feed them, but unscrupulous White Eyes sold the agency rotten beef. Or if the agent was in league with the ranchers, he used government money to pay for animals that didn't exist.

"So I went to talk to these people, knowing if I didn't convince them to return, the soldiers would find them and kill them." Ladino steepled his fingers over his nose. "But this band was different—"

"Your grandmother was with them," Adela whispered.

"Yes," he admitted, lowering his hands. "The tattered calico tunic and skirt she wore hung like a burial shroud on her frail bones. The bluecoats I worked for had done this to her." He shook his head. "While I was trying to convince them to come back, Smeet and six soldiers rode up and started shooting. Everyone scattered, but Smeet and his men rode them down. Smeet shot my grandmother in the back. The rest were slaughtered—even the children."

"The children?" she asked, her voice stricken.

Ladino nodded. "I killed four of the soldiers before Smeet shot me."

Her gaze wandered to the scar from the bullet wound on his shoulder. "Why didn't they kill you like the rest?"

"One of the soldiers, Hawley, was a friend of Smeet's. He convinced Smeet not to kill me—to take me back instead. They court-martialed me for murdering the soldiers. Smeet testified that after I left to talk to this band, he heard these 'cutoffs' were responsible for a raid on the Coghlan ranch. They weren't, but who do you think they believed—me or Smeet?"

"And that's why you want Smeet dead?"

"Yes. And that was why I killed those soldiers. Because White Eyes outnumber the Apache, our revenge is to take ten or fifteen lives for the life of one Apache. It falls to the surviving family members to take their revenge on anyone they can—men, women, and yes"—he shot her an expression of apology—"even children sometimes, just like White Eyes. But I had seen what haphazard murder could cause, and I only wanted to kill the ones responsible. Like Smeet."

"And what about the two soldiers you didn't kill that day?"

Ladino clasped his fingers between his widespread legs. "After I was released from Alcatraz, I found one of them in Yuma." He paused, measuring her probable reaction. "I slit his throat."

Adela flinched, covering her mouth with her hand.

"The other one, Hawley, I found near here," he went on. "He's the man who had the article about the blackmail attempt. He showed remorse, so I spared his life."

"And because he spared yours," she added, lowering her hand.

"At the time I cared nothing for that. I was responsible for the massacre. I had led the soldiers into their camp."

"But you didn't intend to," she rushed to reassure him.

"It doesn't matter what I intended. I did it. Their deaths are my fault. My own grandmother was murdered because of me, because I had betrayed my people. I believed I could help them by joining the White Eye army."

"But you said you had been so careful, how did they follow you? How did they find the camp?"

Ladino looked at her, the uncertainty of that point nagging him as it always did. "I don't know." The kerosene flame flickered, marking the passing moments. "I thought I had made sure only an Apache could track me." He shrugged. "But Smeet knows Apache tricks—he's an experienced trailer."

"It was not your fault."

"A true Apache warrior would have seen it as a trap. A true warrior would never have allowed himself to be followed into a family camp."

"You have to forgive yourself—"

"There is no forgiveness for an Apache. And an Apache wouldn't ask. There is only right and wrong and living forever with the consequences of your actions." He heard his own voice grow soft, deadly. "And there is revenge."

"But your kind of revenge is vigilantism. It's—"

"Against what your White Eye church teaches." He wanted to spit on the floor. "If there has been justice for the Apache, I haven't seen it. My people have to take it. Hypocrisy is all your church teaches. 'An eye for an eye' next to 'turn the other cheek.' And then what is it you once said to me? 'He who lives by the sword shall perish by the sword.' " It's a split-tongue religion for a split-tongue people. I want no part of it."

"When you take the Bible out of context, of course it sounds that way."

He smiled at her, his expression mirthless. "I can see I'm getting nowhere with this. I shouldn't have even tried." He stretched out on the bed and turned over, dismissing her.

"No. I understand. I do."

Seconds later he felt her touch his shoulder at the same time he felt her weight on the mattress. When he turned his head and looked over his shoulder at her, she pulled back her hand.

"Then why do you fear touching me now?"

She only stared at him, her expression startled.

"If you're a nun and a nurse, and I'm only your patient, it shouldn't matter. And if you were only trying to show me your concern, a touch shouldn't matter. So why does it matter, Adela? Because I'm Apache—or because you're a nun trying to hide her hypocrisy?"

"I merely thought you might not appreciate my offer of comfort. I didn't want to offend you."

"My Apacheness isn't contagious, and I'm not going to fall apart just because you happen to step on a nerve."

"You know what I think?" she said, standing up and stepping away. "I think you don't know what you want."

"I know perfectly well what I want." Ladino rolled over and darted out an arm, clutching a fistful of her frock. Though pain ripped through his head and stomach, he pulled her close. "Come here, little split-tongue. Let me show you what you want."

Adela pried his grip from her skirt and twisted back his little finger. When he tried to pull his hand away, she twisted harder. Ladino bit off a curse.

"You're a better man than this, so why don't you take out your anger and frustration on someone else." She released his hand and slid out of his reach.

Ladino heard footfalls scurrying across the landing. "Sister Adela!" cried Sister Michaela.

Adela's attention spun to the door. "I'm with Mr. Ladino."

Michaela burst into his room. "Come quickly—your mother—"

"She's worse?"

"No—no. I think she's better, praise be to God." Sister Michaela closed her eyes and crossed herself. "She's awake and lucid, and she's asking for you."

Chapter Fourteen

After Michaela stepped out of the room, Adela stood for a moment at Ladino's bedside, too stunned to move. She turned her head to look at him. The animosity in his golden eyes had liquefied to compassion.

"Adela," he said, reaching out to her.

"No." Adela held up her hands. "Don't . . . touch me." She shook her head. "Just—don't."

She fled, her heart beating triple time. At the doorway she turned, looking back. Fury had once again replaced all softness on Ladino's features. He reclined and turned over, away from her, his body straightening into a rigid column beneath the white sheet.

Adela strode out to the landing, her hands clutched at her waist. In the lamplight spilling from her mother's room, she could see the concern on Michaela's face.

"Are you all right, Sister Adela?"

Adela nodded. "You can go to bed now, Michaela," she said, her tone distant and authoritative. "And thank you," she added, trying to soften her demeanor.

"You'll wake me if you need me?"

"Yes." She offered a smile. "Now go."

When Michaela rounded the landing banister and disappeared down the hallway leading to their own rooms, Adela turned into the tower chamber and crossed to her mother's room, her stomach knotted in apprehension.

Adela roused her dozing mother by stroking chestnut hair, streaked with gray, off her brow. "Mama?"

Minna opened her eyes, and a sleepy smile unfolded across her face. "I wasn't dreaming," she whispered. "You really are here."

"Yes," Adela answered, swallowing. "I'm here. I came to see how you were doing."

"Have they found him yet?"

A fist of dread clutched Adela's heart.

"Have they found my baby?" Minna repeated.

Midnight silence gathered, yet the clock on the mantelpiece ticked away the seconds until she would have to respond.

"No," she admitted at last. "Not yet."

Minna's face crumpled. "But I told . . . Captain Grisham . . . what I knew about the Apaches. He said they'd go after them."

"I just spoke with Captain Grisham, Mama, and he says they should have him back any day now."

Surely God could forgive a lie to spare her mother's heart.

"The Apache woman nursed him," said Minna, her voice weak. "I think she lost her own baby, so I thought she would understand how I felt and give him back to me. But she didn't." Minna shook her head slowly on the pillow as tears soaked into the bandage on her cheek. "She wanted him for herself." She looked up at Adela. "That's two babies taken from me. After you, I didn't think I deserved another one. And now look what's happened."

"Mama, don't talk like that." Adela smoothed her mother's hair harder, faster. "Captain Grisham is going to bring back your baby. I know he will." Realizing her brisk attention might be hurting her mother, she pulled her hand away.

"Before Mr. Westbrook . . . was killed," Minna continued, unmerciful in her need to speak, "we decided if anything were to happen to us, we wanted you to care for our son. We knew you'd love him and give him a home—even at the convent if you had to."

"Mama, *please*. You're going to get well, and before you know it, you'll hold your son in your arms again."

Minna squeezed her eyes shut as if she were desperate to ward off belief in Adela's lie. "I was on my way up to see you, Adela. I felt I was finally in a position to face you again."

Adela shook her head. "Mama, I don't need an explanation—"

"I wanted to apologize. I wanted to ask permission to become part of your life."

"Mama—"

"Tell me how you're doing, Little Rapunzel. The letters from the Mother Superior always seemed so impersonal—a progress note and nothing more. Tell me what I missed." Another tear rolled down her cheek, clinging in the grids of the gauze bandage. "Were you ever a happy little girl after I left? Did you laugh and play and run with other children the way I imagined?"

"Mama, I can't talk like what happened never occurred."

The purpose in Minna's eyes grew intense. "You deserve a mother who'll listen to you, Adela. I'm listening now. Won't you please help me to know you?"

Adela couldn't speak for the emotion lumped in her throat, yet what choice did she have? She had no pledge from God that Minna would ever recover enough to speak of such things later.

"Who are your friends, Adela? Do you have friends?"

Ladino's face leaped to mind. She couldn't understand why, except that before anger had destroyed their tentative attempt at trust, she had felt as if his wounded heart had called to its companion within her. If it weren't for the ungodly attraction to him she battled, Adela wanted to believe they could be friends.

Struggling to put such conflicting emotions and thoughts about Ladino out of her mind, she called herself back to memories of her childhood days at the convent.

"Yes," she answered finally. Already her thumb began to burn as she rubbed it with the other. "I had a friend once. Her name was Rebecca Adler." She shook her head and rose from the bed. "Mama, I'm sorry, I just can't do this."

She felt her mother's hand grasp her fingers, lacing them together. "Please, Adela. Sit back down and talk to me. Don't let me regret I never knew you, too."

Adela looked down at their clasped hands, then into her mother's eyes, seeing her own lonely self reflected in their hazel softness. She lowered herself to the edge of the bed, her back stiff, her feet poised for escape.

"Tell me about Rebecca," Minna said. "Was she another orph—child at the convent?"

Orphan. Her mother had almost said it. The word plunged like Ladino's knife into her heart.

"No," Adela answered. "Her father was a German merchant."

"Then did you meet her at church?"

Adela shook her head. "They were Jewish."

"Jewish?"

Her mother's curiosity sounded almost casual, as if they spoke like any mother and daughter trying to catch up after years of separation. Yet their feigned normalcy made this whole situation more bizarre than Adela felt capable of coping with right now. But for her mother's sake she had to try.

"So how did you become friends?" Minna asked.

"Rebecca was a student at my school."

Minna's brow wrinkled. "A Jewish girl?"

Adela nodded. "Many children who went to our school weren't Catholic or . . . or orphans."

Minna remained quiet for a moment. "So were you just friends at school?" she asked at last. "Or did Rebecca ever invite you to her home?"

Hearing an intensity that went deeper than the question itself, Adela was slow to respond. "Sometimes she invited me home," she replied. "Usually when her mother asked the sisters for my help with some housecleaning chore. Afterwards, Mrs. Adler would make a donation to the church."

Adela didn't want to mention the times another *niña de caridad*—charity girl—had been sent in her stead. Adela had always feared Rebecca would like the other girl better, that the new girl would take Adela's tenuous place in the Adler home. Now Rebecca was gone. She had moved back East, married the son of a family friend, and built a home of her own.

"Were her parents like some of the people I used to work for?" Minna grimaced. "Or did they make you feel welcome?"

"They always made me feel welcome, Mama," Adela replied, even though she felt the old remorse return. How many times had she been the sole cause of her mother losing her job? Too many to count. Most of her mother's employers had claimed a woman couldn't work when she had a child needing her constant care. No one ever seemed to wonder how a woman alone could support herself or her daughter if no one would hire her.

"And were you close . . . to any of the sisters . . . ? Any

who were . . . like a mother to you?"

Adela studied her mother's eyes. She found pain, but she also discovered understanding. "Sister Blandina came to teach when I was thirteen. She's been almost like a mother to me ever since."

"I'm glad." Minna squeezed her hand. "Is she the reason you've decided to become a nun?"

Adela looked down at her fingers still intertwined with her mother's. "Yes," she ventured, "but it's nursing that calls to me most. I like knowing I can help people. I feel as if I make a difference in the lives of my patients. I feel—"

"You feel wanted, like I never made you feel."

Adela winced. "You did what you had to, Mama."

"But I betrayed you, even though it killed me to leave you there. I never wanted to leave you behind."

"I know." Adela forced a smile and gripped her mother's fingers. "But we're together now. Sister Blandina tells me all things have a purpose. It's just hard to see sometimes."

Since when did she believe the words she'd just spoken? And how could recent events possibly be in God's plan? She couldn't continue to think along that path, or the resentment she always tried to hide, tried to ignore, would return full force.

Her mother's face took on a faraway glaze before she closed her eyes. "Jonathan Junior didn't even cry when I left," she said, smiling miserably as she opened her eyes again. "I know he's a baby and didn't—doesn't—even understand. But it still hurt. Is that foolish of me?"

"No, Mama," Adela whispered, stroking her mother's fingers.

"I want him so much, Little Rapunzel. I used to lie here with him beside me, and his father—Mr. Westbrook—used to lie beside me and . . ." She looked up at Adela and smiled

216

wistfully. "Well, we were so happy. But that doesn't help you, does it? And it doesn't help me, now."

She shrugged, the effort costing her a grimace of pain. Adela reminded herself to give her another dose of laudanum soon.

"Do you ever question your decision to become a nun? Has there ever been someone besides Sister Blandina and Rebecca that you've been close to? A man? Someone who could give you a real family like you deserve?"

Thoughts of Ladino's untamed passion seared across Adela's heart, leaving ashes of doubt in their wake. Yet she had to put from her mind the rush of emotions he always evoked. She could not let herself contemplate a life with him, or children. The uncertainty of his nomadic nature could never offer her the safety and security she craved.

"No." Adela shook her head. "My family is at the convent."

"Are you truly happy there?"

Adela fidgeted. "Yes."

Minna looked thoughtful. "I have something I'd like to give you," she said, her voice drooping with exhaustion. "It's in the clock on the mantel."

Though suspicious of her mother's intent, Adela rose and moved to the fireplace. She'd never really looked at the wooden timepiece on the mantel before, but as she studied its rounded top and the side scrolls that dripped teardrop finials to an embellished base, she wondered what secrets the timekeeper hid.

"You'll have to take out the pendulum, but behind that is a false back."

Adela opened the glass door and stopped the pendulum. Sudden silence filled the room, leaving her with a sense of loss as she unhooked the brass weight from its mechanism and set it aside on the mantel. She then felt inside the empty cabinet below the clock face with its laughing phases of the moon, but could find no evidence of a hidden panel.

She turned to her mother. "How does it open?"

"The spring switch is on the waning moon's chin."

Adela touched the tiny lever and the panel swung open. Inside nestled a coil of gold and black onyx beads, each one an intricate carving of a full rose bloom. Adela held the rosary in her palm, staring at the dainty decades as she strode across the room and sat on the edge of her mother's bed once more.

"It was your great-great-grandmother's," said Minna. "Blessed by the Pope."

"It's beautiful," Adela whispered, awed to hold an heirloom generations old when she'd grown accustomed to knowing no blood relatives. She tilted her palm, letting the beads slide over her fingers and fall like rain until the cross rested in her lap.

"Your great-great-grandmother was a Benedictine nun."

Adela's attention snapped to her mother's face.

"Do you remember the fairy tales I used to tell you?" She didn't wait for an answer. "I did wrong by changing the end of Rapunzel. I realize that now."

Still clutching the chaplet beads, Adela slowly lowered her hands to her lap. "Wh-what do you mean?" she asked, alarmed by her mother's apparent relapse into delusion.

"Have you seen the painting on the easel in the tower room?"

"Yes."

"For a year it's been sitting there unfinished." She smiled, touching Adela's knee. "Do you know why?"

"No," Adela ventured, her stomach tightening.

"The angle was all wrong for me. I just couldn't paint

the fountain from my tower. I needed to get down and look at it close up. I had to feel it and experience it to appreciate it. I kept that painting to remind myself of that." Her smile faded. "As rough as our life was, as awful as our final day together turned out to be, I'd never trade a moment of the time we shared. But I wish I hadn't spent so much of that precious time talking about how happy we'd be if only we had a safe home like Rapunzel's tower. We had each other, and we had love. What else is there?"

Minna sighed. "In my version, Rapunzel refused to go into the woods with the witch." She frowned distractedly, yet her voice took on a profound quality that belied her dwindling strength. "She would have appreciated her prince so much more if she had."

Adela followed the stream of parishioners flowing out of St. Vincent de Paul Catholic Church. As she stepped outside the cool adobe church into the June sunshine, she saw Ladino sitting on the front porch of the Westbrook home, watching her.

Over the last few days he'd grown stronger, spending as much time as possible out of doors, although this was the first time she'd seen him on the front porch. She wondered if he had only wanted to bedevil her because he knew she had gone to Mass.

While his condition had improved, her mother continued to languish, some days lucid, some days delusional. Today had been one of her better days, and Judith had insisted Adela get out of the house, away from her "children."

"Dear Sister Adela, it was so good of you to come," said Father Bourgade, his French-accented voice interrupting her thoughts. "I must apologize for not speaking with you before Mass." Turning, he searched all around him.

"Where is Sister Michaela? I grew accustomed to seeing her in regular attendance."

"Michaela was called back to Santa Fe," she answered, wondering if she'd imagined the remonstration in his tone, or if she only heard her own conscience reprimanding her for neglecting her spiritual duties. "I'm sorry for not attending church more frequently, but I've been caring for my mother night and day."

"*Bien entendu!* How foolish of me." His expression turned thoughtful. "I have not seen Dr. Clayburgh's buggy in front of the house in recent days. He has not been checking on your mother?"

"No." Adela couldn't hide the resentment in her voice. "But we're managing." Hoping to ease away, she took a step down the stairs.

"Have you heard any word from Fort Bayard?"

"No. But they claim they're still looking."

"Well, perhaps you will hear something soon."

"Yes, perhaps." She smiled, taking a step. "Thank you for your concern, Father," she said, stepping down once more.

"Sister Adela," he called.

Adela grimaced before she turned. "Yes?"

He stepped down until he stood even with her, and as he glanced across the street, his eyes narrowed. "Who is the man sitting on the front porch? I have not seen him before, and Sister Michaela never mentioned him."

"He was my patient in Santa Fe. He's still recuperating."

Multitudes of explanations clamored in Adela's mind, begging for confession, but she remained quiet, afraid of unleashing her shame. She doubted her attitude would be so dismissive if Ladino weren't watching her every move. She knew it shouldn't matter, that perhaps she should try to show more interest in the priest's company, but she suspected Ladino would only be able to see through her pretense.

"There is a maid in the house with you, *n'est-ce pas?*"

"Yes, Father."

"*Bien.* That is wise." He looked again at her, his smile transforming into the deep sincerity of his calling. "I have kept you long enough. Visit me if you need to, Sister."

Adela genuflected. "I will, Father. Thank you." She turned, relieved to be able to hurry down the last of the steps and rush across the street.

The moment she reached the gate in the picket fence, she could discern an unfathomable smile on Mr. Ladino's lips just before he lifted a glass of lemonade to his mouth. Ignoring the flutter of nerves in her stomach, she squared her shoulders and strode up the walk beside the fountain.

"Doing penance so early in the morning?" he teased as she stepped up onto the porch. With a lift of his chin he indicated the priest. "He's still watching us."

Setting his glass on the table between his chair and another, Ladino lifted his hand and waved at the priest. Adela watched Father Bourgade lift his hand, hesitate, then return the greeting. His cassock flapped as he strode inside the church doors and shut them behind him.

"What a wicked man you are!" she exclaimed, battling an incredulous smile despite the twist of mortification within her.

"And he thinks you're not safe with such a wicked man?"

Her smile faded, and she ignored his question. It only summoned similar questions to her own mind.

"You're out early," she remarked, all traces of humor gone as she trained her voice to a professional tone. "And on the porch no less. That must mean you're feeling even better."

He gazed at her, the expression in his golden, mountain-lion eyes thoughtful, as if he had something to say, but didn't quite know how.

Fearing what he might voice, she pretended not to notice as she sat down in the chair next to him and stared out at Market Street, which ran between the Westbrook home and the church. Even so, her true emotions churned inside her.

Ever since the night he had shared his past with her, she had found it that much harder to be near him without thinking of his intense passion about his grandmother's death, or the guilt and duty that had driven him to murder. And ever since he had clutched her skirt, insinuating his lust for her, and accusing her of wanting him just as much, she had been haunted by memories of the gentle kiss they had shared in Santa Fe. How could one man express such contradictory emotions? How could she respond in such a way that left her so confused about her feelings?

"Adela?"

Startled, she turned to face him. His contemplation had turned to earnest determination. She could no longer pretend not to recognize his urgency.

"Yes?"

"Now that I've recovered enough to travel . . . I've decided to head out tomorrow or the next day."

She had known this day would come, but she had denied its reality just as surely as she tried to deny the likelihood of her mother's death. She stared at him, and her throat squeezed shut on every one of the responses tripping through her mind.

Tomorrow?

But you're not ready.

You might still need my care.

Instead of saying any of these things, which she recognized as paltry excuses, she merely nodded. She stared at her motionless hands in her lap, too bereft even to toy with her thumbs.

"I'm tired of sitting at camp like an old grandfather," he explained. "I need to go . . ."

His voice droned on, but Adela didn't want to hear him, didn't want to listen to her own conscience reprimand her for caring so deeply. She listened instead to the birds singing in the sapling branches near the fountain.

Ladino grasped her chin, lifting and turning her head until she looked at him. "Did you hear me?"

Adela blinked, forced to acknowledge the reflection of her own disappointment in his eyes. He released her chin, and despite the heat, she silently called back the warmth of his fingers on her skin, missing him already.

"I was telling you how I want to bring back your baby brother. Let me do this for you, Adela," he entreated. "If he's alive, Smeet has him. And I'll make him pay for this."

"Oh, Ladino . . ." She shook her head. "I would give anything for my baby brother to be upstairs in my mother's arms where he belongs. And I know you have every reason to hate Smeet; I understand that. But don't you see? If you added my reasons to those you have already, I would feel as if I were sanctioning his death. I couldn't live knowing my problems had given you another excuse to have your revenge."

"So you want to leave your baby brother in Smeet's hands, rather than admit you want to see justice done?"

"Justice isn't for us to command."

"That's right. 'Justice is mine,' saith the almighty White

223

Eye God. But what kind of justice causes your mother so much pain?"

Adela lurched out of her chair. Her frock caught on the corner of the table between the chairs, toppling it. Ladino's glass of lemonade crashed to the porch floor and shattered. Yanking her handkerchief out of her pocket, Adela dropped to her knees and began to pick up shards of glass, ignoring the wetness soaking into her skirt. Soon Ladino's shadow loomed over her chore, and he began to help.

Yet even as they placed broken pieces into her handkerchief, Ladino continued his tirade. "If you still can't see what Smeet did to me and my family, look what he's done to yours. He's destroyed it. What happened to the anger you felt at the Apaches? The anger you felt at Pajaro? You were ready to blame me and punish me for what the Apaches did, yet you want to sit here and wait for a ransom request that may never come."

Halting her task, Adela glanced up. "The cavalry is still—"

"Lie to me if you want to, Adela, but don't lie to yourself."

The gold fire in his eyes radiated more heat than the summer sun, but Adela was too angry, too hurt, too confused to give him an answer of any kind. Instead, she dropped her gaze and continued to pick up pieces of glass.

Ladino gripped both her wrists. "Look at me, Adela."

She let her arms go limp and did as he commanded, feeling a flutter of panic when she found such atavistic fury in his face.

"Do you want Grisham's failure or my success?"

"I want a broom. I want to clean up this mess."

Again she recognized that unfathomable something shift into Ladino's expression as he leaned closer. He released his grip and placed his hands on either side of her face. Adela could only stare as his gaze consumed her, inflamed her.

And then he kissed her, shattering her like the shattered glass over which they knelt. Adela choked back her emotion as she tried to concentrate on birdsong—anything but this. Yet Ladino's wild onslaught demanded her complete attention as he slid his tongue over her lips, slicing them open even as he sliced her heart and sent slivers of hot sensation down her spine and into the forbidden reaches of her body.

When he broke away, she scrambled up, her legs on the verge of buckling. Shaking out her habit skirt, she glanced across the street and let out a shaky breath of relief when she didn't see the priest. Ladino pushed up from the floor as well, and she didn't know how many moments of silence passed between them before she braved a peek at him.

"Do you still want that broom?" he asked, his voice whisper-deep with emotion. "Or do you want my help?"

Emotionally exhausted, Adela said nothing. She rubbed her thumbs, struggling to calm her shattered nerves.

Conscience told her she shouldn't allow herself to contemplate his words at all. It was not her place to question or act. She should let God hold and shape His purpose as He saw fit.

But another still, small voice urged her to take control.

"I—I don't want Smeet dead. But if . . . if I did want your help finding him . . . where . . . where would you look?"

"Albuquerque," he answered, ripping away her opportunity to pull back her experimental words. "The railroad would provide a quick means of escape. From Albuquerque, he could go north or south, and from one of those directions he could then travel to California or back east."

"Are you certain he's in Albuquerque?"

"No," Ladino admitted. "But with Smeet's options right now, it would be the best place to look." He stepped close and touched her cheek, shocking her with the contact. "If your baby brother is still alive, I promise to bring him back to you. This time let me take care of you, *shitsíné*."

Mesmerized, Adela stared, afloat on his black pupils in a sea of gold. "What does that mean?"

"It's easy to translate words, but difficult to translate the emotions that go with them." Ladino held his hand out to her and quirked his lips up at one side. If a mountain lion could smile, Adela was sure she saw one now. "Let's get the broom and clean up this mess."

Late that evening, Minna's condition disintegrated. She muttered restless complaints to Adela that the sheets hurt her skin, and what urine she'd been able to pass had been smoky, tainted with blood. Adela had continued to give her the *curandera*'s tea in hopes it would reduce the swelling and cleanse the kidneys. Minna now lay spread across the bed, panting shallowly and groaning with the agony of a full-blown case of uremia.

Adela yanked the bellpull to summon Judith, then rummaged through her black bag for the ingredients she would need to make the purgative.

Judith peered in one of the double doors. "Yes, Sister?"

"I need you to bring up a tub and start heating enough water for a bath." She rushed across the room to the secretary next to the fireplace. Flipping down the writing surface, she found paper and a pen. "And I need Jaime to get these compounds from Dr. Clayburgh," she said as she scribbled the names. "If he doesn't have both, I at least need the citrate of caffeine—it can be used alone." She strode back across the room and handed the list to Judith. "If Jaime can't find Dr. Clayburgh, have him convince the druggist to open his shop."

"Yes, Sister Adela." Judith glanced over at Minna, who continued to groan and clutch at her gown. "I thought she was doing so much better."

"I did too, Judith. I didn't expect this." Adela grimaced. "I should have. I should have been prepared."

"Don't be so hard on yourself. You're doing your best."

Adela nodded distractedly. "Go, Judith. Hurry."

"Yes, Sister." She rushed from the room.

An hour later, just as Judith brought up the last bucket of hot water to fill the tub, Jaime returned. "The doctor wasn't home," he reported, "and neither was the druggist."

Determined not to give in to her feelings of helplessness, Adela summoned her strength to reply in a normal tone. "Thank you, Jaime. Would you build a fire?"

"But, Sister Adela, it's summer—"

"Jaime . . ." Judith warned.

"Yes, ma'am," he said, trudging out of the room.

Ten minutes later flames burned at the mouth of the hearth, turning the room into a furnace. After Jaime had gone back to bed, Adela and Judith pulled Minna up into a sitting position and removed her nightrail, wrapping her in the bed's top sheet for modesty's sake.

"Go get Mr. Ladino, will you, Judith? I don't think the two of us can lift her into the tub."

Judith rushed from the room. Moments later she returned, and Ladino hurried in behind her, the buttons on his shirt mismatched with their holes. He looked at Adela, and in their moment of silent communication, she felt an instant sense of relief. Just his presence gave her the extra emotional strength she needed.

"Would you lift my mother into the tub, Mr. Ladino?"

He offered a grave nod and rolled up his sleeves as he strode to the bed. Despite her mother's pain-filled struggles and the weakness Ladino still suffered, he took Minna under the arms and at the knees, lifting her and carrying her to the copper slipper tub before the fireplace. As if Minna were a wounded fawn, he lowered her into the water. Ladino and Judith stood by as Adela pulled the crazy quilt off the bed and covered the tub up to Minna's neck in order to sweat the poisons out of her system.

The shock of being placed in the water woke Minna, and she looked up at Adela. "Have you heard any word yet?" she mumbled. "Anything at all about Jonathan Junior?"

A broken sigh escaped Adela's throat as she smoothed the sweat-soaked hair away from her mother's face. "We're going to find him, Mama. Don't you worry. You'll be holding him in your arms sooner than you think."

Minna's face wrinkled with unshed tears. "I want my baby."

"I know, Mama," whispered Adela. "I know."

After a few minutes of nonsensical rambling, Minna's eyes drowsed shut once more, and her head lolled on the rim of the tub.

While Adela moved an armchair close to smooth her mother's brow and whisper encouragements in her ear, Ladino added wood to the fire, and Judith changed the bedsheets. Thirty minutes later, Adela removed the quilt, and Ladino gently lifted Minna. The sheet clung to her still-swollen body, drenching his shirt and trousers as it puddled water on the Turkish carpet. Minna's incoherent murmurs had lessened, enforcing Adela's belief that her pain had eased.

"Would you put her in my chair, Mr. Ladino, so Judith

and I can dry her off? And afterwards can you help us put her back in bed?" She glanced up at him, taking comfort from the soft compassion in his eyes that belonged only to her.

Without answer, he set Minna in the chair, then turned to face the doors as Adela removed the wet sheet from her mother's body. From the nursery attached to the bedroom, Judith brought a length of toweling and helped Adela rub Minna dry. Adela fetched a clean nightdress and slipped it over Minna's head, struggling with her mother's inert body as she worked her arms into the sleeves.

As Judith hauled out buckets of water, Ladino carried Minna back to the freshly made bed. He placed her in the middle of the mattress and even pulled up the top sheet to cover her. His extra display of care filled Adela with a gratitude so expansive she could barely contain it.

"Thank you," she whispered, placing her hand on his forearm, willing some of her emotions to find their way into his heart at their contact. "Why don't you go back to bed?"

Ladino touched her cheek, caressing her skin with the backs of his fingers. "Will you be all right?"

She nodded, not trusting herself to speak.

"Call me if you need me."

Again she nodded, and a tremor shook through her as he grasped the back of her head and pulled her toward him. She closed her eyes as he pressed his lips to her forehead. When he released her, she looked up at him, meeting his reassuring smile with one of her own. Quietly, he turned and walked out the double doors. As she watched him stride across the tower room, his clothes still wet, a wild, yearning ache engulfed her heart. At last she recognized the emotion for what it was.

Love.

Love for the wild Apache who had given his gentleness without thought of himself when he had carried her mother's swollen body.

Ladino dreamed his mother was crying.

She held his father's head in her lap and sobbed, while the soldier who had killed him looked on, his face shocked at seeing such an emotional display from a blonde white woman over the death of a savage. Ladino watched his mother take the knife from the sheath at her waist. She hacked off her hair until the ends looked as ragged as the bullet wound in his father's chest.

He looked up into his grandmother's face. She also cried, but her tears were contained as she, too, took her knife and sliced off her hair to mourn the death of her son.

Ladino shifted positions and the dream faded, yet the crying grew louder. Tortured grief. Soul-wrenching loss.

He opened his eyes, and still he heard the sound.

Only a loved one's death could create such a sound in the human throat.

Adela.

Ladino bolted upright. As he shoved aside the covers and pushed out of bed, his faulty equilibrium tilted the room uphill. He struggled into his trousers and buttoned them quickly, stumbling out of the room. The disorientation always seemed worse in the middle of the night and when he first woke, but Minna's kerosene lamp spilled its dim glow into the tower room and as far as the landing, lighting his way.

Even before Ladino entered Minna's chamber, still hot from the earlier fire, he saw her vacant bed. Following Adela's sobs, he stepped over the threshold, and just to his left he noticed the nursery door standing wide. The small room was lit from within by another lamp. He tiptoed into the room and pulled up short.

Minna sat in her rocking chair next to the crib, a blanket clutched to her chest as if it wrapped a baby inside. Adela's black-bonneted head rested in her mother's lap, and her back heaved as she sobbed.

Horror of the dead and their lingering spirits gripped him. But he shoved the ancestral fear aside and crept into the room. Adela continued to sob, oblivious to his presence. He edged closer still and reached out, taking her by the shoulders. She made no struggle at all as he lifted her limp body from the floor and pulled her into his embrace.

"She woke up," Adela wailed against his chest, her body shuddering. "She asked for tea. I was only gone for a few minutes."

He glanced over Adela's head at Minna, whose mouth curved in a tiny smile. Maybe it was a shadow from the lamp, or maybe she had truly found peace in her White Eye heaven.

Without a word, Ladino bent down and put his hands behind Adela's knees. He lifted her against his chest, and she pressed her damp face into his neck and shoulder. Fighting to keep his dizziness at bay, he carried her into the tower room and sat down in one of the wing chairs. Draping her across his lap, he held her close and kissed the top of her head as she vented her misery, soaking his bare chest with her tears.

No matter what Adela thought of his savage ways, for this, if nothing else, Ladino vowed to make Smeet and Pajaro pay.

Chapter Fifteen

Adela sat in front of Mr. Leeds's desk, staring out the window at the dappled leaf patterns falling on the happy faces of people passing by on Market Street. All were oblivious to her pain, and she felt the oddest urge to run outside and scream to get their attention, to ask if her mother's death just two days ago had even caused a ripple in their complacent lives. Yet she clenched her hands in her lap, keeping herself silently, obediently contained.

"Sister Adela, have you heard anything I've said?"

Adela turned her attention to Mr. Leeds, who removed his reading glasses and laid them on his walnut desk beside Jonathan Westbrook's will.

She grimaced in apology. "I'm sorry."

Clasping his hands together, he leaned forward in his chair. "It was inconsiderate of me to ask you to come this evening, so soon after the funeral. Would you like to wait until tomorrow?"

"No. No, I really must get through this." She rested her elbow on the padded arm of her chair and propped her chin on her hand.

Mr. Leeds put his glasses back on and read the will from the beginning. Adela tried with little success to absorb the myriad "ifs," "ands," "wherefores," and "wherebys."

He must have seen her vague expression when he glanced up, because he stopped reading once again. "Do you understand what that means in layman's terms, Sister Adela?"

She shook her head.

"I'll tell you what applies in this particular instance. Since Mr. and Mrs. Westbrook are . . . deceased"—he rubbed his nose—"that means you have been named Jonathan Junior's guardian as well as the administrator of the Westbrook estate until your brother reaches maturity." He paused for several moments before continuing. "In the unhappy event that he is never found, or if he is . . . dead . . ."—he cleared his throat—"you will then be sole heir to the Westbrook estate. Excluding a sizable pension for Judith, the estate exceeds three million dollars."

Adela gaped as her hand fell away from her face.

He sighed. "Which presents us with a dilemma. It's my understanding that when you profess your vows, anything you inherit becomes the property of the Catholic Church."

"But I—I haven't inherited anything," she insisted.

"Not yet. But if Jonathan Junior—"

"He's alive."

"It's all well and good to have faith, Sister Adela, but it's been weeks since the Apache attack, and we've received no further word of whether the Mexican authorities have captured Pajaro. Under the circumstances—"

"I believe Nigel Smeet might be in on the kidnapping."

The lawyer removed his glasses again, frowning as if unable to follow her line of thought. "How could that be possible?"

Adela took a deep breath and began to explain. When Mr. Leeds listened to her tale, showing none of the scoffing attitude she'd suffered from Captain Grisham, she felt the tangled mass of anxiety in her chest begin to unravel.

"So you see," she finished, "because this Pajaro and Mr. Smeet have been involved in schemes with each other in the past, it's possible they're involved in this one."

"Yes, it is possible," he conceded. "But there is still a good chance Smeet *doesn't* have your brother," he reminded gently. "After all, there has been no request for ransom."

"I know. I-I've considered that." Adela dropped her gaze. "But I'm afraid this goes much deeper than money. I think Smeet may want revenge."

Mr. Leeds remained quiet for several moments. "You might be right." His chair creaked as he shifted positions. "Even so, what purpose is revenge if the man doesn't benefit in some way? Nothing that has happened thus far could be of any real advantage to Smeet. Mr. Westbrook is dead, and now . . ."

At his shrug, Adela nodded, hoping he wouldn't finish the comment. "Do you think it's possible Smeet hasn't contacted anyone concerning ransom because he hasn't been sure whom to contact?" she asked. "Perhaps he never intended for Mr. Westbrook to die. And . . ." Adela cleared her throat. "And now there's just me. Do you suppose he'll read the obituary and act once he realizes I've been here caring for my mother?"

"It's possible." Mr. Leeds sighed. "In the meantime, if this is all a mistake, and Pajaro still has Jonathan Junior, I'm sure Captain Grisham will continue to do his best."

"Grisham has been utterly ineffectual," she retorted. "Mr. Ladino *knows* Smeet. He has his own reasons for wanting to . . . find the man. He's offered to go after Smeet and rescue my baby brother."

She continued to fight her guilt over this offer, especially since she still found it difficult to accept the fact that anyone would be malicious enough to use an infant as leverage . . . or a tool to exact revenge. But after all Ladino had told her about the man, she finally understood his de-

234

sire for vengeance against Smeet, even if she still couldn't condone it.

An idea began to form—a plan Adela couldn't believe she would consider if not for Jonathan Junior's sake.

"Help me understand the conditions of the will a little better, Mr. Leeds." Her thumbs shook as she rubbed them along each other in her lap. "If I'm the administrator, does that mean I control the funds—that I can use the money the way I see fit?"

"Within certain limitations. I'm afraid you must have my approval on any amount you choose to spend."

Adela nodded. She might not yet feel truly confident in her decision, but she no longer felt helpless.

Mr. Leeds scooted closer to the edge of his chair. "So how much does Mr. Ladino want for going after Smeet?"

"How much does he want?" Adela repeated, confused.

"Yes." Mr. Leeds cocked his head to one side. "I assume that is why you asked if you had control of the finances."

"Oh," said Adela. "I don't know. I—I hadn't thought about that. He didn't mention pay . . ."

For a moment she stared at the paisley patterns on the carpet, wondering if she had misconstrued Ladino's intent for offering his help. After all, she had told Mr. Leeds he was a bounty hunter, and Smeet was a wanted man. Not only that, but she would have so much less to feel guilty for if Ladino considered it a business proposition rather than a personal promise. Yet the possibility that he might have comforted her so tenderly the night of her mother's death only to make money on her grief . . .

"No," Adela began, "I wanted to know about the finances because . . . because I've decided to go with Mr. Ladino, and—"

"Go with him?" He stood and came around his desk

until he stood before her. "You can't be serious!"

Rising from the chair, Adela stepped beside it, curling her fingers around its padded back for support. "Yes, I am."

"But why?" he asked, his forehead furrowed. "You'd be putting yourself in too much danger."

Adela paced to the window. "I can't go back to Santa Fe knowing my baby brother is still out there somewhere. My mother wanted him back more than anything. Now she'll never see him, and he'll never know her." She swallowed the sob that clung to the back of her throat. "I'm his only family now. I'm also a nurse. If he's been hurt, I want to be there to take care of him. And if something were to happen to Mr. Ladino . . ." She swallowed again, unable to finish the thought.

"What would you like me to do?"

Adela clasped her hands behind her back. "Mr. Ladino believes that when Smeet planned all of this, he might have considered escape by train, probably from Albuquerque, so I imagine that's where he'll want to investigate first. But in case he's wrong, I'd like you to hire men to watch the main depots throughout the Territory. I don't want to lose any more time or take any more chances. I just hope it's not too late." She sighed. "As for our traveling needs, Mr. Ladino already has a horse, but I don't think there are any others in the stable."

"No, they were both killed during Pajaro's attack."

Adela responded with a grim nod. "Then I want you to purchase a good mount for me. And I'll need to send a telegram to Mother Eulalia." This last she murmured under her breath.

"I'll do what I can today, but I'll probably need tomorrow and the next day to get everything in order. Can you convince Mr. Ladino to wait just two more days? Perhaps in that time we'll hear from Smeet."

Dropping her gaze, Adela nodded. "I'll see what I can do."

Lying in bed that night, staring into the low flame of the kerosene lamp, Adela thought about raising a child by herself. She, who had envied him his happy, safe, secure home. Now he would never know his own mother, and what few fragmented memories Adela possessed would have to suffice as his legacy.

If he was still alive.

She felt more lost and alone than ever before. And for the first time since her mother's death she acknowledged her fury. Not since she'd beaten Abbie's corncob head against the wall had she felt such rage. She'd learned to contain the depth of that dangerous emotion these last fifteen years, to hide it so well she could pretend it didn't exist.

Adela flung back the sheet and swung her legs over the side of the mattress. She stared at the cheval mirror across the room, hidden beneath the quilt she'd obediently tossed over its face.

She closed her eyes, envisioning herself reflected in the looking glass as she screamed at God for his sadistic meddling. He had thrown every one of her hopes and dreams on a funeral pyre. Now all she had left were memories, a baby brother she might never see, and in the guise of Ladino, the strongest temptation she'd ever been forced to deny. And now He forced her to think of them all at once, to confront every fear with no hope of success. But it was her fault. She'd done the wrong things, made the wrong choices, listened to herself instead of following His instruction.

Opening her eyes, she rose from the bed and padded across the gold-fringed carpet to the mirror. Draped on the burgundy wing chair next to the cheval glass, her black habit waited, watching her, warning her not to do what she was about to do.

Adela ignored its calling and pulled the quilt away, letting the heavy patterned material slide to the floor at her feet. She stared at her full-length reflection, tempting God . . . testing Him. Taunting Him with her brazen disrespect.

Ladino.

With trembling fingers she touched the buttons at the neckline of her nightdress, then pulled her hand down until her palm rested between her breasts. Closing her eyes, she clutched at the material, pulling it tight against her skin, feeling warmth from her body radiate into her curled hand as she tried to imagine what he might have felt when he'd touched her like this.

Startled, she opened her eyes and met the reflection of her shame. She glanced up at the white night bonnet on her head, yet another symbol of consecrated virginity. On impulse, she grabbed her habit and held it before her, looking at herself in it, trying to remind herself of the vows she would soon take. All that came to mind were endless ceremonies: Lauds, Matins, Compline . . . each office arranged at a specific time, ticking her life away.

Adela flung her habit over the mirror as she pulled open her bedroom door. She knew where she was going. To Ladino. She had put off telling him of her decision, knowing they would argue if she did. So why did she go now, in the middle of the night? Why didn't she wait until morning and stop him before he left? Because deep down, her heart denied everything but his wild call.

The lamp on the table at the landing cast its fragile glow around the corner, and she gravitated toward that small light in the darkness, chastising herself for setting out on this course, even as she hurried down the long hallway.

Opening his door, she peeked around the edge, expecting to find him asleep. Instead, light from his bedside lamp glinted off the tattoo on his forehead then diffused over his cheekbones, casting its flame into his drowsy golden eyes. He leaned up on one elbow, and his long mahogany hair slid over his shoulder and chest, pooling on the white sheets in front of him. Adela stared, her eyes wide at the sight.

Frowning, he blinked, and she knew he had just lit his lamp. "I woke up when I heard you in the hallway." Drugged with sleep, his low voice resonated deep in his chest. "Is something wrong?"

Adela pulled in a shaky breath and released it slowly. "No. I—I was just going downstairs to make myself a cup of tea, and I thought I'd check on you." Heat suffused her neck and face at the lie. "I'm sorry if I woke you."

He shrugged one shoulder. "Did you want to talk?"

She hovered in the doorway. "No, I—"

"I don't mind."

Indecision plagued her, but finally she pushed the door all the way open. "All right, I . . ."

Words failed her as he swung his legs over the side of the mattress, keeping the top sheet draped over his hips and thighs, yet revealing several inches of golden brown skin low on his hip just above the drape of the white sheet.

How many hot summer nights had she wanted to slip out of her gown and feel the cool sheets slide across her naked skin . . . ?

Her nightdress. Oh, Sweet Mary. She had come to his room wearing only a gown of thin cotton.

"Would you like me to get dressed?" An enigmatic smile tugged at his lips.

Adela stared at her bare toes visible beneath the hem of her nightdress. To say yes would be an admission of guilty thoughts. To say no would only tempt her to think them. To refuse to enter the room now would call even more attention to her own semi-clad state.

"N-no. You're fine." She stepped into the room and closed the door behind her before she could change her mind. Her pulse raced when he appraised the length of her body, his expression hooded like that of a watchful cat. She embraced herself, squeezing her upper arms as she shifted her attention to the east window. A slight breeze fluttered the lace panels.

"Rain," he said.

"What?" she asked, compelled to look at him again.

"When the wind blows from the east, rain usually follows."

Adela couldn't help but watch him as he turned to face the window. The breeze teased his hair, and she envisioned him as some elemental god. He communed with the wind to summon the rain, while at his side the small fire from the lamp worshiped a muscular body hewn from warm golden earth. Adela stepped closer, and closer still, envying the breeze its fingers through his mahogany hair.

Lost in the fantasy, she reached out to touch the long strands, but when he turned and looked up at her, she pulled back. What was she doing? This was insane!

"What is it, Adela?" The unfathomable emotion in his eyes clutched her heart in its undertow.

"I—I . . ." Her voice faltered; several moments elapsed

as she fought for the proper words. "I need to speak with you about something I discussed with Mr. Leeds today." Clasping her hands, she circled the nail of one thumb with the tip of the other. "I've been named Jonathan Junior's guardian and the administrator of his estate until he reaches maturity," she said, not knowing how else to begin.

"Don't you want to be his guardian?"

"Of course I do. I want to give him a home. Especially now that he has no family but me." She continued to toy with her thumb. "That's why I want to accompany you when you go after Smeet."

Grasping the sheet and knotting it around his waist, Ladino rose from the bed. "No. I promise I'll bring him back to you, but you can't go." Towering over her, he gripped her arms. "I can't be responsible for you, Adela. I need to do this on my own."

"But he's my baby brother," she argued. "And if he's injured, how are you going to tend him?" She forced herself to speak the next bitter words. "How are you going to have your revenge if you have to care for an infant?"

Defeat and remorse clouded Ladino's expression. He released her and strode away, gazing out into the blackness beyond the window. Adela felt her heart collapse. She'd known her last words would be the ones to sway him into considering her side, yet she took no satisfaction in her victory—if it could be called a victory at all.

"If I go with you, you won't have to worry about getting him back to me and losing valuable time," she said, her voice a whisper. He didn't turn. She pulled her lips between her teeth, considering her next words. "And if it's pay you want—"

"Pay?" He turned on his heel, staring at her as if she'd offered him sackcloth and ashes and expected him to be grateful for her charity. "Did I ever mention or imply wanting money?"

"No," she murmured.

"Do you really think I don't give a damn about you or that baby?"

"No," she murmured again, softer this time.

"Then why the hell did you ask me that?"

Because your anger sets you on familiar terms with me.

Like water seeking the easiest course—if not always the smoothest—Adela felt shamed by the fact that when they fought, she found him easier to resist. Yet his fire also warmed her, made her simmer with life even if he did sometimes scorch her with his heat. And that's why she had come here tonight. She wanted to feel alive. Yet because she feared the depth of her feelings for him, she couldn't seem to keep her own weaknesses from goading her into hurting him.

"Why did you ask me that?" he repeated.

"I—I don't know," she said, unable to look at him—unable to be completely honest with him. "Because I-I'd like to keep this a business arrangement between us."

A short bark of sarcastic laugher escaped his lips. "That would be so much easier for you, wouldn't it?"

Adela tried to ignore his implication. "Mr. Leeds is buying a horse for me, and I also had him see about hiring men to watch the train depots in case Smeet tries to get away somewhere."

"You what!" He stalked toward her like a caged wildcat. "I wanted to take him by surprise."

"If Smeet is in Albuquerque, as you think, you can still take him by surprise," she argued. "But if we—"

"We?" He shook his head. "You're not going."

"—miss him," said Adela, raising her voice to be heard,

"perhaps someone else will see him and be able to catch him." In her own anger, she found it easier to meet his furious stare. "And I *am* going."

Several moments passed until his eyelids slid halfway closed, hinting at his resignation. He sighed. "Can you be ready to leave in the morning?"

Adela glanced at her hands. "That's another thing. Mr. Leeds needs a couple of days to get a horse for me and hire those men. In the meantime, he thinks Smeet might contact me concerning ransom."

Ladino shook his head and laughed. "You're still hoping that bastard will come here, aren't you? Adela, he'll just send one of his men, and then I'll have to hunt him down anyway. Damn!" He stepped closer, clasping her shoulders. "I'm tired of waiting."

"So am I," she murmured, her voice full of defeat. "I want to find my baby brother. He's the only family I have left."

"Adela . . ." he whispered, embracing her.

She pushed against his chest. "Please don't . . ."

Holding her close despite her struggles, he pressed her head to his shoulder. "I'll wait the two days," he whispered, stroking her head. "We'll go together."

As Ladino's crucifix dug into Adela's chest above her heart, branding her with the heat it had absorbed from his body, she could only think of her fury at God.

God. He had taken her jealousy of her little brother, and her attraction to this half-breed, and He had twisted it into His will to punish her. He'd taken her mother, He'd taken her brother, and now she feared He'd take Ladino, too. God would allow Smeet to kill them all, leaving her behind. Imprisoned in grief and duty. Alone.

She didn't know when Ladino's comforting embrace became something more, but as he continued to hold her, murmuring soft Apache words, she felt his hand move from her head to the small of her back. He pulled her hips tight against him, and through her nightdress and the sheet tied about his waist, she felt his masculinity harden against her lower belly. When she pulled back to look up at his face, he brought his hands up under her chin and began to untie her bonnet strings.

"Ladino . . ." Shaking her head, she reached up and covered his hands with hers.

He caught her fingers and pulled her hands away, pressing them instead to the ridges of muscle covering his ribs. Lowering his mouth, he teased her lips with his breath. Eyes open, she watched in wonder as his gaze radiated such feral appetite she felt as if he wanted to devour her very essence.

"Let me see your hair," he said, lifting his hands once more to the strings at her throat. "You only tease me with glimpses."

This time Adela swallowed her fear and let him untie the streamers. Why? Why was she allowing this to happen? She closed her eyes, steeling herself as he pulled her bonnet away from her head and tossed it on the nightstand. As the air rushed its cool, exploring fingers across her scalp, Adela felt as if he had ripped away a layer of her identity, leaving only deep insecurity in its place. What if he didn't like what he saw? What if the person she truly was beneath her bonnet no longer appealed to him?

"Your hair is short," he uttered in sad surprise. Adela's heart dove to the depths of humiliation. "Did you cut it to mourn your mother's death?"

Adela opened her eyes and looked up at him. She searched his face for some clue of how her appearance affected him. "No, my hair was cut when I became a novice. Do you think—? Is it ugly?"

Ladino smiled, his expression wistful. "No." He lifted both hands to her head and pushed his long fingers into what she knew must be a flattened mass of curls. As he lifted the locks away from her head and let them fall, she watched his lips curve into a smile. "No. Your hair is beautiful." A glow of appreciation warmed his eyes. "Like you."

Braver now, Adela smiled as she reached up and touched the soft strands of hair at his temple. She smoothed her hand down the long lock as it covered his chest and felt the smooth, hard expanse of muscle laced with scars. She fingered the hard nub of his nipple beneath the silken strands. A tremor shook him, and Adela felt it move through her own body, slowly becoming a burning ache as it settled deep within her womb.

"And your hair is beautiful . . . like you," she murmured.

"What do you want, Adela?" he asked, measuring her in his wary gaze. "This?" He settled his fingers on the row of buttons on the front of her nightdress.

Adela swallowed as he undid three and then stopped, looking at her, asking her with his puma's eyes how far she wanted to test her calling. "I—I . . ." Her voice faltered and she couldn't say all that she wanted to. *I want to be loved. I don't want to feel this pain anymore . . . this anger . . . this guilt.* "I want . . . to be free."

"How free?"

Free enough to take command of my identity, my womanhood, my soul without thought of the consequences.

"Free enough not to care about anything."

"Nothing is that free for long, Adela. Freedom has a price." He stepped away and untied the knot on the sheet, letting it fall to his feet like the quilt at the foot of the looking glass.

Ladino wore only the crucifix. The myriad scars on his fully aroused male body added erotic mystery to his sleek, animalistic beauty, while the new slash across his stomach shouted danger. "Touch me if you dare" his stance proclaimed. He stepped close once more, and Adela closed her eyes, feeling the insides of his wrists caress her nipples as he undid more buttons. A shudder of unease mingled with tremors of desire. But before she could pull away, he touched his lips to hers, and then he trailed his kiss to her cheek, her nose, her ear. Tingles raced down her arms in the wake of her nightdress sliding to the floor.

Stunned by the heat of his naked skin pressed against her own, Adela remembered the few times she'd dared to savor the sensuality of rubbing her soft inner thighs against each other at night. She wanted to touch him like this forever, to let his warmth melt into her own. But did she dare allow herself to burn for him now and throughout eternity? Could she welcome his fevered plundering of her womanhood . . . of her very soul?

Shaking, Adela pulled away. "I'm sorry," she whispered. "I—I don't think this is what I want after all." She covered herself as best she could with one trembling hand while she knelt down and grasped her nightdress with the other, slipping her arms back into the sleeves.

As she fumbled with the buttons, he covered her hands with his. "Are you sure?"

His voice warmed her like sun-drenched honey. Glancing up, she was instantly snared in the heady danger of his eyes.

"Yes," she replied. "No," she admitted, her voice low. "I'm not. I'm not sure at all."

As he pulled her with him, closer to the bed, she couldn't bring herself to stop him—didn't want to stop him. He sat down, splaying his hands across the top curve of her bottom as he pulled her between his legs—just as he had before their first kiss. That memory mingled with this experience in her mind until she lived them both, past and present.

Never taking his eyes from hers, even though she couldn't bring herself to hold his gaze for more than a second or two, he leaned down and slipped his hands beneath her gown at her ankles. He glided his hands up her calves, dipped them into the backs of her knees and then up the sides of her thighs until her nightdress bunched at her hips. He smiled with mischievous promise as he put his head under her nightgown and let the material drop around him, hiding his face from view.

Adela gasped when his mouth touched the flesh between her breasts, the same flesh he had claimed that night in the hospital when he had grabbed her nightdress. She released a throaty moan when he laved the cleft where her breast met her ribs, then circled his tongue ever closer to one hardened nipple, never quite touching it. As his hot breath continued to fan her body, Adela felt the fear, the exhilaration, the aching anticipation of some wild emotion she couldn't quite identify . . .

Freedom. Giving it a name seemed to give it a life, a fiery longing to escape her body and become itself.

When he pushed her away slightly and traced his lips down her stomach, her legs began to tremble. And when he flicked his tongue into her navel, then dried the moisture with a hot breath, every joint in her body melted.

Before she knew how or when, he had removed her nightgown. Leaning back on the bed, Ladino pulled her

Kelley Pounds

with him, sliding her atop his body. Slipping his smooth, hard thigh between hers, he flipped her over, leaving a sensation in the pit of her stomach like falling in a dream.

His hair fell down around them like a dark curtain, and he held her hands above her head as he moved his mouth over her body, continuing to torment her with the moist laving of his tongue. Adela shivered when the strands of mahogany silk caressed her cheek, her neck, her breasts, the insides of her arms . . .

Ladino stared down at her, his eyes amber bright. "Is this freedom you want worth a little pain, *shika?*"

Adela nodded, and as he released her hands from above her head, she moved her palms over his shoulders, feeling the thick strands of his hair glide over his skin. She twisted her fingers in his long tresses and pulled his face close. "Tell me what that means—*shika.*"

"My lover. My forbidden, illicit lover."

The words, his whispered voice, his warm breath against her skin sent chills throughout her body. She pulled him even closer, tilting her head to meet his kiss. Ladino teased her lips with his tongue, refusing to enter. Adela groaned, opening her mouth, begging him to meet her halfway. At last he touched the tip of his tongue to hers and moved his other thigh between her legs.

Holding his weight with one hand, he cupped her throat in his palm. "I haven't had a woman in seven years," he said, his fierce whisper heavy with desire. "And a woman like you?" He slid his palm down between her breasts. "Never . . ."

He lifted his torso off her body and sat back on his heels. In a mixture of modesty and longing, Adela tried to pull him back to her, but he resisted. Soon she no longer cared as he placed both hands on her breasts, circling

248

the nipples in his palms.

Adela shuddered, instinctively raising her legs up against his torso. Still watching her, still demanding her attention on his face, he smoothed his hands down her stomach. She could feel his rib muscles contract against her inner thighs as he pulled his hands even lower. At last he splayed his fingers across her belly and slid both thumbs into the cleft of her woman's flesh.

She gasped, trying in vain to pull her knees together. Her body went rigid, all thought concentrated on the warm pressure of his thumbs as he touched the place so secret she rarely dared touch it herself. He remained still, staring down into her face. Frightened, she gazed up at him, studying the savage strength of his smooth chest partially hidden behind the curtain of hair.

Just when she was about to speak, he began to rotate his thumbs. Slowly, a new tingling warmth suffused her. Her legs quivered with need under each measured stroke.

"Touch me," he whispered, then grasped her hand and moved it between them, curling her fingers around his manhood. He groaned, and Adela felt a contraction in her palm. His eyes closed and his face contorted as if in misery.

"Did I hurt you?"

His eyes still closed, he shook his head. "No," he managed in a breathless whisper.

She began to caress him, rubbing her thumb across the moist tip of his arousal, teasing him as he teased her, until finally, Ladino guided his manhood to the very place where his thumb had been. Lifting her, he slid deep inside her. Adela cried out as searing pain mixed with heightened erotic sensitivity.

Groaning, Ladino began to move within her. The pain subsided, yet Adela could not overcome her fear. She'd

gone too far. Regret nipped at her conscience. He seemed
to sense her reluctance and stopped, moving a hand up to
cradle her cheek, brushing his thumb across her lower lip.

"I'm afraid," she whispered.

"The freedom comes after the pain, *shika,*" he whispered. "*Shilhú'ash.* Go with me and we'll find it.
Eim'báhshay," he whispered, the sound a caress along her
ear. "*Eim'báhshay,*" he repeated, the word itself a seductive
whisper. "Make love to me, *shitsíné.*" He began to move
again, and Adela's fear slowly gave way to renewed trust as
he continued to whisper in her ear. "Hold me like I'm
holding you, Adela. It feels so good to be inside you, to be
one with you like this."

He slid one of his hands down between them, caressing
her with a finger even as he stroked inside her, moving
within her. Adela whimpered and felt herself tighten around
him. He groaned, a look almost of pain filling his eyes as
Adela began to move with him, her rhythm awkward as she
strove to meet his thrusts, desperate to become part of him
as he was part of her.

"Don't think, *shitsíné,*" he whispered. "Don't try to control," he said, increasing the pace. "Just feel. Let yourself
feel. *Shilhú'ash,*" he said again. "Go with me."

She hooked her heels at the backs of his knees and
opened her thighs fully, understanding at last, tilting to
meet each stroke without thought. Instinct took over and
she let her body guide her. He moved both hands to clutch
her buttocks. She tilted even more, understanding on a
primal level that he wanted to be even closer to her, closer
to her very soul.

He thrust harder, guiding her, helping her, pulling her to
meet him. Something began to happen, to unfurl inside her.
Bloom upon bloom upon bloom of sensation.

Freedom. It cascaded over her body like a waterfall . . . like Ladino's hair caressing her naked skin.

Freedom. She felt it even in his weight as he pinned her beneath him, holding her so tightly, so tenderly she cried.

Half an hour later, Ladino kissed her forehead as she lay beside him, her head nestled within the crook of his elbow. He wanted to hold Adela like this forever. If he remembered nothing else, he wanted to remember how soft her skin felt next to his . . . how incredible he had felt wrapped inside her. He felt a tingle in his eyes as he smoothed his hand down her body, from breast, to waist, to hip, reveling in the power of his rediscovered masculinity as she clung to him in sleep, clutching his hair while tiny aftershocks rocked her body.

Ladino had never thought himself capable of feeling this immersed in emotion for a woman. He didn't know if it was love he felt for Adela, but he hoped he'd at least given her a taste of the freedom he had experienced in her body's embrace.

A strange weight on her waist and the sound of deep sleep breathing not her own pulled Adela awake. Slowly she opened her eyes. Soft lamplight emphasized the darkness still bathing the window, and projected on the wall she saw the silhouette of her body nestled within Ladino's embrace.

How long had she slept? She couldn't be certain. Long enough for images of Ladino's lovemaking to torture her dreams . . . to writhe in bed with her, to crush her beneath pain and self-condemnation until her heart and soul knew no peace.

Carefully, so as not to rouse him, she tried to lift his arm from around her waist. He groaned, clutching her even

251

tighter. Did he really want her so close to his side? Did she really mean so much to him? Did she really want to leave him?

No. But she had to. She'd blasphemed God. She'd lost her vocation. She'd chosen to believe in the transitory illusion of human comfort, when she should have been open to God's divine healing. The only way to put her heart right again was to gather the shredded remnants of her faith and confess to Father Bourgade.

Adela lifted Ladino's arm again, and this time he turned over, muttering in his sleep. She slipped out of bed and hurried on tiptoe to the nightstand close to Ladino's head. Plucking her nightgown from the floor, she yanked it over her head. And as she put on her bonnet, tying the strings beneath her chin, she allowed herself a tearful study of Ladino's sleeping form.

If she couldn't allow herself to continue loving him, perhaps she could make amends to God by preventing Ladino from committing violence in order to save his soul.

She only hoped her own soul deserved redemption.

Chapter Sixteen

Nigel read the obituary once more and smiled to himself as he tossed the *Albuquerque Daily Journal* atop the growing pile at the end of the kitchen table. Like alley cats on rats, the nosy reporters had somehow managed to pounce on the details of Jonathan Westbrook's will.

"Well, little Master Westbrook," he began, looking down at the bundle of bargaining advantage on his lap. "Didn't I tell you things would look up for your new father? Your mother is dead, as she deserves to be, and your sister, the silly little nun, will be the perfect target for my ransom demands. Tell me, my boy, should we ask for all of it, or should we be content with a third?"

Jonathan Junior dropped the watch fob he'd been playing with and stared up into Nigel's face. Still too heavy for his tiny neck, his head wobbled in a movement imitating agreement.

Nigel smiled. "You are quite right. Even a third would buy us a grand house in London."

The infant smiled, revealing toothless gums, and Nigel was helpless to fight the unexpected burst of affection. He hadn't believed a man like himself capable of fatherly emotions. But he had decided that by raising the boy as his own, a part of Jonathan Westbrook would always belong to him . . . a part that would never betray him or refute his existence.

Jonathan Junior turned his concentration back to the chain looped at the front of Nigel's vest. Nigel took the watch out of his pocket and flipped open the lid. The ticking entranced the baby, and he gurgled as he touched the crystal, trying to close his fingers around the black pointed hands beneath.

"Soon we will have the time of our lives, Master Westbrook."

The infant gurgled in response.

If only other parts of his life could change for the better so neatly. Nigel had hoped their greater distance from the opium dens would deter Perry's roamings, but short of locking the bloody fool up with the Apache woman, Nigel couldn't keep him home. Just two hours ago he'd sent Ben to fetch Perry yet again, hoping to avoid being manipulated into going to town himself. The prospect didn't seem likely.

Nigel snapped his watch shut and replaced it in his pocket. The child frowned and fussed, drooling down the front of his nightdress and over Nigel's hand as he grasped at the fob.

"Now, now," Nigel chided, taking out his handkerchief. He wiped his fingers and the infant's chin. With a squall of rage, the Westbrook heir voiced his disgust at the assault, turning his face away. "You mustn't grow impatient," Nigel scolded. "Patience is a virtue, and it's best you learn that now if you wish to have your way in life."

Still the baby howled, and Nigel tried to cover his mouth like he'd seen the Apache woman do. The infant's rage increased, adding fuel to Nigel's hateful envy of the woman's affinity with the child. He tried shifting positions, but the babe's shrill screams rent his eardrums and sliced a shudder down his spine.

"Are you hungry? Is that what's wrong?"

Nigel shifted the boy to his shoulder, and the new position quieted the infant into a weak whine accompanied by hiccups. Nigel yanked a skeleton key from a nearby hook, and after some one-handed fumbling with lock and knob, he opened the Apache woman's door. Light from the kitchen spilled to the corner where she huddled, untied for the last three days.

On the first day of her new "freedom," she had broken up the washstand, hitting Nigel over the head with one of the legs. He'd given her a sound beating, and then he'd removed every last piece of furniture, including the bed. In order to make escape impossible, Nigel had even nailed boards over the windows. The woman hated him for her prison of perpetual darkness; he could see it in her bruised face and vicious glare as she pushed up from the floor.

"It's time to feed the child so I can put him back to sleep."

Nigel grabbed the lamp from the shelf outside her door and met her in the middle of the room. As he handed her Jonathan Junior, he noticed her broken nails and bloody fingers. No doubt she'd been trying to claw the boards off the windows. Nigel smirked, but she avoided his attention, flicking a speculative glance instead to the kerosene lamp in his hand. Obediently she turned back and sank down against the wall in her familiar corner.

Realizing who held him now, who fed him, the baby's whimpers ceased. Resentment curdled in Nigel's gut.

The door slammed in the other room, and Nigel heard just one set of footfalls across the plank floor. Damn! That either meant Perry was unconscious again, or that he'd have to go fetch the bloody fool himself after all.

"Mr. Smeet?" Ben asked, his voice proclaiming exhaustion.

"In here!" Nigel barked.

Ben strode into the room, and Nigel noticed a spot of

blood marring the skin beneath his nose. "The chinks threw me out."

"Bloody hell! Are you completely worthless, or just stupid?" Nigel backhanded Ben. The boy staggered, barely catching himself on the edge of the open door. "Damned politician's bastard! I should have put a stop to his games long ago." Reining in his anger, he lowered his voice. "Have you saddled my horse?"

"Yessir."

"Watch the Apache bitch." Nigel handed Ben the lamp and stalked from the room.

As Nigel rode back to the adobe, he saw fire shimmering against the dark silhouette of the Sandia Mountains. Even from here, he could smell the smoke. He spurred his mount into a lope, leading Perry's horse behind him, with Perry himself lashed facedown across the saddle. Perry grunted and groaned at each impact, but Nigel concentrated on deciphering the position of the enormous orange glow. Was it the roof of the adobe on fire? The sense of foreboding in Nigel's chest gave him his answer.

When he reached the yard, flames writhed and roared, devouring the wooden roof. While the boarded windows of the Apache woman's room remained dark, the other windows glowed like eyes from hell. The fire licked out the open door, but hadn't yet reached the *chamiso* bushes or the stables.

Nigel's mount reared as he vaulted off its back. Yanking the animal's head down by the reins, Nigel tied the horse to the hitch rail. As he ran toward the house, heat seared his lungs. Just outside the doorway he found Ben's body, the stolen gun and belt clutched in one out-flung hand. Grabbing Ben by the back of his red flannel combinations,

Nigel dragged him away from the house, scanning the yard and surrounding landscape for any sign of the woman and child.

Nigel flipped the young gunman over on his back. "Ben!" he shouted, slapping the boy's face until he coughed and sputtered his way to consciousness. "Ben, where's the woman and the boy?"

"Gone," Ben rasped, pushing up on his elbows.

"In the fire?"

Ben shook his head. "Gone. Escaped." This time he coughed so hard he leaned to the side and retched, but nothing came up.

Nigel knew the boy needed water before he would be able to explain, so he rushed to get the canteen from the saddle and hurried back. After uncorking the vessel, he handed it to Ben. The youth drank, taking ragged breaths between swallows.

"Took me by surprise," Ben choked out. "The baby woke up." More coughs wracked his frame. "I took him in to her. Didn't know she'd be that strong—or that fast. She hit me in the head."

"With what?"

"Floor plank." Ben coughed, retching again.

Visions of the woman's bloody fingers clawed Nigel's memory, taunting him for his stupidity.

"And th' baby." Nigel grabbed Ben's shoulders and shook him. "Where's Jonathan Junior?"

"Took him with her," he squeezed out before dissolving into another coughing spell.

Nigel stood up and paced. "Damn that bitch! I'll kill 'er when I find 'er." The Cockney had slipped back into Nigel's voice, but he no longer cared as he turned on his heel and rushed back to Ben. "I'm goin' after 'er. And

257

you're gettin' on the train to Silver City. You'll meet that nun, and you'll get that million dollars. That Apache bitch will not ruin my plans. With that money I can live like a bloody king! And I will raise my son. *My son,*" he repeated, shaking his fist. "*Mine.*"

"What about . . . Perry?"

Reminded of Perry's inert body still draped over the horse, Nigel stopped. Behind him a window exploded, and the fire whooshed its way to freedom amidst shards of shattered glass. Smaller fires bloomed to life among nearby bushes and trailed vines of destruction across the grass.

He stormed back to Perry's horse and untied the knots in the rope. Perry's drugged, emaciated body slid off the saddle and slumped at the feet of the skittish animal.

Nigel turned a livid gaze to Ben. "Get up."

"But—"

"Get up," he repeated. "You'll 'elp me toss the wretch into 'ell where 'e belongs. Bastard's cost me everything, and I'll be damned if I'll let anyone take me for a fool again."

"Mr. Smeet, please!" Ben struggled up, still clutching the gun belt. Another coughing bout seized his body, doubling him over. "No . . ." he croaked out, shaking his head.

Nigel slid his pistol from his shoulder holster and aimed it at the boy. "Take a look, Benjamin. The bloody fool will be like this the rest of 'is wretched life. Ye'd be doin' 'im a favor," he cajoled, even as he clicked back the hammer. "One worthless man is already dead at your 'ands. What's another?"

Pressing his finger on the trigger, Nigel measured Ben. Terror warred with indecision on the boy's face, and Nigel saw his hand move to the grip of the half-breed's gun. Nigel lowered his aim and pulled the trigger, shooting the dirt at

Ben's feet. Ben jumped back, dropping the gun belt to the ground.

"Don't ye dare cross me, Benjamin."

"But, Mr. Smeet—"

Aiming at Ben's chest, Nigel cocked the hammer. He pressed his finger on the trigger, preparing for the moment of crisis when the gun would explode. "Come 'ere, Benjamin."

The boy's expression changed from horror and disbelief to the crush of defeat and self-loathing. Skirting Nigel, Ben walked forward, nearing the unconscious form in the dirt. Nigel re-holstered his gun, and together they lifted Perry by the arms and legs and carried him to the burning house. When they drew as near the searing blaze as they could, they tossed Perry's body through the door and into the flames.

Perry's screams rent the air, and Nigel laughed. "Burn in hell!" he bellowed. His laughter deepened with satisfaction as he exorcised the last shred of weakness from his soul and baptized himself in the fire of complete power and control.

Waking up before the others, Adela packed quickly and slipped downstairs, determined to cross the street to St. Vincent de Paul's before she left with Ladino. The moment she stepped out the front door, her hand still on the knob, she heard a moccasined foot slide across the porch floor.

"Where are you going, Adela?"

Ladino's soft inquisition sent tremors to her toes. She turned and met his eyes. "I'm going across the street."

"Why?"

"To speak to Father Bourgade." Trying for an attitude of nonchalance, Adela turned and pulled the door closed behind her.

"Why?" he asked again.

She looked away, embarrassed by the half-lie about to escape her lips. "It's . . . customary . . . to go to confession before one travels. One never knows how dangerous a journey will—"

"Bullshit. *One* is lying to me."

Adela swallowed and forced herself to look at him. "All right. I—I need absolution," she admitted, her determination to tell the truth overcoming her fear. "What I did the other night was wrong, for more than just the obvious reason."

"Because you plan to become a nun?"

Adela nodded. "It's more than just that. I . . ." She swallowed again. "I was unfair to you."

"I'll be the judge of that." He rose from his chair. "Why don't we go inside and talk about this."

"I wasn't the one lying in wait on the porch," she shot back.

"You've been avoiding me. How else was I going to get you to talk to me but to catch you by surprise?"

"All right, let's go in the parlor." She led the way back inside, dread wrapping around her like a shroud as he closed the parlor doors behind them.

"Now why do you think you're not being fair to me, Adela?"

"It was wrong. A spiritual weakness. Instead of seeking comfort where I should have . . . with God, I—I went to you."

"It's not wrong to reach out to another person when you're grieving, Adela."

"The way I did it is."

"You told me you wanted to be free."

"I know," she admitted, twisting her hands and rubbing

her thumbs. "And you told me that nothing is that free for long. Well, you were right. Our . . . night together . . . might have cost me everything."

Adela couldn't admit it to him, but she was afraid her love for him had demanded her very soul in payment. How could she love him and live the life she'd planned for herself? How could she make amends to God for turning her back on Him in such a grievous manner?

Ladino stepped near and lifted the cross of her gold and black onyx rosary nestled in the folds of her habit skirt. His proximity brought back memories of the east wind and its promise of rain mixed with the scent of their passion.

He fingered a gold bead and looked up at her. A derisive smile curved his lips. "Is this supposed to impress the priest with the wealth of your new conviction?"

"No," she answered, pulling the chaplet out of his hand. "It belonged to my great-great-grandmother," she explained in a voice laced with sorrow as she let the beads dangle from her belt once more. "My mother gave it to me."

He fell quiet at that, and Adela wanted to feel vindicated, but she couldn't. She wondered only how her ancestor had felt when confronted with these emotions. Or had her great-great-grandmother never truly wanted to be a nun as Adela did?

"It's to remind me of my promise to God and to myself," she added, turning her back on him and facing the cold fireplace. "The other night I forgot that promise."

"And you think confessing to some priest is going to change what happened?" He grabbed her arm and swung her to face him. "I washed the sheet after you left, Adela, so no one else would know but me. Nothing will burn that memory from my mind."

Adela stared up at him, unable to speak at first, to explain. Her words hid, forcing her to search for them and pull them out like stubborn children. "I know nothing will change what happened," she whispered. "But the reason—" No. That wasn't right. How could she explain? "Remember I told you that one night not to take your anger out on me?" She sighed. "Well, that's what I did. I was angry—"

"Angry at me?"

"No. Angry at myself," she admitted. "Angry at God for taking my mother away from me. I wanted to punish Him for punishing me." She rubbed her temple with her fingers. "I . . . I want to become a nun. I've wanted to take vows since I was fourteen. I know what we did was . . . *seemed* . . . beautiful—"

"If it was so damned beautiful, why are you trying to deny it now?"

"Because . . ." She pressed her hand to her forehead. *Because I could lose myself in the kind of freedom you give me, and that terrifies me.* "Because it goes against every vow I've ever wanted to take. The convent is the only home I've ever known. I want safety and security, and I have that there. That's what I've worked for, and when all of this is over, that is the life I want to go back to. You're not what I want in my life."

"You want prison."

"The convent is not a prison. And being a Sister of Charity is a worthwhile calling. It's what God has chosen for me to do."

His lips tilted in a mocking smile. "You get yourself mixed up with God too much. You want prison, yet you blame it on God."

"That's not what I'm saying!"

"So go confess then, if it makes you feel better to put

262

your guilt off on a priest," he said, his voice a cruel slice on her heart. "Tell him everything we did together, Adela. Tell him how I made you feel. Tell him about the damn bloody sheets!"

"Ladino—"

"Apologize to the priest." He stalked from the parlor, his long hair lifting on the breeze with each angry step.

Adela thought about going after him, but as she heard him tramp up the stairs, she decided such an action would only be a further blow to his pride as well as her own. Instead, she stiffened her back and walked out the front door, her stride never faltering as she crossed the street.

Only when she mounted the steep steps of St. Vincent de Paul's and opened the massive front doors did her heart begin to race. The cool adobe interior smelled of age, musty earth . . . and sanctity. An old woman knelt in one of the pews, her voice a fervent song as she recited her rosary.

Steeling herself, Adela turned to the confessional ornamented with red velvet curtains and Gothic spires. She took one step closer, and then another, until she stood with her hand poised on the curtain. Father Bourgade would never tell, but what would he think? And what would she think once the priest knew her weaknesses—her love for an earthly man and her faithlessness to her God and Savior.

"Enter, my child," she heard him say in his French accent.

She couldn't do it. She couldn't share what had happened between Ladino and herself with another living person. Blasphemy! God would find a way to punish her for this, too, but she wouldn't punish herself—at least not with a confession to Father Bourgade.

Adela stepped away from the curtain and made her way slowly up the center aisle, keeping her eyes trained on the crucifix above the altar table. When she reached the rail, she genuflected deeply, solemnly, making the sign of the cross. She kneeled and then lay prostrate before the altar, listening to the old woman's musical voice as it filled the nave.

"Forgive me, Father, for I have sinned," Adela whispered, her breath stirring the dust on the rough wooden planks of the floor. *"Mea culpa, mea culpa, mea maxima culpa."*

Ladino found the horse he'd ridden to Silver City in the stables behind the Westbrook home. He'd just yanked the saddle cinch tight and was leading the gelding out the door when he saw Judith burst out the kitchen door and run across the yard.

"Mr. Ladino!" she yelled. "Some little boy brought this message for Sister Adela. He ran away before I could ask him any questions." She handed Ladino the sealed envelope. "Do you think it might be about the baby?"

Ladino didn't answer as he slid his bowie out of his moccasin and slit the flap. Still holding the knife, he read the note.

Meet me behind the Sugarman boardinghouse on the corner of Bullard and Broadway at ten o'clock tomorrow morning. Bring one million dollars. Do not notify the authorities or I'll kill the baby. I will approach you only when I see that you're alone. Don't make a mistake or your baby brother dies.

So. She'd gotten her ransom note after all. Ladino wanted to laugh at the irony of it, but all humor had withered in his heart. He handed the note back to Judith, who scanned it and stared up at him with wide eyes.

"From Smeet?"

Ladino nodded. "But you can bet he didn't come here

himself. Not after the failed blackmail attempt." He shoved his knife back into his moccasin, his purpose renewed tenfold as he led his horse down the gravel carriage drive to the front gate.

Judith kept pace, trotting at his side. "What do I tell Sister Adela?"

Ladino stopped, staring at the open doors of the church. Like a childish fool, he waited for a moment to see if Adela would emerge and see him leaving, but he waited in vain.

"Tell her I've gone to find Smeet's lackey."

"Are you coming back?" she asked. "Sister Adela will be upset that you left without her."

He turned to Judith. "Then tell her I'll be back when I have the baby." Sending one last glance at the church, Ladino mounted and kicked his horse into motion through the open carriage gate.

Ignoring the startled glances as he rode down Bullard Street a few minutes later, Ladino found the Sugarman boardinghouse. Right across the street stood the two-story Meredith and Ailman bank with its large windows and cast-iron face. He smiled at the logic; a room on the street side of the boardinghouse would afford a perfect view of a woman in a black habit entering the bank to make a withdrawal. More so, whoever spied on the bank would never believe a nun wise enough to suspect she was being watched. They didn't know Adela. Still, he didn't doubt that the person Smeet had sent would be keeping a close eye on the bank even now, knowing the message had arrived at the Westbrook home.

Guiding his horse to the hitch rail, Ladino glanced up at the second-floor windows of the boardinghouse. In the middle window he saw a young man's pale face peeking around the edge of a curtain, watching the comings and goings across the street.

He knew that face. It was the damn coward who had left him for dead. What was more, it appeared he worked for Smeet.

He dismounted, ignoring the ogling of passersby as he continued to stare at the face in the window. As if called by the silent, shaking rage in every muscle and tendon of Ladino's body, the youth looked down and met his gaze. Shock and terror fluttered across the coward's face, and the white curtain whipped back into place.

Guessing the kid would attempt to escape out the back, Ladino looped the horse's reins around the hitch rail and vaulted up onto the boardwalk at the corner of the boardinghouse. He raced to the back of the building and hid under the stairs. Drawing his knife out of his moccasin, he crouched, ready to pounce.

He didn't have to wait long for the clatter of boot heels down the rough staircase. When the boy hit the last step, Ladino sprang. He yanked the kid around and slammed him up against the brick wall under the stairs, shoving the knife against his throat. Ladino sized him up, noticing his own black leather gun belt slung low on the coward's hips.

"I—I thought you were dead!" The youth's Adam's apple grazed the blade as he swallowed.

"You think a dead man could slit you from ear to ear?"

The adolescent shook like a deer, and like his mountain lion namesake, Ladino couldn't resist toying with his prey. He pushed the knife closer to the boy's throat, reveling in how his hatred burned Adela's softness from his system.

"H-how did you find me?"

Ladino laughed low in his throat. "It's not how I found you, but how you found me—again," he said. "I believe this is mine." He yanked at the buckle on the gun belt, loosening it. When the rig fell free, Ladino whipped it out and rolled it up with one hand, then held it to his side. "What's your name, kid?"

The coward swallowed again. Ladino drew a tiny bead of blood on his throat, and the boy closed his eyes. "Ben," he whispered.

"Did Smeet send you down here?"

"Smeet? Who's Smeet?"

Ladino flipped his knife to the other side of the boy's throat. Ben pushed his head back so hard against the brick wall, Ladino thought the boy would choke on his own tongue.

"And what about the baby?" Ladino asked. Ben's eyes opened wide, and Ladino smiled. "I know all about what Smeet is up to, and you're going to tell me what you came to tell Sister Adela."

"You know the nun?"

Ladino ignored his question. "*Where* is the baby?"

"Smeet has him near Albuquerque." Ben's gaze scuttled away, then back again. An Apache might look away out of respect when speaking to someone, but Ladino recognized a white man's lie when he saw it.

"Where is the baby?" Ladino repeated, drawing a shallow, inch-long line of blood on the liar's throat. "If you don't tell me now, you'll never talk again."

"The Apache woman took him," he admitted.

Stunned, Ladino frowned. "What Apache woman?"

"Umm . . . uhh—"

"What woman, damn it!"

"I—I think Smeet called her One With No Relatives."

Duu Yáabit'ékédán. She'd only been a child in Estrellito's band, no older than Judith's boy, Jaime, when last he saw her.

"She was with Pajaro. She'd lost her own baby—"

"Where did she take him?"

The boy looked down at Ladino's hand, then back up into his eyes. "I don't know."

Ladino nicked another line, longer this time. Blood trailed down Ben's neck, soaking into his collar.

"I'm tellin' you, I don't know!" The adolescent's voice rose in panic. "He was gonna trail her. He figured she'd head south."

"To Pajaro's stronghold?"

"I guess."

"And where's that?"

"Somewhere in the Guadalupes, but not even Mr. Smeet knows exactly where."

"You sure about that?"

"If he does, he never told me." The boy squirmed. "He plans to kill the Apache woman when he finds her. Pajaro is still supposed to be in Mexico, but Smeet won't want to take any chances. He'll try to catch her before she gets too far."

"And just when was the baby supposed to be delivered?"

Ben shuffled his feet.

"When?" Ladino repeated.

"Mr. Smeet wasn't gonna bring the baby. H-he was gonna take the money and head east on the train, then go to England."

"Just what was he planning to do with the baby, abandon him? Murder him?"

Ben shook his head. "No. He was gonna keep him."

Once again Ladino felt shoved off balance. "Keep him?"

"Yeah. Thinks he wants to be the baby's father."

Ladino couldn't imagine Smeet feeling any brand of human emotion. To think of Smeet raising the child as his own son defied comprehension. What would he teach the boy? Hatred?

Of course if the woman were successful in getting away and taking the baby back to the stronghold, Smeet's plans would be ruined. But that would make him a desperate man—a dangerous man.

"When did the woman leave?"

"A couple of days ago. About three in the morning. Smeet found a few tracks headin' back through the Sandias."

Ladino knew that meant the woman would continue to use the cover of the mountain chains running south. She'd know where to find water and how to locate hidden supply caches.

"I'll let you live, Ben," said Ladino, drawing a deliberate line across the boy's throat—not too deep, just enough to cut his point home. "But if I ever see you again, I'll slit your throat. Remember that next time you look in the mirror."

Adela shut the front door quietly behind her, not wanting Ladino to know she'd come back just yet. She needed a few more minutes alone to collect her thoughts before they left. On second thought, perhaps she should apologize. How would he react when she told him she hadn't been able to confess?

Hoping he would still be in his room, she hurried up the stairs before she could change her mind. His door was closed, so she knocked. "May I come in?"

No reply. Was he so angry with her he refused to speak? She turned the knob and pushed the door wide. Only an eerie silence met her intrusion. She peered inside and saw that the bed had been made.

Knowing he would be ready to leave, the sight shouldn't

have alarmed her, yet she couldn't shake the sense of dread that choked her breath. She rushed across the room and opened the nightstand drawer. All that remained was her old handkerchief.

Empty. His knife was gone.

Adela sank back on the bed, fighting tears as she held the thin square of material he'd left behind—a blatant message that he had no more use for her softness or her hypocrisy. The betrayal and panic of being abandoned yet again wrenched her heart. This was why she'd never wanted to love him. Not only did he have a nomad's soul, but his only purpose in life was his drive for revenge.

Maybe Ladino had talked to Judith before he'd left. Adela shoved the handkerchief in her pocket and rushed from the room. She sped down the stairs and through the dining room into the kitchen. Judith stood at the worktable, peering out the window as she laid strips of dough in a lattice pattern across the top of a dried apple pie.

"Have you seen Mr. Ladino?"

The woman jumped. "Oh! Sister Adela, you're back. I've been watching for you, but I must have missed you crossing the street."

"Where is Mr. Ladino?"

"He—he left, but a—"

"Without me?"

"Yes. But a message came. A request for ransom."

Before Adela could speak, the door swung open and Ladino stepped into the kitchen. He stopped short, staring at her, his face devoid of emotion.

Judith's gaze jumped from him to Adela. She quickly finished weaving her dough lattice and put the pie in the oven. "I'll go check and see if the clothes on the line are dry." She wiped her hands on her apron and hurried out the still-open kitchen door, shutting it behind her.

Adela focused on Ladino. "Where did you go?" she asked, chiding herself for the accusing anxiety in her voice. "Judith said there was a message."

Ladino nodded. "I was getting ready to go after Smeet myself when it came." He stepped closer. "I found the coward who attacked me. Smeet sent him to get the ransom. But Smeet no longer has your baby brother."

"What? Who does?"

"An Apache woman from—"

"An Apache woman?"

Ladino grabbed Adela by the arms and gave her a quick shake. "Let me finish!"

Adela gasped, speechless. As Ladino stared at her, she thought she saw in his eyes a hint of the same emotion she wanted to exorcise from her own mind and heart. He released her and stepped several paces away, until he stood near the kitchen window next to the worktable.

"I'm going after the Apache woman," he said at last. "She escaped Smeet and she's headed south. The boy thinks she's going to Pajaro's stronghold in the Guadalupes. I'm going to try to intercept her in the Sacramentos before she gets too far south. It'll probably take me six or seven days to reach the Mescalero Reservation." Ladino crossed his arms over his chest. "I came back for you if you still want to go with me."

Adela could see the emotion it had cost him to make his decision. She knew he wanted nothing more than to forget about her, to leave her behind. Yet he had come back. As angry as he had been, he had kept his promise.

God forgive her, but despite her fresh vows, Adela discovered she loved him even more.

"I'll get my things."

Chapter Seventeen

"I shouldn't have gone back for her . . ."

The words echoed in Ladino's mind, keeping time with each climbing hoofbeat of Adela's horse as she followed him high into the rugged San Andres Mountains.

For the last four days he'd done nothing but question his sanity. With just the horses and a fire to keep them company, Ladino had lain awake each night watching her sleep in the orange glow. Despite his anger, or maybe because of it, he had been forced to call on every drop of his willpower not to steal around the fire and arouse her in her sleep. He fantasized about making her beg for what he alone could give her . . . for what she alone could give him. He wanted her to admit it and then invite him to awaken the fire he found only inside her body.

Ladino shook his head to disburse the erotic images, reminding himself that she had come for her brother's sake, and her quiet resolve should be enough to convince him to keep his distance.

His horse stumbled and he swayed in the saddle. He pushed himself upright, then peeked over his shoulder to see if she had noticed. Too late he realized she had.

"Are you all right?" She urged her horse toward him between yucca plants, juniper trees, and boulders.

"Fine."

"Are you feeling dizzy?"

"I said I'm fine." He reined his horse's head away from her. "We'll make camp when we get to the top of the next rise."

A snake's rattle sounded. Adela's horse reared and screamed. She screamed too, grasping her horse's mane and crouching low over the animal's neck as it bucked. Ladino tried to reach over and grab her mount's bridle, but the horse swung its head out of his grasp. One high kick of the beast's hindquarters tossed Adela over its head. She tumbled down the hill and crashed over the rocks, sliding, twisting, her breath bursting from her lungs in short grunts. Her horse bolted away, dragging its reins through rocks and bushes.

As he urged his mount down the hill, Ladino saw the rattler slither away, twitching its tail in short rattles of warning. The unusual behavior sent a shiver of gooseflesh down his arms.

When he reached Adela, she had come to a stop in a heap at the base of a juniper tree. A grimace of pain tightened her face as she pushed herself into a sitting position on shaking arms.

He vaulted off his horse. "Are you all right?" he asked, crouching beside her, steadying her with his hand on her back.

"I'm . . . okay," she pushed out, then bent over her knees and coughed so hard Ladino thought she would faint. Finally she pulled in a good breath. "Oh!" she exclaimed, picking something up and dusting it off—a corncob wrapped in a bedraggled scrap of calico. "Abbie."

"Abbie?"

"My doll. She must have"—another cough wracked her body—"fallen out of my pocket."

"Your doll?" He noticed a faintly painted face, but other than that, nothing about the cob looked like any doll he'd ever seen. "It doesn't have any hair." The comment was out

273

of his mouth before he thought.

"Neither do I," she quipped, pocketing her doll.

And then her expression changed, her huge brown eyes filling with a shy embarrassment. Despite his concern, memories of their lovemaking filled his mind. Shoving those thoughts away, he lifted her chin with his finger and peered at her face.

"Pretty scratched up," he said of the bleeding contusions on her forehead and chin. Noticing how her habit sleeve had fallen limply around her wrist, he took her hand and folded her cape up over her shoulder, revealing several deep scrapes above the garter that held up her white undersleeve. "These wounds need tending."

"Well, we'll have to . . . do it without my medicine," she said, coughing to the side before glancing back at him. "My bag of tricks just . . . trotted away." Her eyes widened. "Oh, no!"

"What?"

"My rosary is in my saddlebags! We have to get the horse."

"To hell with the horse!" He wanted to shoot the animal, but he knew he was just as much to blame. "The worthless beast will wander back on its own."

"Are you sure?"

He nodded. "Let's get you somewhere more comfortable." Wrapping his arm around her waist, he helped her stand. Her body shook, and a triangular flap of material dropped open in her skirt. Holding her up as she walked, he guided her to a sheltered area within a group of boulders and trees.

The site provided one of the best vantage points in the San Andres range. After the sheer drop-off only a few feet away to the east, vast dunes of white sand spread out in the

Tularosa Basin. Far beyond that rose the Sierra Blanca and Sacramento Mountains where the reservation beckoned, like Alcatraz Island in a sea of false freedom.

"Thank you," Adela murmured as he helped her sit down on the largest boulder.

"I'll get my canteen so we can wash away the blood." Ladino turned back to his own mount.

"What about saving the water to drink?"

"I know of a spring nearby, and a cache," he assured her. "I'll go after more water and some supplies so you can mend your habit." He fetched the canteen and brought it back. "Do you have something to use to clean your wounds?"

She let out a choking laugh. "I'm layered in material. I'm sure I can . . . find some small corner that isn't too dirty."

Ladino uncorked the canteen and offered it to her. Adela took a quick swallow and handed it back. "Thank you," she said, then wiped her mouth on the back of the habit sleeve still intact. "Deplorable manners," she said, her grin sheepish.

Bending over, she lifted the dusty hem of her habit and peeked up at him as she ripped the first strip from her petticoat and put it in her lap. A few moments later, he took one of the strips and doused it with water. He was just about to bathe the gash on her arm when she touched his hand, stopping him.

"I can do it," she murmured, taking the pad. She lifted her arm so she could see. The cut continued to bleed, so she pressed the pad over it and rested her arm at her side.

"I'll wash your face." Ladino wet another strip from her lap. He dabbed at her forehead, and then at her chin, trying to ignore the fact that she watched his face as he worked.

"There," he pronounced. "Anywhere else?"

At last she dropped her gaze. "I think I have a scrape or two on my legs, but I'll tend to them."

"Has your arm quit bleeding yet?"

Raising her arm, she lifted the pad. "It appears so."

"I'll get some *nopal*."

"*Nopal?*"

"Prickly pear," he explained. "It makes a good poultice."

He turned and found a cactus nearby, just down the hill close to where she'd fallen. After removing his headwrap and spreading it out on a rock, he carefully cut off several leaves, setting them atop the red cloth. Once he had enough, he bundled them up and carried them back to where she sat. He stripped the spines from one of the pieces with deft strokes of his knife, leaving only a juicy fillet in his palm. This he placed over the gash on her arm, tying it in place with another petticoat strip.

Busy slicing more pieces of cactus, he was startled by a feather-light touch on his forehead. He looked up and found her studying his tattoo as she traced it with her fingertips.

"Does the H stand for half-breed?" she murmured, lowering her hand to her lap. "I've always wanted to ask."

"Yes," he replied, trying to keep his voice emotionless as he went back to slicing.

"Why do you always keep it covered?"

He glanced up at her, propping the handle of his knife on one knee. "And have everyone know I was a convict? It's bad enough being a half-breed without proclaiming the fact with the tattoo."

"And you don't—with your long hair and the way you dress?"

"That's my choice," he said. "The tattoo was forced on

me. I don't like seeing the expression on people's faces when they see it. It's like having my power taken away from me all over again. At least when people see me in the clothes I choose to wear, they see what I want them to see."

He sliced another piece of *nopal* and placed it over the abrasion on her forehead. "Hold that there for a minute."

While she pressed the fillet to her wound, he cut a strip of petticoat to length. Trying to avoid touching her fingers with his own, he covered the *nopal* with the fabric and wrapped the makeshift bandage around her head. As he knotted the material, she gazed up at him from within the circle of his arms. Her face was so close, her expression so earnest and endearing, that another wave of emotion crashed down on his heart. He averted his gaze and backed away, smashing a piece of prickly pear between forefinger and thumb.

"And here's some for your chin." He smeared the substance on the smaller abrasion. "No bandage for that one." Fighting deeper emotions with an attempt at humor, he grinned and said, "If I cover up any more of your head with material, you won't be able to open your mouth to boss me around." Feigning a speculative expression, he reached for another piece of petticoat. "On second thought . . ."

Scowling, she yanked the strip out of his hand.

Ladino laughed, the sound soft at first but growing louder the longer he looked at her, with the bill of her bonnet jutting out like a bird's beak above the bandage.

"What?" she demanded. "What's so funny?"

"Nothing." But under his breath he made a bird noise.

"It's not polite to mock the wounded," she said, favoring her injured arm as she wrapped the length of petticoat around his neck and pulled him close. So close his laughter faded to silence. So close he could smell the faintest hint of mountain lilacs beneath the dust from her fall.

He pulled away, meeting no resistance as she let the strip of petticoat slide from her hand.

"You said you had injuries on your legs?" he asked.

"Yes, but I can tend them."

Ladino nodded and cut up more pieces of cactus, leaving them in his headwrap on the rock for her to use. Slipping his bowie in its sheath, he noticed how she stared at the western horizon, her face echoing a growing concern. The sun was sinking fast, and a lavender glow settled around them. Darkness would soon swallow even that small light.

"Ladino," she began, turning her attention back to him, "could you build a fire before you go?"

Fear peeked through her words like a frightened child peering from behind her mother's skirts. Her vulnerability intensified his longing, his desire to teach her how to love and survive his world.

He nodded, and when he returned with dried grass, twigs, and dead tree branches, he used his knife to dig a hole for the fire.

"Why do you do that?"

"If you build your campfire in a hole," he explained as he sheathed his knife and piled dry grass and kindling, "it's harder for those at a distance to spot your camp."

Adela nodded, lips compressed, upper arms clenched in white-knuckled hands.

Ladino lit the tinder with a match he'd fished out of a moccasin fold. Blowing on the tiny flame, he nursed it to life until it devoured the twigs and started on the branches.

"How long will you be gone?"

"An hour, maybe two if I look for a rabbit or something else for us to eat." He pushed up and rested his hands on his hips. "Know how to use a gun?"

"Yes," came her whispered admission.

He lifted his eyebrows. "Who taught you?"

"My mother. When I was five."

The mixture of shame, grief and fatalistic disapproval in her voice puzzled him. He imagined Adela as a child holding a gun, shaking with fear and aversion, yet determined to master the weapon if only for her own survival. The similarity to his own childhood weapons training brought back the ache of old memories.

"Maybe you should have been born Apache," he said, unable to make up his mind whether he offered the comment as a compliment, or as an admission of kinship—of understanding. Perhaps both. "You're a remarkable woman."

"It certainly doesn't require any remarkable strength of character to consider taking another person's life."

He realized she spoke out of fear; she hadn't meant to hurt him, but he still felt as if his beliefs had taken another slap in the face.

"You don't think so?" He crouched beside her, taking his knife from its sheath on his gun belt. He let the firelight play along the blade. "Have you ever stared into an enemy's eyes and seen the blood lust only your death will satisfy?"

"Ladino—"

"Until you've seen it, until you've had to make the decision to kill or be killed in the face of an enemy, save your judgments and platitudes about character."

She stared at him with such naked emotion he felt as if his own knife twisted in his chest.

"I didn't mean it as a judgment against you."

He ignored her, shoving his knife into his moccasin. Removing his gun belt, he laid it on the rock beside her and stalked away from the fire. "I'll be back soon."

He jumped on his horse, reined the animal around, and rode into the encroaching shadows. Once hidden, he turned and watched her through the trees. She slapped her palms against the rock, then with a howl of rage she shoved his gun belt off into the dirt.

Guilt gnawed his conscience. Why had he treated her so callously? Had her words spoken to him too deeply? Damn! but his vulnerability to her approval intrigued him, maddened him . . . *frightened* him.

Almost as much as returning to the reservation, knowing he risked a new kind of imprisonment for her sake.

Far to the northeast, lightning lit the blackened sky. The storm was too far away to hear the rumble of thunder, yet the sudden bursts of light added to Adela's fear. Here, the birds had quit singing, and only the crackle of the fire and the song of crickets filled the night.

A rock fell somewhere behind her, cracking against another, followed by the fine spray of rolling pebbles.

"Ladino, is that you?"

No answer. Only silence. She turned back to the fire, telling herself it was just a rabbit, or maybe a deer. Nevertheless, she added another stick of wood to the flames, hoping a larger blaze would keep predators at bay.

She heard something else, something that sounded like a sharply exhaled breath followed by a rhythmic thump against the ground. Chills chased down her spine.

"Ladino?" She picked up the gun belt from the ground and fumbled the pistol out of its holster. "Is that you?"

The scraggly juniper to the north of the fire moved. A new shape emerged beside it. A huge shape. She raised the gun, aiming in the shape's general direction, ready to pull the hammer back with her thumb.

Exhaling a breath of exhaustion, her horse plodded into the firelight. A sigh of relief escaped Adela's lips, and her shoulders sagged.

"You scared me!" She re-holstered the gun.

The gelding moved closer. It nudged her good shoulder and began to rub its forehead and nose up and down her arm. Her fingers still trembling, Adela scratched him beneath the strap of leather under his forelock.

"Serves you right to be tired of that bridle, you beast!" The gelding blew into her face. Adela laughed, tucking her cheek into her shoulder. "Is that what I get for name-calling?"

She got up and removed the saddlebags, digging through them until she found her rosary safe inside. Taking down the two canteens and her medical bag from behind the saddle, she set them on the ground beside the fire. After leading the horse away, she hobbled him and removed the bridle, hanging it from a tree branch.

"You'll have to wait until Ladino returns before the saddle comes off." Finding a rock with a bowl-shaped depression in its surface, she filled it with water from one of the canteens. After the animal had finished the water, she poured a little more. "Now that's it until we see what Ladino brings back."

Once she'd cared for the horse, Adela returned to the rock by the campfire. She dug her scissors, needles and thread out of her medical bag, then undressed to her chemise and petticoats so she could mend her habit. About an hour later, just as she had dressed and put the implements back in her bag, Ladino returned.

"You're back!" she exclaimed, too relieved at seeing him again to think about the rift between them.

Along with saddlebags, canteens and binoculars, his

horse carried a rabbit, a couple of unfamiliar leather bags, and a long, membranous tube wrapped around its neck.

"I see your horse found you," he said, as he dismounted and led his mount to where hers was hobbled.

She nodded. "I gave him some water, but not too much in case you weren't able to get any. And I couldn't remove the saddle."

"That's fine. I'll do it," he said, untying the rabbit from his saddle horn and dropping it on a flat rock near the fire. "In the morning I'll take both horses back to the spring before we leave." He unwound the tube, then looped it around a tree branch.

"*What* is *that?*" she asked, wrinkling her nose.

He held up an end. "Horse intestine filled with water."

"Cleaned out before you filled it, I hope."

He nodded, smiling. "I found it and a couple of parfleches in the cache," he said, removing the leather bags and lifting them to show her. "One contains dried mescal patties, the other jerked venison." He took down his saddlebags and canteens, setting them by the fire. "I also found some needles made from maguey thorns. I can show you how to use yucca fiber to mend your habit."

"Oh, I had needles and thread in my medical bag."

He glanced at her habit. A trace of what looked like disappointment tugged at his lips. "Good."

As he grabbed his gun belt from the rock, he studied her with a thoughtful expression. Adela blushed, but held his attention with all the innocence she could muster, realizing he must have seen her tantrum. He said nothing, and after buckling the belt around his hips, he grabbed the headwrap and tied it around his head, hiding the tattoo once more as he went back to the horses.

Adela watched him remove the saddles, and as she

studied the play of muscles beneath his shirt, she remembered how those same muscles had bunched tight beneath her hands with each thrust of him inside her. Admonishing herself for her self-betrayal . . . her soul-betrayal . . . Adela returned her attention to the fire.

Moments later he returned and grabbed the rabbit by its ears from the rock. "Know how to skin a rabbit?"

Adela shook her head. Ladino shrugged and went about doing it himself, silent for several moments as Adela watched him.

"You didn't have your gun. How did you catch it?"

"Snare," he answered. "What do you do about food when you go on your solicitation trips—do you take it with you?"

"Sometimes," she answered. "But when we visit mining camps, someone there usually provides our meal. Or sometimes a miner will travel with us for a time and hunt if we need food."

"If someone always provides for you, why are you afraid of being out here?"

"I didn't say I was afraid."

She forced herself not to shudder as she watched him clean his hands and knife on a tuft of grass before sliding the blade in its sheath on his gun belt. He obviously noticed her discomfiture, for he flashed her a shrewd smile. Grabbing the stick he'd set beside him, he speared the skinned rabbit and held it over the fire. After a long silence, Adela felt compelled to question him, even if doing so gave away the truth of her fear.

"Aren't you afraid of anything?" she ventured.

He offered an ironic smile. "I'm Apache, remember? I provoke fear. I don't experience it."

"Really, Ladino. Everyone's afraid of something."

For a brief instant he gazed over the fire at her before returning his attention to the rabbit on the spit. He turned their meal over the fire, and several minutes of silence passed until the meat had finally turned golden brown, and the juices, no longer pink, sizzled and smoked as they dripped into the flames. He pulled the rabbit back.

"You really want to know what I'm afraid of?"

She nodded.

"Having to depend on others for the food I eat." He pulled a leg from their meal and offered it to her.

"Why?"

"It destroys the pride and spirit to always take what those in power give."

She took his offering, passing it from hand to hand until it quit burning her fingers. "Are you saying that my spirit has been destroyed by taking what people provide for me?"

He shrugged. "No. I was only making a general comment. Enjoy your supper, Adela." An enigmatic smile touched his lips, revealing a glimpse of white teeth.

Holding the warm leg of rabbit, she stared into his unusual eyes. Understanding came slowly, and she realized he meant everything he had just said as a double-edged peace offering—a tit-for-tat apology. He may not have appreciated what she'd told him earlier, but he understood—just as she understood his belief about charity being equated with power over the powerless.

Eating the portion of rabbit he had given her, Adela watched him eat his. She noticed again tonight how he didn't toss the bones away as she'd seen so many other men do. Instead, he set them aside in a neat pile, next to the discarded skin, and she knew he would later carry everything away and dispose of it almost respectfully.

"Ladino . . ." When he glanced up, still chewing, her

courage faltered, but she pushed through anyway. "Remember when you said you might tell me your other name someday . . . ?"

"And you want to know now," he said as he studied her face. " 'Idui Bndaa'," he answered, setting aside a bone.

"What does that mean?"

"Eyes of the Mountain Lion."

Stunned, she stared at him. How many times in her own mind had she compared him to the animal? More than just the color of his eyes, she found the essence of the beast in the way he watched people like a mountain lion watched its prey.

Like he watched her now.

"What are you afraid of, Adela?"

She continued to share his gaze, unable to admit that being with him like this frightened her. Not only because of the feelings she continued to harbor for him, but because she feared this wild place he called home. These deserts and mountains he loved were her monsters in the closet, her fear of the dark—her own memories of blood and death and guilt.

Yet for her baby brother's sake, she had found the willpower to venture into Ladino's wilderness. Now if she could just convince herself that Jonathan Junior was the only reason she had come. That inability terrified her more than anything.

"Before my mother left me at the convent," she began, "we used to travel from town to town as she looked for work. We spent many nights just like this. Alone, with only a fire to keep—" She stopped, swallowing the lump in her throat as she listened to the sounds of night. The breeze through the brush and grass. An owl. The distant howl of a coyote. "To keep the wild animals away," she finished, thinking once more of her blood-spattered dress and the dead man's bloody coat wrapped around her tiny body. But she couldn't share that—it was too close to the heart of her fear. "I was terrified a bear or mountain lion would eat me while I slept."

Ladino smiled. "Now you have a mountain lion to protect you."

Adela stared into his eyes, and for a moment the dancing flames between them created the image of a mountain lion sitting on the rock across from her. A sleek, golden brown wildcat that sensed her every weakness, yet protected her from harm.

"Experiences like that will only make you stronger out here," he said. "They teach you what to expect—what to prepare for." He breathed deeply, and Adela became aware of the earthy, desert musk scented with undertones of cedar and piñon. "And you're free."

Free.

Her feeling of security vanished, along with her appetite, and she added her bones to the growing pile. Ladino offered her more rabbit, but she shook her head and looked away, studying a shadow of firelight flickering in the bushes, wishing she could see the enchantment in Ladino's world instead of being repelled by its treachery . . . Wishing the freedom of sharing his love didn't come at such a price.

"You know," she blurted, anxious to change the subject, "my mother used to tell me fairy tales so neither of us would think about the dangers out here."

"What are these fairy tales about?"

"Princes and princesses, witches and evil spells."

He lifted an eyebrow. "Stories of witches and evil spells kept you from being frightened?"

She laughed, the sound wistful to her own ears. "Some

of them were a little scary when I was six," she admitted. "But they're really just stories to pass the time," she said, remembering the first time her mother had told her the story of Rapunzel. Lost in grief now, she had to force her smile to remain. "Most of them begin with the words 'Once upon a time,' and they're always full of magic, giants, and talking animals."

"Sounds like the stories I heard as a child."

"Really? Tell me one."

"They're more than just stories. The Apache teach their children proper behavior through the legends told around the fire." He finished the last few bites of rabbit and set the bone aside with the rest. "I'll tell you the story of White-Painted Woman and Child of the Water. There are many versions, but this is the one I grew up hearing."

Ladino put another log on the fire and blew flames back to life. Resuming his seat on the rock, he appeared to be thinking.

"*Níaguchilááda,*" he said at last. "In the beginning time, nothing existed except for *Bik'éguindan-n*—Life Giver."

As Ladino spoke the name of his god, his gaze caught hers, holding it, forcing her to remember the day he'd told her she was beautiful . . . forcing her to remember his kiss.

"Life Giver decided to create," he continued, his voice softer now. "On the first day, he created *Sha*—Sun—and Mother Earth and the moon and the stars. He also created wind, Old Man Thunder and Little Boy Lightning." As if to emphasize his point, lightning lit up the northeastern sky. "And he created the rainbow to remind us of his beauty. On the second day he created all things that fly and crawl: birds, snakes, lizards, insects. On the third day he created all the four-legged animals: the buffalo, deer, elk and antelope. And on the fourth day, he created man—the Apache.

Since that time, four has been a sacred number to the people."

Adela leaned forward, cupping her chin in the palm of her hand. She'd never thought the Apaches would have such a rich history of their own creation, or that it would be so similar to her own.

"Life Giver created man last, not because he was strong and made to rule over the animals, like the White Eye Bible teaches, but because he was weak. The animals were meant to take care of him and help him live by providing food and clothing. Without everything that had been created before, Man could not exist."

Several moments of silence passed. Adela considered prompting Ladino, but sensed he would consider any interruption rude.

"Now in those early days, there was a woman," he continued. "Her name was White-Painted Woman. She was beautiful and chaste, and she refused to marry. A giant lived in those times, and monsters. And then a terrible drought brought famine. The People starved because there was no rain. They believed they would be saved if a willing virgin sacrificed her life. White-Painted Woman went away and lay upon a rock to await her death. In the night, a gentle, female rain fell upon her. She conceived a baby and called him Child of the Water."

He paused, and the firelight undulated shadows on his face, increasing the atmosphere of intimacy.

"To keep Child of the Water safe, White-Painted Woman dug a secret place, like a tiny cave, for him to hide in. She covered it with a flat rock on which she built her campfire. The giant came to her fire often and saw tiny footprints in the dirt, but no child. He accused her of hiding that child. She told him she had made the footprints herself because she wished for a child to ease her loneliness. To prove her words, she knelt, and with the side of her closed fist she pressed a footprint into the dirt. With her fingertip she added five little toes."

Ladino moved around the fire and knelt beside her, making the baby footprints in the dirt. How small they were, how real they appeared. Fear gripped Adela's belly as she thought about her baby brother somewhere out there alone with the Apache woman, who ran, hiding from Smeet.

"For many years White-Painted Woman convinced the giant she was alone, until—Adela, what's wrong?"

Adela lowered her face, staring at her reddened thumbs.

Ladino lifted her chin with his fingers. Shooting sparks in the starlit sky reflected in his pupils. "We'll get him back," he promised, startling her as he always did with his uncanny ability to sense the nature of her thoughts. "Perhaps even now your mother looks on from the Land of Ever Summer, guiding us."

"Oh, Ladino, what if we can't get him back?" she wailed. "What if he's dead?"

He said nothing for several moments. Then he grasped her hand and pulled her up from the rock. "Come with me. I want to show you something."

Adela allowed him to lead her away from the fire, over rocks and around bushes and trees until they neared a precipice that dropped into blackness below. Adela gasped, yanking her hand out of Ladino's grasp, refusing to be led any farther.

"Look," he said, lifting his chin to indicate the moon that had just begun to peek over the far distant Sierra Blancas and Sacramentos—his ancestral homeland.

As she edged closer to Ladino, the gibbous moon cleared the mountaintop, bathing the Tularosa Basin in an ethereal glow. The white sands in the middle of the valley shimmered like a diamond-encrusted veil tossed across snow.

"Séi higaya," he said.

"Séi higaya?" she repeated, her tongue tripping over the stressed vowels and unruly consonants. "White sands?"

Ladino smiled, lifting an eyebrow. "More or less."

"It's beautiful," she exclaimed.

"Like flowers and trees, but wilder, more dangerous?"

His teasing words rocked a tremor through her, and she realized what he was up to. "I wish you wouldn't do that," she said as she turned and began to stalk back to the campfire.

He followed her. "Do what?"

"You know what," she shot back over her shoulder. "You always twist my own words to taunt me. I don't know how you do it. One minute I feel safe, and the next minute you say or do something to rip the rug right out from under me. It's cruel."

"It's also effective. A weapon you use yourself." He caught her arm and pulled her around to face him. "You remember when you spoke of flowers and trees to me, don't you?"

"Of course I do. I'm not the one who was hit over the head."

"So are you still frightened?"

"No, damn it, I'm angry." The words popped out of her mouth before she could stop them. Shame burned the back of her neck.

"Good," he said, mocking her with a smile. "Anger serves a purpose. When I see your fire overcome your fear, I have faith you can withstand what's ahead of us." He released her arm and stepped around her, striding back to the campsite.

Nonplused, Adela stared after him.

Her stomach clenched with the sudden discovery that he had once again slipped through her defenses and forced her to explore another facet of her true character. She, who had always wanted to defy death, to master her own life—she, who railed against God and those in the church who tried to mold her thoughts—was as powerless as she had always been, because as much as she protested, she was afraid to let anything but false control rule her life.

"He's alive, Adela. And we will get him back, but we need to get an early start tomorrow," he said. "The Apache woman will be moving quickly, and we don't want to miss her."

He turned then and looked back at her, his form a silhouette in the firelight. "Always remember, Adela. Even the most dangerous, unpredictable things can be beautiful. And faith is the most dangerous and unpredictable of them all," he said, his voice a deep rumble in the night.

Chapter Eighteen

Ladino led the way up the mountainous freight road that paralleled the course of the Rio Tularosa. As their horses climbed, the arid landscape of the Tularosa Basin dropped behind them, giving way to pine- and spruce-shrouded mountains, lush vegetation, and hide-and-seek views of Sierra Blanca peak.

Home. When he'd been cooped up in that cell or busting rock with a ball and chain attached to his leg, he had clung to sanity with memories of his early childhood in the forests beneath White Mountain. Yet when the terrain leveled off and he saw Blazer's Mill in the heart of the meadow, surrounded by the buildings, barns, and stock pens comprising the Mescalero Agency, he realized once again that those days of freedom were over—for everyone.

Coming home without honor symbolized its own brand of imprisonment, a resurgence of guilt for helping to destroy a way of life. Nothing slammed the prison door shut quite like seeing Adela's pity as she took in the ragged children and dogs playing amongst tepees and brush shelters. To her these humble homes represented a backwards, impoverished culture, the part of him she couldn't quite accept . . . the part of himself he wasn't sure he was brave enough to face.

Her expression changed to one of pleasant surprise when she looked ahead at the row of small, identical buildings standing along the road opposite the agency compound. "Houses?"

Ladino nodded, trying to keep his anger and hurt in check. He knew he shouldn't blame her. She couldn't help his bitterness concerning the White Eye imposition. What pained him most was having to admit to himself that he'd gotten used to the Westbrook home in Silver City. He'd even found it comfortable. Maybe that was why he resented her attitude; it reminded him once again that only half of him belonged to the Apache way of life, where living for comfort was considered a weakness a person could ill afford.

Drumming hoofbeats sounded from the distance and grew louder. A bare-legged Apache man dressed in a shabby white shirt and brown vest rode toward them from the agency buildings. He reined his bay horse up short before them, sending a cloud of dust into the air.

"What have you and this woman come for?" he asked in Mescalero, indicating Adela with a lift of his chin. "Tata Crooked Nose must know of all who come."

Surprised by the man's blunt manner, Ladino could only stare. "Tata Crooked Nose?" he asked at last.

"Agent Llewellyn," the man clarified in English, then switched back to his native tongue. "I must take you to him."

"I have no wish to see the agent," Ladino returned, trying to train his voice to a more polite tone than the younger man had used. "I want to know where I might find the camp of my father, Nantan Estrellito. I seek his wise counsel."

He called Chief Estrellito by the polite form of "father," a term of respect even though the chief was a distant cousin—his grandmother's only living relative.

The man shook his head. "First you speak to Tata Crooked Nose. If he agrees, I will lead you to the camp of our father."

Frustrated, Ladino turned to Adela and translated.

"Perhaps Mr. Llewellyn can help us," she said.

"I haven't met an agent yet willing to help anyone but himself."

"Then maybe *he* has seen the woman," she said, indicating the young man who had come to meet them.

Ladino turned back to the Apache, but reproached himself for even considering Adela's suggestion. If the woman had been banished, or even if she belonged to Pajaro's band for some other reason, Ladino knew he risked suspicion of holding evil power himself just by asking about a woman who associated with a witch. He would get nowhere if the man believed that.

"Take us to Tata Crooked Nose," Ladino said, resigned.

When they neared the white clapboard agency buildings, Ladino noticed how Adela studied the women who strolled past. Some carried parcels of flour and beef in burden-baskets with straps across the tops of their heads, while others held babies in cradleboards on their backs. Her attention turned to the long line that snaked away from the commissary. Though a few men stood here and there, mostly women and small children dressed in combinations of buckskin and faded calico comprised the line.

"Issue day," Ladino explained. "I remember a time when the women had pride and confidence in their faces. Now look at them."

Ladino recognized many of the older women as they studied Adela, their eyes full of destroyed hope and guarded distrust.

When their attention shifted to him, he saw their recognition. He felt their hostility. Yet he rode on, pretending to ignore them. His wrongs were his own to bear. To appear friendly or apologetic would reduce him to less than nothing in their eyes, a man to be ridiculed. Only in withdrawn acceptance of his own guilt could he ever hope to redeem himself.

The line of women parted, and when the guide led them through the gap, Ladino's lungs burned as if he breathed their animosity. Adela must have sensed it too, because she glanced over at him, her brow creased with concern.

He wanted to warn her that the behavior she witnessed now was nothing compared to the reaction he expected from Estrellito. Even so, he felt obligated to face his kinsman, if only to allow the man a physical outlet for his disgust and condemnation. He doubted the chief would consider him—the worst coward and traitor—worthy of help, much less the more violent act of retribution demanded by custom. Even so, for Adela's sake, for her brother's sake—for the sake of his grandmother's memory— he would try.

At last they reached the south side of the largest two-story building. A porch ran its length, and a white picket fence contained a lawn. As the Apache dismounted, Ladino swung off his own horse and lifted Adela from her side-saddle. Even touching her in this small way set fire to his imagination, yet he couldn't allow his severe façade to falter by acknowledging her questioning expression in front of the others.

As their guide led them to the agent's office, Ladino's chest tightened. More than anything he wanted to ride out of here and never return to accusations and suffocation. But that would be the coward's way. He would not dirty his honor further.

The office door stood open, and as Ladino and Adela darkened the threshold, Agent Llewellyn lifted his head. Surprise crossed his face, and he pushed back his chair and stood. He wore a sling on his left arm, disguising the tight fit of his blue military coat across his barrel-shaped paunch.

"Come," he said, motioning them inside. As Adela stepped into the office, the agent's pale, thin eyebrows arched in greater surprise above his crooked nose. "Sister!" he said, assessing her patched habit before sending a measuring glance over Ladino's form as well. "Please." He gestured toward two chairs facing his desk. "Have a seat."

Adela sat first, and Ladino followed suit, grateful she had taken the chair farther into the room, leaving the one nearer the open door for him.

Agent Llewellyn sat in his own chair and rolled it back to his desk. "How might I help you?" he asked, looking first at Adela before sending another thoughtful expression Ladino's way. As if just remembering their guide's presence, the agent then looked up at the man in the doorway. " *'Ixéhe,* Loyal Dog."

Ladino noticed Llewellyn's thanks seemed sincere despite how he'd spoken the Apache's name to his face. Loyal Dog proved his name as he stepped inside, leaned against the wall, and folded his arms across his chest.

When the agent returned his attention to Adela, she spoke.

"I'm Sister Adela Fremont from Santa Fe. I don't know if you've heard of the Westbrooks of Silver City, but I am the late Mrs. Westbrook's daughter."

Sympathy flooded his features. "I was deeply sorry to hear what happened, and so close to Fort Stanton, no less. My sympathy." He leaned forward. "Have you received news of your brother? The last I heard, Pajaro had escaped to Mexico."

"As a matter of fact, sir, that's why we've come. You see, Pajaro kidnapped my brother on behalf of a man named

Nigel Smeet. The Apache woman who was with Mr. Smeet as my brother's caretaker has escaped, and we believe she's taken Jonathan Junior and is headed for Pajaro's stronghold. We came here hoping to intercept her. At the very least, we hope you might have information that will help us find her."

Llewellyn turned to Ladino, his expression thoughtful, as if he tried to decide what to make of their companionship. "And you've hired this man to help you?"

"Oh, no, sir. Mr. Ladino agreed as a favor to me."

"What band are you from?" Llewellyn asked Ladino in Spanish.

"I speak English, Llewellyn; I'm half-white."

Ladino immediately regretted his rash bluntness as he waited to see what reaction the mention of his mixed blood would stir.

Llewellyn leaned back in his chair. "Half-white, you say?"

Ladino returned the man's regard, but refused to speak.

"You're the one who was sent to Alcatraz," the agent continued. "The interpreter from Fort Stanton. I've heard of you. El Ladino Greñudo." He paused, his expression thoughtful. "And I've seen your name listed here in the old agency books."

At the prospect of the man enforcing the law and confining him to this reservation, panic-stricken fear assailed Ladino.

"I won't stay here." He stood up so fast his chair scooted across the floor. He pivoted toward the door, but Loyal Dog pushed away from the wall and blocked his path.

"Now hold on a minute, Mr. Ladino." Llewellyn strode around his desk, gesturing Loyal Dog back to the wall. He then turned and leveled his gaze on Ladino. "I just said I'd heard about you. I didn't say I believed everything I heard. And I said nothing about making you stay. Why don't you have a seat?"

"All I want is to speak with Nantan Estrellito."

"In good time." He gestured toward the vacant chair now skewed with the neatly arranged room. "Please."

Coaxed by the man's soft-spoken yet authoritative manner, Ladino straightened his chair, sat down, and curled his hands around the ends of the arms. He dug into the wood with his fingertips. When he glanced over at Adela, he saw a more intimate understanding of his true fear than he wanted to acknowledge.

"Let's get a few things straight, Mr. Ladino. I'll tell you right now I've heard all about the court-martial proceedings. I know all about Smeet. If he were still in the military . . . well, I'm not a violent man, but I'd horsewhip him myself and take pleasure doing it."

Adela's skittish glance and sympathetic smile touched on Ladino for a moment before she leaned forward in her chair and turned her eager attention to the agent. "You really don't believe all that's on record about Ladino's court-martial?"

Ladino recognized her efforts to defend him, to make him more comfortable in Llewellyn's presence, and he resented it. Not only because his outburst had made him look the fool, but because after all he had told her, explained to her, he couldn't believe she'd be naive enough to think an Indian agent would give a damn about his reasons for killing White Eye soldiers.

"I haven't been here long, only a little over a year, but I've heard plenty of stories among the Mescaleros about the slaughter and the court-martial." Llewellyn returned to his desk and sat down. "Granted, Mr. Ladino here isn't a popular man among his people, but from what I've gathered, I don't believe he could have been involved with Smeet the way the records claim."

Ladino stared at Llewellyn in amazement. How had this White Eye earned the confidence of the Mescaleros in such a short time?

The agent continued, seemingly unperturbed by Ladino's intense regard. "And because I've also heard many stories about Pajaro's involvement with Smeet, both past and present, I'm inclined to want to help you. Unfortunately, I haven't seen the woman you're looking for."

"What about Estrellito?" asked Adela. "The woman was from his band, so perhaps he can help us find her. Or if he hasn't seen her, maybe he knows the location of the stronghold—"

"In the Guadalupes?" Llewellyn interjected. "Personally, I think all those barren hills and canyons look alike. And the caves . . ." He shook his head in bewilderment. "If Estrellito knew, don't you think I would?"

"What makes you think Nantan Estrellito would tell you?" Ladino challenged.

"Chief Estrellito's on our side now, Mr. Ladino, and the military wants nothing more than to get its hands on Pajaro, but no one can touch him." Llewellyn sat forward in his chair. "Why would Estrellito protect Pajaro by keeping the location secret?"

"It's not a question of protecting Pajaro, it's a question of betraying one's own people."

"I realize that, but things have changed since you left. Estrellito wants peace, and he's even shown support of the police force I've recently established."

"Police force?" asked Adela.

"Yes. By having the Mescaleros oversee their own justice according to the rules—"

"White Eye rules," Ladino interrupted, then clenched his jaw.

The agent stared at Ladino. "Yes, White Eye rules," he agreed, his voice deep with inevitability. "But you see, I'm trying in any way I can to eliminate the need for military intervention. We both know how disastrous that has been for your people in the past."

"And how is this police force working, sir?" asked Adela.

"So far, pretty well." He nodded toward the Apache man standing near the door. "Loyal Dog is a sergeant. He was with us when we caught Give Me a Horse, the crack-shot horse thief that managed to wing me." He lifted his injured arm. "He also helped us catch some rustlers trying to make off with Chief San Juan's cattle. Granted, the authorities only took our efforts seriously because these same men had stolen several from John Chisum's herd, but we caught them here on the reservation, and that's progress."

Progress. Ladino tried to deny the word by withdrawing his ripped emotions within his chest, but he knew change would never be denied. And Llewellyn, though arrogant, was the first agent he'd met who seemed sincere in his desire to help the Mescaleros.

This revelation forced Ladino to acknowledge the part of him that wanted to try once again to help his father's people, the Indeh—the dead—find some harmony in an altered world. It might mean giving up his freedom and remaining here. And unless he could perform some heroic deed for his people, or win their forgiveness some other way, it would certainly mean ridicule and hatred. First, he had to find Smeet. He had to find Pajaro and the baby. Then he would decide whether he would allow himself to fully trust this bluecoat and become a willing prisoner.

"But that's beside the point." Llewellyn sighed and shrugged. "I'll certainly be the first to admit I don't see everyone who sets foot on this reservation. And as for Pajaro's stronghold in the Guadalupes, well, maybe Estrellito will tell you more than he's ever let on to me." He cast a glance at Adela. "Will you be staying here while Mr. Ladino goes after the Apache woman?"

Adela cast a quick glance at Ladino. "No. But thank you."

"Well, all right then." He stood at his desk and gestured toward Loyal Dog. "He'll take you to Estrellito's camp."

Loyal Dog led the way south and east, across the clearing and into a canyon that pushed deeper into reservation lands. For the next few hours Adela hung back, studying the mountains rising all around and listening to the breeze whispering through the pine and spruce trees, while Ladino rode ahead with their guide. The men spoke to each other in Mescalero. Each vocal pause, each tone spoken at the back of their throats, each syllable drifted back to her, blending with the birdsong and the trickle of water in the creek. Just like Latin chant blended with the scent of incense as it drifted to the vaulted ceilings of St. Francis Cathedral.

For the last week she had watched Ladino absorb his surroundings like a thirsty man who'd gone too long without water. He was a nomad in his element . . . his home. Until this moment she had been drowning in wide open spaces and praying to find her brother so she could go back to her own home—the close-quartered safety of the convent. But somehow, a deep sense of rightness—of belonging to these mountains—settled in Adela's heart, taking her by surprise, offering her a glimpse of the comfort and peace she had known only in the convent. How could that be?

She was still contemplating the subtle change within herself when she heard the chatter of feminine voices. A cloud of smoke drifted through the trees, carrying the scent of food cooking over an open fire. Soon, the canyon they had traveled from the agency opened into a small meadow. In the dim light of dusk, a central campfire illuminated ten or eleven tepees and brush shelters, all with their doorways facing east to welcome the rising sun.

Children played at the edge of the campsite, skipping, tossing rocks, battling one another with sticks. She smiled as she watched a boy, about six years old, drop into the tall grass and disappear, then reappear a short distance away, pouncing on an unsuspecting playmate like a young wild animal stalking his prey. At their approach, the women around the fire ceased meal preparations and turned. The children quit playing and bunched together in groups.

One little girl, about three, bent to the ground and picked up a rag doll with long black hair. She ran to the center of camp and threw her arms around the legs of a man who had just emerged from the shadows beyond the fire. The Apache man hefted the child to his leather-clad hip, and the little girl fingered one of the long silver earrings that dangled down the front of his bare brown chest. He patted her on the back, soothing her fear as she stared at them, her young eyes filled with a defiant bravado.

Despite her own nervousness at being amidst an atmosphere of suspicion, Adela couldn't help but smile again. The little girl's obvious faith in her father, and his devotion to her, tugged at her heart. Glancing over at Ladino, she saw that he too watched father and child, his expression akin to longing.

Though she knew it was folly, Adela imagined him with

a child on his hip. A little girl with fair skin and chestnut hair who would laugh and place her tiny hand on Ladino's golden brown forehead, smoothing the lines through his tattoo.

As if sensing her attention, Ladino's gaze slid to her. They shared a moment of silent communication before her smile faltered and she looked away, shaken to her soul by the glimpse of a future that could never be.

Loyal Dog swung a leg over his horse's neck and slid to the ground. Stepping forward, he greeted the group. Remaining quiet, Ladino also dismounted and stepped forward, his face revealed in greater detail by the firelight. All turned their attention to him, and then the women glanced from one to another, their tones and attitudes growing hostile as they whispered amongst themselves.

One young woman remained quiet as she studied him, the expression on her face unreadable except for the glimmer of recognition in her large brown eyes. If the woman knew him, why wasn't she participating in the callous talk with the others?

Ladino turned his back on them and strode to her side, his own brand of bravado apparent in the catlike grace and control of his movements. Adela leaned over and put her hands on his shoulders, feeling his muscles bunch beneath her palms as he grasped her by the waist and lifted her down. Letting her hands continue to rest on his shoulders, she met his gaze. Anguish glimmered in the depths of his eyes even as his lingering touch burned through her habit and bindings, finding the soft flesh beneath. But then he stiffened, pulling away as he slipped once again behind the austere façade he'd displayed at the agency.

Several more men approached the fire from the darkness beyond, and one man, older than the others, led the way.

His obsidian eyes peered from leathery folds of brown skin, his sharp nose pierced his face, and his mouth cut a grim line above a heavy, square chin. Gray had begun to streak his jet black hair, which hung in uneven lengths to his buck-skin-clad shoulders. Everyone fell silent as the man saun-tered up to Ladino and stared into his face, his stance aggressive even though he stood six inches and fifty pounds shy of Ladino's powerful six-foot-one frame.

The man Adela assumed to be Estrellito spoke in Mescalero, his voice a guttural knife thrust of sound. Silver earrings, similar to those of the man holding the little girl, shook across his shoulders.

After a polite pause, Ladino spoke, and Adela could see he was careful to keep his eye contact fleeting, unobtrusive in order to show utmost respect, just the way he had ad-vised her to do before their arrival at the agency. Yet she felt an odd sense of pride when she noticed how he showed no sign of submission, no gesture of apology as he stood be-fore the chief.

Adela also noticed how the one woman who had re-mained quiet earlier crept closer, her head cocked in in-terest and her gait awkward, as if one leg was shorter than the other. The woman's intense study unnerved Adela, and she shifted her attention back to Ladino and the chief.

Chief Estrellito replied, his tone still sharp as he cast his attention to Adela. He glared at her with such fierce ani-mosity she flinched. With one last abrasive comment and a noise of disgust in his throat, the chief turned on his heel. For a moment he met the woman's penetrating gaze, but then he dismissed her regard and strode away through the others who parted for his progress.

Ladino stood in resolute silence while those in the fire-light cast a few last glances at him, then ignored him completely as they invited Loyal Dog to join them. Adela cringed, her heart aching for Ladino's shame and embarrassment at being shunned by the group.

At last he turned and stalked back to her, and Adela wanted to say something, anything to ease the pain he tried so valiantly to hide. "Ladino, I—"

"No one here has seen the woman or your brother," he snapped. It was obvious he wanted none of her soft sympathy to ease his humiliation. "We'll make camp somewhere else." He grabbed his horse's reins and was about to wheel his animal around when the Apache woman limped to his side.

"No," she said, frowning as a few around the fire turned to look at her. "Come. Bring your horses." She turned and hurried away, her awkward gait doing nothing to slow her progress as she led a path into the shadows where the chief had disappeared.

Surprised that the woman spoke English, Adela glanced over at Ladino. "Who is she?"

Ladino cast a contemplative glance after the woman's back. "Laughs Like the Wind," he said in a distracted tone. "Daughter of Snake Walker, the medicine man." With that he followed the mysterious woman, leaving Adela behind to follow or not.

Frustration to know more gathered in her chest. Having no choice but to keep silent for now, Adela traipsed after Ladino, leading her own horse. As they passed the fire, some of the men and women watched them with resentful curiosity, but none intervened, though Adela sensed they knew what was taking place. Why was the medicine man's daughter going to such lengths to help them?

When they reached the far edge of camp near the dusk-blackened skirt of trees, Adela saw Laughs Like the Wind standing near a dome-shaped brush shelter. As she and Ladino drew near, the woman studied Adela from the toes of her awkward shoes upward, her main concentration settling on the bonnet.

The woman turned her attention to Ladino. "You and your wife may stay here. In my shelter."

Adela opened her mouth to protest being mistaken for Ladino's wife, but Ladino put his hand on the small of her back. His fingertips glided across the top curve of her bottom in such a husbandly gesture of possession Adela couldn't speak for the flutter of sensations racing up her spine. When she caught her breath, she realized his action was a caution not to correct the woman's assumption. But why?

"That is generous of you," said Ladino, speaking English in return. "But we can't let you do that."

"Your mother was kind to me when I was small and my leg first wounded," the woman said, her voice heavily accented. "I wish to return her kindness."

"But what about . . ." Adela paused when she realized she didn't know if it would be considered rude to speak the chief's name, even in his absence. ". . . the others?" she finished, sending Ladino a glance of uncertainty. "Won't they disapprove?"

"Dis . . . approve?" the woman asked, her expression puzzled.

"Yes," said Adela. "Won't they be unhappy if we stay here?"

The woman sent a dismissive study over Adela's shoulder at those gathered around the fire. She laughed, and the soft, quiet sound did indeed remind Adela of a teasing breeze. "They expect me to do as I please." When Laughs Like the Wind turned to Ladino, Adela noticed again an odd intensity—a silent, private communication that made Adela feel cut off, unwelcome. "Stake your horses," she said, lifting the leather flap to enter the shelter. "I will build a fire inside and gather my things."

"Your things?" echoed Adela, her voice rising in alarm. For days she'd been alone with Ladino. But the thought of sharing this woman's tiny shelter with him in the proximity of so many witnesses who must also think she and Ladino were married made her heart beat like a hummingbird's wings. "Surely you don't mean for us to put you out of your home."

Laughs Like the Wind straightened. "Tonight I will sleep in my father's house. He will not be there anyway . . ." She glanced over at Ladino, and a fleeting smile touched her lips. "Not when I tell him my brother has come." With that, the woman disappeared into her shelter.

Adela turned to Ladino. "What did she mean by that?"

A deep, contemplative frown creased his brow below the red headwrap. He shrugged, but Adela sensed he understood more about the woman's mystery than he was willing to reveal.

"Let's see to the horses," he said, stroking the white blaze down the nose of his mount.

If Ladino weren't as nervous as Adela, he would have laughed at her antics just to break the strained silence between them. Now that they sat across the fire from each other, alone in the shelter, Adela would not look at him. She studied everything in the small dwelling *but* him. She gazed at the domed ceiling, where pliable pine boughs had been lashed together and chinked with mud. She moved her attention to the floor, where the stumps of the boughs had been entrenched in the earth. She combed her fingers through the fur of the deerskin on which she sat, as if she'd never felt anything so soft or comforting.

No longer did he feel the urge to laugh. Instead, a restlessness grew within him—an overwhelming need to put a stop to the sensual play of her fingers through the fur before she drove him to an action both of them would later regret.

He burned with frustration to discover that no matter what she did, he wanted her. He would always want her. Even at such inconvenient times as this.

Because he knew her insecurity so well, it being so close to his own, the perfect barb leapt to his tongue. "Is this shelter more comfortable than you expected?"

More animosity colored his words than he'd intended, and for the first time since they'd entered the shelter, she met his gaze.

"Yes," she replied, but then her expression became contrite. "I mean . . ." She pulled her hand into her lap and rubbed her thumb in her usual nervous manner. "Yes," she said again, her tone resigned. "I must admit it is."

Her gaze wandered again, and this time she reached out to touch a bundle of dried herbs resting in a shallow basket woven in a star motif. Other baskets, in different sizes, shapes and designs took up one small section of the dwelling, their arrangement neat and pleasing to the eye.

"It's cozy." Her lips shook as she smiled. "I like it."

"Laughs Like the Wind built it."

"By herself?"

Ladino nodded, his optimism growing when he recognized the awe in Adela's face as she studied the construction with new interest.

"It's Apache custom for women to build the shelters," he explained. "A good wife and mother provides a comfortable home for her husband and children."

"Does Laughs Like the Wind have a husband and family?"

He shook his head. "When I was sent away she had just lost her husband. No children."

"Oh," Adela replied, regret knotting a frown on her brow. "How was she injured?"

"Attacked by a bear. Her leg was mangled."

Adela cringed, and for a moment said nothing. At last she found her voice. "She said something about your mother?"

He nodded. "Snake Walker was a widower, and at that time Estrellito's band traveled with Cadete. Laughs Like the Wind grew attached to my mother, and the medicine man surprised everyone by allowing my mother to care for his daughter while she recovered. That's how she learned English."

As if summoned by their discussion, Laughs Like the Wind ducked through the short doorway, her hands laden with a bowl of stew and a round piece of fry bread. "I brought food for your wife," she said, her expression severe with *'in'ch'indi*.

Understanding that he was being told without words to fast, Ladino acknowledged her appeal with an imperceptible nod. Smiling, Laughs Like the Wind then held the bowl and bread out to Adela.

Accepting the offering, Adela cast Ladino a quick expression of curiosity and concern. "Would you like to share with me?"

"No, thank you."

Adela studied Laughs Like the Wind, and Ladino knew Adela believed the woman had been told not to feed him. She was right, but not for the reason she suspected. Estrellito and the others had nothing to do with the fact

309

that he was being made to go without food. He wished he could explain, but he knew Adela wouldn't understand.

"You must keep up your strength," she argued.

"I'm not hungry."

"But you haven't eaten since noon yesterday."

Ladino met her insistence with stubborn silence. Until this moment he had declined meals for no other reason but his anxiety over returning home. Wondering what Snake Walker might want with him that required him to fast, Ladino couldn't deny the dread mingled with excitement and a sliver of hope. A ceremony of some kind? But for what?

As the tension between him and Adela persisted, Laughs Like the Wind cast a sheepish glance between them. She pushed up from the ground and hobbled out the small door, muttering something to him in Mescalero—something about searching for her father.

Adela toyed with the crude antler spoon, then finally propped it against the rim and set the bowl aside, balancing the fry bread on top. The new determination in her eyes warned him of her intent to put an end to his subterfuge. "All right, if you won't eat, at least answer me this. Why did you let Laughs Like the Wind believe I'm your wife?"

A weighty throb in Ladino's stomach took him by surprise, especially since he'd thought himself prepared for this question.

"The Apache have very strict ideas about a woman's morality," he answered. "I didn't want her to think you a loose woman because you travel alone with me."

The emotion in Adela's soft brown eyes fluctuated between guilt and gratitude. "Oh," she said. "Thank you. But I'm not sure I deserve such a gallant lie, considering . . ."

"Considering what happened between us?" he finished. "You weren't alone that night, Adela." He draped his arm across his upthrust knee. "And maybe it's not exactly a lie."

She gaped at him.

"Among the Apache, there are no fancy wedding ceremonies. No priests. No proclamation of vows. Perhaps just a blessing as the couple crosses the threshold into the home built by the bride." Seeing the alarm on Adela's face heightened by the dancing flames, Ladino offered a wistful smile. "Don't worry, Adela. I haven't tricked you into a secret marriage pact. True commitment can only be made in the heart." He glanced away and grabbed a small stick of wood, adding it to the fire. "You made no promise to me."

For long moments she said nothing, and he felt as if his words stretched between them like a lit fuse to the hidden keg of meaning she so obviously wanted to avoid.

"What will you tell them when you come back without me?" she asked, her voice soft with apprehension and a hint of regret.

"Who says I'm coming back? I'm not welcome here." He pushed at one of the woven baskets with the toe of his moccasin. "Besides, this place is a prison, full of hopelessness."

"You say that, but I think deep down you want to be a part of these people. Perhaps a day will come when you will be welcome again. What will you say then? You'll have to explain."

"Not if you return with me," he quipped. In that moment he realized he was only half-joking.

"Ladino—"

"I know," he said. "You'll marry the church." Hoping to hide his disappointment, to circumvent his blunder, he forced a teasing smile to his mouth. "If I come back, I'll tell them you put my belongings outside our shelter, divorcing me."

At her look of bewildered shock, and a pain he couldn't

fathom, he reached around the fire and lifted her bowl, holding it before her. The fry bread teetered on the edge. "Now eat before it gets cold—before you drive me to begging for food like a dog."

"I thought you said you weren't hungry."

"Just eat."

Adela took the bowl and set it in her lap. She lifted the fry bread and was just about to tear it in half when he stopped her with a gentle touch on her hand.

"Don't break the circle," he warned. "Eat from the whole."

For a moment Adela stared at his hand. Then she lifted her lashes, peering at him from beneath their half-closed length. Lost in the desire she so easily ignited, Ladino moved his hand to her face. He caressed her cheek with his fingers and brushed his thumb across her lips.

With her caught like a rabbit under his mountain lion's spell, he leaned forward. She didn't move, but continued to stare at him in fascination as he brought his lips close to hers. He was about to kiss her, when her gasp of alarm shattered his trance-like concentration. He recognized her horror as she stared at something over his shoulder.

Turning, Ladino saw framed in the doorway an old man's body hunched over a walking stick. Wizened black eyes shone within sagging gray brows and a crisscrossing pattern of wrinkles. Snake-like images painted each cheek, and atop his chest-length, iron-gray hair, the ancient one wore a buckskin medicine hat decorated with eagle feathers and downy white fluffies. Out one side of the cap jutted the open jaws of a rattlesnake, fangs extended, while its body coiled around the old man's head amidst the eagle's plumage.

Snake Walker.

With the man dressed in full ceremonial regalia, Ladino found it easy to believe that the ancient one had witnessed many events not only outside his own lifetime, but from outside his own body.

"You, my son, are the one whose return I saw in my dreams, coming at the time of the full moon with a woman to find a woman," the medicine man said in Mescalero. He held out his gnarled hand to Ladino. "Come with me. You have much to see and learn."

Chapter Nineteen

Shock seized Ladino's chest, stealing his breath. Compelled by the uncanny force of Snake Walker's presence, he stood and ducked out of the shelter.

The entire camp had gathered to witness the medicine man's summoning. If not a mood of approval, Ladino at least sensed no belligerence. He felt as if a fresh breeze had fanned his long-banked desire for acceptance into a bonfire of hope. Still, even though the medicine man had seen him in a vision, Ladino knew better than to add too much fuel to his vulnerability; any weakness could burn him alive.

A soft touch on his arm severed his enchantment. He turned to Adela, who now stood at his side, her black-clad body silhouetted in the firelight spilling from the doorway.

"Where are you going?" she whispered, her eyes wide as she stared at Snake Walker. "What does he want with you?"

"I'm not sure, but he may have news of One With No Relatives." A movement distracted Ladino, and he turned to see Snake Walker striding away. "I need to go with him to find out."

Adela nodded. "Be careful."

He brushed the backs of his fingers against her cheek. "I will."

With that assurance, he turned and ran after the medicine man, who had almost disappeared in the shroud of trees. At last he caught up, in awe of Snake Walker who, though twisted with age, moved with the swiftness of a man half his seventy or more years.

As they climbed the mountain on the eastern boundary of the canyon, the full moon rose higher, lighting their path in its cool glow. When they reached the crest, the silvery orb's face seemed close enough for Ladino to trace with his fingertips.

After sharing several moments of silence, as was the Apache way, Ladino could no longer contain his curiosity. "Is it really true, Wise Father, that you saw my coming?"

"You've grown rude like the White Eye with your disbelief and your foolish questions." The old man turned to him, a challenge sparkling in his ageless eyes. "I'll ask one of my own. Was your woman badly injured in her fall from the horse?"

Shock seized Ladino's midsection, throbbing in his still-tender wound. The rattlesnake. He had been trapped in the concrete world of White Eye beliefs too long.

"No," he answered, his voice solemn, full of newfound respect. He forced himself to listen as crickets and a breeze through the pines whispered to half-lit shadows. This time he would let Snake Walker choose the moment to fill the silence.

"You've forgotten much, my son." With those cryptic words the old man walked away.

Moonlight winked along the length of an eagle feather in Snake Walker's cap as he weaved his way along the mountaintop. At last Ladino followed in the ancient one's path, which led to a brush shelter in a clearing amidst the pines. The lodge had been painstakingly built, joints chinked with mud between interwoven branches. A stack of firewood stood just outside the leather-flap door facing east, toward the face of the moon and the rising sun.

Snake Walker set aside his staff and shed his clothing, piling it carefully near the doorway. The medicine man moved with the fluidity of his namesake as he lifted aside the leather flap covering the doorway and slipped inside the lodge.

For a moment Ladino hesitated, his heart pounding to a frenzied beat. A plume of smoke rose like a mountain spirit from a hole atop the shelter, taunting him to conquer his fear, beckoning him to learn his fate.

At last he undressed, baring his body and his spirit for a ceremony of rebirth. Taking a deep breath, he swept aside the drape and entered the shelter. The flap fell shut behind him, sealing him with the medicine man inside the tiny womb.

Hunched at the waist, Ladino followed a sunwise path around the fire that burned in a pit next to a pitch-coated basket of herbal water. Sitting down opposite Snake Walker, Ladino breathed in the heat that emanated from the red, glowing rocks nestled within the depths of the flames. The sloping interior walls enveloped him in painted buckskin that depicted images from his spiritual past. The four phases of the moon painted on the hide marked the sacred four directions, and other religious designs—stars, crosses, snakes, even mountain lions—called forth neglected memories of the deeper meanings each symbol held in his life.

"You wish to know why I have brought you here," stated Snake Walker. "Why a man spurned by his people, a man who cannot decide which path to walk in his life, should be so chosen."

"Yes, My Father. But I have so little time," Ladino ventured. "I don't have the customary four days to fast in the proper way and retreat by myself to seek answers."

"You think I do not know this?" Beneath folds of leathery skin, Snake Walker's eyes glittered with indignation. "I am no foolish coyote to be lectured about the rites of the People."

Chastised, Ladino fell silent. He soon found himself assessing the differences and similarities between them. Though he couldn't deny the satisfaction of latent power he felt within his own firm body, he admired the patience and endurance evidenced by this man's wrinkled skin. Decades of hardship, strength, and wisdom had been distilled into rope-like muscles tougher than sinew and a mind that refined all thoughts to their purest meaning.

"I was once like you, my son," Snake Walker said, echoing the essence of Ladino's thoughts. "That is why I have been given this ceremony for you. The injuries you have suffered only hide the true injury you must heal. To do that, you must remember. Your mind must accept what it has not been able to accept before."

Snake Walker's words slithered against some formless, nameless pain buried deep in Ladino's memory, and he began to feel an odd pulling sensation, like the strong, undulating muscles and cool scale of a snake as it glided across the back of his neck. His eyesight blurred. He shuddered, blinking to clear his vision. Lowering his head, he peered into the fire, into the deep blue flames that coiled along the bottom of a log. Even here he could not escape the ancient one's commanding presence.

That this man would share a special ceremony with him alone should have given Ladino a profound sense of homecoming and acceptance. But as he lifted his gaze once again to the face of the wizened old man, his anxiety only intensified. He struggled to keep his focus from penetrating too intensely, unwilling to allow the old one further into the depths of his uncertainty.

"I know the truth behind your pain, for I have walked

your path in my dreams." Snake Walker looked away then. He used a pair of deer antlers to place several glowing stones in another portion of the pit. He then set aside the antlers and sprinkled sage atop the stones. "Yet I would be wrong to tell you where it began and where it leads. That is for you to discover." At last he glanced up. "You must surrender, my son. *Shilhú'ash*. Go with me."

Snake Walker's words sliced a shiver down Ladino's spine. He continued to fight, but in the end it was the shade of his own voice, his own urging of Adela during their lovemaking that reminded him how fear could be the threshold to freedom.

"Let my spirit strengthen yours," Snake Walker urged. "The woman you seek cannot hide if you trust yourself and your vision."

He swiveled and retrieved a water drum from behind him, bringing it and its loop-ended drumstick to his lap where he nestled it between his knotted legs. Sound receded completely, only to be saturated moments later by a rich bass vibration from the water drum—a vibration that matched the slowing rhythm of Ladino's heart. The medicine man began to chant in a voice as old as time even as he took up a gourd ladle and dipped it into the basket of water. His mesmerizing drumbeats never faltered, his voice never diminished as he poured the water over the glowing rocks.

Steam hissed, spiraling up into the air and rolling across the low ceiling like storm clouds. Another ladleful followed, and then another, casting the pictures on the surrounding painting into a hazy world all their own. Ladino closed his eyes, drawing in deep, lung-scorching breaths of sage-scented fog. He could feel the pull of sweat from his skin, as if his very essence was being sapped from his body, leaving him light-headed and floating on Snake Walker's song and the hypnotic beat of the drum.

Ladino didn't know whether an instant or an eternity had passed when the chanting faded into a silence that blended with the darkness. He opened his heavy lids and gazed at Snake Walker through the sinuous mist. The ancient set aside his drum and arranged several shallow gourd dishes close to his folded legs. Ladino recognized the contents of one as *hoddentin,* the yellow pollen of the tule reed. The fog shifted, and Ladino identified another substance as galena, the mineral cubes pulverized into gray powder. The old man mixed several drops of water from the basket with the galena, stirring the compound into a thick paste.

Setting this aside, Snake Walker measured several pinches of the yellow tule pollen in the palm of his hand. "Open your mouth," he ordered. Ladino complied, and Snake Walker placed a pinch of *hoddentin* on his tongue. "This will nourish you and give you strength for your journey." The medicine man then smeared pollen into his hair. "This will heal your broken thoughts." Finally he fingered Ladino's eyes closed and smoothed the pollen across his eyelids with the pad of his thumb. "This will help you see things that have been invisible to you before."

Snake Walker chanted a prayer, and the vibrations of the medicine man's voice rumbled throughout Ladino's body. The ancient one pinched up more of the *hoddentin* and drew a sunwise circle on Ladino's chest, beginning and ending in the east. He then drew a cross, dividing the circle into four equal parts. Still chanting, he removed Ladino's headwrap. Then, dipping his finger in the galena, he painted a silver moon disc over Ladino's tattoo. Peace flowed through Ladino, and he closed his eyes.

An hour passed, maybe longer, as Snake Walker painted Ladino's face and body, then created more steam, chanting while he beat his water drum. Ladino yearned to become a part of the sound, to drift in search of truth, yet part of him wouldn't release the last shred of resistance. Deep inside he clung with every fiber of his will to the reality of lungs burning with moist heat and a stomach raw with hunger.

But as the medicine man resumed his chant, his primordial voice seemed to come from everywhere and nowhere at once. Bit by bit, Ladino began to release his mental grip. The heat drained his strength and he began to sway. Memories, scene upon scene upon scene, began to spiral through his head. At last his mind relinquished control and separated from his body, allowing him to float on the intoxicating steam to another time and place.

He opened his eyes and saw their amber depths reflected over and over again in the crystal Snake Walker held before his face. The old one continued to chant, and Ladino stared into the crystal . . . waiting . . . waiting . . . waiting for his vision to come.

When his eyes were about to drowse shut again, a mountain lion's face burst into the crystal, with stars of firelight and rainbow light reflected in its pupils. As the cat gazed at him, Ladino felt as if he were being pulled inside his own soul.

Just before he became of one mind with the mountain lion, the cat's face shrank until Ladino could see its entire body outlined against the mouth of a cave. It was morning in this vision world, and Ladino sat cross-legged atop a hill amidst tall green grass. The cougar turned, twitched its black-tipped tail, and looked over its shoulder. Without words, without a voice, the animal beckoned silently for Ladino to follow just before it leapt into the cave's black void.

Ladino pushed up from the ground and ran toward the black hole. When he stepped inside, nothingness greeted his feet. He plummeted. His stomach lurched to his throat, and he could hear himself screaming, even as the cougar also screamed from some other place within the abyss.

The vision suddenly changed and he was chasing the puma across another meadow. When he lagged behind, the animal would stop, glance back over its shoulder, and twitch its tail, beckoning Ladino to follow before it bounded off once again. Ladino's lungs burned and his breath came hard and fast as he ran, desperate to keep pace with his spirit guide.

At that moment he realized that he heard only his own heavy breathing and heartbeat amplified in his ears. Though the grass and the branches of the distant pine trees swayed, telling him a breeze blew, he heard no sound.

The mountain lion led him to a secluded place where four cubs hid among rocks and undergrowth. Somewhere along the journey, the cat had changed. No longer representing Ladino's soul, his spirit guide, the cat had become a mother . . . a mother asking him in 'in'ch'indi, the voice of silent communication, to study her cubs.

Three were small and weak, passive, their eyes still blue as they stumbled, crying to their mother. Their faces called to mind people he had known: Cadete, the murdered chief; the medicine man who had fallen from the tree; and the third cub, the strongest of the three weaklings, reminded Ladino of himself.

The fourth cub was large and aggressive, its eyes black, unnatural. It snarled, then cawed like a raven. Ladino stepped back in horror as the beast circled its mother from west to south to east, its anti-sunwise path denoting chaos and violence.

For the first time, Ladino noticed the rough, dull texture of the mother cat's fur, how thin and lank she was, as if the one unnatural kitten had drained all life from her, and in so doing, the life from its siblings.

Ladino looked back at the kitten, watching it transform into a full-grown raven. The bird burst into the air, then swooped low over the puma's head, snapping at her ear until blood ran down the fur along her cheek. The cougar growled and pawed the air at the traitor who was no longer in disguise, but the raven only taunted her with a *tok, tok, tok* as it veered away again.

Her remaining cubs forgotten for the moment, the mountain lioness bounded after the evil bird. Ladino chased her, jumping four narrow streams right behind her until finally they came to the clearing he knew so well. It was autumn now, and brown grass swayed in the silent breeze.

The site of the massacre.

His gut clenched.

"No," he heard himself say. The pain in his stomach threatened to double him over, so he turned and fled back across the first stream. He was about to jump the second when the mountain lion leaped in front of him, halting his escape.

The huge cat twitched her tail and lowered her body into a crouch. Her stomach tightened and lifted with a warning growl. When he refused to turn, she flattened her ears and wrinkled her nose, baring four vicious, talon-like teeth.

Despite his trembling limbs and thudding heart, Ladino still refused to look upon the scene of the tragedy, terrified of his inability to control what he might see. Instead, he lowered his own body into a crouch, preparing himself for the mountain lion's attack.

The cougar bared her teeth again, but instead of the eerie scream, Ladino heard his grandmother's breeze-like voice issue from her open mouth.

"Go back, 'Idui Bndaa'. Go back."

Ladino shuddered, but stood his ground. The cat's body melted, became hazy for a moment, then slowly reshaped itself into his grandmother's form. Ladino's heart wrenched to see her reservation-issue rags hanging on her skeletal body.

"I have tried to show you in a gentle way, but you cannot see," she said. "You must go back, *shich'iné*."

Aching to touch her, to hug her, Ladino lifted his arm. He stretched out his fingers to her, coming within a scant inch of her cheek, so close he could feel the weak warmth and energy emanating from her body. Just before contact he curled his fingers back into his palm and dropped his hand to his side. To touch her would pull him irrevocably into the Land of Ever Summer. He would cease to exist in This World of Shadows . . . the real world . . . the world in which he had left Adela.

"Go back, my grandson. Face your fear. See the truth."

Taking a deep breath, Ladino turned his body, one halting step at a time, until he faced the stream he had just crossed. He jumped it and landed at the massacre site once again. Lifeless grass still swayed in a soundless breeze, unchanged. The raven dipped and glided over the meadow, its caw a cruel jeer. Four times the bird scraped its wing along the ground as it flew, and four times a river of red sliced through the deadened grass.

Blood.

Ladino heard the breeze now. The mournful sound filled his head. He flinched as screams rent the air. Horses pounded the earth. Gunshots cracked like thunder. And then they appeared. The People. The small group of Apache women and children. He saw his grandmother, old and feeble as she ran to him, emaciated arms outstretched. A soldier rode down on her. Smeet. He shot her in the back. She threw up her arms before falling to her knees and slamming to the ground on her face.

Guilt and shame, misery and hatred drove Ladino from his body, pulling him up into the sky. Though he looked down on himself standing amidst the butchery, he could still feel the impotent shock and fury slice through his heart. Insanity ate away at his reason until he became a wild man, whirling into action. Growling like his namesake, he pounced on one soldier after another, yanking them off the backs of their horses and slitting their throats in his effort to reach Smeet.

"We led them here. We led them here," the raven heckled, adding its sadistic *tok, tok, tok* of laughter.

The taunt drove Ladino back into his body, leaving him to stand in a river of blood. The huge black bird flew across a changing landscape toward an enormous gaping hole in the rocky earth—a cave spawned of the desert heat and desolation of the Guadalupe Mountains. Pajaro stood at the edge of the black, cactus-toothed mouth, laughing as he held out his arm to the raven. The bird landed on Pajaro's wrist, its wings spread wide as it opened its beak in a sneer.

Ladino looked down and saw something partially hidden in the bleached grass and clumps of *sotol*. The mountain lioness, his grandmother, dead and bloody at the witch's feet.

"I knew where your grandmother was that day." Pajaro laughed, the ugly sound simmering in his throat. "I told the soldiers because I wanted her dead for denouncing me to Cadete! Knowing you have blamed yourself has only added flavor to my revenge." Again the witch laughed, and as he stepped back, disappearing into the cave, his last words echoed from the depths. "Come after me, 'Idui Bndaa', you foolish coyote, and I will destroy you, too!"

Ladino could not move. Still standing in the river of blood, he heard a throbbing, pulsing, echoing sound, like the beating of his mother's heart in the womb. He felt as if the current were sucking him under, drowning him. A crimson tide of rage bubbled up inside him, filling his heart, filling his lungs, filling his mouth until the sound burst forth in a vicious roar.

He charged out of the river after Pajaro, splattering thick, bright red rivulets on the dead grass, like an infant born in the wilds. As he reached the dismembered cougar in the mouth of the cave, he watched its shape shift once more into the form of his grandmother, her corpse sprawled facedown as if she had just been felled by Smeet's bullet and Pajaro's betrayal.

Ladino jumped into the cave, once again plummeting through the blackness. As he fell, the roar of outrage shuddered throughout his body—throughout his soul. Flailing his arms, he continued to fall, until he was aware of a misty haze and a glow far below him. Firelight. Suddenly, he became one with the steam and burned with the heat of the flames as he reentered his own body inside the sweat lodge.

He jerked and threw his arms back to catch himself. Opening his eyes, he was startled to find the medicine man facing him, still beating his drum, still holding the crystal. As if cued by Ladino's returning thoughts, the old man opened his eyes. His shoulders slumped and he lowered the faceted stone.

"Your guilt is cleared, my son," whispered Snake Walker, all strength drained from his voice. "I will see that your father's people no longer blame you." Squinting, the ancient one cocked his head. "This cave. Do you recognize it?"

"Yes, My Father," Ladino replied, his voice solemn.

"The Abode of the Evil Ones." Snake Walker nodded, his expression grave. "It is fitting that One Who Speaks With Birds would choose the forbidden place to flaunt his contempt for our ways." He reached out and traced the yellow pollen circle divided into four equal parts on Ladino's chest. "*Nda'i Bijuul Siá'*. The completion of Life's Living Circle waits there for you, my son. You are reborn. Follow your heart. Claim your vengeance."

Adela tossed fitfully beneath the lightest fur on her pallet. Long ago she'd stepped outside and watched the full moon set, plunging the world into an atmosphere the color and consistency of ink. Now she could see a patch of metal-gray sky through the smoke hole. By slow degrees the patch turned blue, until golden light soaked through the thin skin over the doorway, filling the shelter with the promise of the rising sun.

It's dawn! Why hasn't he returned? Is he hurt? Dead somewhere? Murdered by that crazy old man? Where could Snake Walker have possibly taken him?

The first quivering notes of a man's chanting drifted to her from somewhere within the camp and stilled her frenzied thoughts for just a moment. Otherworldly in its emotion and spiritual intensity, the song called to mind mornings at the convent. The sound would have been peaceful, comforting, if not for the fact that Ladino's continued absence had sharpened her panic and frustration to a razor's edge.

She imagined herself berating him for keeping her waiting. For making her wonder and worry, alone and afraid.

As if conjured by her thoughts, the door flap lifted and

he strode into the shelter, sunlight rushing in after him. When he let the skin fall shut behind him, Adela gasped at the sight of the changed man before her. All outward evidence of his white ancestry was gone. Beneath his unbuttoned shirt, painted symbols covered his bare chest with its multitude of scars, transforming him into her dark fantasy image of a pagan god.

Intense.

Primal.

Savage.

Simultaneous thrills of desire and alarm shot through her body, smothered by the heavy pain of an emotion she could only identify as grief. Grief for what? For seeing such obvious evidence that she had lost her tenuous hold on his immortal soul? No, she'd never had, nor would she *ever* have, any real control over him, any more than she could master her own heart where he was concerned. She mourned because once again he was beyond her understanding, beyond her reach . . . and too far beyond the aching need for safety that tortured her spirit.

Feeling confused and vulnerable in her position on the ground, Adela threw back the fur and pushed up from the pallet, smoothing her habit and straightening her bonnet.

"I've prepared my horse, and Snake Walker has provided me with food." Ladino stepped closer to her around the fire's dead ashes. "I leave right after Nantan Estrellito finishes the Morning Song."

She'd never seen his face set in such a fierce mask of purpose. At first she could only stare at him, still under the spell of his transformation as she noticed the painted disc covering his tattoo. Then she saw the dark circles under his eyes and the almost imperceptible wilt of his shoulders, and her nurse's instincts rescued her voice.

"As invincible as you seem to think you are, you've over-extended yourself. You need to rest, Ladino."

"No. I know where the woman is headed."

Adela rushed toward him, but the change in him stopped her short of her desire to lay her hand on his arm. "Did the old man tell you where Pajaro's stronghold is?"

"The 'old man' is Snake Walker, the medicine man, and no, I figured it out for myself."

"How?"

He glanced away for a moment, his jaw clenched. "Snake Walker helped me see things the way I should have seen them from the beginning. The way I had been trying to see them, but wouldn't allow myself."

"How?" she asked again.

He wouldn't meet her gaze. "Visions."

"What do you mean?"

"I saw the location of Pajaro's stronghold in a vision."

"You mean you remembered it," she corrected.

"No, I dreamed it," he said, his voice more defiant now. "Pajaro spoke to me. I saw him in the mouth of the cave. I recognized the cave."

She nodded. "You remembered it."

He grasped her shoulders and shook her. "Damn it, Adela, mock your own faith, doubt your own faith, but *don't* doubt mine! I was at the site of the massacre. There was blood. Blood everywhere. Rivers of it." His face twisted into a vicious snarl. "And Pajaro was there. I didn't lead the soldiers to my grandmother's camp that day. He did."

The desperate pain in Ladino's voice and the shine in his eyes stole Adela's voice. He continued to hold her arms in his bruising grip, but she didn't protest, so trivial was her pain compared to the glimpse he had revealed of his.

He released her and stepped back. Adela watched him

fight for control of his tortured expression.

"I want the bloodiest revenge I can inflict." He clenched his jaw. Even so, a tear escaped his lashes and streaked through the paint on his cheek. "I want four thousand rivers—no, four *million*—to run red with the blood of Smeet and Pajaro."

"Ladino—"

"No!" he shouted, holding up his hand. "No more preaching your civilized White Eye ways, Adela."

"But—"

"I'm leaving you behind," he announced. "I want no more interference. No more distractions." Still facing her, he stepped back, closer to the leather flap. "No more responsibility for anyone's life but my own."

"But I need to go with you." Panic unlike any she had experienced in fifteen years clenched her throat. "My brother—"

"I said before that I would bring him back, and I will. But you will stay here," he ordered. "Safe."

"No!" She rushed to him and clutched his arm. "Ladino—"

He shook off her grip, flipped aside the skin over the door, and disappeared, leaving her no chance to refute his command.

Adela gritted her teeth against a scream of rage. She would follow him, no matter what he did to try and stop her. But if she could just convince him he could trust her not to do something foolish, perhaps he wouldn't want to leave her behind.

But how could she trust his heathen Apache vision?

How could she not?

She would not allow herself to be abandoned again, even if it meant facing yet another wilderness with a man she wasn't sure she could believe—a man whose violence she could never hope to control.

Once again her choice had been burned down to the terrifying essence of faith.

Chapter Twenty

Adela swiped a sheet of perspiration from her forehead and squinted up at the cloudless sky. Four vultures floated on the air currents above them. The carrion birds had been following them for three days, waiting, Ladino said, for them to drop dead in the blood-boiling heat.

As dizziness swirled through her head, she relinquished her study of the sky and resumed her climb. Still trudging along some thirty feet below Ladino, she led her horse amidst clumps of prickly pear cactus that clung to the belts of gray-brown rock like tortured souls clawing their way out of hell.

Though the lingering humidity gave evidence of rain several days past, nothing flourished in the Guadalupe Mountain wasteland except ocotillo, *sotol*, cactus, vultures, snakes . . .

And Ladino.

Like the black-tailed rattlers she'd seen sunning themselves on a rock this morning, he appeared perfectly within his element. But then he'd packed away his shirt and trousers in favor of a calico breechclout. With his gun strapped around his hips, and his long hair gliding down his sinewy, golden brown back, he looked more Apache than ever.

He scanned the ground as he moved, crouching occasionally to study a group of rocks, or to touch the broken twig of a greasewood bush as he searched for sign of the Apache woman's passing. He'd lost her trail yesterday, and since then he'd set a relentless pace, even though he'd insisted on walking to save the horses from collapse. Adela shared his desire to find the woman before she reached the stronghold, but she didn't know how much longer her own body would last before *she* collapsed.

Propping his foot on one of the rocks, Ladino surveyed the identical hills surrounding them, oblivious to the display of muscular inner thigh he presented for her view. Exhausted she might be, but even her aching muscles couldn't distract her from the sheer magnetism of his physical presence.

Adela forced her attention to his face. "Have you found any sign yet?" she asked, shielding the right side of her face from the glare of the late afternoon sun.

A grim frown crossed his features. "Not yet."

"Can we rest soon, then? I'm tired," she said, dismayed by her whining tone. "And hot."

He scowled down at her. "Get rid of your habit. Too much modesty counts for nothing out here."

"I can see that," she shot back, furious to admit he was right. Three times already he'd suggested she peel down to her chemise and petticoats, and this time she was tempted to do just that.

"You should have stayed at the reservation."

"Maybe so," she snapped. "But you're stuck with me."

He measured her with a dispassionate glance, obviously still angry, even after eight days since leaving the agency. Sliding his gaze away, he turned and forged a path toward the crest of the hill. As Adela watched each long stride, she couldn't help but admire his body's sensual grace . . . or the hard muscles defining the curve of his buttocks.

Wishing she could move as freely, as comfortably, she heaved an indignant sigh and stopped her horse. Unbuttoning and removing her habit cape, she draped it over the saddle. Ducking behind her mount, she removed the rest of her habit, including her breast binding, this time sighing in relief as hot air cooled the perspiration on her sore, chafed skin. After stuffing everything in her saddlebag and re-adjusting her chemise and petticoats, she donned the cape again, buttoning it down her chest.

Just as she'd finished rearranging her clothing, he reached the summit and stopped, turning to watch her. A smug smile teased his lips while she panted and clambered, tugging her horse's reins as she sought purchase in the loose rock. At last she caught up to within ten feet of him and fell to the ground under the full force of his arrogant gaze.

"I see you finally took my advice."

She answered his mocking smile with a glare, still gasping for air as she crawled the last few feet.

"I warned you what you'd be in for when you chased me down and threatened me with Llewellyn's police force." As he offered his hand and helped her up, he smiled again, this time with more compassion. "Look," he said, pointing to the canyon below.

"Water!" she exclaimed, too excited to maintain her fury. Her gaze devoured the sight of a shallow creek tumbling over small rocks and around boulders before it hid in the shade beneath desert willow trees and thick underbrush. "*Cool* water!"

"We'll rest for a while when we reach the bottom, and then you can stay there while I scout the area."

Leading his horse, he turned and angled down several feet to the right, then to the left, his nimble feet dodging clumps of cactus as he hopped from one belted ledge of limestone to another.

Adela dusted herself off and followed, holding her petticoat out to the side so she could see where to place her square-toed shoes.

"You know these mountains well." Her breath came in short gusts as she waved one arm to keep her balance.

"When I was little, we used to come here every year to gather mescal."

"How long has it been since you were here last?"

"About twenty years."

"Twenty years? And you came here as a child?"

She scoured the vast network of hills and canyons that stretched for miles in every direction. Distracted by the thought of how easy it would be to get lost, she almost didn't see the wand of ocotillo about to slap her in the face. She leaned aside at the last moment to avoid the sharp claws hidden beneath the flame-colored blooms and mouse-eared leaves.

"It's not my childhood I've had trouble remembering."

Adela stumbled, her concentration shattered by the unintended meaning his words about childhood memories held for her.

"That's amazing," she managed to say once she'd regained her footing.

"Apaches have long memories. Maybe because there is no written language."

Ladino leaped off a steep ledge and his horse followed. He looped his mount's reins around the saddle horn. The free animal headed straight for the water. Adela's gelding whinnied, tossing his head and pulling at the reins in her hand. She too secured the reins out of her horse's way. Freed to follow his leader, her gelding jumped from the ledge and trotted down the last few feet of the slope.

Adela gathered handfuls of her habit skirt and crouched on the ledge, preparing to ease her body down to the slanting earth a few feet below. Ladino turned and offered his hands to lift her down. Though reluctant to accept his help, she placed her hands on his shoulders as he gripped her beneath the arms. She tried to avoid his gaze as he lowered her to the ground, but his proximity filled her senses with such heat and heady musk that she found herself snared in his eyes.

"Thank you," she murmured, her hands still resting on smooth, firm skin that glistened with perspiration.

He didn't move away, and the expression on his face caused her spine to melt and pool in the deepest recesses of her womanhood. He leaned closer, still watching her, still holding her captive without any attempt at force. Just before he touched his lips to hers, she regained her senses.

"Thank you," she said again. Twisting out of his arms, she set off down the slope again. He followed her, and by the time she reached bottom and the pool where the horses watered, her knees were weak and shaking. Even so, she forced herself to ignore the desire that lingered as she absorbed the drastic change in her surroundings.

"This is beautiful!" She managed to work her mouth into a smile of gratitude and appreciation as Ladino reached her side. Two birds caught her attention then, flitting amongst bright lavender willow blossoms. Their playful flight stirred the sweet, musky scent of the orchid-like blooms, while their chirps and trills mingled with the gurgle of the creek. Eddies in the current had lapped away at layers of limestone to form pools where pale green leaves danced circles, then dodged boulders as they floated downstream. Still smiling, she turned again to Ladino. "Is this where we camp tonight?"

He smiled, gazing at her instead of their surroundings. "I have a better place in mind just a few more miles up this canyon."

"A better place than this?" she asked, hopping from one stone to another, away from him, until she reached the rock island in the middle of the creek from which grew the largest, bloom-laden willow.

His smile remained, unperturbed. "Near a small water-fall."

"A waterfall? In these mountains?"

"Now that you've seen this, is it so hard to believe a waterfall can exist in such a forbidding land?"

She followed his hand gesture as it swept from water, to tree, to turquoise sky. Even the vultures hadn't dared destroy her vision of the perfect oasis. For some reason, the small detail of their sudden absence disturbed her, but she couldn't fathom why.

"No," she admitted. A smile fluttered across her lips before she looked away and knelt down for a drink.

As she cupped her hands in the water and brought the cool liquid to her mouth, she watched surreptitiously as he strode to one of the pools and crouched with his legs wide-spread. His breechclout hung down between his thighs and trailed on the ground as he swished his hand in the water, skewing his reflection.

He'd explained his unusual action to her the first time she'd seen him drink from a pool near a mountain spring. His god had made no two things alike, he had told her—not a blade of grass, nor a grain of sand—and therefore the Apache found it presumptuous to be fascinated with their reflections. Yet he had asked for a mirror that day in the hospital when he'd been afraid she had cut his hair.

What a paradox he was. Many of his beliefs were similar to the teachings of the Church, and still he sat before her like a watchful puma scanning his surroundings for danger even as he brought water to his mouth in cupped, human palms.

She knew those hands had killed, yet as she watched him now, she recognized once again a devout respect in his simple movements, a natural devotion not repressed by complicated ceremony or the masquerade of celibacy.

He took another drink and wiped the back of his hand across his lips. Resting both elbows on his knees, he raised his head and captured her gaze.

Disconcerted, she rose quickly. To disguise her abrupt action, she lifted her face to one of the willow blossoms. She closed her eyes as if enjoying the sweetness, when in fact she fought to calm her stomach and steady the continued weakness in her knees.

"What's wrong, Adela?" His movements lithe, he sprang from one stone to another until he reached her beneath the willow. She backed away, but came up against the tree and rapped her head on the trunk.

"Nothing."

"Nothing?" He grinned, his eyes alight with understanding as he pulled her lower body closer to his and pressed her shoulders against the tree. "Nothing?" he repeated. "We've been driving each other insane since Silver City, and you say it's nothing?"

"Ladino—"

She tried to protest, but her words were obliterated when he claimed the kiss she had denied him before. The moment he touched her lips with his hot tongue, all thought abandoned her, leaving behind only the instinctive need to press her hips even closer to his. She succumbed to that need, inciting a moan from both their throats. His kiss deepened. So intense was her physical reaction she felt as if he were opening the very center of her being. It was that fear of losing all sense of self that gave her the strength to break contact.

She pulled away, her mouth still open, her lips still tingling. He watched her, his gaze intense with desire. Mortified, she shoved out of his embrace and escaped to the other side of the tree.

He didn't follow, but continued to watch her, his breathing fast and heavy. "Are you angry with me?"

"No," she answered, her voice a low murmur as her gaze slid to the horses. Both had drunk their fill and were now grazing a nearby patch of grass, whisking away flies with their tails. "No, Ladino."

She brought her gaze to meet his golden eyes for a moment before her focus fell to his bare chest and shoulders, where sweat glistened on his bronze skin. No matter how much she tried to deny it, to change it, her love for him had grown stronger, her body's response to him heightened even more by a sense of pride in his wisdom, his capability and his spirituality. And when she wasn't consumed with memories of their lovemaking, of the terrifying contradiction of freedom and enthrallment she felt in his embrace, he almost lulled her into feeling . . . safe.

Almost.

She sighed and looked away, up at the sky. Once again she noted the absence of the enormous gliding birds that had been following them, waiting for their demise. Once again the odd sensation of something being very wrong needled her, pulling her thoughts away from the conflict and confusion of her emotions for the moment. She frowned as she searched the air for their ominous companions.

Ladino sighed. He bent down, picked up a rock, and skipped it across the pool. "I'd better see if I can find some sign of the woman." His voice was still husky with thwarted passion. "Chances are pretty good she came by here."

His words strengthened her nagging awareness of the subtle disharmony surrounding them. "Ladino . . ."

"What?"

"Something seems very . . . strange." She stared at the sky until she heard him move, coming nearer.

"What is it?"

"It's . . . it's the vultures," she said. "They're gone."

Instead of looking at her as if she had lost her mind, his startled attention flew to the empty sky. When he looked back at her, she swore she saw embarrassment and a glimmer of admiration.

"I'll see if I can find out what's diverted their attention. Maybe they've found her for us." Touching her cheek, he smiled. "I still say you should have been born Apache."

He removed his knife from its sheath and shoved it in his moccasin. He then unstrapped his gun belt, handing it to her in the ritual now familiar between them. Adela folded the belt around the holster and held the rig close to her, watching him scale the rocky hill as if he ran on level ground. Such decisive agility made her understand the depth and importance of his compliment for the first time.

What was more, she now realized that he had helped her begin to discover that same spirit of confidence in herself. And of all places, this subtle change had been taking place in the wilderness—the birthplace of her darkest nightmare.

Startled awake by the whinny of a horse, Adela straightened from her slouch against the boulder and instinctively felt for the holster in her lap. Dusk threatened the small pocket canyon near the head of the intermittent creek, and the meager sunlight cast long shadows around the rocks, brush, and trees. She searched for their horses, finding them a few feet away, still hidden between a couple of boulders and tied to the stake she had driven beneath the shade of a red-barked manzanita.

Adela heard another whinny. This time she realized the sound came from the direction of the creek. Should she call out in hopes it was Ladino? Maybe he'd discovered a stray horse from a nearby ranch. Or perhaps he'd caught a wild one.

No matter how many excuses she made, she knew instinctively there would be no familiar face emerging from the underbrush this time. She was alone. She had no one to depend on but herself.

Clutching the gun, Adela scrambled up and rushed over to the horses. She crouched behind one of the boulders and set the gun aside while she rummaged between the saddles she'd removed earlier. When she found her saddlebag, she jerked it to the top of the pile, fumbled open the buckle, and yanked out her habit. Stepping into the half-buttoned skirt, she shoved her arms in the sleeves, then shrugged her shoulders into the frock. After yanking the folds of her cape out of the neckline of her habit, she groped the remaining buttons into their holes. Dressed now, she grabbed the pistol and whirled to the ground beside the saddles, her chest heaving with exertion and suppressed panic.

Again the horse whinnied, accompanied by the murmur of a man's voice. Adela fought to hold the weapon steady as she removed it from its holster. The horses perked their ears in the direction of the creek, and her gelding let out a throaty nicker.

"D'you hear that?" came a young man's voice, closer now.

A shod hoof rang on stone, and Adela estimated their distance at thirty feet. Almost at the mouth of her little hideaway.

"Hear what?" This voice sounded older, exasperated.

"Sounded like a horse," came the harsh whisper in reply.

Her horse nickered again. She glared at the wide-eyed animal and slowly cocked the hammer, cringing when it clicked into place. The sound, small as it was, heated terror at the base of her skull and sent chills down her spine and arms.

"There it is again, Cal." It was the younger man, and from the clarity of his voice, she knew they'd reached the opening of her canyon. "And I thought I heard a gun being cocked this time. Over there."

Oh, dear God. Adela closed her eyes, and the creak of leather met her ears. After that she heard only silence broken by an occasional shuffle in the underbrush. Clutching the butt of the pistol with both hands, she leaned to the side and peeked around the boulder.

Horses. Two riderless horses, ground-tied and grazing.

Her heart beat so fast and hard she could hear it in her ears. Maybe they were harmless, but because she was alone, vulnerable, with Ladino miles away, she wasn't about to give up what little advantage she had. She waited for another noise, but all she could concentrate on was the memory of her mother's ear-rending screams—and then the gun blast.

She flinched as if the sound had just this moment shaken her world, yet the silence outside her memories became so taut she could no longer stand the strain. She had to do something. Anything. Even now she knew the two riders were searching the area, creeping closer from the shelter of one bush or boulder to another.

Should she fire distress shots and hope Ladino would hear?

She'd give her position away if she did. And once she

fired the gun, she'd be committed to a course of action she was afraid she wouldn't have the courage to sustain.

Still, she knew they would eventually find her, and if she didn't fire the shots now, when she had the chance . . .

Adela pointed the barrel to the sky, squeezed her eyes shut, pulled the trigger, thumbed the hammer back, shot again. Three times the pistol barked and jumped in her hand.

Within the echo of her own shots, she heard the click-click noises of two rifles being simultaneously levered into play from opposite sides of her hiding place.

"We see your horses," said the younger man from somewhere off to her left, beyond the boulder. "Come out and show your face!"

Adela swallowed what felt like her heart as she maneuvered Ladino's belt around her waist and buckled it. Still shaking, she fumbled open the loading gate behind the cylinder with her thumb. After she'd pushed the three spent shells out of their chambers with the ejector rod, she clumsily pulled three more from the loops on Ladino's belt. Her fingers trembled so badly it took several moments to shove fresh bullets back into the empty chambers. Closing the gate, she took the gun in both hands again, squeezing her eyes shut for a brief moment as she swallowed once more, this time in preparation to speak.

"P-please don't shoot. I'm—I'm a nun." She hoped to call on the universal respect people usually felt for the religious.

"Stand up so we can see you and we'll hold our fire."

With the rough boulder biting her back, Adela pushed herself slowly to her feet, turning toward the voice as she moved. She saw the young one near the horses beneath the manzanita tree, no more than ten feet away. Blond and fresh-faced beneath a battered gray hat, he couldn't be more than seventeen. Just a little older than the boy Ladino had killed. She shivered, suddenly understanding just how dangerous and intimidating even a boy years shy of true manhood could be.

"Hell, you *are* a nun!" the youth exclaimed, his grin of surprise turning into a leer as he studied the gun belt buckled loosely around her hips.

As Adela leveled the weapon at his chest, alarm raised the hair at her nape.

"Hey, Cal, get a look at this gun-totin' nun," the boy said, his demeanor detached, as if he faced the quivering barrel of a loaded pistol every day.

Something moved in Adela's peripheral vision, and she shifted just enough to see the one called Cal emerge from behind a boulder shaded by a locust tree. The older man's dark complexion, black hat, and clothing blended with the encroaching shadows.

"Come on, Rupe," he said. "She don't have nothin' we want."

"No?" The one called Rupe cradled his rifle in his arms, his complete indifference to her threat a taunt in itself. "Nice gun ya got there, Sister." His gaze dropped to her hips. "Nice belt, too. Looks right purty on you. It'll look even better on me."

Adela backed away, realizing too late she was distancing herself from the horses—her only means of escape.

Rupe advanced again, crouching near the saddles. He plucked up something, and as the black and gold beads dangled from his fingers, Adela realized he held her rosary. It must have fallen out of her saddlebag when she'd removed her habit.

"Looky here, Cal," he said, holding the beads. "Why, I'll

bet Lupita would like this." He bit one of the gold beads. "Pure gold!" he exclaimed. "Hell, there's no tellin' how appreciative she'd be if you was to give it to her."

Cal shook his head. "I don't think so."

"Aw, why not?" Playful disappointment laced his tone.

"For God's sake, Rupe, she's a nun."

"You suppose she's packin' a shooter like that to protect her virginity?"

"Your mama shoulda slapped your face a time or two, pup." An indulgent smile belied Cal's rebuke.

A smirk teased Rupe's lips as he stepped closer, and Adela retreated, clicking back the hammer. Rupe stopped, but malice smeared across his face, filling his grin with evil purpose.

Have you ever stared into an enemy's eyes and seen the blood lust only your death will satisfy?

Ladino's words echoed in her head.

Shoot to kill. If you're going to hold a gun on someone, be ready to follow through, or they'll take it away from you, and you'll be the one who dies.

Still, Adela didn't know if she could consider taking another person's life again, even to save her own.

"Let's go, Rupe, we don't have time for your shenanigans."

Rupe shook his head and leveled his rifle at Adela, the rosary dangling like a cruel jeer from his trigger finger. "Not until I have that gun of hers." His gaze traveled her body. "And I'm going to enjoy unbuckling that belt, too."

"Back off, or I'll kill you," Adela said, her voice deep and throaty, filled with a purpose and confidence she did not feel.

"You're playin' with fire, pup," Cal warned.

Rupe only smiled wider as he charged Adela.

She pulled the trigger, and a wave of shock spiraled up her arm. Rupe screamed, and his gun fell to the ground.

"Damn bitch shot me!" he yelled, clutching his arm. Blood oozed between his fingers and ran down his hand, staining his striped shirt as well as the rosary he still held. Murderous hatred replaced the shock in his eyes, and he charged her again.

This time Adela didn't shoot, but dropped the pistol as he grabbed her and wrestled her to the ground. He stretched the rosary across her throat, and the beads bit into her neck. Adela's heartbeat pounded in her temples as she clawed at her attacker's eyes, knocking his hat off with her frantic struggles.

Suddenly Ladino's face sprang into view above Rupe's head, and a long silver blade appeared at his throat.

"You're playing with more than fire, you little son of a bitch."

Chapter Twenty-one

Ladino yanked Rupe up by the hair and hauled him back against his chest. He fought to restrain his fury as he held his knife against the boy's throat. Adela scrambled to stand, coughing as she clutched her own throat, her face and neck smeared with the coward's blood.

He had almost waited too long before stepping in.

"Drop the rosary, Rupe," he said into the youth's ear, refusing to acknowledge the horror twisting Adela's expression.

"Cal?" Rupe pleaded. "Help me? Please?"

"Drop it!" Ladino ordered.

"He can have the rosary," Adela said, her voice a taut rasp in her throat. "I don't need it."

"That's not the point." Ladino met Adela's gaze, defiant as he pressed the knife closer to Rupe's jugular. "One little slice, and it's all over."

Cal aimed his Winchester at Ladino, his movements slow, as if he'd just recovered from a stupor induced by the surprise attack.

"I wouldn't do that if I were you," Ladino warned. "You couldn't shoot me fast enough to save Rupe's life. Besides, you know as well as I do your friend started this." He smiled at Cal, pivoting on his heel and pulling Rupe's stumbling body between them. "But if you'd like to shoot him now to make up for your earlier cowardice, I'd be glad to hold him up for you."

"Ladino, please," Adela begged. "I don't want the boy dead."

"You're not the one holding the knife."

She flinched. "P-please, let him go."

"The minute I do, Cal over there is going to blow my head off, if he doesn't blow yours off first. Do you want that to happen?"

Adela glanced over at Cal. When Ladino saw the beseeching look she gave the man, an inexplicable jealousy scoured through his system, all because he knew the coward had the ability to give her what she wanted most. A peaceful end to the violence.

Cal shifted and lowered his rifle. "Drop the rosary, Rupert. Now. I already told you we don't have time for this."

Rupert did as Cal said, opening his hand and letting the rosary fall from his bloody fingers. "All r-right," he said. "I d-dropped it. Now, let me go."

"Sounds more like an order to me. Don't you know Apaches don't take orders from White Eye runts like you?"

"Ladino, *please*," Adela repeated, the desperation in her voice edged with anger.

Ladino ignored her. He refused to soften.

"We don't want no problems," said Cal. "The pup's just a bit feisty and knot-headed's all."

Ladino dragged Rupe with him to Adela's side. He released the kid, thrust him away, swept up the pistol from the ground. At the look of awe on Cal's face, an upswelling of pride and triumph filled Ladino's chest. He'd moved with such speed his actions had appeared to occur simultaneously to the white man's untrained eye. He hefted his bowie by the tip of its blade, ready to throw at the boy, while he aimed the gun at Cal.

"Now, drop your weapon, Cal, and get the hell out of here, before I kill both of you."

Cal, his expression somber but sensible, lowered his Winchester to the ground and began to step backward toward the mouth of the small pocket canyon. "Come on, pup, let's go."

Rupe glared at Ladino and then at Adela as he clutched his wounded arm and stumbled away, showing an immature bravado by turning his back on Ladino as he followed Cal to the creek. Soon Ladino heard staccato hoofbeats as the two men rode away.

He turned to Adela. "Are you all right?"

To his surprise, she glared at him and unbuckled his gun belt, letting it drop to the rocky ground. She turned toward the horses, but she had just taken two steps before he grabbed her arm and whirled her to face him.

"What the hell's wrong with you?"

"How long were you hiding?" she blurted. "How long did you test me to see if I was capable of killing that boy?"

Ladino released her. "How did you know?"

"How—long?" she repeated, enunciating each word.

As he watched the moisture streak down her face, tracking through the dust and blood on her cheeks, his own anger quickly replaced his shame and astonishment.

"I told you to shoot to kill, Adela," he said. "Any hunter knows maimed prey is dangerous prey."

"But he wasn't prey, Ladino, he was a man!"

"A *dangerous* man. Damn it, he was strangling you!"

"And you didn't try to stop him until it was almost too late."

"You mean I didn't stop you from pulling the gun on him, don't you? I didn't take the decision to save your own life out of your hands until you had already given up. You would have let him kill you. That's what this is about. I didn't save you from yourself."

Deep furrows sketched across her forehead, and she tightened her lips into a contorted grimace of anguish. With her fists balled at her sides, she spun on her heel and strode to her horse. Growling her impotent rage, she gripped her blanket and saddle, hefting both to the gelding's back.

"I hate you for doing that to me!" she yelled, whirling to face him, her habit skirt billowing around her ankles. "I hate you for manipulating me because of some twisted need to prove a point and make me accept your ways. You want me to be a killer. You want to soothe the conscience your mother tried to instill in you by turning me into what you are—some kind of savage, callous *animal* bent on murder!"

Ladino felt her words like the thrust of his own knife in his heart, and a startling cruelty welled into the wound and out of his mouth before he could stem the flow. "Yes, and you wouldn't want me, you wouldn't be so fascinated with me if I were as meek and mild as one of your damned priests! Admit it, Adela. You hide behind that habit—"

"No!" She shook her head. "You're wrong!"

"—You're afraid of anything outside your convent walls, so you pray and confess and pretend to live a meaningful life—"

"My life *is* meaningful!"

"—but you know something is missing. Don't you!"

Adela's chin quivered, and suddenly her whole body began to shake. "You just don't understand," she whispered.

"Looks like we're even," he ground out.

"I just can't believe hurting and killing people will make my life more meaningful, like you think it will make yours."

"I just want you to understand what it takes to survive out here."

"I don't *want* to survive out here!" Her neck went limp

and her forehead drooped against the saddle. "I've already lived like this, and I *hated* it." She brought her arms up and cradled her head in her hands to shield her face from his gaze. Her gelding stretched its reins tight against the stake as it turned its head to look at her. The animal uttered a soft nicker, as if to comfort the weeping woman, and Ladino felt remorse twist the knife of pain Adela had already driven into him. Even the stupid beast knew to offer solace, while Ladino only stood by and watched, aching to touch her, wishing he could say or do something to make amends for his harsh words and his betrayal.

The rosary. She'd forgotten to pick up her rosary.

Ladino strode back to the site of the attack and lifted the string of beads from the rocks and grass. Gold roses winked, greedy for the fading twilight, and the black onyx roses, dull and slick with blood, looked like Apache Teardrops. His teardrops. Unshed. Uncertain. Sitting like rocks in his throat.

He trudged to the creek and swished the beads in the current. The dark stain clouding the water reminded him of the blood-filled rivers in his vision. Yet instead of fouling the stream, the blood dispersed and rushed away, leaving the water clear and pure once more. He wished his own taint could be so easily washed away in Adela's eyes. But as surely as this rosary and its testament against violence had been her legacy from her mother, the beads of his own birthright—death, mourning, fury, and vengeance—were irrevocably intertwined, sullying the decades of his life.

No matter how much his own mother would wish otherwise—no matter how much it hurt for Adela to hate him for his blood lust—he could not change. Not yet. Not until Smeet and Pajaro were dead. Even then he wondered if his pain and restlessness would ease, if he could live a life with some semblance of peace.

Ladino's shoulders slumped, and he sighed as he draped the wet rosary across his knee and untied his headwrap. He swished the red cloth in the water, twisted out the moisture, grasped the rosary and stood up.

When he returned to the horses, he found Adela yanking the girth tight on her sidesaddle. The gelding stood patiently, his muscles twitching only to shimmy away an occasional fly as she locked the buckle in place. Ladino stepped on a twig, snapping it in two, and Adela jerked her head in his direction. Anger hardened her eyes, now swollen and red-rimmed.

"You forgot your rosary," he said, offering it to her.

She studied the string of beads, then turned away, lifting her saddlebags behind the blanket roll. "I don't want it anymore."

Feeling her words like a personal rejection, he stiffened, grew defensive. "Why? Because it had the boy's blood on it?"

"Yes."

He stepped closer, dangling the beads from his fingers, taunting her with them. "Look, Adela. Blood washes off."

Her gaze flew to his face, and an angry challenge blazed in her eyes. "But the memories of blood never come clean, do they?"

Ladino had nothing to say. He wished he could hate her for this—for stripping his spirit bare until all he had left for protection was a shroud of aching vulnerability.

"Would it be so bad to be more like me?" He despised the guilty, groveling undertone of his voice. "Do you find me so repulsive?"

"I don't find you repulsive," she answered softly. "In fact, I—" She shook her head and lifted her hand to cover the words she would not utter. Her gaze drifted up to his tattooed forehead, softened, then returned to his eyes. A new tear followed the path others had cleared through the blood and dust. She lowered her hand. "It's just that I can't understand you, Ladino. Where does the killing stop? Who pays last for your pain? If you ask me, I think you're paying the highest price, with all that is good and kind in your heart."

"Nothing good and kind can exist in me until Smeet and Pajaro are dead."

"But you're wrong—"

"Here, wipe your face and neck," he ordered, holding out his wet headwrap. "You have the boy's blood all over you."

Stricken realization burst into her eyes. She lifted her hands to her throat, then fluttered her fingers up to her cheeks.

"Here," he repeated, his offer gentler this time.

She grabbed the cloth, and his gut clenched as she scrubbed her face and neck so savagely that red blotches stained her skin, more violent in appearance than the blood had been.

As she shoved the soiled fabric back in his hand, trembling fingers betrayed her struggle for control. "Saddle your horse," she ordered, dismissing the subject and the rosary still dangling between them. "And pick up those guns if you have to. I want to get away from this place. I'm cold."

Though waning, the moon was still large enough, still close enough to trace silver light across the hilltops and light Ladino's path as he led the way up the canyon toward the falls.

Adela had been eerily quiet for the past hour, and each

352

time he glanced back, he saw her still rigidly seated on her horse, with one hand clenched around the opposite shoulder as if to ward off the shivers wracking her body. Her gelding stumbled over a loose rock, and she clutched the reins tighter, but her mesmerized study of some obscure spot beyond the horse's mane never wavered. With her shoulders hunched as if the blanket of newborn stars threatened to collapse and smother her, she looked like a child. A lost child, exhausted, half-asleep, yet scared and cold, even though the warm air whispering around them had to be close to seventy-five degrees.

He pulled back on the reins, stopping his mount. The horse jerked its head up and pranced its forefeet as Ladino urged it to turn in its tracks.

"Are you all right, Adela?"

Her gaze drifted up and found his face, but it was almost as if she didn't see him, as if she were looking at someone else. When she nodded, the silver moonlight caught the moisture in her vacant eyes, and chills sliced across the back of his neck.

"It's just a little farther," he added to reassure her—and himself. "Half a mile. Can you make it?"

"Yes," she answered, her voice tight and thin.

His chills multiplied, chasing an instinctual foreboding down his spine. He'd seen the momentary madness seize others—knew it had seized him the day Smeet murdered his grandmother. How much longer until the last fiber of her frayed self-control snapped?

How would he handle the consequences when it did?

"Damn," he muttered under his breath, frowning.

He turned his mount and pressed his moccasined heels into the horse's flanks, urging the animal to a swift walk over the rocky terrain. As he had hoped, her gelding met the quicker pace. Soon, puddles dotted the canyon floor, left behind where the waterfall-fed creek seeped into the rocks and disappeared. Not much farther now. He could hear the water's soothing sigh, and as they rounded a bend, the moon above the concave cliffs of the canyon spilled its light into the gentle veil of cascading water. Swallowed by the large pool at the bottom of the fine spray, the light resurfaced in gentle ripples across the moon's reflection.

He'd get Adela into the shelter of the cave behind the falls, build a fire, make her as comfortable as possible until she could regain her warmth and collect her wits.

But when he glanced back at her again, dread sluiced over his shoulders. She repeatedly wiped her hand down her arm and then frowned at her palm, as if it were soiled and wouldn't come clean.

"Damn," he muttered again, his worried frown deepening until he could feel the day's accumulation of desert grit clenched in the creases of his skin.

At last he led the way across the point in the rocks where the pool overflowed into the creek bed. On the limestone bedrock beneath the limbs of a walnut tree, Ladino leapt from his horse and looped the reins around the saddle horn. He turned to Adela with the intention of helping her down, but she had already dismounted and was hopping on one foot, her other hung up in the stirrup. She fell, thudding to the rocks, and her foot came free. Before Ladino could offer his hand, she scrambled to her feet and ran, splashing into the pool beneath the waterfall.

Stunned, Ladino watched the chest-high water float the hem of her cape in a circle around her as she ripped loose the bonnet ties beneath her chin.

"I want it off of me. Off!" she screamed, flinging the bonnet into the water, where it floated on captured air pockets. She fumbled frantically with the buttons on her habit cape. "And I want this coat off, too!"

Coat?

Ladino unbuckled his gun belt and let it fall to the rocks as he plunged into the pool, his high-stepping strides sending giant sprays into the air.

A ragged cry ripped from between her clenched teeth as she slipped the last button free and yanked the cape from her shoulders. The material pooled like a black stain on the water.

Ladino waded closer. Her cape slipped past his bare skin, and he grabbed it out of the water, tossing it to the limestone bank. Feeling his way over the moss-slick rock beneath his moccasined feet, he closed the distance between them.

"It's so heavy," she whispered, her childlike voice full of disbelief. "So heavy." She yanked at her mended sleeve, and the sound of ripping material joined the whisper of falling water. "Please . . . help me . . . get it . . . off." Her voice jerked with panicked sobs.

"I'm going to help you, Adela." Ladino swallowed, moving his hands to her throat and the first button in the long row down the front of her frock that disappeared into the pool. "I'm going to help you." His own fingers trembled as he worked each black disk out of its hole. Finally he pulled the habit from her body. The garment streamed water as he heaved it to the bank next to her cape. "There," he assured her. "The coat is off. It's gone."

She shivered in her wet chemise, her fists clutched to her breasts. "I didn't want him to die. I didn't want him to die," she said over and over again under her breath, shaking her head. "But I was so cold," she added with a whisper. "So cold."

Ladino frowned, confused. "Adela?" he prodded, but she ignored him. A low, whimpering wail keened from her throat. "Adela, listen to me." He grasped her upper arms. "That man you shot didn't die." She refused to look at him, so he shook her, once, to get her attention. "He didn't die."

"But he did," she argued, her tone bewildered. "I saw." When she lifted her gaze to his, her expression reflected such childlike pain, such betrayal, he felt it like a spear in his heart. "You said blood washes off," she accused. "I can't get it off." She shook her head weakly. "I can't get it off."

"Then I'll help you," he promised softly, still confused, but willing to do anything to bring her back to him. "I'll help you wash off the blood."

Chapter Twenty-two

Tightening his grip on her bare shoulders, Ladino moved with her slowly, closer to the fine spray near tumbled boulders at the base of the canyon wall. As the breeze caught droplets of cold mist and splashed them into their faces, Adela flinched, struggling in his hold.

"It's just water, Adela," he soothed. "Just water."

What have you done to her, you savage son of a bitch?

"Let it flow over you. Let it cleanse your heart and spirit." When his mind formed his next words, a shaming twinge of hypocrisy collided with an intense longing he didn't want to think about, didn't want to understand. "Let it baptize you until you're free of blame."

His words seemed to draw the tension from her body until she stood pliant in his embrace and allowed him to move with her into the heart of the spray. Refreshed by the gentle wetness coursing over his own body like female rain, he lifted his hands to Adela's head and tunneled wet fingerpaths through her hair. She closed her eyes and lifted her face to the moonlit veil. A sigh escaped her lips, and her expression changed from trepidation to a relief so rapturous Ladino's own ragged breath emptied from his lungs. Rivulets ran like cleansing tears over her cheeks and down her nose, and she opened her mouth, taking the desert life force inside her as if she were White-Painted Woman preparing her body to conceive.

Ladino shuddered with the primal desire to protect her, to cherish her . . . and more. So much more. He smoothed one hand down her cheek, chasing the moisture that caressed her face, until her chin rested in the frame of his forefinger and thumb. Cupping the slim arch of her neck in his palm, he continued to cradle her head in his other hand. Watching her, aching to be absorbed within the depths of her body and soul, he slid his thumb across her chin, caressing the bottom of her lower lip.

When she straightened her head and gazed at him with rationality restored to her eyes, her own passion kindled, his chest tightened and his breath caught in his throat.

Reason and restraint fled as he covered her mouth with his. She moaned, and the water she had warmed on her tongue spilled across their joined lips, down his chin, and over his wrist.

Like a phoenix risen from the ashes of some mysterious nightmare of death, she returned the hunger of his kiss with an appetite that startled him. All shreds of the honor and gentleness he had hoped to show her exploded into shards of raw lust. She was alive, she was lucid again, and she wanted him as much as he wanted her.

He didn't want to think beyond this moment.

With the water still coursing over their bodies, she tightened their embrace, twining her arms about his neck and pressing her body close. Her chemise clung to his chest, arousing his senses to the warm, soft woman's flesh beneath thin, wet cotton.

She broke away from his kiss and gasped for air. "I don't know how you do it," she whispered. "I don't know how you make me forget everything but you. Nothing but the moment matters when I'm with you like this."

Spreading her hands wide, she sluiced water down his arms until she broke the surface to tease his hips with her fingertips. Before he realized her intention, she untied the leather thong holding his breechclout in place. The wet calico drifted away, and water enveloped the hard length of him, tightening him until gooseflesh gripped his thighs. His desire should have been squelched, but when she moved one hand between them and began to caress his rigid manhood with the backs of her fingers, he shuddered as his stomach clenched and new life engorged him.

Gripping her thigh, he pulled her leg up until it rested at his hip. For a moment she stopped stroking him and met his gaze, her expression startled. Moments later, understanding filled her eyes and teased her lips with a seductive smile as he took her mouth again. He unlaced her shoe and shoved it off her heel with his fingertips. The shoe bounced off his calf and drifted down his lower leg. Gliding his tongue across her upper lip, he caressed the bottom of her stockinged heel with his fingers, then moved up her calf, into the crease behind her knee, up the bottom of her thigh and in . . . gliding across her buttock until he found the divide in her pantalettes.

She broke away from his kiss again and stared into his eyes while he teased his fingers along the soft folds of flesh partially covered by tight material. When he slipped one finger beneath the edge of the fabric and eased it away, her breath left her in a shuddering sigh. Watching her, losing himself in her eyes, he slid his finger deep within her soft cleft, then slipped it out slightly and toward himself until he found the focus of her pleasure. As he began to stroke her, she closed her eyes and her leg quivered as she hooked her heel around his thigh and rocked against the pressure of his finger.

"Do you want me, Adela? Here? Now?"

She nodded, then whispered, "Yes." The word ended

with a hot breath followed by a warm, suckling kiss on his wet shoulder.

As stroke after stroke heightened her whimpers and brought her closer to climax, his entire body tightened until he thought he would die with the sharp pain of his desire. Growling low in his throat, he gripped her other thigh and lifted her, shoving off her shoe even as he brought her down on him, entering her in one swift thrust.

Her own wild cry ripped into the air with his. Gripping his shoulders, she arched her upper body away from him. As the water rained down between them, she began to move, abrading his bare hips and thighs with the fabric of her stockings and pantalettes.

He clutched her to him and carried her out of the pool, where he sat down on the rocks smoothed by decades of flowing water. With her astride him, he reclined slowly, holding her at arm's length. She looked suddenly frightened and insecure, yet breathtakingly erotic in her wet, thread-bare chemise and tattered petticoats.

"You take the lead, Adela," he said softly.

At first she only stared down at him, but when he reached up and ran a finger from her chin, down her neck, to the erratic pulse in her throat, she closed her eyes. And as he thumbed her budded nipples beneath the wet fabric, thrusting his hips at the same time, her head fell back and a cry escaped her throat.

Slowly, she began to lead him with her own rhythm . . . circling, grinding, sweetening, pulling, coiling the sensations within his body until he was oblivious to the hard rock surface beneath his hips and back. He felt the muscles in her thighs begin to tremble, and with a cry of need, of desperate frustration to be fulfilled, she collapsed on top of him, biting the shoulder she had suckled and kissed earlier.

Further aroused by the wild nip of pain, he took over. Clutching her head with one hand and splaying his other over her bottom, he drove himself so deeply within her he felt he could fuse her body with his into a single flame.

"*Shilhú'ash*, Adela. Go with me. *Eim'báhshay.*"

She nodded, and her breaths came in hot, whimpering pants against his ear as she shared the cataclysmic promise of splintering mind, heart, and spirit.

So close. So close. One more rotation. One more, and then his release ripped his body asunder, tearing a cry from his throat. Her cry burst free at the same moment, and their voices mingled, piercing the blanket of stars above the moonlit canyon.

Much later, as he floated back to himself, he could still hear and feel her quick breaths against his ear.

Only now each breath caught as she fought back a sob.

He sat up with her, then gripped her head and forced her to look at him. Tears streamed down her face, and a wet curl of hair teased her eyebrow. He smoothed it back with the others rioting over her head and cradled her cheeks, wiping away her tears with his thumbs.

"Adela, what's wrong?"

"I—I love you so much, Ladino," she whispered, her voice lurching with emotion, "so much, but—" She gulped and wrenched her head away, pushing herself off his lap. "I can never be free to love you the way I want to."

He pushed up from the rocks and stood before her, placing his hands on her shoulders. "Adela—"

"Please don't touch me any more. I can't stand it."

Before he could respond, an anguished sob burst from her lips and she ran into the thicket of wild grapes along the curve of the far canyon wall. Even the loud thrashing of her escape couldn't drown out the sounds of her misery. He poised himself to follow, but an instinct—an intuition—stayed him. As much as maimed prey was dangerous prey, he also knew wounded animals preferred to nurse their injuries alone and in peace.

He decided instead to tend the horses, gather their things, and climb up to the cave where he could build a fire. He'd find her later—if she didn't see the firelight and seek him first . . . when she was ready.

The sound of the waterfall whispering past the cave opening couldn't soothe Ladino's worry. He gazed through the veil, but saw nothing but darkness beyond the firelit droplets. No sign of Adela. Just a few more minutes and he'd go after her.

He heaved a sigh, picked up a long stick and prodded the scraps of burning mesquite. Sparks jumped into the columns of aromatic smoke like shooting stars, arcing toward the ceiling before they died into ash. He was just about to stand when he heard movement. A rustle of soft material against one of the bushes that clung to the ledge outside. And then she emerged, her body framed by the cave opening, the skin exposed by her threadbare white chemise aglow in the firelight. Water fell behind her as she stood with one black-stockinged foot atop the other, clutching her arms with her hands to cover her breasts.

"I was getting worried," he said, rising.

She opened her mouth to speak, but made no response as her gaze strayed to the back of the pocket cave, where he had stretched a rope and hung up her habit to dry, along with her bonnet, cape, and shoes, as well as his breechclout and moccasins. After a quick glance at his trousered legs and bare feet, she returned his regard, her face flushed with embarrassment.

"Are you cold?"

"A little," she murmured.

Ladino grabbed a blanket and draped it around her shoulders as he urged her into the cave and close to the fire. She offered a tentative smile as she sat cross-legged on the ground, careful to keep the blanket tucked close about her.

"Are you hungry? I found some mescal patties in a cache at the back of the cave. Would you like some?"

"No. Thank you."

At a loss, he sat down across the fire from her, and several moments of silence passed as he watched her stare into the flames. At first he thought she had slipped back into a state of shock, but the concentration in her eyes was too intense, her anguish too tangible. Instead, she seemed to be gathering courage.

"Thank you for giving me time alone. Time to think." She glanced up at him at last. "And I'm sorry if I worried you. I worried myself tonight." Her laugh sounded tight and insecure, ashamed. Then she sobered as if she had gathered the strength she needed at last. "I apologize for losing control," she said, her tone bewildered. "I don't understand what came over me. I could hear myself talking— about coats and blood, and—and I knew what I was doing was mad, that I wasn't a little girl anymore, but I couldn't stop myself." She shook her head. "Not only must you think me a hypocrite, you must think me insane."

"No."

"No?" she replied, her voice incredulous. "How could you not think so, when I'm not even sure?"

"Because I know what it's like when the pain you've fought so hard to control suddenly rebels against the smothering numbness inside. The detachment that makes everything bearable, that hides the ugliness of the truth, suddenly becomes a prison your soul must escape. The emotions you release can be destructive." *As they were, and are, in me.* "But they can also heal."

"Yes," she said, her voice thoughtful, and the rapt expression on her face told him he'd helped her grasp some mysterious understanding of herself that she had denied before. "And I want to thank you for—for . . . doing what you did. I know you don't believe in what you said—about baptism and water washing my heart and spirit clean—but when you were in the pool with me, washing me, caring for me . . . loving me . . ." She returned her gaze to the fire. "I did believe. You made me feel more loved and forgiven and safe than I've ever felt in my life. For a while you made me forget. I truly was free." She shivered. "But freedom has a price," she continued softly.

"And the price of your freedom is a murdered man's bloody coat," he observed, meaning no cruelty. He only wanted to understand.

She nodded, shivering again, clutching the blanket tighter. Ladino rose and circled the fire toward her. He sat down behind her, gathered her in his arms, and pulled her back against his chest. Though she didn't fight to get away, her shoulders remained rigid. He waited, knowing the longer he held her, the more she would relax, the more she would relinquish control—the easier it would be for her to speak without looking into his eyes.

"Who was he?" he whispered into her ear. "Tell me."

The fire crackled, flames undulating as cinders leaped toward the ceiling. Water drizzled past the mouth of the cave, and a moist breeze carried the sweet fragrance of willow blossoms on the waves of mesquite smoke.

"I was six," she began, her tone resigned to confession. "It was November, there was a couple of inches of snow on the ground, and I was cold. Neither Mama nor I had a coat. Or a blanket. And we didn't have any food." As she relaxed into his embrace at last, he accepted her weight, and the shuddering in her shoulders eased. "He was a drifter with nowhere to go. Like us. He said he'd share his food if we let him share our fire. I could tell Mama was nervous, but she agreed because we were both so hungry. Despite his wild looks—his long, dirty hair and stained clothes—he seemed nice enough. Nice enough that after I was full for the first time in weeks, I fell asleep by the fire."

She fell silent, and Ladino made no attempt to question her, knowing she needed to set her own pace. As they gazed into the fire, her head alongside his, her curls tickled his cheek.

"Later," she continued, "a ripping sound woke me, followed by soft laughter, a muffled whimper, and some shuffling. When I opened my eyes, the man was on top of Mama, covering her mouth with his hand. She was struggling, clawing the snowy ground, reaching for something. He'd taken off his gun belt, and Mama's fingers shook as they came within an inch of his pistol handle. I didn't know what to do. I was terrified. That's when I saw her little gun, tossed in the snow just beyond the ring of firelight. I guess he'd found it and thrown it out of her reach. Her gun was too far away, so I grabbed his pistol and put it in her hand."

Adela swallowed, and Ladino felt her breath picking up speed.

"She shot him, and the blood—" She shuddered and said no more for several moments. "Mama pushed him off, and even though she was crying, sobbing, she wrestled his coat off his body. Her hands shook as she searched the pockets and put his money and pocket knife in her skirt pocket. Then she draped the coat around me." Another shudder wracked her body. "I was crying now, too, and I threw a fit and tossed the coat on the ground. I told her it was bloody and heavy and I wanted it off me. She put it right back on, buttoning every single button up to my throat. I'd been complaining of the cold, she said, and that man had died to give me his coat. The least I could do was wear it." Adela shook her head. "She'd never been so harsh with me. She was like a different woman. Now I understand why. But then . . . ?" She shrugged.

"The next morning we reached Santa Fe, and she left me in front of the convent with a promise to buy something warm for us to drink. She never came back. That was the last time I saw her until I went to care for her in Silver City."

Several seconds passed with nothing but the crackle of the fire and the whisper of the falls to keep company with the silence.

"For a long time I thought she blamed me—that she was punishing me for what had happened. Ever since then I've promised myself I would never be responsible for another person's death. I wanted to atone, so I became a nurse."

Ladino tightened his embrace. "You were doing what you had to do to survive, Adela. To stay alive. To save your mother."

"In my mind I know that, but in my heart . . . ?" She rolled the back of her head on his chest until his chin rested atop her damp curls. "You were right about me from the beginning. It's not my vows holding me back. I'm hiding. And my life does feel meaningless sometimes. Especially now, when . . . after . . ."

"Adela, I spoke those words in anger."

"Yes, but you were right. And I'm afraid I can't change. I can never be the person you want me to be. I can't even be the person I want to be because there's something missing. Call it faith, or trust, or whatever you like, but I don't have it. Even in God. Especially in God." She shrugged, but he knew the movement was anything but dismissive. "The closest I've come is being with you these last weeks. With your bullying and prodding, I thought I was beginning to find some strength and faith in myself. But when I was alone, facing that boy with a loaded gun in my hand, I realized I couldn't count on myself." She sighed. "I don't have the courage to survive in your world."

"I'm sorry I made you doubt me, Adela. But you do have courage. I've only known a handful of women in my life with your mettle. I wanted to show you that you have what it takes to survive."

"Yes, but is survival at any cost worth the price?"

Her words pierced him, forcing a sigh. "You have to decide that, because even if I vowed before your White Eye God to protect and defend you with my life, I couldn't promise I would succeed."

"I know," she said, defeated. "Sometimes love isn't enough, is it?"

Her head lolled on his chest, and he held her in silence, not knowing what to say, yet realizing her words held the breadth and depth of her entire life's experience in its miserly fist, imprisoning her within her fear. For her the risk would always be too great, the terror of abandonment too severe.

Long after she had fallen asleep and he had gently laid her down and moved around the fire to study her as she slept, her words haunted him.

And her face. Whether illuminated by the flame of a kerosene lamp, or by the fire in this cave, Ladino realized that seeing her face in such light awakened his longing for a settled life. A life filled with peace. A life in which each night he could watch her across a fire, across a thousand fires for just as many years. He imagined echoes of her features in the faces of their children. He imagined a little girl with a long-haired doll who would race to his embrace in the bright circle of a communal blaze.

But she had expressed it so clearly.

Sometimes love isn't enough.

And sometimes, he added to that, *awakenings are more cruel than rude.*

The next morning, dressed in her dry habit and stiff shoes, Adela climbed down the tumbled boulders beside the falls. Ladino stood in the shade of the walnut tree, saddling his horse. Her gelding stood ready, and he nickered when he saw her stride near. Ladino lifted his head and looked at her, his expression impassive. Unfathomable. As if the intimacy they had shared last night had never happened. Or didn't matter.

But she knew that wasn't so.

She swallowed, forcing herself to smile at his implacable mask. In the sunlight she noticed shadows beneath his golden eyes. Even the vertical lines framing his sensual mouth seemed more pronounced.

"You know, with all that . . ." *happened yesterday,* she had been about to finish before she stopped herself. "You never said if you found the vultures or any sign of the woman." She swallowed, hoping to control the quiver in her voice. "Did you?"

"The vultures had found the remains of a cow," he responded, his voice cool, impersonal. "Some meat had been sliced away with a knife. And I found the woman's moccasin prints as well as grass discarded from a cradleboard.

That means your brother is still alive, but it also means One With No Relatives is no longer making an effort to hide her presence."

"Do you think that means she believes Smeet has given up?"

"Yes."

"What do you think?"

"Smeet will never give up. I think he's ridden ahead to wait for her at Pajaro's stronghold—the Abode of the Evil Ones."

Chills clenched her nape. "Abode of the Evil Ones?"

He nodded. "Many lifetimes ago a medicine man went into the death hole and never returned. Some say they hear his drum beating deep inside, but only the Evil Ones come out at night, spiraling into the sky like smoke. It is taboo for anyone to enter the cave."

"That's only superstitious nonsense," she scoffed.

"Is it?"

"Then why does Pajaro—?"

"Because he's a witch—'*Ént'íin*. An evil man with no honor. And because he has no respect for our ways, he is unpredictable. He'll be twice as formidable as Smeet."

"If we even encounter him. He may still be in Mexico."

"We need to be ready, just in case." He startled her by touching her cheek. "Adela—"

She silenced him by turning her head and pressing a kiss into his palm. "Don't worry, Ladino. I'll be all right. You've prepared me well." Before he could respond further, she hoisted herself into the saddle. "Let's go. We have a lot of ground to cover if we want to reach Pajaro's stronghold before dusk."

Chapter Twenty-three

The death hole gaped like a hungry maw, its limestone lips and cactus teeth still blurred as Ladino tried to focus the binoculars. Something moved in the left half of his view, making quick progress as it neared the point where the mesa top had collapsed and rock-littered earth descended into the throat of the cave. One more adjustment and diluted detail sprang into crisp clarity. It was the woman. She picked her way through prickly pear and *sotol,* carrying the *ts'ál* on her back.

"What is it?" Adela asked. Her touch on his arm made the picture jump and quiver. "What do you see? Is it her?"

"It's her."

"What about Jonathan Junior?"

The dim evening light and the shadow of the cradleboard hood made it impossible for Ladino to discern the babe's face, but he did see a pale arm wave in the air near the gourd rattle.

"He looks fine from here."

"Oh, thank God," she whispered. From the edge of his vision he could see her beside him, peeking over the top of the boulder behind which they hid. "Any sign of Smeet, or Pajaro?"

A rock dug into his belly as he shifted the binoculars. For a moment he caught sight of the far escarpment edge. Beyond and below the sheer drop-off, flat desert floor stretched for miles into Texas. Angling the glasses lower again, he found the vantage point above the cave's protected entrance and looked for a hidden sentry among the layers of rock and tangled creosote bushes. No one. Pajaro had not returned from Mexico, or someone would be at least partially visible, keeping watch.

But what about Smeet? He slowly circled the mouth of the cave, then scanned the entire horseshoe-shaped depression before the entrance. He could see nothing but tumbled rocks, desert vegetation and an occasional juniper tree. No sign of Smeet. No horse. Nothing out of place. Just One With No Relatives moving ever closer to the black void.

But then what had he expected from an ambush—beating drums?

"No sign," he answered, but his hair crawled on his scalp.

The woman lurched and fell.

"She's down!"

"What?"

"She tripped over something. A hole or . . ."

"What?"

As Ladino watched, Nigel Smeet exploded from the earth and vegetation, holding a rope in his hand—the rope he must have hidden and yanked tight just in time to trip the woman. Before she could scramble to her feet, Smeet rushed toward her, dirt clouding off of his body. She whipped out her arm, and Smeet jumped back to avoid the slice of her knife.

The infant's frightened screams rent the air.

"That sounds like a baby crying!" Adela's frantic voice obliterated the distant sound. "What's happened? Is he hurt?"

"I don't think so. Not yet. Stay here."

"But—?"

"Just stay here." He thrust the binoculars at her and ran,

stooped over, for his horse hidden next to hers behind a juniper.

Smeet might expect trouble from the south, but he'd be less prepared for a surprise attack from the north.

Especially an attack by a dead man.

Ladino leapt into his saddle and raced down the slope as the woman and Smeet continued to fight. Smeet clenched her knife hand in his fist, then backhanded her across the face. Her head whipped to one side, and she stumbled and fell backward. The knife flew out of her grip, arcing hilt over blade through the air. Ladino kicked his horse's flanks, urging the animal into a full gallop as he ripped the air with a war cry.

Smeet stared, his eyes wide, his face pale as he mouthed the words, "Oh, bloody hell!"

One With No Relatives turned to look at him, then took advantage of Smeet's surprise and scrambled to her feet. She ran, weaving through cacti and jumping over boulders.

Smeet chased her, and Ladino pounded the earth behind them, pursuing them beneath the vaulted roof of the cavern mouth. As he gained on Smeet, he heard hoofbeats behind him and turned in his saddle. Adela rode toward him, her head low over the horse's neck as she dodged the startled cave swallows that screeched and swooped from their nests in the surrounding walls.

"Adela, no!" His voice echoed in the immense void.

Her gaze jolted to his and he saw the fear in her eyes, yet she didn't slow her pace. Her body remained set with grim determination.

"Damn it, Adela, go back or you'll get yourself killed!"

"Catch Smeet, I'll follow the woman!" she shouted back.

A string of expletives burst from Ladino's mouth as he launched himself off the back of his horse, tackling Smeet.

Adela thundered by, and the combined pounding of horses' hooves shook the ground beneath Ladino's body, filling the air with a hollow drumming sound. Dust clouded over him and Smeet as they rolled and slid farther into the throat of the cave.

Ladino ended the roll on top of Smeet, but Smeet grabbed a rock and smashed Ladino alongside the head. Ladino crumpled. Blackness feathered the edges of his sight as Smeet wrestled out from under him and stood. He felt blood trickle through his hair as he fought to focus on his enemy's sneering face.

"So, you filthy half-breed, you aren't dead after all!"

Smeet kicked Ladino in the groin. Ladino groaned, his body shriveling into a fetal position.

"I'll just have to take care of that myself. But shooting's too bloody good for the likes of you."

"Oh, dear God! Ladino!"

Adela's cry startled him. He shook his head to clear his vision, searching for her, but he found the Apache woman instead. She vaulted over the ledge at the far left corner of the cave, then jumped from one limestone boulder to another among the many that had fallen away from the cavern wall. As she disappeared below his range of vision, he found Adela at last. She had dismounted to follow the woman, but was now scrambling back up the slope toward him.

The ominous click of a pistol hammer jolted his attention back to Smeet. "On the other hand, shooting the nun will bring me great pleasure."

Ladino pushed himself to his knees and threw his torso at Smeet's legs. Smeet toppled, and the gun exploded, the shot echoing with his yelp of surprise. Smeet tumbled down the slope toward the ledge. He grasped for a clump of *sotol* to stop himself, but missed, grabbing the ledge instead. His

373

lower body rolled over the edge.

"Help!" he cried, his face twisted with panic as he clawed for purchase in the rocks.

The world trembled as Ladino reeled to his feet and started downhill toward Smeet, unsheathing his knife as he ran. He imagined Smeet begging before life ebbed away beneath the slice of his blade.

"No, Ladino!" Adela struggled up the hill. "Please don't—"

"Damn it. You're not going to change my mind! I've waited too long for this."

"And I've waited too long to find my brother."

Ladino didn't respond. A cry of anguish and frustration tore from her throat, and she turned, racing back downhill to the place where the Apache woman had escaped. From the edge of his vision, Ladino noticed his horse had found hers. Both animals nickered, prancing and tossing their heads as Adela jumped from ledge to boulder and descended into the cave.

"Pull me up, you bloody savage!" Smeet demanded.

Ladino moved with purpose toward his enemy. The man's struggles ceased and his eyes widened, focusing on the knife. A perverse sense of pleasure filled Ladino, erupting in a smile. Reaching the ledge at last, he stepped on Smeet's fingers, then crouched down and placed the blade alongside the man's jugular.

"It's a long way down," he said, sighting along Nigel's body into the dark chasm gaping beneath the man's feet. "You should beg instead of giving orders."

Below and to the left of Smeet's dangling form, he caught sight of Adela as she cleared the boulders and drew near a finger-like ledge within jumping distance of a narrow, perpendicular shelf. When she stopped and looked up at him, realization clubbed his dazed brain. What if the woman hid in some unseen place beneath the hollow ground on which he stood? What if she lay in wait, ready to push Adela to her death?

"Stay there, Adela," he ordered, his voice laced with panic. "Wait for me."

"I've got to catch her, Ladino. She's getting away."

Ladino's hand shook as he held the knife to Smeet's throat.

"All right," Smeet whined. "*Please* pull me up. Then you can shoot me. Just don't let me fall. Please don't let me fall."

"What makes you think shooting's any better for you, you miserable son of a bitch?"

But as Ladino stared into his vanquished enemy's face—into gray eyes full of terror and supplication—he couldn't use his blade. His need to see the man beg and suffer deadened into ashes beneath the greater need to help Adela.

As he jerked his bowie away from Smeet's throat and reached out to pull the man up, a strange sound emerged from the depths of the chasm—a sound like a million beating wings. Echoing, throbbing, pulsing with no discernible rhythm.

The sound of *Nu'bil*. Chaos.

A bestial whirlwind spiraled, anti-sunwise, from the death hole. The Evil Ones swirled around Smeet, tangled in Ladino's hair, flapped their wings against his legs, and thumped his chest. Afraid he would lose his balance and tumble into the void, Ladino threw himself down on his stomach and gripped Nigel's arms over the limestone edge.

Fire sprang to life from the shelf opposite Adela—a torch held by an unseen hand, reaching, *stretching,* for Smeet's legs.

"She's going to set him on fire!" Adela yelled.

Flames raced up Smeet's trousers, but it was Adela who caused Ladino's heart to stop beating as she leaped through the cloud of beasts swarming over the black void. His heart remained suspended in his throat until she landed on her hands and knees on the opposite ledge. Relief pumped triple-time into Ladino's chest, sending his blood whooshing past his ears.

A raw scream burst from Smeet's throat as the flames engulfed his body. He released his hold on the ledge and clawed frantically at Ladino's arms. Ladino winced as fire singed his skin. He fought to sustain the extra weight, but Smeet kicked the air, his frenzied movements jerking his body out of Ladino's already tenuous grasp.

"Oh, dear God!" Nigel cried. "Help me! I'm going to—"

Smeet's shoulder seams ripped and gave way, leaving nothing but the remains of burning sleeves in Ladino's hands. Shrieking, Smeet plunged into the abyss, illuminating the jagged rocks around him and setting hundreds of spiraling bodies on fire as he fell.

Gooseflesh crawled over Adela's neck and shoulders as Smeet's screams echoed through the chamber. She straightened and looked up at Ladino through the swarming cloud of bats. Behind him, the strip of sky had darkened to a purple bruise flecked with spiraling black bodies. Only the burning scraps of material in Ladino's hands illuminated his face as he stared down into the chasm, his expression unreadable.

"Daaiinaa," he said, his voice somber. "It is finished."

He dropped the burning sleeves, and they drifted into the darkness amidst the counterclockwise swirl of winged creatures.

Called back to their purpose, Adela cast a quick glance toward the place where the woman had stood beneath Ladino's ledge, holding a torch, and found that she had disappeared.

"Ladino—the woman!"

He sprang to his feet, and his balance wavered, swerving him near the edge. Adela gasped, covering her mouth until he straightened, racing across the slit of black-speckled sky to the corner where she and the woman had descended into the cave.

He scrambled down the tumbled rocks to the finger-like projection over the chasm, then hurtled through the cloud of bats. He slammed against the wall, but righted himself by gripping the rock.

"Did you see where she got the torch?" he asked, his voice almost inaudible beneath the sound of flapping wings.

Adela shook her head. "No."

"Maybe there's a pocket in the wall." He blinked, then scanned the area. "Damn, it's getting dark. But I can still see a shadow up there." He lifted his chin, indicating a large spot high on the wall, darker than the surrounding rock.

Before she could respond, he began to scale the wall, feeling the rock face for small holes, using them for finger- and toeholds. A stray bat fluttered in his face and he swatted it away with one hand. His foot slipped, and Adela gasped. He searched for another toehold, and the sound of his moccasins scraping against rock made her cringe. As she held her breath, she couldn't help but wonder if the Apache woman had done the same with Jonathan Junior strapped to her back.

"Found some," he called. "I'll toss a couple down."

One torch landed on the ledge in front of her, rolling toward the chasm. Adela scrambled after it, picking it up just before it seesawed over the edge. The other landed at her feet. She clutched both to her chest, her breathing quick and shallow with worry until Ladino climbed down and stood safely beside her once more.

He took one of the torches and lit it with a match he'd taken from a fold in his moccasin. Then, with his torch, he lit hers.

"Let's go." He turned and charged ahead, his balance still uncertain.

Adela ran after him, fighting to keep her own balance over the rock-littered floor. Soon they slowed down, and the sounds of bat flight faded, replaced by a silence so infinite she felt as if they had entered a void where nothing existed beyond the immediate glow of their torches. Clammy, suffocating darkness swallowed each exerted breath and wrapped like a shroud around her body until black almost became a presence. A promise of death. An implosion of the soul.

This, she decided, *is the true birthplace of nightmares.*

"Are you sure you've never been in here before?" she whispered. "That you don't know where we're going?"

"No. I told you—entering this cave is taboo."

Now she understood why. She started to shiver, chilled as much by fear as by the drastic drop in temperature.

"Then how will we find her? How will we find Jonathan Junior? How will we find *anything?*"

When he turned to face her, the torch dancing light and shadow on his features, Adela gasped.

"We will find the woman, Adela. We will recover your brother safely, and we will get out of here. Alive."

"How do you know?"

He offered her a self-deprecating smile, but the expression in his eyes revealed how twisted he felt by his own terror—his dread of evil forces, of breaking custom and suffering the consequences. "I don't," he said simply, then turned and moved on anyway.

As Adela followed Ladino deeper into the cave, she took a deep breath and let it out in an effort to soothe her panic.

Dripping water echoed around them, and their torchlight illuminated pools with surfaces so calm they looked bottomless. From the midst of the pools, enormous pillars rose like icicle-draped totem poles, their reflections making them appear twice their true height.

"I see torch glow," Ladino said, leading her beneath rock daggers and translucent draperies striped with mineral deposits. "Up ahead to the left. Beyond those broken columns."

As she followed him across a natural rock bridge, the gorge beneath their feet swallowed the torchlight into nothingness. Her heart pounded in her throat. She'd been frightened when she'd jumped the chasm at the cave's entrance, but crossing this void in all-consuming darkness gave her terror new life.

"The light isn't moving," he whispered. "She must have stopped."

"Why?"

"She probably doesn't know we've followed her. I'm sure she believes only those under Pajaro's protection are able to enter this cave and live." He paused, his expression thoughtful. "We can work this to our advantage."

Ladino crept closer, his moccasined feet silent as he moved over the rocks. Adela followed, treading carefully as the passage narrowed between jagged, broken cave formations. When they cleared the doorway, an enormous cathedral-like room opened before them. Adela breathed her awe, for in the center of the room's vaulted ceiling, a huge hole opened to the sky, revealing hundreds of stars. Moonlight bathed thousands of ceiling daggers and at least twenty central pillars in a silver glow.

At the foot of one of those pillars crouched the Apache woman, unaware of their presence. Her torch stood clamped between several rocks on the floor. She had just settled Jonathan Junior back into the *ts'ál* and was tying the leather straps.

Ladino spoke in Mescalero, his voice booming in the vast chamber. The woman gasped, gaping at them both. She grabbed the cradleboard and stood, clutching the babe to her chest. As Adela and Ladino moved toward her, the woman shifted her weight as if to flee, but Ladino barked a command. She stopped, and Ladino spoke again, this time at more length. As they drew nearer, the woman's attention flew to Adela, an expression of awe warring for prominence with terror.

Adela frowned at Ladino. "What did you tell her?"

"I told her you were *'isdzá 'izee 'iil'in*—Woman Who Makes Medicine—and that your power is stronger than Pajaro's. That's why we were able to enter this cave. I told her you had been sent to find her in a vision from your mother, who lives in the Land of Ever Summer. That your mother is the woman whose baby she stole."

Adela gaped at Ladino. "But that's ridiculous. I have no power. My mother didn't—"

"Aside from killing the woman, the only way we can hope to get the baby away from her is to frighten her with her own beliefs. No matter what you believe, to her Pajaro is a witch. Without his protection she believes she would not be alive right now. Only one as powerful as Pajaro could enter this cave, and only one as powerful as Pajaro would have courage enough to be sent on such a mission by a spirit from the dead."

Adela considered his logic. She stepped closer to the woman until the two of them stood within an arm's length. She spoke to Ladino. "Tell her I've been sent to take my brother home where he belongs."

Ladino translated. The woman clutched the cradleboard closer, and her expression swayed between defeat and defiance. In the end she shook her head, her short hair swinging about her chin as she voiced her refusal in harsh, guttural tones.

Adela needed no word from Ladino to understand the woman's response. Frustration threatened to overwhelm her, yet some hand of instinct seemed to guide her—to offer her one more tactic.

"Her hair is short," Adela said, swallowing the emotion that suddenly clogged her throat. "Ask her who she mourns."

Ladino stared at her, and for a moment she thought he would refuse. Finally he translated.

Tears pooled in the woman's black-brown eyes and streaked through the dirt on her face. She gritted her teeth and her eyes hardened. Disappointment and despair crowded into Adela's heart, but then the Apache woman's expression broke, and when she answered, Adela recognized the misery in her voice.

"She mourns her husband and her infant daughter, killed in a raid by Mexican soldiers four months past." Ladino's explanation came almost as a whisper. "The soldiers tortured the baby, then cast her on the campfire. They ruined her beautiful little body for her new life in the Land of Ever Summer, and Pajaro wouldn't let her go back to the site to give the bones of her daughter and husband a decent burial. She resents him for this, but she has nowhere else to go. She has no other family."

Adela ached for the woman's pain and loss. Though One With No Relatives revealed little of her heartbreak except the tears that clung to the edge of her firm jaw, Adela knew she felt the injustice—the abomination—like a fire of rage across her soul.

In an insight born of desperation, Adela handed her torch to Ladino and untied the ribbons at her throat. She slid her bonnet off her head, revealing her own short hair. As she had hoped, the woman's attention fixated on the cropped tresses, her eyes filling with confusion, curiosity, and even a hint of what looked like respect. Adela knew her action was a cruel trick to play on the woman's grief, and she was about to compound that cruelty by using words that ripped her own heart to shreds.

"Tell her . . . tell her I understand her wish to keep the baby. I understand what it's like to be alone, to have no one—no relatives but the baby she holds."

Again Ladino stared at her, and she wasn't sure if he would speak. When he did, the woman's face softened even more as she gazed at Adela. When she replied, her tone suggested interest and concern.

"She wants to know if you cut your hair in the Apache way to mourn your mother's death."

As the woman watched her, waiting for her reply, memories of Minna's suffering bombarded her, laying bare the fury and bitterness she felt for the ones who had subjected her mother to such a cruelty. But for the woman who held her baby brother so lovingly, so possessively, she felt only compassion.

"Yes," Adela answered. She followed the word with a nod, no longer able to meet the woman's gaze for the guilt of her half-lie. Even as she glanced away, she knew the woman would probably accept her avoidance as a sign of re-spect for the intimacy they had shared. The thought left her heart hollow with the disgrace of her deception.

A moment passed before Adela realized the woman was speaking again, her soft, nasal voice low, resigned to sorrow.

Lifting her attention to Ladino for the translation, Adela caught the sparkle of elation in his golden eyes even as he spoke in somber tones. "The woman says she loves this baby as much as she loved her own daughter, but because she is a hunted woman, a member of Pajaro's band with no-where else to go, you have made her see that she can't keep him. To keep him would only bring him death. Her life is too uncertain. She wants more for him." Ladino paused, glancing at the woman himself before turning back to Adela. "She will return him on the condition that you keep the new cradleboard she made for him. She has said many prayers over it, for his safety and health. It is a home to him. The only thing she has to offer to show her love."

Adela bit her lower lip to quell the sudden quiver of her chin. "Tell her I'm grateful to her for keeping my baby brother safe. And tell her . . ." She faced the woman more fully. "Tell her that I've been told her daughter is safe and whole and happy, living with loving family members in the Land of Ever Summer. Her daughter knows how much she is loved and missed."

Ladino voiced the message, and the final shards of the woman's stoicism crumbled. Her face twisted with emotion as she handed the cradleboard to Adela. She gripped the gourd rattle dangling from the hood and shook it before Jonathan Junior's face. He reached for the tan ball, gurgling as he smiled up at One With No Relatives. She returned his smile, even through her tears.

" 'Idui Bndaa'!" a man's voice echoed like thunder, shattering the intimacy of the moment. Adela whirled. Ladino dropped one of the torches and whipped around, knife at the ready. Four Apache men stood at the mouth of the narrow passageway. The one in front, dressed in a cavalry coat and breechclout, stepped forward. Adela shivered and clutched Jonathan closer to her as torchlight reflected in the Apache's cruel eyes and illuminated the black plumage of the raven on his shoulder.

Pajaro.

Ladino tensed, fighting the residual dizziness that punished him for turning too quickly. He crouched, ready to spring as Pajaro sauntered forward.

"So, you have followed your vision and found me," Pajaro taunted, speaking Mescalero. "Or rather, I have found you. Once again I have caught you unaware."

"Being caught unaware does not make me fully unprepared."

The raven spread its wings and opened its beak, projecting its owner's disgust. Pajaro glanced at Adela, and a mocking smile spread over his face. She lifted her chin, and he laughed, returning his attention to Ladino.

"You have your father's taste in insolent women. But why should I expect more from the bastard half-breed son of a slave, and a stupid, prideful coyote?"

Ladino clenched his teeth, leashing his emotions before he spoke. "You're angry because my mother wouldn't respond to your attention when you were a foolish young boy just out of baby grass. You envied my father's prowess, his status as a warrior, and his possessions. Your soul has been stained by lust for your own cousin, and your heart is eaten by spite. You have no honor, and you have earned no respect. You have to steal fear in its stead. You are a tyrant, not a true chief as Cadete was."

Pajaro shook his head, still smiling, yet the atmosphere around him seemed to radiate his fury. "You are worthless, 'Idui Bndaa'. Weak. *Duu nk'échiida.* Like the rest of your family. Like your grandmother, clothed in her *honorable* reservation rags. That is why she is dead, and I still live."

"And that is why I intend to avenge her death on you."

Pajaro lifted his eyebrows. "And when it is you who dies, what happens to your woman? What happens to the baby?"

"I will not die."

A sharp laugh burst from Pajaro's throat. "You are just as stupid and prideful as your father was."

"Are you afraid to accept my challenge?"

Pajaro's lips tightened into a thin line. As he handed his torch to one of his warriors, the raven flew from his shoulder and landed high atop one of the columns, its wings outstretched. Moonlight stroked its feathers and tinged its sharp beak with an eerie glow as it settled its wings to its sides.

"All right, 'Idui Bndaa', I am ready."

"This is between us," Ladino reminded, securing his torch among some fallen rocks, "to be settled in the Apache way." He removed his gun belt and let it fall to the floor. "Your men will not interfere except to bind our wrists."

Pajaro's eyes glistened with sly amusement as he unsheathed his knife. "My men will not interfere."

He turned and muttered a command to one of his warriors, who stepped forward and knotted Ladino's wrist to Pajaro's with a rawhide thong.

"Ladino, what are you doing? He'll kill you!"

"Stay out of the way, Adela."

The moment Pajaro's man stepped back, Pajaro

whipped his knife at Ladino's stomach. Still distracted, Ladino jumped away. Twisting sideways, he narrowly escaped the blade. As Ladino battled dizziness, Pajaro jerked him forward again. The witch laughed as he stabbed Ladino in the thigh, then flicked the blade up across the inside of his biceps.

"What a foolish coyote you are, 'Idui Bndaa', to let me cut you apart bit by bit." Pajaro's face split with a malevolent grin. "At least your father's blade was swift and sure, not limp and weak like yours."

Ladino growled his rage and swung Pajaro around, pulling him off balance, scattering their audience to one corner of the cave. While Pajaro stumbled, Ladino brought his knife arm across his chest and whipped it back, aiming for Pajaro's neck. Pajaro ducked and leaned back, but not far enough. Ladino's blade slashed his enemy's face. A gash opened at the top of his cheek, just a quarter-inch under his eye.

The quick movement cost Ladino. Pajaro's face became two masks of hatred instead of one. Ladino blinked to clear his vision and watched blood stream down Pajaro's cheek. The witch lowered into a crouch and advanced on Ladino, his breath coming in slow, sinister gusts. Ladino began to circle, avoiding him, trying also to avoid Adela's gaze as she watched him, her free hand clutched to her mouth. He continued to move, waiting for Pajaro's impatience to provide an opening.

"You fight like an old woman, like your grandmother, 'Idui Bndaa'. Biishe could finish you."

The raven screeched and dived from the column. "Biishe!" the bird cried, repeating its name as it swooped at Ladino's head. Ladino ducked, and Pajaro chose that moment to stab at his belly. Ladino jumped back, but stumbled over a rock and fell, pulling Pajaro with him. Before Pajaro could straddle him, Ladino rolled, twisting his body up in the arm of his nemesis and smashing his elbow into the face of the witch. Pajaro grunted. Ladino leapt to his feet, jerking his foe with him.

Again the quick movement cost him. Ladino blinked to settle his sight, and Pajaro pressed his advantage. Again and again he slashed and stabbed at Ladino. He missed each time, but drove Ladino closer to a point where the rock surface changed into a huge depression that looked like it had once been the floor of a shallow pool.

As Ladino jumped back to avoid yet another jab, what he thought was solid rock cracked like eggshell and gave way beneath his feet. He threw his arm back to save his balance, and his knife hurtled out of his hand. He heard Adela's gasp and his own yell as his body plunged then yanked to a stop, still attached to Pajaro by the rawhide binding their wrists.

Instead of finishing him, Pajaro crouched at the edge of the hole. He levered his blade beneath the thong and cut one loop. Ladino's body dropped an inch, and nausea jolted into his stomach.

"No!" He grasped Pajaro's knife and tried to wrest it away, but Pajaro sliced his palm.

Ladino jerked back his hand. Before he could react again, the raven swooped, screeching as it flapped its wings in his face. Pajaro cut another loop. Ladino's body dropped another inch. The bird pecked and clawed Ladino's upraised arm as he struggled to fend off the attack.

"Ladino, here!" Adela's voice. Too close.

"Get back, Adela!"

He felt the hilt of his knife in his palm. Though blinded by the frenzy of the raven's attack, he tried to locate her; he needed to see that she was safe. She screamed. Ladino found her then, sprawled on the ground. Blood stained her mouth and nose, the result of Pajaro's backhand.

Killing rage filled Ladino. He howled a war cry and lashed his blade at the raven, stabbing it in the breast. The bird plunged into the hole behind him.

Pajaro yelled his fury. With renewed vengeance he sliced at the final loop binding their wrists. Just as the leather snapped, Ladino caught his nemesis behind the knee with his knife. Pajaro crumpled backward, and Ladino severed muscle and ligament as he used the Apache's leg for leverage to climb out of the hole. At last he rolled onto solid rock. Pajaro's feral, blood-smeared face was a blur in his eyes as the knife arced toward him. Ladino dodged the blow and jabbed his knife upward, straight into Pajaro's chest.

The witch collapsed atop him, lifeless. Ladino disentangled himself from the body and stood. Stumbling to Adela, he reached down to help her to her feet. With no regard for the blood that smeared his body, she threw her arms around his waist, and her body shook with sobs.

"I thought I was going to lose you," she whispered. "I couldn't let him kill you. I couldn't."

Ladino stared over Adela's head at Pajaro's warriors and spoke to them in their native tongue. "Will any of you challenge me to avenge this man's death?"

The three men looked from one to another, but said nothing. His breath still coming in heavy gusts, Ladino waited, but none of them made a move toward him. One of them gestured at One With No Relatives. After one last glance at Jonathan Junior on the ground nearby, one last smile at Adela, she joined them.

Ladino pressed a kiss to the top of Adela's head. "Let's get out of here."

Chapter Twenty-four

"She's leaving me," Ladino murmured to the baby he held in the cradleboard. "Take good care of her for me, Little Squirrel."

Jonathan Junior gurgled his response, then shoved his fist in his mouth as if he were eating a nut. Ladino smiled wistfully and lifted his gaze, ignoring the stares of train passengers milling about the platform as he watched Adela. The Cristo Rey Mountains framed her slender form as she turned from the ticket window and strode toward him, her sturdy shoes clicking across the wooden planks.

"Did the conductor find a place for the goat?" he asked when she reached his side.

Adela nodded. "In the baggage car behind us." She smiled, her lips quivering. "I only hope Nanny is less interested in trunks and valises than she was in saddlebags."

Ladino couldn't bring himself to share her attempt at humor, even though the milk goat's appetite had been a constant source of amusement and exasperation since they'd bought her from a goatherd near the Slaughter Ranch.

Afraid she would see the naked emotion in his eyes, he glanced down at her habit, noticing for what seemed like the hundredth time that she had cleaned it since reaching El Paso, and she'd mended the rip with black thread. Only because he stood this close was he able to tell her habit had been ripped at all. Only because he knew her did he remember why.

Memories. After today, they were all he would ever have. *Stay with me, Adela. I love you. Don't go.*

He wanted to say the words. But he wouldn't. He wanted her to be happy, and if her happiness couldn't include him and his uncertain future, then he would have to let her go. If she ever came back to him, it would have to be because she wanted to, not because he had begged.

The train whistle blew, and a cloud of acrid black smoke puffed from the smokestack and drifted back, settling around the passengers still standing on the platform.

"All abooaard!"

Ladino's gut clenched as Adela reached for Jonathan Junior. His bandaged hand brushed hers as he handed her the cradleboard, and when their gazes met, he saw tears hovering on her lashes.

"I'll miss you," she whispered. "Please think of me kindly."

"Dákuji," he said, his voice hoarse with emotion. "Always."

She smiled, stepping back several paces before she turned and strode away from him, farther down the platform.

"Adela, wait!" Ladino rushed forward, removing his bowie from its sheath and cutting his medicine bag from his neck. "I want to give you something." He sliced a long, thick lock of his hair, then cut a length of the medicine bag thong and tied it around the hank of hair. He held it out to her. "To remember me by."

As she stared at the gently curling lock, her chin trembled, and she pulled her lower lip between her teeth. When she raised her eyes to his, her tears finally broke their bounds. She took the lock of hair from his hand.

"Perhaps you can use it for your doll," he suggested,

feeling foolish because his heart almost burst with the desire to beg after all. "All good Apache dolls must have long hair."

Instead of the quick quip and smile he expected, she threw her free arm around his neck and pulled him close, holding him with such fierce desperation he couldn't imagine where she found the strength. When he overcame his shock, he closed his eyes and clutched her close, breathing deeply to imprint her scent on his memory.

At last she pulled away and reached up to touch his cheek. "Thank you," she choked. "I'll make a proper Apache of Abbie yet." She opened her eyes wide, making room for tears before any more fell. "And here," she said, pulling her handkerchief from her pocket and handing it to him. "To remember me by." She smiled, trying to force a cheerful expression when she knew he felt like he did. Miserable.

The whistle blew again, and Jonathan, who had taken the first whistle in stride, began to squall. Swaying gently and whispering to comfort the child, Adela moved away. Ladino studied her profile as she offered a shaky smile to the porter, who helped her step up into the car.

A gust of engine steam drifted back along the train, obscuring Ladino's view as he watched her through the windows, seeing her carry the cradleboard down the center aisle. The puffs came quicker, harsher, louder until the train began to move. Adela had found her seat, and now she leaned out an open window. She held up the cradleboard and waved one of Jonathan's arms. Then she waved herself as the train picked up speed. At last the entire train passed him by, leaving nothing behind but the echo of a distant whistle.

"Daaiinaa," Ladino whispered, pressing her kerchief to

his nose and breathing deeply. "It is finished."

Adela tilted the cup of breakfast tea to her patient's lips. He sipped the last drop of the liquid, then rested his head back on his pillow. She patted his arm and smiled.

"Thank y', Sister," he mumbled, his eyelids drooping.

"You're welcome," she said, setting his empty cup on the tray that rested on his cot.

She continued to stare out one of the many windows on the ward to the dusty streets and adobe buildings below. In the month since her return, yet another brick Victorian had begun to take shape atop a hill on the outskirts of town. So much change, and yet her life felt empty, leaving her to fantasize about pine trees, clear streams, and a waterfall that cascaded from a sheer canyon wall.

With a sigh, she lifted the tray and turned her attention away from the window, only to find Sister Mary Francis, the newest brown novice, in her path.

Adela jumped, and dishes clattered. "You startled me."

"I'm sorry," Mary Francis murmured. "I came to tell you that Sister Blandina wants to speak to you. She's in her classroom."

Adela frowned, wondering what Blandina could possibly want to discuss. Something about Jonathan Junior? At last she nodded and smiled. "Thank you, Sister. Could you take this?"

The girl accepted the tray and hurried down the ward's central aisle. As Adela watched her go, she surveyed the rows of cots, searching for the fragile sense of belonging that continued to elude her. It was gone, destroyed by new sisters, new schedules, new patients. None of them anything like Ladino.

She rushed from the room and made her way downstairs

and outside where she lingered for a moment, enjoying the sun. It was just before the morning recess, and little girls' voices lifted in song drifted from Blandina's classroom. The sound called to mind another morning song when Adela had awakened in the shelter built by Laughs Like the Wind. Nostalgia brushed past her on a cool breeze.

She stood and listened for a moment, until finally the singing stopped and Blandina's voice carried over the giggling wave of girls that rushed out the door.

When Adela stepped inside Blandina's classroom, she found her mentor sitting at her desk holding Jonathan Junior on her lap. Blandina murmured to the baby, who investigated a row of blocks on Blandina's desk.

Adela smiled. Where she had struggled for acceptance, her baby brother seemed to take it as his due. Being the only baby—and the only male child at that—her brother had more than his share of older sisters and mothers. Yet Adela felt nothing but gratitude for the affection her peers lavished on him—especially Blandina.

"Sister Mary Francis said you wanted to speak with me?"

Blandina lifted her head, and Adela could see a slight puffiness around her hazel eyes.

Adela rushed forward. "Sister Blandina, is something wrong?"

"Not really." She glanced down at Jonathan, who held up a wooden block for her inspection. Blandina nodded, said "Block," and he returned to his play. She lifted her gaze. "I wanted to tell you that I received orders to open a school in Albuquerque. Pauline, Mary Josephine, Gertrude, Agnes, and Mary Aloque will all be accompanying me."

Adela plunked down on the piano bench near the desk and stared at Blandina. "When will you be leaving?"

"We're hoping to open the school in September, so I imagine we will be leaving within a week's time."

"That soon?"

"I'm afraid so."

Adela stared at Blandina as a million emotions collided in her heart. The two strongest emotions were grief that her mentor would be leaving, and worry about a future she would have to face alone. Yet beneath everything grew a fledgling understanding—of herself and of her disillusionment. The realization struck her that as much as the convent had changed, as much as it would continue to change, she was the one who had changed the most.

"Adela," Blandina began, "others tell me you haven't been yourself since returning. Is there something you'd like to discuss with me?"

Jonathan Junior grew impatient with the blocks. He held his hands out to Adela and made grasping fists. She lifted him from Blandina's lap and brought him to her own, where he pawed at her pocket. He pulled out Abbie and cooed in delight. Adela had honored Ladino's request and secured his hair to the head of the corncob doll.

"You still have Abigail?" Blandina asked, her voice soft with nostalgia.

"Yes." Adela offered a wan smile, trying with little success to hide her grief. "Jonathan's grown fond of her."

"I don't remember her having hair." When Blandina touched the mahogany tresses, sudden understanding exploded in her expression. "Are you still planning to profess your vows in December?"

Adela didn't answer at first. Instead, she tickled Jonathan's stomach, willing his happy gurgles and laughs to lift her tortured spirits. It did no good. More than anyone else, she owed Blandina her honesty.

"I don't know," she whispered. "So much has happened. And now that you're not going to be here, well . . ." She shrugged. "I'm not so sure I belong here anymore."

"Perhaps you're just frightened," offered Blandina. "It's understandable to be concerned about such a deep commitment, and it's normal to question your faith every now and then."

Allowing her gaze to drift around the room, Adela shrugged again. "I don't think it's my faith I'm questioning anymore, Sister Blandina, at least not the way you mean. I think it has more to do with what I need to face in order to be honest with myself and with God."

She shifted the baby to one leg. As she bounced him, he continued to play with Abigail. She'd noticed he liked to rub the soft hair between his fingers. How many times had she done the very same thing? Remembering. Wishing.

Regretting.

"The church needs more women like you, Sister Blandina."

"And more like you, Adela."

She shook her head. "No. The church needs women who know exactly why they became Sisters of Charity. I've always looked up to you because you've never had reservations in your faith. This is your life. This is God's plan for you. But I'm not you, Sister Blandina; I think I finally understand that.

"I've lied to everyone here," she continued. "But most of all I've lied to myself. It's not that I haven't been happy, or that I don't want to serve God, it's just that I know now I can't serve Him as a nun." She cleared her throat and closed her eyes, saying a silent prayer for the courage to continue. "I've hidden behind my habit because I was afraid to leave the convent—afraid to live with the uncertainty of life. I can't stay. I hope you can forgive me."

Jonathan's gurgles filled the strained silence, until at last Blandina spoke. "Oh, Adela," she began, her voice quivering. "Normally I would be disappointed in one who has come so far in her training only to turn back. But you've come to mean so much to me, I can't find it in my heart to be angry with you for discovering the ability to understand yourself."

Blandina's words helped the enormous burden to unfold its layers and layers of cloaking from around Adela's heart.

"What will you do if you don't stay here?"

Adela smoothed her fingers over the blond swirl on Jonathan's head. "I could live in Westbrook House and take care of Jonathan. I would be well provided for there. It's a beautiful home . . ."

"Or you could take what you've learned of Apache culture and use your nursing skills at the Mescalero Reservation."

Blandina's expression filled with an intimate knowledge that disconcerted Adela, forcing her to acknowledge the truth. She had spent too much time alone with Ladino, and Blandina had to know she had shared too many of her deepest emotions with him to have remained chaste.

"Yes, the thought had occurred to me."

"Do you think you would be accepted?"

The double meaning of Blandina's words startled her. She wasn't sure how to respond. She would never know if the Mescaleros would accept her, nor would she know what Ladino's reaction would be unless she traveled to the reservation to find out.

"I could try. I've learned to respect their beliefs, which aren't so different from our own, and I would like to help them."

"Then perhaps that is what you are meant to do. I know you've heard it said many times before, but the Lord does work in mysterious ways . . ." Blandina offered a teasing smile, the kind of smile she would share with an equal.

So much acceptance in such a small gesture made Adela want to cry. "And it isn't for us to question which direction He leads," she finished, repeating the lesson Blandina had been trying to teach her for so many years. The lesson she had finally learned.

Blandina's expression grew somber. "You do know that when you present your decision to Mother Eulalia, you will be shunned and considered an outcast, don't you?"

"Yes."

"And you're prepared to face that?"

"Yes."

Blandina's eyes took on a bright sheen. "Well then. No matter what the others do or say, I hope you'll find some way to stay in contact with me."

Adela nodded, and her throat tightened. "I'd like that. You've been like a mother to me, and a dear friend. Thank you."

"Well," Blandina said in a dismissive tone, as she sniffed and rose from her chair. "Since we'll both be leaving soon, and I won't get to see Jonathan for very much longer, would you mind if I took him for a walk in Archbishop Lamy's garden?"

Adela handed Jonathan to Blandina. "Of course not," she said. "That will give me the time I need to face Mother Eulalia."

Two months ago the prospect would have terrified her. Now, as she watched her mentor walk out the door, Adela smiled, her spirit soaring with the realization that she was free. Free to live. Free to take risks. And the first risk of her new life would be to face Ladino.

Adela rode among several others in the wake of a freight wagon train entering the Mescalero Reservation. Once again it was issue day, and a flurry of activity surrounded the agency buildings. Along the white fences, children played with dogs, while their mothers lined up at the commissary window.

She smiled, glorying in the September breeze that tousled her shoulder-length hair. She'd had enough of black bonnets and blacker restrictions. And somehow she knew her mother would approve of the dress she wore. Lavender. A color that showed respect in mourning, but allowed her to embrace a life completely different from the one she'd left behind.

Jonathan Junior rode in front of her on the saddle, as intrigued by the activity around them as she was. True to her promise, she'd kept the cradleboard, though Jonathan preferred riding free of restraint.

She had spent two weeks in Silver City helping Mr. Leeds clear up legal issues concerning the Westbrook estate, and when she'd told him of her plans, he had been stunned. She understood, knowing he wondered about the sanity of a woman who was willing to take an infant who was heir to millions of dollars to live on a poor Indian reservation. Eventually she had convinced him that she had every intention of giving her brother all the love and care he could possibly want, no matter where their home happened to be.

But the prospect of living on agency land depended on Ladino. She'd sent him a telegraph, telling him what day she planned to arrive. She prayed he would be here to meet her.

As they drew closer, she searched for him among the other men, and when they rolled into the agency yard she spotted him standing next to Agent Llewellyn. Her heart leaped in her chest, ready to explode with the magnitude of her love.

Dear God, she hadn't realized how much she had missed him until now, as she watched him study each incoming wagon with an intensity that bordered on obsession. He still loved her. She could see it in the disappointment that stained his features when he didn't find the woman he expected—a woman in a black habit tucked safely away on one of the wagons. She smiled. That woman no longer existed. She only hoped he would accept the woman she had become.

The train of wagons stopped, and Adela reined up behind them. Holding Jonathan in her arms, she dismounted in the midst of the other riders and tied her horse to a fence. Carrying her brother on her hip, she strode toward Ladino through a cloud of dust. When she stood within a yard of him, she started to cry, and the face she loved so well blurred in her sight. He looked at her at last, his expression a dismissive perusal until his gaze reached her face. Disbelief glittered in his golden eyes, and his lips twitched with an uncertain smile.

"Ah, *shitsíné*, you came. And your hair . . ." He stroked a tousled curl that touched the corner of her eye. "It's grown."

"We'll make a proper Apache of me yet—if you want me to stay."

"Is that what you truly want?"

"More than anything."

"But I don't know how hard life will be for us here. What about Little Squirrel?" He caressed the curls on Jonathan's head. "What if I can't give you both the kind of security you need?"

"You've given me more than security. You've awakened my will to survive. You've awakened my heart. You've awakened the fire in my soul to its true calling. All I need now is your love."

"You have it. Always."

"Dákuji," Adela repeated in Mescalero, and her tears fell freely as Ladino enveloped her in his embrace.

Epilogue

Adela snuggled deeper under the blanket, smiling as she listened to Ladino chant the morning song outside the shelter she had built for them. His rich voice greeted the first dawn of their new life together as a married couple, and a warmth unlike any Adela had known before spread through her body and enveloped her heart. She closed her eyes and allowed herself to drift on the sound as the last note of the song echoed across mountaintops, carrying its prayer to the rising sun. When Ladino had finished and was quiet, the voices of the birds filled the silence.

He crawled back inside her lopsided shelter and lay down beside her, crooking his elbow and resting his head on his hand. The sun's first rays stretched through the dwelling's east-facing opening and bronzed the length of his body, still naked from a long night of lovemaking.

Adela reached up and stroked her fingertips over his smile, which was laced with sated contentment. "I have a surprise for you."

"Oh?" He kissed her forefinger as it brushed past his lips. "I have a surprise for you, too."

"Oh?" she echoed, teasing him. "You first."

He rubbed his hand down her bare arm and laced his fingers into hers atop her hip. She waited for him to speak, but he kept silent, staring at her as if everything rested on her reaction.

"This must be some surprise," she said.

He smiled and squeezed her hand. "Llewellyn has a

401

house at the agency for us. I've decided to become one of his police officers."

Now it was Adela's turn to stare, unable to speak.

"Wouldn't a house make you happy, Adela?"

"Oh, Ladino, I won't lie to you," she said, her heart expanding beyond bounds even she couldn't believe existed. "I would love a house. Especially since we have my brother to raise. But are you sure about wanting to be a police officer? Have you made such a serious commitment just to please me?"

"No. My decision is for both of us. And I want to help my people." He slanted her a teasing smile. "Besides, I grew accustomed to sleeping in comfortable beds. Even when I was tied to them," he added, lifting a brow.

"Well, there is that," she conceded, trading him a wicked grin. "But for right now you'll just have to make do with a bedroll on the hard ground. And all I have to tie you to . . . is me. Forever." She pulled her hand from his and walked her fingers up his bare chest. Finding a scar, she traced it. "Make love to me again, Ladino."

How she could ignite his desire after the night they had just shared, he couldn't fathom. He lifted a single brow. "Where's your bonnet? You haven't been the same since you took it off."

"I certainly hope not." She laughed. The gentle sound soaked to the deepest part of him like female rain. *Female rain.* Strong and steady and enduring, with just enough thunder and lightning to energize his soul.

"How would you like an Apache name?"

"I would love one." She tilted her head at him, and her growing chestnut tresses fanned over her shoulder. "But right now I want my husband to share my body." She leaned forward and bit his ear. "*Eim'báhshay,* Ladino."

Her seductive voice obliterated his control. He slid himself between her legs and glided inside her in one smooth stroke. She was wet and warm, and she clutched him tightly within her, so tightly he released a shuddering breath against her ear.

"Ladino?" she whispered, as he began to move within her.

"Hmm?"

"I'm going to have our baby."

He stopped and gazed down into her face. In the soft glow from outside, he could see the moisture in her eyes. Filled with a tender happiness he'd never hoped to earn, he showed his appreciation of her gift with the gentleness of his lovemaking.

"*Eim'báhshay,*" she whispered in his ear again, nibbling. "Don't hold back."

Chills raced down his legs and he surrendered, thrusting deep within her. Adela's body soaked up everything he had to give like dry earth soaked up rain, and still he wanted to give and take more. At last Ladino felt his release melding with hers in shaking muscles, ragged breaths, and cries carried to the heavens on the rays of the rising sun.

Long afterward, she lay with one leg draped over his. "So what Apache name have you decided to give me?"

"Female Rain," Ladino murmured at the top of her head. Keeping her leg draped across his, he turned and leaned up on his elbow to nibble her neck. Tasting the salt on her skin, he teased his tongue over one breast and worked his way down to her belly, kissing the slight swell that was their unborn child before he lifted his face and met her gaze. "The only kind of rain that can completely quench a forest fire, or bring a child to life."

403

From atop a nearby mountain peak, the haunting cry of a cougar added her song to the morning air.

Adela smiled. "I think your grandmother approves."

Author's Note

Sister Blandina Segale, Hermana Dolores, Sister Eulalia, Sister Mary de Sales (who later became the first woman doctor licensed in the Territory of New Mexico), Archbishop Lamy, Father Bourgade, Agent Llewellyn, Chief Cadete, Estrellito, and many of the other characters in this story truly lived, although their personalities in this book are my own invention.

As for places, I used fictional license where Pajaro's cave is concerned. I wanted to use Carlsbad Caverns, but the final confrontation scene I envisioned there would have been physically impossible. So, since there are over 200 caves in the Guadalupe Mountains, I decided to blend Mescalero legends pertaining to Carlsbad Caverns with facts about limestone caves in general to create a cave setting all my own.

About the Author

Kelley Pounds is the daughter of a writer and rancher from central New Mexico, so her love for the West and its stories came naturally. Her favorite memories from childhood include listening to her dad's bedtime tales about wild horses in the Manzano Mountains, running barefoot in the foothills, hunting for arrowheads, and exploring ancient Pueblo ruins.

Today she and her husband own a cattle ranch about an hour's drive from her beloved Manzanos, where they're raising their daughter to love the land as much as they do.

She can be reached at P.O. Box 8, Corona, NM 88318, or you can visit her website at www.kelleypounds.com.